Until the Sun Breaks Down:
A Künstlerroman in Three Parts

Until the Sun Breaks Down:
A Künstlerroman in Three Parts

II. The Recluse Finds a Way

Joseph Nicolello

RESOURCE *Publications* · Eugene, Oregon

UNTIL THE SUN BREAKS DOWN: A KÜNSTLERROMAN IN THREE PARTS
II. The Recluse Finds a Way

Resource Publications
An Imprint of Wipf and Stock Publishers
199 W. 8th Ave., Suite 3
Eugene, OR 97401

www.wipfandstock.com

PAPERBACK ISBN: 978-1-7252-6977-4
HARDCOVER ISBN: 978-1-7252-6978-1
EBOOK ISBN: 978-1-7252-6979-8

02/16/21

Damascius (translated by from *Commentary on Plato's* Phaedo, *The Golden Chain: An Anthology of Pythagorean and Platonic Philosophy* (World Wisdom, Inc.), edited by Algis Uzdavinys © 2004. Used with permission.

M.M. Bakhtin From THE DIALOGIC IMAGINATION: FOUR ESSAYS by M.M. Bakhtin, edited by Michael Holquist, translated by Caryl Emerson and Michael Holquist, Copyright (c) 1981. By permission of the University of Texas Press.

II. The Recluse Finds a Way

And when a man leads a Dionysian life,
his troubles are already elided and he is free from his bonds
and released from custody, or rather from the confined form of life;
such a man is the philosopher in the stage of purification.

—DAMASCIUS (B. 480)

Only that which is itself developing can
comprehend development as a process.

—BAKHTIN

1

As he in hot pursuit of the truth must first let the skeletons take up their shovels, the next morning William crawled out of the deformed bunk-bed as birds began to chirp through a window not quite closed, beside the debris of roach stubs, matches, a pocket knife, and stood beside the tall aluminum door overlooking fifteen snoring, drunken men, crooked bodies sprawled across one another, interlaced with long coats and quilts, permeating the dense atmospheric wreckage with a thick, liquid revelry. The pilgrim observed an olive branch from which an Israeli flag, that had served as a cover, had fallen; and stepping over the flag and across the limbs crossed one another in a tanned, dampened maze, or patchwork of soon-blazing sunlight, took the olive branch as his walking stick. He then took the finger-length remains of a bottle of wine and drank it down, looked to the sky, drank again, and when the bottle was finished and the blindfolded body before him was snoring, he left, singing,

Let dead poetry rise up again, O holy muses, since I am yours. Sing, sisters of the sacred well, and let the underworld's chips fall where they may.

Slight overcast swept across the darkened sky of formulating navy-blue shades, there in that second realm where the spirit purges. He thought of Helena, of home, of desolation, and slung his bag over his shoulder and took off for the exit door.

In a two-dollar pair of hiking boots, sweater with rolled sleeves, and a second-hand pair of pants, William took off at once down the last somber streets of San Diego and for a moment longed to return to New York, or hop a boat to Europe, before the desire to remain in motion voyaging north overtook such fantasies, fleeting as the allure of palm trees. Familiarity announced itself a safeguard, transparent, for he with fate on his side, cultural fluorescence, the willingness to live free of any master's self-enslaving chains, and the pilgrim passed on through the vacant streets of shadows, hundreds of sleeping homeless bodies in place of where the night's action had taken place, and a street-sweeper echoed, shuffling the metallic distance. William looked northward, and saw four stars in the transforming sky, moving from darkness to light, and felt not unlike the first man: 'O Lucan, with thee I recall the first breast, rendered now a holy Bay, transfixed and weightless safeguarded by soft mud' and progressed through the cloudless aspect of unchained air that, moving further north, became like liquid oxygen. Thus he walked by one art gallery and another. It struck him that nothing within the frames registered; objects without meaning, eyes without a mind. Art was something of the past, for the culture of irony had eclipsed artistry; and naturally, a people who give up on art have simultaneously given up on themselves. And from the agonizing tint of unchanging mediocrity charging each sterile slogan, be it chemical or visual poison, both, from hieroglyphic degeneracy around one iron aluminum scaled corner into the realm of heteroglossia, as in following her traced voice to its origin, he encountered a figure he'd never seen the combination of outside of some multisided screens:

Here was a being altogether missing in the Jerusalem morning: a being composed of such an array of identarian buttons—black, Muslim, feministic, abortion-advocating lesbian clad in metallic sunglasses, beltless denim overalls downturned before her protruding, tattooed pelvis.

"You look like you seen a ghost, boy. Where you tryin-a get to?"

"Train."

"Here, drink dis rum wit me."

"Yes."

"I just left seminary—I know, I know. Yeah, the burka is new. Yo—I tried to find Jesus. I mean why would I not want to? They did of course recite something or another about Jesus and the poor, though this was later revealed as a linguistic painkiller en route to the $30 torn towels and burned sheets one was forced into buying. The sheer economics of it all was nauseating and not even God could lighten the load. One had to either be well off or naive, perhaps both, relegating the rest—the masses—to hope in another life. Fa real, Christ would have despised the ordeal; and as I sought neither to have my sorrowful bank account drained by millionaires wearing crucifixes nor give up on Christ altogether, I considered flipping the tables out beside the glowing ATMs. Alas, they were bolted into the ground, and so instead I vanished, praying I would bump into a real man who would dissuade both my departure and my inadvertent celibacy; of course, I received nothing but a compliment from a retarded jock, and left it at that. Now I'm going east, first to New York City, then Harvard. Not yet though, I ain't goin nowhere till next week. Drink till den."

"I am come, my sister, to break the laws of the abyss."

William sat absorbed, bedazzled, the warmth of rum channeling through his virgin veins.

She made a thumb motion to her Newport; he proffered his light. She gave him an ear bud, and some haunted music from an album portraying something of a lighthouse with searchlight at night, cast in the fog of smoke, blue-purple hue, spherical light guided to an unseen end.

The naval base stood towering behind them. Sounds of the invisible machines cast through the streets of dawn as if prolonged whispers of a malformed farewell. Dying birds, burning eyes; a cab pulled up and she got in without goodbye.

He took a greedy sip, nose held, of the brown burning liquid. Between the drained bottle, sticker peeled, and the rum cup, he unfolded a poem:

> Harvard Avenue
> *Expansive sky,*
> *Train window*
> *& memory of sea:*
> *divided by brick/*
> *June breeze tossed thick*
> *from tree to rustling tree.*

He awaited her return for naught. He took to tuck the poem in his pocket, standing to go, though it slipped through a hole unbeknownst to he in pursuit of the station.

Smoke plumed above titanium walls within and throughout cranial motions. Languid families of birds set flight beneath the fading moon.

Through the gates and windows of closed-down shops William overlooked displays of magazines, dietary supplements, brochures, swimming trunks, glow-in-the-dark beer signs, the gray door of apartment buildings struck with illegible spray-paint and peeling stickers passing in such a merciless array as to become conclusive companions, or, rather, mocking bystanders. Futility rushed through the city even at dawn and choked him as in a flash; William felt detached from humanity, and doubted he'd blink an eye were he told that morning the whole of it would tonight be wiped out.

Rip Van Winkle stood in the organic market before the cash register rubbing his eyes before lit, exposed bulbs. Newspapers lay in stacks still held together by colorless plastic cables, from which fresh ink and warm paper scents rose through and within the glass doorway.

SUICIDE BOMB AFGHANISTAN 19 DEAD—LETTERMAN CONTROVERSY—CIA—UNIVERSITY OFFICIAL—CELEBRITY SEX TAPE—POLICE WILL NOT BE—TERROR ATTACK—TERROR PROBE—CAR CRASH KILLS COUPLE

"Look at this," William said to the man, who fell from his wooden stool with shock before receiving William's inquiry. "How much longer can this hysterical world go on?" He was conscious of his delirious, sleep-deprived state, and felt intoxicated. Then the old man grinned, as William whispered, "It is time to do something about all of this."

"Yes, yes, my friend, the world these days is in ruins. We need a new voice, a new generation, young like you," said the solitary turbaned man at his cashier, briefly tugging with angst at his long half-white beard. The man readjusted his silken shawl and poured two tall cups of steaming black coffee.

On a small television set the same headlines ran across the screen; the man turned to it, shutting it off with one fierce motion of his wavering, emaciated, liver-spotted hand. "Who has guided you, or what has been your lantern, coming forth from the deep night that makes the valley of Hell forever black?'"

"I voyage north today," William said, "To San Francisco."

"Where from?"

"East."

"I travel the entire world, my friend, and everywhere I go there is riots and disasters and all of it. You must listen to your heart, see everything, and all wonderful days begin with good company, and you do what please you. You cannot please everyone. The world in need of revolution, and if there no revolution, then there must be the revolution of the self." He looked to William with solemn eyes and slid the cup his way across the marble countertop. "To be young like you again; now go, you take free; the sun rising—go find the others—we need you," pointing to the newspapers, "Bye my friend. Bye. I see your eyes, see you. I say prayer now."

"In all of my time in Southern California," William thought to himself as we walked through to the street, "That was the first fine person I met."

Before the doors to the station a middle-aged man stood with what appeared his wife, both clad in maroon jogging suits, an earbud in one another's ear, panting, chugging from a half-crushed water bottle. The man broke off the small woman's deep voice to correct her in numerical configurations regarding automobile and life insurance. William knew by the look in their eyes that the contempt for true artistry in his society stemmed from a planted hatred seething within such persons of a society wherein the archaic, the inane, is holy, and pacifistic rebellion against such blatant futilities is unfathomable due to the colossal, unending bombardment of worthless slogans, inventions, and characters from reality-television programs and their malevolent, vomitous commercial breaks which the men and women of the streets had declined and fell unto imitation, in the conscious sense and otherwise. There were but two ways to deal with televised propaganda, and that was either with an anvil or with distance. Does true ignorance ever feel at a loss for anything? A means of which one can figure one's self out. Do the imitative propaganda empires' pitiful topics barraging each imitative American street resemble any trace of authenticity worth living for, or must one go headfirst into physical slobbery and psychological catastrophes if one is to blend in? It was not that the man before him stepping away from the copper doorhandle leading to the interior of a worn-down, diminutive museum giftshop of a train station was insubstantial as a human being, nor that he reminded William of Mr. Kant, but that all of these men and women were beginning to resemble one another with frightening consistency; Helena had not just turned into her mother, but she had lost her identity in the burning wheel of modern life, and had lent her intellect and beauty to a culture of convenience; it is as convenient to let someone break down as it is to click what is called a mouse; thus she would never suffer again, though nor would she experience the inner richness once sought through individuality and temperament, for in that case one would be prescribed to pharmaceutical drugs. The rarity of a Nielsen, of a Octavia, became evident to William as he waited beside the velvet rope in line, overlooking black and white photographs, his consciousness returning with a nihilistic strain, like melodious words dancing across the piratical back pages he once wrote, internalized, and had taken with him to the streets of the mind.

He'd misread the schedule and the train would not be departing at once, nor would it be straight to San Francisco. Ms. Fellows had contacted a friend of hers with a restaurant somewhere in the city whom William would be in touch with, as Nielsen had contacted his brother. William held the piece of paper within his wallet as agonizing time passed by, the long colorless streets through tinted windows beginning with the ferocious daylight heat at once. The trip would be a train-ride back to Los Angeles, a bus to Bakersfield, another train to Emeryville, and a last bus ride over the Bay Bridge into downtown San Francisco. He looked over his crumpled map and let waves of intuitive pleasure rush through him, waves of pleasure that reoccurred as he stood to pace the ground the way he had always done in subways, the rate of his thoughts taking him from the bench and placing him to and fro across the ragged marble, concrete grounds. Old wooden benches, brusque antique clocks, and long glass doors through which the trains began to pass in, to and fro, as overhead operative voices relayed looming departure estimates. Centurial couples with tubes in their noses sat hand in hand beside bright children pulling at their parents' limbs insistent upon vending machines and going to the gift shop. Still the fountains seemed metallic in taste and William did not understand how such conductors with their gray beards tainted with corncob pipe smoke could drink such water.

An indulgence in its own right to go without a phone, William reflected, to go on with the confidence to disavow standby and all its tangled knots. Time broke down again and one could reclaim attentiveness and reflect upon structural details of space and matter around him. Primitivism seemed dead on arrival. He felt an ascension concurring within his spirit as he paced the station, overlooking the distant buildings, black and white photographs, and he knew somehow he would have to deal his generation a blow, one less bitter than irrefutable in richness and vision, though nonetheless a blow, one from which its unconscious would never recover.

~

"Los Angeles-bound train now boarding!"

He tore himself from a deep sleep and golden daylight had spilled inside like melting gold through the concealed windowpanes. Looking over the empty station William followed the half-dozen passengers on board to a seat of his own within the caboose. Boot heels and wheeling luggage clicked and rang through entranceways and exits. His sunburn had at last dissolved into a tan and the long shower and shave at the hostel had done him right. It was a fine feeling away from the computer, also, where one had to inform everyone of all one had ever known of what he enjoyed or what he would do today. Without such contrivances, one could go in alone; no impulsive, thoughtless embrace of compulsory thoughtlessness, but the obscure, exclusive joy of language and death. There were universities in San Francisco; there were also streets and people upon them. He no longer wanted everything at once anymore as somebody sang, 'LAST CHANCE ABOARD!'

It began as a smooth, acclivitous ride and remained so as again he was headed alongside the Pacific. The streets of agony and resentment and physical, psychological anguish faded into a blending archival finality of unfamiliar glances, of disenchanted recognitions.

"Good morning, sir, may I get you anything?" asked a pleasant, fleshy redhead with gapped tooth to whom William smiled, paralleling her tone:

"Glass of orange juice, please."

She scribbled on a notepad and walked through clicking doors. Again the glorious, glittering Pacific Ocean was unfolding before him, with each second passed, all its vast body spreading further, further. From his bag he brought forth a bottle of champagne, uncorked it, poured mimosas and let time pass over familiar land with an occasional window-side return-gaze to the sea. There were smiles here and there. He tilted his reflective glass to one such woman and for the rest of first lucid quarter enjoyed himself.

~

Los Angeles seemed as if a miscalculated dream; a scorched, historical, and geographical array of telephone-crucifixes laid out across flattened land. From a downtown payphone William gazed about the streets of smog, all the stretching land appearing as a strange, chemical reaction beneath the low light-blue sky of elongated dissolving clouds.

"Man Ray lives in downtown San Francisco and his restaurant is in Japantown, he wants you to call him. His wife is in Thailand and he says you can stay with him a few weeks."

"Aha!" William said, spitting down at soda cans along sparkling concrete.

Ms. Fellows gave him the phone number, wished him well, and concealing her anxiety let William go; he spoke next with Nielsen. More had happened already in two hours than it had in two weeks, he realized, and was surprised to get a hold of Nielsen Nielsen so early; it was just morning on the East.

"Been up all night. Carson's gone mad again, he's returned. I have been doing nothing, seldom getting out bed. Think I lost ten pounds in a week."

"Well your voice sounds fine. Hang in there, old chap."

"My brother wants to meet you then. He's living for free at a house in Fisherman's Wharf, working at the adjacent hostel café. You can stay with him, but just don't mention my name around there. Last time I was there I went out with a real bang."

"What happened?"

"Oh," Nielsen said, "I'll just write you a letter about it when you have an address. I knew San Diego wouldn't work out."

"No one knew anything."

"No, I mean I couldn't see you staying in southern California. That's where I was abandoned. I was glad to have been abandoned there."

"What should I expect from San Francisco?"

"Where are you now?"

"Los Angeles."

"Just enjoy the coast," Nielsen said. "Call me in a few days and tell me what has happened in San Francisco. It is not a place where nothing happens, let me tell you that," he reaffirmed, "It is a place where one's week beats anyone else's year, but it is also much more than that. There is not much like traveling whereupon the destination is sort of unfathomable save in essence. And remember, for good or ill, whatever the future brings, William: you who would seek chaste eyes must first burn with Sabbatai Sevi and an earlier book of Gomorrah."

"I will take your word. Today is the first fine day I've had in weeks. Get some sleep. I'll call you when I'm with your brother."

The line for the Bakersfield bus was a block long and curled around the hot asphalt and the driver was just beginning to let everyone on as William returned. The bus appeared as if it would fill to the brim as William walked alongside the line and dozens of defensive eyes peered into his, their uniform eyes emblematic of geographically condemned bipedals. He stood beside the body that was temple to the first set of downcast, unbeknownst eyes he noticed ahead of untold, sweating numbers that had been waiting an hour and dared not look back.

"You know da line start back dare," a woman hissed beside the driver, handing in her ticket.

William looked back with them as if unaware of any prolegomena to persecution. The mob pointed to the back of the line as the bus driver told them to shut their mouths and move ahead. Commotion formulated amidst the lot as William neared in beside the drugged man just before him.

"Ay wait," the driver said.

"Me?"

The piercing eyes of wolverines glared from window-seats.

"You ane got no otha bag?"

"Just this pouch, sir."

"Ha," he said, his golden teeth and jewelry shining. "You a light travel. Ticket?"

An old woman with nostalgic, attic perfume and beige hearing aids sat beside William, bulwarking his targeted identity. Commotion began outside of the bus as the last were let on, the rest to wait hours longer in the scorching heat. A near-riot unraveled outside as the police, en masse, rolled in.

"May I ha' ya attention; we got us a five-hour bus ride through the desert. It's mad hot outside. Any of dat, I mean even a peep, you getting offa the bus and gonna walk to Bakersfield cause it's scorching outside, and I ain't dealin' wih dat."

Whispers subsided through the aisleways and the assertive driver nodded, starting the engine. In the parking lot a brawl had started, with purses and sneakers soaring through the perimeter of fists and mace, and in a swift turn all the station was out of sight.

Out of the smog at 80 MPH, straight ahead into the trancelike, burning yellow desert—few cars, trucks were on the highway at all and for some time no matter which way one looked the desert was a bronze mirror of itself, intersected by sweeping plains of dry, towering, fleeting mountains with occasional dilapidated patches of grass serving as interims, the journey at once became a lucid, meditative trance with no sound at all save the constant rumbling of the motor, the distant sound of headphones, a ring-tone, all of the bus fixed upon the the scorched atlases each way one looked. He looked to his map of California, traced his pencil over the names of Bay areas, noticing that in the city furthest west a man could go, Fisherman's Wharf was the closest, if not on, the Pacific Ocean. Bliss overtook him as he gazed upon the hastening desert, and as the woman beside him fell asleep amidst an online game of checkers he found himself removing the half-full bottle of champagne from his bag to drink to the rumbling, incessant, victorious drum beat of the motor.

Children whispered some seats back:

"Look ma! That's a coyote!"

"There ain't nothing there. Where? No, no. Lay down."

There were misshaped, misplaced odd cracked clay boulders, and splintered wood sprinkled with sand; to the left immeasurable, golden space.

"No baby, that's just some left behind things. Someone had a fire it looks like."

"No, that's them I see some!" one of little girls lisped.

William looked left again and saw nothing. Then, out from behind the mound of rubble to the bus's right, a mother coyote crawled out, its ears arched like antennae, its dirty-blonde coat still in the vast space. The glimmer of her eyes projected even from the quickened distance, solitary within the desert, its body unmoving until her eyes could turn no further. The girl rapped upon the leather seat with her small hands, smacking at the window.

"Mommy, *look*!"

The coyote could never begin to catch up but there, just in sight behind her, crept from the mound a pack of baby coyotes. The children began to giggle with their mother, stopping for a moment, and beginning up again.

'Something about the baby and the woman,' thought Baron Fellows; 'Them, and Schopenhauer.'

"A baby coyote, mommy! A baby coyote!"

"Where are they going!"

"They're all going safe home, like us, little ones."

"Do coyotes have houses?"

The kids snickered.

"Do coyotes cook dinner in the kitchen and use toilets and drive cars?"

"Yes, why of course!"

"You're lying mama, you're lying!" the toothless girl sang.

"No dear, they go to the mountains. Their homes in the mountains, in the night. They're out here looking for something to eat. That mama's gonna have supper for her children tonight. Maybe rabbit, fruit, vegetables, elk, squirrels, or little mousies like you!"

"Eek!" they squealed with a shiver, "Eek!" and in a moment fell sound asleep within their mother's arms.

The lime green exit signs passed by with titular unfamiliarity as William drank the warm and flat Baron De Beaupre Brut, creating an excellent atmospheric balance and a fine counter to the unremorseful air-conditioning blowing from reprehensible ventilation shafts. Half of the passengers wore blankets beneath cream-colored dimmers and hat holders, luggage holders clicking against the weatherbeaten ceiling plastic, falling safe asleep below.

From there it was a ride of stimulated dreams which fell from the memory upon awakening as timeless shades of feeling shed their respective skins, elevating consciousness rushed through his mind, heightened by the unchanging proximity of the towering California sun, in the form of a near illegible note scrawled on the back of his Jerusalem grocery store receipt:

> But as in landlessness alone resides the highest truth, shoreless, indefinite as God—so, better is it to perish in that howling infinite, than be [??] dashed upon the lee, even if that were safety!

And on a second, final slip of paper, one inscribed in pre-Hellenic days, in the abstract hours of Octavia, indeed written in her cursive hand with surgical precision in the last fragment, the first line typewritten on an antique piece bought out on Manhattan Avenue in Greenpoint:

> Gird this man with a smooth rush and wash his face so as to remove all grime—the sun will show you, rising now, where to take that train that traverses sea and mountain, and that easier ascent than has hitherto been carried out—for I had read de Voragine and know the sea rush at the crown of thorns, I too, in my temporal, condemned way, seek out an uprooting and rebirth of myself.

2

THE TRAIN WAS COMING in on time. Bakersfield terminal was a concrete platform the size of a football field with spherical cement benches one could rest upon. There was an old-fashioned trolley station of a shopping center just beneath the array of arrival, departure grids. Batches of shade distilled the hot afternoon as William looked out upon the long, cloudless sky above triangular glass-frames held together by brick encasing. He kept an eye upon a pacing, beautiful Armenian woman with long brown hair and a flowing, multicolored-pastel dress of disarrayed octagonal shapes walking with her luggage clicking on behind her, held by a thin, hairless arm. Her rich hair flowed in the Southern California wind. She then approached him, avoiding his eyes, and sat down feet away, her antique-brass luggage between them.

"This side go to Emeryville?" said William, following an innocent cogitation.

"Yes."

"How far is that from here?"

"A few hours," she said, looking always ahead at the open space. As soon as William looked away, she turned to him and from the corner of his eye she was older and perhaps more beautiful than he had expected, with the last of youthful freckles scattered upon her frail cheekbones. White and rosy cheeks of lovely Aurora! She bared no immediate satisfaction in her examination of his youth, concluding, "You've got a spot of something on your face."

He licked his fingertip and wiped at his right cheek—champagne; she nodded. He pondered what had made him think that here was an Armenian woman—had the sight of her simply collided with a journal entry from Vasily Grossman, to the power of daybreak champagne?

"Your dress is colorful. How far is Emeryville from San Francisco?"

"Just over the Bay Bridge. Quick. It's a little shuttle bus. Don't they say it on your ticket?"

"The ink cut off."

"It's very close. Where are you coming from?"

"San Diego," William said, noticing just beyond the fence and plants the young mother from behind him tucking her children into car-seats with tales of wild coyotes and partings of the hair, "But now I'm to see friends in San Francisco."

"I grew up outside of San Diego; I teach in Oakland," she said. "I love San Diego."

"Let's get a drink," William said. "We've got a half hour." He felt quite young, or as if he'd given away some secret that may've not existed in his tonality, phraseology.

"Where, in the station? They're all horrible over-priced places."

"I'll buy a pint of whiskey and we can cut it with water and bring it on the train."

"What if we have a drink here and miss the train?" She smiled as if out of courtesy. Buses unloaded behind them as the platform filled with another 70, 80 passengers. There was a plain disquietude that is afternoon to become evening in the air, and restrained gusts of wind sifted throughout the platform. "I don't even know your name. What is your name?"

"William. Who you?"

"Michelle," she laughed.

"I'll go buy us a drink and bring it back," William offered, "And if I miss the train then I am a fool and you're fine anyway."

"You can do that. You ought to buy socks also."

William looked down at his pants-ends coming up before the tip of his boots. All the while he hadn't noticed his lack of socks.

"It saves on laundry this way, though," he stood, and walked to the station and across the tiles to the tobacconist counter.

"A pouch of Bali-Shag."

An enormous bald man met his eyes, receiving his rumpled bills, and pressing them out replied:

"Where you headed? Where you been?" He slid the pouch of tobacco ahead with extra matches from a clapping set of reddened, plump hands.

"Neither," said William, crossing over to the wine shop.

Inside the quaint, wooden-walled shop a group of raucous gentle-men kept the cashier company drinking a chilled bottle of white wine and smoking foreign, hand-rolled cigars in three-piece suits.

"Good afternoon, gentlemen."

"Good afternoon."

"The same."

"Good day, kid."

"Pint of Old Grand-Dad, sir."

Combed sugar-white hair shown beneath fluorescent bulbs as the faint handheld radio played on. Tigran Mansurian: *Requiem.*

The paunchy cashier turned to place the bottle within William's bag; a group of conductors, in off-hours, he gathered. One polished his pocket-watch with a paper napkin.

"Where you headed, boy? You look like you just stepped out of the *Inferno.*"

"It'd been much worse, I admit," William said.

"You've still got a red tint."

"Red as wine; burgundy!" jousted one of the men, breaking into a jagged, raucous fit of laughter which broke out into the entranceway and caught the attention of a dozen passersby.

"You come from the desert?"

"He looks as if he were fasting, also!"

"A saint!" roared one of the men in an iron tone, "A saint on our hands! Here, give him wine!"

The cashier poured out a tumbler of wine and they drank together, pouring another, and letting it pass down. Synchronicity in sighs, warmth of the blood.

"No, no," concluded William, "I've just left San Diego is all."

"Ah, ah-hah," he prophesied, "Then ye did just escape the inferno. Abandon all hope no longer."

"I could never have believed that death had undone so many," William recited from memory, proposing a last toast to the men, glancing to the clock.

"Where do you go now," cried a round, sweating man through yel-low-white whiskers. "You know we once conducted all the Western lines."

"Emeryville is next, and then to San Francisco by night."

The man who had most animatedly responded to William's recita-tion set his glass, his cigar down in a cracked casino ashtray as smoke passed through the uncovered lamps like mist through the sun, his face growing intoxicated with daydream as the other men watched on, as if affirming whatever the man was to expound based upon the concentration of his glazed, cheery eyes rising from his coarse, interlocked hands.

"That was always the best part of the trip, no matter where I went beforehand or how I got there," he said, his eyes retracing youthful days in that simultaneous state of sorrow and tribute, reflected gratitude, "My wife would meet me there on Market Street, always just before dusk."

He paused for a moment sighing and poured another round. They took them down with a collective 'Ah.'

"Good luck, kid," the cashier saluted. "Stop back in and get where you're going safe. Get—safe; did I say dat right?"

"Ah," the sentimental man wiped his eyes with the same paper-napkin, cutting William's farewell off, "He'll get to San Francisco safe alright; the boy's got a pint of Grand-Dad and a train on a summer day. What else is there?"

William trotted through emerging floods of people and doorways to the platform, looking back once to watch the old men hang their bearded heads down through pluming clouds of smoke.

The train had arrived. Michelle stood beside a pillar and eyed William from a distance as he approached with confidence; each instance he looked to her eyes she seemed colder, yet still contingent. He stood beside her as she typed on her phone, tucked it away.

"Are we boarding now?"

"No, it's the next train."

"Where does this one go?"

"Through to Houston, Texas."

"Oh," William said. "Want to have a drink in the food court?"

"You're a little rummy, a lush," smiled Michelle, "But so am I. You just look young, so young. How old are you?"

"29."

"No you're not. You don't look 29. You don't even look 22."

"Nobody looks their age, though; they just look older or younger than a legal procedure. Isn't it so strange? Our number-image associations seem beyond outdated."

"What do you mean?"

They sat down again upon the bench.

"I mean that things like age, and net worth, and everything just break down into numerical assumptions after inevitable time, yet numeric theory is, by default, assumptive; the age rationale never quite fits together as well as the amount of energy we put into the equation."

"Your lips are all red. What happened?"

"I reunited with some old friends at the wine shop."

"There is a wine shop?"

"I told you," William said.

"It is too soon to start drinking."

"I spend a good bit of time in New York City; thus I do not understand what you mean by that. I had a glass of wine with some conductors. We should go back and see them."

"What would I want with some old conductors? Let me try on your glasses," Michelle said. "Your prescription is so strong! You are *blind*."

"I assume you are a guidance counselor," William said.

"I am, in fact. And what do you do for a living?"

"I am going back to school someday. Quite, well, come to think of it—perhaps not. Either way, I want to be a ribald garbageman when I grow up."

"That is all?"

"Yes."

"In what sense?"

"I intend to flip a coin," William said with a sonorous ardor. Michelle spoke of the 'Vitality and ethical vigor' of her profession over the increasing chorus of voices crashing together on the platform as William watched the faces pass by perspiring and full of restraint, frustration, contempt, yelling into phones and talking to themselves, lunging ahead to the nearest vacant wicker bench, the long California sky hovering over them in its pastel blue, symmetrical oblivion. A blind woman lofted breadcrumb to a group of birds that had earlier been upon the station's clay overhead, making experimental music with her brittle gray stick. Hovering electric headlights flashed through the wavering heat.

"You are not paying attention," Michelle said. William decided she was insane and did not believe anything she said. Her eyes and fingers never left her cell phone.

"No, please, carry on," he implored. "I am listening."

The train pulled in much more tardily than the usual bullet-silver Amtrak line William had rode thus far. The middle-afternoon train to Emeryville was single-leveled, far shorter, and had a simplistic iron build which neither reflected light nor anything at all. Its horn blared once just before touching down, and with the release of steam, which whistled and rose to and fro in gusts of cylinder-precision, the doors clicked open.

"All aboard!"

"It was nice meeting you," Michelle said, standing to go.

"Goodbye."

William walked ahead through the crowd with his bag over his burnt shoulder, Michelle fresh in his mind after a brief pause at his quick dismissal. He walked about the car drunk, feeling energetic, going first to the dine-car for coffee.

He walked back out through the clicking doors; within the second car Michelle sat, her luggage in the seat beside her. She looked to William, to her phone, and applied earbuds. He found a seat some cars back and poured whiskey into the coffee and let the land unfold before him euphoric as the blood rushing through his veins for the first time in a very long time flowed with whiskey's fire.

"Price of freedom is worth the threat of rattlesnakes. O sediments of time, unchain me, thy Goethean son."

A burly, white-bearded man slung the bathroom door open; one of the quieter men from the Bakersfield wine shop.

"You," he bellowed, in a voice that smelt of whiskey and which soothed and awed William. "You, when in doubt, read Schopenhauer." The man adjusted his conductor hat and lapel and golden chain-cuffs across navy-blue nylon, toppling over at a bump in the tracks. He scratched his bearded neck and grunted.

"What's the arrival time in Emeryville, friend?"

"Yar," he coughed, building his recurring cough to a near-asthmatic attack, gargling and gaggling phlegm through an unopened mouth as William watched him in awe, wanting to know everything about him. "We be there in two hours."

"Wait, Emeryville in two hours?"

"The wine has ye stewed," whispered the man. He laughed. "Time passes on burgundy. I have tasted time, and it tastes like dung. You know what, what a wise man said."

"What did he say?"

"He said he wouldn't go to Heaven if there was no wine."

He waddled, stormed some feet to an open area to latch onto to a steel pole and look out over the passing land.

"You say two hours till Emeryville?"

"Ye deaf," he hacked, breaking into a near-seizure against the aluminum walls. He regained his composure and scoured, overlooking a distant prison complex, whose barbed wire shone in the late-afternoon sun. "I miss me wife. I miss her my dear. No, no you want none of this. Oh, I've had a big lunch."

"I miss my wife also," William said, bringing a conspiratorial look to the man's corpulent face.

"Men don't get married young as you anymore. What, ye hath child?"

"No, no."

"Ah," he groaned, scratching at his neck with an animalistic rapidity, "You isn't old enough to understand all these things. Smile more often, flip your lid wherever you land, because I'll tell you now, and I'm no degree-framing winner nor shall I ever choose so, but the closest an unattached man can come to death in this life is through a routine his soul finds unfitting. Them speaking of comfort cannot even spell the term with confidence. Ye head back now, before I begin a book, I'm a bit woozy, encroach," he gagged, "But we'll get where we're going, and all be well. Life is nothing but a severe, incomprehensible interruption. Contempt ought be the law of the land, but contempt leads to skepticism. We can't have people thinking, now can we? The name's Conductor Francis Aaron Fuccello. The longest story told: 'To earn one's living or to live one's life?'"

William extended his weak, thinned hand to the broad-armed, staring conductor who winked, his open mouth admitting several dented and missing teeth of silver. With a mutual nod he unlocked an anonymous door and they had separated. The message of God, Fate, William marveled, in the conductor's slanted, ominous eye.

When he returned to his seat he found Michelle sitting down, overlooking the last of the desert which the train had begun to accelerate through across the agonizing sand, advancing upon the beginning of a valley, sloping mountains and riverbanks of flushed greens, an immediate rejuvenation of the land and of the soul, the flesh and the oxygen of being. Michelle's side profile, thin and tan and reflective, made a fresh counterpart to all which lay before him.

"Hello, William."

"Good evening."

"I will now take you up on that drink. Last night I drank so much, like the night before and the night before, and I promised myself I wouldn't today," she laughed, turning to William as he sat down beside her, inhaling a fresh cider-sort of perfume, looking down upon her thighs wrapped in a rustled, denim fabric. She landed him two glasses of seltzer water and ice cubes. "I was tired of thinking of having a drink. It seemed much more plausible and pleasurable to have a drink than sitting around thinking about it."

"Even with a young-old lush like me," William smiled, carefully pouring her drink.

"I felt terrible earlier. Strangers are so difficult when you are feeling bad, don't you think?"

Still, she seemed quite mad, but William did not mind at all. What was the good of assumption? Had her mouth not just twitched? He reached up to his formulating beard, his bald head still burned and soon to flake. He knew himself wounded, human as anybody. His company was nice in the form of a beautiful woman, now seeming as if in her mid-thirties, for champagne made everyone seem a little younger and whiskey a little more alive and the disintegration of the desert through their window in the late afternoon while lush forestry blossomed around them made perfect sense, the escape from Hell. It was the way her amber eyes widened so with each completed sentence that invoked madness, and it was the vision of the passing California land through windows which invoked the coming up for air for once suffocated souls. Peace reigned, a darkened heart still alongside the sea, like people thinking along their path, who go with their heart and with their body remain, their eyes set on the glittering reflexivity of Mars.

"I never thought of that. I do understand, though."

"Are you sure we can just drink out in the open like this?"

"I don't know where else to drink."

"Cheers!" whispered Michelle, smiling for the first time, and turning to the unfolding deliquescent landscape, the sun breaking through mountains as Michelle began to tell a story concerning the night prior, as the potent whiskey cured her hangover at once and she even draped her arm around William for an instant as he slept upon her bare shoulder, weary and worn out.

～

"Good morning, sleepy-head," she whispered. William looked about him; the familiar panel-gray interior of the car, the faded ivy-green cushioning outlining the plastic backs of chairs and trays. And while William had not thought of angels since the very end of *Uncle Vanya*, with now his olive branch pressed against his breast, in a moment heard one singing the song that disdains all human means, a cathedral towering nearby, and a little bird atop its spire.

Then suddenly through the window immense clouds such as he had never seen broke at once across, amidst several shades of blue sky, and distant yellow-orange aura glowed across unfamiliar lands, islands parted across the water reflecting the sky's expansive, encompassed shades of colors coming together and drifting apart where between mountains he recognized at once, microscopic, what appeared the Golden Gate Bridge standing still before vanishing sun whence its surreal, ominous glow reflected in the water seemed to reflect again the clouds, creating a hallucinatory projection of paralleling liquids lit by the tranquil sun in a bath of light, and the clouds became one with the ocean at dawn, reflected in the mountains projected past the bridge, as if to land's, to eternity's end.

"We'll be there soon," Michelle said, "In forty minutes or so." She handed him her glass of whiskey and they looked on to the Bay entranced. The sight of it reaffirmed any doubt William had ever fathomed, breaking the chains of any regret he'd had in young adulthood, his near past vanquished, for through its abstract, marred route it had come to this, this crystalline moment, and there was no other way! He could not remove his sight from the bridge, the centerpiece of waves broken across the sky within blackened forestry, shadows of snow-white cliffs and amber clouds. It was the last streaks of sunlight stretching breaking through the last of the lilting clouds, closest to the sea's midnight hour, the reflection then as having reached the day's end of expansion of light on earth that thrust him into no other reaction but to cry tears of joy. He looked away, to avoid the immensity of his sudden consciousness.

"It will be nice to arrive," William said with difficulty; the words would not disassociate themselves from the land, the sea ahead, as the train broke faster still to its destination, racing against the dusk, to San Francisco, U.S.A. He again looked away, and still thought his heart might explode. "It has been a long day." He longed to absorb the moment alone.

"I slept a little also!"

No wonder Nielsen had been so weary to leave, and no wonder he'd been sympathetic for Carson's having conned him to stay those years ago! What would a man not do to walk across that bridge at dawn with his friend back home, at dusk with his love to the other side, to the riverfronts and piers, to the lighthouses and hidden bars, to the abandoned bunkers and climbing trails!

And this, of all visions, nothing more immense had he seen in his life, not a city more surreal at dusk from a distance, for this was no Manhattan, no, but the effects were powerful from a distance—he then knew the city was still far off, unforeseeable, and the feeling evoked within him, the raw power, redemption in the waves breaking against the sunlit Golden Gate, so then what were all of the lights in Manhattan anyway but workers in offices late at night!

He became fanatical with ideas and prophecies rushing through him—so this was the furthest west a man could go, there it was, looming angelic transposition, ye old San Francisco—William lost control of his body and excused himself for a moment to the window downstairs, to soak it in alone. San Francisco grew ever so closer as he called Walter at once from Michelle's phone:

"Hey pal, I'll be in Emeryville soon!"

"You're here! Ask the driver for Embarcadero or get off at Union Square—we're leaving now, it'll take us a bit, going for a long walk."

"I will be in touch!"

They spoke on of the ride north as William laughed to himself at the parallel in his voice to Nielsen's as the phone's service cut out. Lower depths of the sky contained a broad band of orange while the clouds sifted as if carved by a specific, rare element of the perceptive mind's eye. Leaves of shadowed hickories and evergreens began to mount and stream at once past the windows of the train. He returned to his seat as Michelle explained to him in an elevated voice her success in the realm of owning, instead of renting an apartment, in the future, of scholarships she'd been applying for at the finest universities, and her eyes at last became still, fixed upon his in an excessive simplicity.

"So then after all of this and college, William, what will you do!"

"I've no ambition but to live!" he announced, drinking his whiskey. Warmth rushed through his body, the circuitry of his brain resuscitated in a sort of cool stillness.

"By what *merit*?"

Ah, glasses; she had placed upon her frail, freckled nose a studious pair of vintage wiry glasses. It did not matter. It seemed like every girl in the land owned a pair of bifocals by now, the larger the set the more cautious one would be.

"It will just happen as it is now. I've no ambition and I've never felt so confident to live in my life."

"But ambition, ambition is everything!"

Cool winds overtook the once-scorching atmosphere as William stepped to the parking lot at dusk, a chilled breeze akin to the first day of autumn in New York when all of the year's most idyllic, crisp breeze and each microsecond of the day is nostalgic in each way, everything around seems photographable, a nostalgia for the present, the architecture renewed, the crystals of doorsteps cast in fleeting shadows of tranquil daylight, doves singing at the edge of chipped wooden parks before retired metal gates of peeling ashen paint, the soul replenished with each vivid, indispensable breath. He looked right, left, his mad attention caught as he stepped through the crowd of dozens. A four-foot tall man in flannel suit with a clipboard gripped in his tiny hands who screamed at the top of his lungs, an estranged dirty-blonde wig wavering atop his head:

"SAN FRANCISCO FOLKS, SAN FRANCISCO—NOW OR NEVER, ALL ABOARD"

One gathered from just out of sight that the driver wielded his arms like windmills in a hurricane as he tore tickets in half, then closer to the chaos, an acne-torn face reddened and possessed and devoid of features at all aside from a downcast mouth that gave a periodical, 'Bah.' Michelle walked to her car waving goodbye with warm wishes and William looked back, placed his hand upon the cold steel railing, and began to walk up the rumbling rubber steps of the truncated bus; pragmatic thought no longer sifted through his mind but an imaginative continuum, the advent of unconscious recitation; if such a pursuit of fate were to prove irrational at the final hour, then the world would prove irrelevant. Some men spoke of the apocalypse with their hands upon your wallet while others were better off knowing nothing lest yearn; both forms, bound by routine, seemed despicable as flight set in. Orange mist overtook the city skyline cut by fulgid seas, the approaching serenity felt when he looked upon the Bay, having passed through so many skylines as to grow bored with them and yet San Francisco still seemed like no other city within closing proximity. The still Bay Bridge perplexed William into a transfixed state of euphoria, as if his mind were made of ever-changing conscientious landscapes. The driver veered onto the bridge before bursting, roaring across yelling and then screaming at traffic as wind rustled through his open window, the rumbling of the motor crashing to an almost deafening rate once, honking and waving fists at passing cars, pulling ahead faster than anyone on the long bridge of ricocheting steel pillars; the thousands of stranded neon bulbs clicked on at once as William drank joyously, his reflection in the window cast in the colored explication of stranded lights cast up, down, perpetual as if a grand, architectural symphony. It was a bridge that delivered one from the past unto the future, desolation unto ecstasy. Goosebumps shot across his body and the mirage of distant neon lights mashed together at a lucid pace with a speed as to disembody any lapse in consciousness. He clicked on the overhead lamp; it came on strong. Wince. He looked at text upon shelves and chairs and away; the text remained identical. He looked to his reflection; his image remained ghostly in a stream of electromagnetic fields. The engine took roar toward a vision of spontaneous combustion. The sun took a bow and bent over the purple-black reflected sky that exhaled the glowing, yellow-white moon. The motorcyclists attempted to zip past the bus at the center of the bridge though could not fathom coming around the gravitational bend. The varied, wind-worn faces dissolved like evaporated past; *finale de la memoria*. The driver thrust his head through the window, his wig held by a stitch, broke, he took his wig into his hand and cried, "GAH—GEH BACK! GET FUH BACK'AN," spitting dry lifeless gobs to the exterior, surmounting ocean wind. The immense, sloping concrete hills of San Francisco beneath glowing Byronic bulbs which began to differentiate themselves from silhouetted lattice, the flickering spaces seen through fleeting metal panel-pillars of the bridge sets of eyes of angular, hovering chrome caught within a sea of traceless fog. Thoughts, hallucinatory thoughts which broke together like music within the reflective, flickering bridge lamp lights. The traffic jams pressed, overlapping as docked and roaming boats and traversing ships spread and drifted from the evening oceanic crest. The Heaven of infinite varieties bound by death became lifeless. The deathless lens of macroscopic youth, prevalence; *wayward my son, wayward*. The pouch of European tobacco came forth from his torn pocket rolling a cigarette upon the windowsill, sweat breaking through, dissolving tasteless. The developing winds of nightfall's gilded ascent, pursued by a nearing existential reassessment as the past's thirst and hunger of multidimensional poverty dissolved without haste upon the click and clack of multi-ton bus tearing over and past the checkered speed ramp, swaying out and around the chiseled concrete bend en route to some mysterious Civic Center, Mission Street Left Lane, Polk Street. The love he had lost all had lost once, and the apparition of paradise regained galvanized the unbeknownst ramparts of the damned behind walking through the clay ruins of shopping centers and parking meter tickets of dread and sleepwalking into permanent death being the physical tiers of derealization. The bartenders hath Budweiser. The patrons hath kaleidoscope. The imaginative glowing entrance unlike former gated pillars; chemical bread and digital circuses. The technological delicacy of taboo bombed unto objective ruins. The political correctness of Rome; the psychological deconstruction of the land; the rebellion of the individual borne of universal agony. Wind that burst of sea-blue sky, an ode to replenished dusk. The spread legs of language lay perceptive torn brick along wallpaper applicable by he whose broken dream then broke through total dawn; the ballot box doth not suffice; abjection, there is no good mourning; halt, gone, forth, again, far past the irresolute slogans of mouthing tongues ye Pacific at dusk, the looming bridge turning and breaking and do not ever bend:

'This gilded city, ye San Francisco, hold my unyielding heart beyond the nothing past now; wrack the mind open timeless let it barge.'

3

MARKET STREET.

Walking along such a crisp strip of auld bricks and old-fashioned miniature pillars, an intoxicating taste of crisp new air, steel prevention chains trickled with mist beside ringing trolley cars, cyclists, navy-blue taxi cab, the streets were crowded, that is not overbearing, and not a fluorescent sign was seen at first glance, and thus William acknowledged at once that he knew nothing of San Francisco other than it was interwoven of closely-knit areas, eclectic with psychedelia, its geography smaller than Brooklyn. He knew no more and watched downtown pass before his window. Bliss, still, to arrive as a stranger.

He could not have guessed, for instance, that as the driver made his first stop at Union Square, that it was Union Square at all, for the Union Square William had known was intense, jam-packed and filthy without resignation as all of the city of lower Manhattan around it. He stepped out and through the bus driver's broken-slang instructions and purchased a map at a newspaper stand just ready to tie up its awnings. The air swept through with increasing oceanic and lucid wisps; upon his second taste he grew further intoxicated without feeling overwhelmed, as if the San Franciscan air were more intoxicating than a drink. He found downtown San Francisco was neither overwhelming nor underwhelming in its streets, but a perfect cross between; it seemed the perfect city to land on a whim.

The bus took off in a loud, elongated fissure of blackened smoke. From the east a cloud of tobacco interlaced with marijuana pressed forth, the scent of a fresh café's steaming coffee; west, chiseled staircases, contours within a projecting sprinkler where children screamed and yelled in choruses of mystery-religions; south, a beige-orange maze of sparkling sidewalk and a tumbling leaflet beside young men and women drinking from a cooler of chilled, bottled beer with fair skin complexions, throwing a set of wooden die and laughing boisterous; north, with the recurring cool, autumnal breeze within his lungs, a group of young women smoking, drinking, reading before a marble fountain upon a set of wicker benches. A single policeman walked through and looked as if he had broader things on his mind. William waved to the women, drank whiskey, and lit a cigarette of success; here he was breathing autumn, and yet it was summer. The women's kind response had a subtle fragrance all to itself, with the docks and piers beyond them ruminating within, beyond the glittering, vast Pacific. He felt not unlike Fyodor descending the gallows. Wind swept through the plaza courtyard. He walked ahead past the fountains and parks to an elegant white tower standing before the swooping lights of the Bay Bridge, distant and glowing across and upon the water like a towering recaptured memory. He walked about granite steps, ponds laden with lucky pennies, the oceanic breeze perpetually filling his lungs. He had never felt more alive in his life, he witnessed, as trolley cars rolled just behind him, ringing their rusty bells to the rattle of loose manholes, packed with people and heading down the center of a long, ancient street. Red-cheeked women walked beside the waterbeds and magnificent milk-white steps at dusk on Market Street, stretching behind them, beyond the last of the towering red sun. He walked down to the harbor as the bridge towered over him, running his eyes along the vivid colors of everything; never had he seen a city so much like its own aesthetic theory, one which could break and catch and dissolve the tears from one's face at once. He knew, in bliss, tears had long been exhausted from his body. He had burnt out his melancholic soul. He was a young man. The romantic boy, his devoid cosmos, slept upon a park bench in the southern, infernal cities. He would now witness the art of life before creating, solidifying his own craft or art.

Interconnected buses turned away from the water barging forth from Mission Terminal and down Market reading 38 GEARY STREET in yellow-green as he continued forth to the water. At the pier he shouted to the Pacific Ocean a hymnal cry for all that is ragged and righteous, to never lessen one's ambitions for subjacent beings.

He sat at the dock's edge breathing in rhythm with a sort of philosophical prayer amidst channeling ships and a thousand voices. For the first time in near memory he felt euphoric without motion. He had gone as far West, as far away from home as possible, and had no reason to return. The last seagulls spiraled into flight before him and vanished into the night sky. All his agonies had led him to serenity. With the false world in ruins he knew not if he was better though that he was braver. Everything around him operated in his favor; he had awoken from one dream into a reality far richer. Empty bottles cracked against the sidewalks as street sweepers hissed through sunset. He thought back to his mother and walked ahead.

Beside the spraying fountains William studied a set of thin, trenchant figurines. Nervous realizations entered William's mind. One cast the appearance of a young Henri Désiré Landru, the other shorter though he had perhaps once been attractive resembling a James Stewart let loose with long, flowing dark hair, though like scenery upon a stage, either was still yet better viewed from a distance. His anxieties returned full throttle as he realized with one's wave that the prior figure was Nielson's brother, the other fellow some stranger. Even from a distance his face resembled a chalk board wiped clean. The two young men neared in on William and he thanked himself for having confided in barreling through his day drinking. These two, at least to the extent of their bloodshot, vanquished eyes, could perhaps be of no help whatsoever; until Nielson's brother Walter greeted William so kindly that the latter at once felt like an utter fool.

"Welcome to San Francisco," he smiled, "And this is Saul." Saul wore torn green sweater and high-water denim trousers while Walter wore black save his hunting boots of tan-dark blue. William embraced them, looking each young man in the eyes, Saul's mouth parted as if to say something perfunctory before returning to whatever was happening in his mind as William and Walter subsided to the preliminaries at dusk.

"It is great to be here," William said, looking around at the tips of encompassing buildings in awe, "I've never wanted to walk so much in my life." He lit his cigarette with rejuvenation and went to speak.

"Let's go for a walk," Walter said. "It's a small city and I'll show you whatever you want to see."

"You've been all over the place," said Saul with drugged laughter, "From what I hear."

The three men set off back down Market Street as the sun shone its last rays of the day upon Earth. Light gleamed off the tracks upon the streets, the shining spokes of passing bicycles as reflected in the sunglasses of passersby.

"Yes," laughed William, "But it's all over now. This city I think is my final destination. I've seen enough."

"You can stay with me awhile," Walter cut in warmly. "I live in a house for free in a part of town called Fisherman's Wharf, it's out by the water, my roommates—"

Although this was what William had needed to hear another looming burst of excitement was boiling within him and anyone's words around him came together in a clouded maze. The three of them passed by the extent of Market Street William had walked along prior and into new, unchartered territory. Hovering signs for the Public Library, Tenderloin, Mission, Polk Street, appeared one after another and William remained stunned at the possibility of true adventure in such a place and the texture of the climate and held the air within his lungs, letting it out and along the brick pathway of Market, where skateboard wheels ricocheted across the brick. He knew then that he did not care if he died along the way, for having in his life felt such a way and having tapped into such a mode of consciousness. Nostalgia for the present; one thing he might compare such climate to was the first day of autumn in New York City (Less a seasonal matter than rhapsodic, ethereal, definitive), as he had prior, though now his mind became a stream of images as Saul took a bottle of wine out of his coat pocket and passed it around:

'When ragged men climb the docks down near brick-broken Water Street in oily jumpsuits that makes one see black and white for a moment, deliverance of another world where oysters and crayfish crack all the way from Norwegian ponds and tugboats break across the Hudson, shadows of the Manhattan Bridge just behind one as the seasons disintegrate, the metamorphosis of oxygen, where cigar smoke barreled from the depths of a swaying tugboat, a distant foghorn crashing against the gated walls like resounding water, ladders coated with fresh lacquer brought back up past the nets for the evening and to the ancient restaurant going to meet the one you love and all of life runs according not to calendars but to one's heart, when the air is pristine laying grounds of crisp orange-red leaves to fall , spinning as the grave to the living ground when upon such a day one can face being and time with the fervent anticipation of life, the past a mountain of needles, and boot-heels clicked upon concrete in vitality of the city dusk. O Octavia, if you could see him now!'

"Man," William said, unable to contain nonsensical arrangements of words within his psyche, "We have to do everything, and see everything, I can't believe it, I just can't believe anything!"

"My brother says you study journalism."

"I was, I will transfer somewhere around here, everything is all up in the air."

"I could never do it," reflected Saul, "Every time I sat down to write articles I felt as if I weren't living; I'd look out of my window and see people on the streets and I wanted to be there."

"Well I suppose with such a thing, no matter what you're writing, I don't mind spending some hours a day working at eternity, whereas most people work an entire life at quite nothing involving themselves at all."

The debauched trio came together in vibrant, absurd tones of laughter as such a city as ye 'ol Frisco Bay could draw out of a young man. Saul lit a cigarette which broke through in William's direction of fresh tobacco and equal parts weed. This stunned him as now it was right beside him along the open street; what stunned him more was the way the structure of the city made it seem so right, so natural. He cast a bewildered eye upon the nearly concealed space cast in the shadow of a fractured sun, where a homeless veteran spoke to himself: "if you had been able to see everything, everything—then there was no reason for her to give birth, so you haven't seen everything, and so she did, immaculately at that: that is the real nucleus of all this." He readjusted a medium-sized cardboard sign, delineated with black marker in an unsteady hand: 'God's presence is always with us.'

An approaching figure with both eyepatch and peg-leg, and wreaking of burnt hair and stained skin, slunk down beside the sign, pronouncing, "I must bolster my hope and make the sick woman speak at last of the morals of genealogy—O the happiness of the dead, no more decision-making!"

Even the dispossessed had a cunning alphabet, and faith as well! Even the worst of the streets could make one smile, witnessing the hitherto invisible, as if the sun next split upon that specific piece of brick ground with a power that came from Heaven—shop windows of watercolor sheep, a talk with Jacques Le Goff, an *Aeneid* warped by rain, and a ringlet of extinguished candles.

"Don't worry," laughed Saul, taking in enormous gusts, "This is San Francisco, we'll come back to that shop, so watch." William followed behind the two madmen as the twisting smoke blew in flashing diagonal grids across unperturbed passersby, from the homeless to the police force, from matted black tambourines banging against hollowed palms to matching lime-green tobacco packaged, grown somewhere just down the highway in those mountains of Santa Cruz, or so William could envision, and walked on drinking the bottle of wine, holes developing at his shoe bottoms.

William took his cigarette and inhaled; and the very moment he exhaled he was high like no other high, and the city then cast in final clouds of night glowed in series of a thousand reduplicating holograms, bit by bit of fractal matter skyrocketing toward imperceptible revelations, acceleration the word breaking through the colors of life, and still after the initial sequences his consciousness returned to find he'd stepped just a quarter of a block. Neon lights of strip parlors and adult bookstores lit up across the way. The merry somnambulist trotted off the last awakened horrors of vagabondage, dissolving into the audible state whence the forgotten cigarette blistering his index and middle finger awoke him. He yelled and toppled into an old man. The old man looked into his eyes and smiled; there stood a parrot on his shoulder.

Saul and Walter roared with laughter on up ahead, and like a dream Saul pulled another bottle of wine from his coat, wrapped in brown paper bag. Pulling the bottle from his lips in a slight doorway he handed it to William.

"You know Napa Valley?" Saul said, entranced. He looked as if a child in that moment. "Where all of the good wine comes from."

"El Norte."

"Let's sit at this bench and drink wine," Walter said.

They sat upon a metal bench between Polk Street and Van Ness and watched the buses and the trolleys go by. William had the warmth of the sun inside him. The wine balanced any exceeding thought-pattern induced by the marijuana which was nimble for in San Francisco marijuana is not antiquated with paranoia thus it was a different drug or recognitional enhancement of a Heaven-like city depending on one's state of mind. William and Saul spoke of similar family backgrounds and heritages and of being poor and shared the bottle swaying on the bench like old friends, singing classical songs at an increasing, voluminous tone—was it Old Man River?—Walter listened on with light in his eyes as a slight crowd gathered along Market. He was abstaining from drinking due to an experience he wished to not speak of which said enough about the experience. He took a phone call and cut ahead toward Polk Street for a moment.

"This is good wine. I feel great. I haven't drank in moments," William sang through Saul's whistled refrained. They stood atop a pillar as the small crowd widened, swaying to the orchestral nihilism. Through indulgence William had begun to absorb the city within himself having first been absorbed by the city. Saul turned to William pausing, stating in a baritone voice: "Together now!"

William outspread his arms to the crowd, stepped down to take the hands of a young girl and the crowd took to song together, Saul conducting with batons of cigarettes and crumpled newspaper. William took back to the bench for a final burst of song which resonated down past Mission Street, past Van Ness the other way, as men from a neighboring restaurant came out with limbs flailing infuriated at the disturbance and nearing in, when the girl and the crowd slipped, dissolved into the heuristic debris of what looked like, around the bodega corner and vanished, a parade.

"You drunk!" cried the man, "Go way!"

By night in San Francisco.

4

"Now William, one second, if you don't mind, we have to go pick something up," Walter returned. "Would you mind exploring by yourself, Van Ness here, Polk Street, and you can take it straight down to the house I'm staying at on the big Fort Mason property in an hour we'll be back." He pointed down the street, as if to implicate his phone call had been important. "Beach is the last street up at the Pacific Ocean. Comrade, give me your hands; come hither." He climbed up the wall and stood: the Embarcadero a needle drop below, far out, William lost in wonder at the chariot of the sun. "From there, or no, rather, if you're not down there in an hour just call me in an hour and we'll come meet you, do you mind?"

"No, no that's alright, I—"

"I'll take your bag, buddy!" said Saul. "You're a good mensch! There are magnetic mountains, and there partially decompressed mountains of concrete—come and see! Oh it's not that heavy," but still he insisted with drunken eyes, and since William had taken with him nothing of great value he removed the bag from his back and he was turning right onto what that woman had said in passing, into her Bluetooth, 'ooo Polk, yes, I see it,' now transported within the heat of the nocturnal moment. The maddened characters were back down the street again cutting a corner to buy whatever they needed; and William felt rejuvenated walking up that unknown Van Ness with hundreds of cars and trucks hurtling the breeze his way. He watched Walter and Saul fade out beneath billboards as he walked further ahead down Van Ness Street, his shadow within lights flashing from estranged corridors bound by broken columns, aluminum pipe and smoke-screens funneling in and out of alleyways, traversed waterfalls of fog, truck depots and hotel signs, café with sizzling dinners and fresh batches of coffee.

'Through a musky barrel of a bar window cloaked behind brownish tapestry graffiti: profile of she, the guide who gave me hope and light. O Heavens.'

He stopped in for a drink and drank from his cold pint glass, swallowing the foreign language of the senses, his eye upon the nocturnal traffic of the street.

The buildings and dual-lane traffic of Van Ness registered acquiescently with his present state. He passed payphones and contemplated calling east though could not do anything but move ahead, sever himself further from the past. The brisk air was getting cold and he pulled his sweater sleeves down and swaying ahead until irrevocable night had fallen, he approached Hemlock Alleyway and at once turned right.

At the end of the alleyway stood a corner with large multicolored Christmas bulbs decorating what appeared a corner bar. Smoke burst from behind the tan wall, the lights shining in the darkness. He walked ahead.

Through a crowd of young drifters and girls in fine leather jackets with rose-red lipstick stood a young man in white button-up shirt tucked into black jeans, his shirt stained with wine and ash. His curled dirty-blonde hair and round red WC Fields nose which did not fit his thin frame at all made him the most appealing-looking patron of all. He stood beside two women whose figure and faces were concealed in darkness.

"Who are you?" William asked on a whim. He knew he felt good from the weed, wine and whiskey, chain-smoking cigarettes, and followed his heart. "You seem just like me."

The young man and the women beside him laughed, the latter more a level of renitence discarded by whiskey. William laughed as the heavy door swung open behind him and faint garage music trickled out into the street.

"What is that supposed to mean?"

"I just got into town an hour ago and this alleyway caught my eye. You seemed like the most decent person in the crowd." The remaining crowd looked half-besieged, the other half ignoring ridiculous drunken banter. "We're the youngest-looking, ragged types here. I've just blown into town from the east, but first Los Angeles and all of that."

"Well, I'm Isaac," the young man said, fixing his crushed velvet vest beneath his arm, extending his hand to William.

"William. I arrived into town about an hour ago. I'm staying with some friend over near Fort Maiden. Do you know where that is?"

Isaac exhaled smoke laughing into fluorescent lights above his head. The women beside him laughed also as if in a state of shock, or confusion, as though something had been interrupted, but upon the very interruption the something's unimportance had at long last made itself clear through fate and hemlock.

"Do you mean Fort Mason?"

"Yes, yes."

"That's where I live. At the hostel house."

William toppled over; Isaac helped him up.

"So then," concealing his sense of shock, his elation of the miraculous, "Do you know this guy, he is my friend's brother I know him not too well, Walter?"

"I am his roommate! Come have a drink!"

The door swung open once more; marijuana flooded through grated fences; there it was: 'You Can Be My Baby'—Red Squares.

Isaac held the door, roaring into the forming night with laughter, and looking once back upon Polk Street, walked into the half-crowded, dimly-lit bar of eyes and voices drowned by familiar guitars, past candlelight and circular oak with an arm draped across his shoulder as Isaac continued to laugh on in disbelief, William casting a confident eye upon the new world of flesh, intellect and indulgence.

"To think," Isaac marveled, tapping the tip of a vacant chair. "To think Walter had just mentioned so last night!"

Beside the grated fence the young women sat down, smoking, and looking at William.

"Janine and Erin."

Erin curled her hair with one manicured hand, extending the other while placing her lips to Isaac's shoulder. She had the appearance of a cute, European waitress in a plain t-shirt and shorts with thong sandals, although she spoke plain English in a high-pitched voice with the vaguest Southern reminiscence.

Janine wore long, flowing black hair with a white dress to her knees, tan sandals with strap behind the ankle, her nails revealing a recent manicure. She drank gin as William, Isaac and Erin bellowed over the music.

"All the way from San Diego! And still going!" Isaac threw a bottle cap at the unlit chandelier, creating an audible clinking sound in the quiet smoking room as the record switched sides. Oceanic wind burst the texture of candlelight upon each face, glowing in turns, as taxicabs crept along Polk Street.

"It's that sort of feeling when you're unsure if you're about to wake from a dream—I've been experiencing it during the past week."

"I know what you mean," Erin said with enthusiasm. Isaac nodded with his mouth concealed, as if licking his teeth or picking at something; whatever it was, he spit it out to the gates while exhaling through his nostrils. Janine leant over to her purse, her hair flowing across her exposed back.

"Tell us of your trip!" Erin shouted, rubbing her palms together.

Janine reverted her attention from her phone and placed her chin within her hands quite close to William; through the smoke he could taste a fresh scent of cinnamon exude from her body. Isaac polished off his whiskey, slamming it down, snapping his fingers, and leaping for another round.

"Don't start without me!"

"How do you all know each other?"

"We went to school together," Erin said, "And I just met Isaac at his house. Fort Mason. We have great, big parties."

"You'll get to know everyone. It is a small city."

"Now tell me!" cried Isaac, "Of everything!"

They clinked their swirling glasses together and drank.

"Oh, I don't know much but the question of variables; the Bay Bridge at the height of dawn, speeding across it on a bus, or the Golden Gate Bridge from beyond Emeryville, standing before the Sumerian sun, playing tic-tac-toe for prostitutes on tablets. Nay, that was a dream. I will have to write travel articles. I am a journalist."

"You don't seem like a journalist," Isaac said.

"How so?"

"I don't know. I don't know, hmm; you were looking for something else when you began traveling, and not just a city to write articles in."

He rubbed at his round nose as William sat contemplative.

"I don't know what I was after, or if I was after anything. Journalism is just a fine way to make money. I believe I'll live off of the money I have for a while, because I've got quite a bit saved," and cut himself off there, as not to sound childish in announcing that his mother had just put a one-time, both pathetic and integral, emergency fund of three hundred dollars into his account for safety. "I think in the long run I will disavow journalism, though," William announced, "For how can I go on critiquing that which I have not done?"

"It sounds like you already have disavowed it, then."

"I'm here is all, to enjoy myself, aimless as anyone with vague artistic goals on my mind."

Isaac broke into pure summer laughter at William's woeful tone, and after an allegorical climax added, almost, "You sought out an artistic existence of any sort in Southern California?"

"No," Erin responded for William. "That's not what he said at all."

"No, please," Isaac sobered up on command, "What I mean is that what has ever come *out* of Southern California? What I'm saying is that the same thing happened to *a lot* of people in San Francisco. You will see it's like America's little Europe, tucked away with a bad image across the land, and the better for us. Let the country think this is some sick, perverted city; that way the idiots stay far away."

Janine and Erin broke away to the bar as Isaac and William carried on.

"And the best part is that you can relax at the house we've got. We live there for free! This summer, and I've been here for multiple summers in San Francisco, is shaping up like no other. The heights of this concrete hill, its extremities unlike that of other cities, which vanquish false sight and blind one with fleeting rhapsody!"

"To that which ye speak of!"

Clink.

"Where are you from?"

"Delaware."

"I've never been there."

"These girls I've reunited with are wonderful. Knew them from college. If they seem edgy it is because I tried to lay them both at once."

"I would try the same," William said. "Where did they go to?"

"To the bathroom."

"Let me buy you a drink, a pint of fresh Anchor Steam to go with whiskey. Don't you think fresh pints of ale go so well with so many voices and clouds of smoke and glasses of whiskey?"

"If you wish," Isaac said. "It would be like Heaven. The night is still so, so young and tomorrow is a bad idea when and if it arrives, so today you cannot take it too—now hold on, I've an idea."

"What is it?"

"You buy Janine a drink and I'll buy Erin a drink and then we can get you to the house and I've got a quart of Jameson there."

"Is Janine single? She looks too beautiful."

Erin returned, embracing Isaac.

"Where are you two going?"

"Erin, dear, is Janine single?"

"Yes. You know that."

"I am checking. Where is she?"

"Ordering a round of drinks."

Isaac and William threw their hands to the air in an identical gesture, sitting back down upon the creaking wicker, circular plush-covered chairs.

"Isn't life so difficult," Isaac said.

"Does our new friend like Janine?"

William blushed and already felt as if he'd been in San Francisco for half a joyous decade, looking out upon the bustling street, the passing headlights and buses and shop-awnings going up and down in clanging succession.

"He was going to buy her a drink and I was going to buy you a drink. Tonight is so beautiful outside. William, why are we alive?"

"Oh Isaac, cut it out."

"I must know!"

"Have your whiskey; William, do you want to know something interesting about San Francisco?"

"Yes."

"Here is the thing about San Francisco: Janine said you are handsome, so don't go anywhere."

"I'll stay put," William said.

A tattooed bar-back returned with a fresh tray of wavering, foamy pints, placing them down one by one, the streetlamps glowing off each glass in fleeting, successive flashes of light measured by retracting doors. Erin looked to William and away as a signal, before turning to speak with Isaac, whose red face glowed with fever and anticipation, his hand motions almost dangerous in such proximity, rivaling the native body languages upon the streets of Manhattan.

"I hope you like Anchor Steam," Janine said. "It is a San Francisco beer."

William lifted his glass to hers, overlooking her mesmerizing face and aligned milk-white teeth.

"It is the best drink I've ever had in my life," said William.

"I can't believe you're to stay at Fort Mason." She looked down around his feet, William following suit, fearing he should have worn, or purchased, another outfit. "You brought no bags?"

"A chauffeur has it taken care of."

"How fancy!"

"One of Walter's friends brought it along for me."

Janine laughed, saying almost euphorically, "You'll see once you get used to San Francisco there is nowhere else to go in California unless you're passing through and feel like taking pictures. Then nowhere else to go in the country but New York."

"I'm from New York."

"I went to school at Columbia!" shouted Janine. She at once put her hand over her mouth. "For my Master's, history and a bit of psychology, before that we went to the state university across the city."

"So you're all caught up," William said.

"With what? School was a waste of time. A Zionist astrologer was just here before you stepped into my life. He concurred.'"

"I know, but what I meant is caught up with the greatest American cities, as you say."

"Oh yes, yes."

"A friend of mine in New York used to get me all of Columbia and NYU English and Literature curriculums and in my spare time I used to teach myself those courses. I believe that was the real education, nixing economical—and hence ideological—bondage, rather than the education involving others and their flapdoodle."

"I can agree with that."

"You'll also have to know I am exhausted."

"You seem fine. Did you sleep on the ride?"

"There were too many transfers," William said, "And also, I longed to see the land."

"How did you occupy your time?"

Janine crossed one thin leg over the other and folded her interlocked hands upon her bare knee. An arrogant trace of overeducation and psychoanalytic tendencies emanated from her cinematic figure, which William found, in a sort of cognitive whirlwind, attractive.

"I thought—"

"What did you think of?"

"I thought of how fine the champagne tasted and how fine the land looked once we got out of the desert and of some interesting kind people I met along the way."

"I haven't had champagne in ages—"

"Champagne!" shouted Isaac, "Quick, finish these drinks!" He leapt to his feet and ran to the bar, catching an array of positive attention from passersby.

"We'll never leave," Erin smiled, drinking her glass, her pinky finger extended, an arrow shot through the ceiling.

"We were supposed to have been to his house two hours ago!"

Isaac returned with four mimosas set between his arms, swaying miniature orange-yellow tides.

"To William!"

"And what was your last name," Erin said.

"Fellows, William Fellows."

"To William Fellows!" cried Isaac so that most of the bar turned around, a blue cab slowed down, and Isaac fell backwards through his chair. The crowd broke into hysterics; he arose with his drink intact.

"No, no!" shouted William, "To you, my friend, Lazarus, and to San Francisco!"

Janine looked him in the eyes as they touched glasses, the rest of the bar behind him—in a moment of silence each patron drained their respective drink—in another, the proper foursome were back out on Polk Street laughing in the summer breeze skipping and yelling down Polk Street, streaming through the night with interlocked hands as Isaac hailed a cab and they took off for the water. Janine pressed against William within the cab and kissed him—they pulled away for a minute to look out upon the Pacific, illuminative sands and piers at night upon the frenzied multicolored lights and harmonious trance of Beach Street, before William took to Janine again.

The four passed around a bottle of red wine upon the broken-down porch overlooking the outlying Golden Gate Bridge, that thing of mouse-pads and keychains, paper plates and programmatic laughter, flicking orange ash to the ground's peeling paint as Isaac and William spoke, the women laughing together sighing joy with intoxication and looking beautiful with nocturnal prowess and youthful wonder outside of the three-bedroom ranch home. No one had a job though everyone had 27 wagons full of liquor, wine, and acres of tobacco, hemp, and hashish; the great recession. And when the money ran out, explained Isaac, you could obtain welfare and food-stamps in San Francisco, or when your library card had too many fines you could sell the books you stole or trade them in for new books on Clement Street. The women branched off into subtle conversation as Isaac leaned over William's way.

"I'll give you a tour of the house then, after we finish these drinks and have a bottle of Jameson. Did you not bring any bags?"

"I ditched most of my belongings in San Diego. That Saul wanted me to roam without my bag, to go along Polk Street or something I believe. At the time I liked the idea of walking around high without a bag, so I tossed it into his arms and marched."

Isaac exhaled, offering a slight shrug of his shoulders.

"For future reference don't lend him anything. I dislike him. He is a bum."

"He seemed too young to be a bum."

"Well, he has places to stay, and I'm sure he was doing you a genuine favor, but I believe he was on both psilocybin and morphine tonight."

William shuddered to think of the slightest effect of either drug on top of the enhancement granted by the combination of alcohol and marijuana.

"But you'd never know," concluded Isaac, "Because that is the sign of addiction. You cannot tell what he's on unless it is nothing and he is anxious and insane, or felled with chemicals in pursuit of a magnetic-destructive illusion of sanity, balance, content with turning blue in a corner. That is the younger generation for you now and always."

William grew nervous before he decided he didn't care about anything and momentarily listened to Janine speak of something entitled the 'Machiavellian Moment.'

"And what about Nielson's brother?"

"Oh Walter is alright; I mean he doesn't even drink. I hear his brother is much different though."

"His brother is a good friend of mine," William said, feeling better at his sudden, slight dilemma, "And I look forward to hanging out with you and meeting this other roommate of yours. Hope fellaheen Walter don't grow jealous."

"He is incapable of that sort of emotion," Isaac replied, "And that is why we don't speak much. His comfort seems to lie within self-inflicted hardship, and people like Harold Smith and I want to go out and live and read everything and see everything and throw all the American Dream by the wayside in pursuit of individual endeavors. Quite an unfashionable concept these days but we can admit that the people of this land are suffering inside out, and perhaps someday we will be the voice of reason. I could tell by the look in your eyes in the bar that you will love San Francisco, and to talk with Harold who arrived here a year or so ago under identical circumstances to yours and meet all of his, our friends before I go North. His girlfriend left him in the desert, so he sold his bicycle and caught a train here. In fact you seem as if his younger brother to me. Brothers of impulse. Pleasant outlaws. Ha! We will have a ball before I leave. In fact my going-away party is tomorrow night. Let me show you around the house."

William could say nothing to the news that Isaac was to move, nor could he enquire whereabouts. His stomach felt leaden for a moment, though he had felt worse, and overlooked Isaac glowing with excitement as he gave William a tour around the quaint home.

Gravid living-room with extensive film collection, innumerable art, photography books and cut-out of Van Gogh's smoking skull on the wall, a desk of a table in a hallway of a diner room with a reading chair, a faded melon couch, kitchenette through which ants crawled igniting some sort of other odd excitement within William who just then thought to himself, 'Garnish thyself in poverty;' it was a perfect little bungalow whereby Isaac had just then announced the couch as William's.

"Get some rest. You'll need it before your day tomorrow, and then the party at night. We will be up all night."

William collapsed upon the couch, asking, "And what shall you and the women do tonight?"

"Similar things as to tomorrow night, last night, and all San Franciscan nights," smiled Isaac, zipping up a black leather jacket before the flickering light of a butterscotch candle which casted subtle shadows upon the beige wall before the grand piano, its pedestal-vase containing sets of hunched dandelions.

"If you see either of those two tell them I apologize for not calling, that I am exhausted, and to leave my bag beside me if possible. I may, no I am going to fall into the deepest slumber I've ever had in my life. I don't know if I am coherent but please relay that message. My toothbrush will be like the coming of Mashiach in the morning."

"Yes, sir," Isaac leaned over to shake William's hand. "We will do lunch tomorrow. I'll take you all over the place."

"Lo spirito della vita deve prevalere, il fratello o," William said with closed eyes as he used the last ounce of strength contained within his body to shake Isaac's hand, as all of the weeks of destruction, rebellion, confusion, doubt, betrayal, agony, poverty, and violent ambiguity had all at once surmised.

The psychological culmination of such plagued irrationality had not won, nor had it been swept aside. Rather it had spit thrust into its face before being converted into a calculated, structuralized revolt against the forces that dance amongst the outer rims of he whose broken dream has taken him wayward, bound by multidimensional exile. He was proud to have survived, he thought with his tumbler of whiskey, and proud to have never returned home, and even more proud to have intercepted his agonies with strength.

Though he could not see it from the couch William again envisioned the seraphic lights of the Golden Gate Bridge before him, the electronic lanterns of the Bay Bridge behind him, thousands of souls traversing through the paradise of San Francisco. He knew that the worst was over, picking at the scars of poverty and sunburn along his arm, combating a serene takeover of unconsciousness though William could not commit to sleep still yet for he knew that for a long time to come the days of his life would contain blue skies, the wisdom of the exiled, the spirit of youth, O wondrous exile as synchronicities are rarest in the chaos of subterranean journey though more rewarding fruits of freedom are amidst, found, signaled along such immense paths, the sway of artistic intoxication O city of orgies, the perfume of those gorgeous, angelic women and O what a feat to at last attain life, individualism, having crushed all foes along the way, every single last snippet of drudgery, of weary exhaustive banalities common-thread as they could be gone, then to fall into a deep sleep, smiling, William Fellows' lips red with Californian wine, calmed mind strange, iterate wonder of this Harold Smith renegade Isaac had mentioned and through a dream the words of that winter-time madman melancholic Saint Gideon as he himself tore off through the night for another Brooklyn doorway, Rockaway Beach, another pursuit of truth in trying, fraudulent times such as theirs he sang: 'Wayward my son, wayward.'

Words broke through his mind as the door swung opened with that crisp, oceanic wind. He half-opened an eye and watched Janine tiptoe to him on bare feet, concealing a precious smile. She stopped at his side, leant down to his lips.

"Come here," William said, and pulled her in.

"I thought you were asleep!"

"Hibernation, my love."

She pressed her body on top of his, exchanging positions through bursts of laughter.

"You will be at the party, won't you?" Janine pulled away, whispering, and brushed her disarrayed hair back with her hand, her shadow rushing across the minimal wallpaper.

"I have little choice; though even if I had numerous choices, I would go to see you."

They embraced again, now warming up a chilly upper arm, resurrecting a thousand little geese.

"Not tonight," she said, "You handsome boy. Not yet. You'll think I'm whore and laugh at me with your boy-friends at the party."

"None but a bitter fool could laugh at a woman so beautiful."

"May I see you tomorrow?"

"Come here," William said, kissing her neck.

"Oh, stop."

"We can go on a date tomorrow; you'll show me around."

"We can walk across the Golden Gate Bridge and have dinner in Sausalito! Oh, also, I heard you saying the most vicious things to Isaac earlier."

"What did I say, nosey?"

"You two speak so ridiculous together!"

"What did I say, though," said William.

"You just said the most correct things about the world. I want to hear more of it. I want to read everything you've written."

"I'm interested in what I said, Janine, but my long-term memory is in ruins. I'll say more things like it to turn you on this weekend, sweet lady."

"First you said something about a girlfriend."

He looked into her dark blue eyes and could see already she was growing attached; the city at night, he gathered, was just so spellbinding that such things could happen without warning. And all the better, and more natural, without warning. He took his glasses from the coffee table and yawningly applied them.

"We are long through."

"Are you sure?"

"Yes."

"Why did she leave you?"

"I needed a woman and she was a child."

"I understand. Kiss me."

He pulled away to observe her flushed radiant face before pulling the blankets over their bodies and kissing her; at once she responded in the hot darkness, handing William her wine, the perimeter lit by her lighter:

"Aren't you going to take my dress off now?"

"No. Put that fire out, you're going to kill us."

"Why not?"

"Why what?"

William wanted to laugh out loud at state of intoxication, if not the state of his life.

"Here," Janine tucked away the lighter. "Why aren't you going to take me now?"

"Because I would think you were a whore on Saturday, like you said."

She asked with timidity if he would.

"We feel the same way in multiple ways," William said. "But kissing you is so much fun. It is such a nice way to end the day. You taste so nice; I want to taste your body in a fresh state of mind. I feel your legs wrapped around me; you feel me."

She moaned, running her hand through his hair:

"You said the nastiest thing earlier."

"What did I say?"

"You said that our generation no longer anticipates anything but wars in obscure countries and thereafter gadgets to keep us distracted from them."

"So what?"

"No one says anything like that."

"Well then they're grotesque. Annihilate them."

"Let's go to sleep."

She lay still for a moment before her hand went first, then began to go down on William. He came up for air as Isaac and Erin ran back outside with their whiskey and stacks of philosophy books, leapfrogging over a sidewalk-seated woman with her head between her knees, clutched tight, wearily unmoving from her ring of scattered needles, around the corner and into the kaleidoscopic night. William waved goodnight and placed his glasses back on the coffee table and inhaling that fresh air streaming through the crack in the window, went back down.

5

'HAVE I TRULY NOT dreamt a thing,' William considered, awakening to a notion of interior consecration that was something he had never known, nor would have believed, existed. For he awoke late in the afternoon beside his bag, all items intact, and a perfectly still house through which blew the intoxicating oceanic breeze of the Pacific. His elation was further amplified by the array of handwritten notes for him on the table, held down with three little unopened bottles of Fernet: Saul explained they'd ended on an adventure, everything was intact, they'd be by later. Isaac would be working across the street at the café until five. Janine would be stopping by at four. The sky was expanding evermore, cloudless; he inhaled the fine fresh wind as if for the first time, stepped out in underwear and plopped down upon the canopy chair. His colorful dreams from the night, the years prior, channeled, suffused into the light of day with the persistence of Olympian runners. He roamed about the still, vacant household, the sun beaming in through each open window where paper-thin drapes sailed to and fro and took a glass of Jameson. Through every window the sky was infinite and gas blue. Janine had even left a witticism of her own!

'The burned books are worth celebrating inasmuch as most celebrated books are almost worth burning.'

He tucked a pen behind his ear, dressed, and took to his drink in the kitchen. On the refrigerator William noticed a delirious, handwritten note addressed to him:

"Ay! Isaac tell me, no, well 6:00 AM! You are sleeping on my couch! No, I've got a bed now! I knocked over my ashtray inside—sorry if I woke you two! Tomorrow I will be at the Hearth, a bar on Geary Street and the best unknown Saturday daylight drinking spot, you see—Isaac tells me we must meet, so we must! Hello Walter! Walk up Van Ness, right out front to Geary one-way street 38 to the numbers look for seven, or eight, or nine, I forget which Avenue but one of the bars on the left-hand side of an extensive street! We'll drink before the party! Isaac's party. Must sleep beforehand. Will try to wake you. See you soon! Love, Young Bacchus from his Stepdame Rhea's eye."

There was an indistinct line arrangement following the text which symbolized a signature and brought a widened grin to William's face. Harold Smith?

He poured another whiskey and took a Rainier Ale from the refrigerator. Warmth ran throughout him at once and he feared he would miss Janine; hadn't Isaac said the party was in two days? But on a Sunday? No, no, tonight—already.

He took a pile of quarters from a large, ceramic jar upon the kitchen counter and bolted through the aluminum back door into the day, leaving his half-gone pint of Grand Dad out on the counter as to compensate. He cut through slight forestry around the hostel building, past map-pried facial inquiries, and unfamiliar hallways, taking a route Isaac had pointed out to him earlier in the prior evening. He looked out upon the sea, out past Alcatraz, and sighed with relief to exist before walking into the cafe. Walter sat behind the desk melancholic drawing something on an old menu sheet. In a sense he symbolized once more to William all of that which he had longed to leave behind, and once again he looked up with dismay, feigning both reality and concern.

"Hey," Walter said, looking up. "Sorry about last night."

"Oh no," William smiled. "I had a nice little excursion and then slept for the first time in weeks. I feel impeccable. Thank you for tending to the bag. How was your evening?"

"We ended up by the Sunset. An area of homes and shops near the ocean. My girlfriend lives out there. I am mad at Harold—doubt I'll be at the party tonight but do as you please."

He looked away, Nielsen's twin brother in the flesh, exaggerated and distraught in his leather jacket and greasy hair, indecipherable homemade tattoos.

"Who?"

"My other roommate. Not Isaac. The one that left you that note."

Walter tucked the sheet of paper aside and lowered the overhead music which had been playing from the speakers, as outdoor chimes twinkled to and fro.

"You are welcome to stay but I don't know if you will be able to stand Harold. I don't know why he didn't just go into his room.

"I was going to kill him," he added to the prior pair of general statements. William observed him, dumbfounded, unsure to as why he'd already become a part of some doldrums or another.

"If something happened, I must have slept through it."

"I told him you were staying over and when I got in at five in the morning and everything was quiet I figured everyone was asleep, you looked comfortable, and so I went to sleep. Then at around five or six in the morning I hear howling from the gates at the other end of the parking lot. A man and a woman, screaming and shaking around signs and gates pretty much belligerent. For a second I heard glass break and more hysterical laughter. I thought for a second that someone had just escaped from the mental institution. Then the voice got closer and I grew nervous, you know, apprehensive. The one other person around is the front-desk person across the street, and this person approaching sounded crazy, their partner in crime no less crazy."

William held back a spreading grin, one of which had origins he could not pinpoint. He pretended to observe the tacky posters along the spacious, salmon-colored foreigner's cafe, and to rub his cheekbones out of exhaustion as means of holding back a smile while Walter spoke with morose rage boiling in his eyes:

"Then I got nervous when they were getting close to my window because the voice sounded familiar. I was just about to fall asleep. To get past those gates out front and to walk down past the side of the house my bedroom is inconvenient for anyone going to the hostel, you'll see, so when shadows began to stretch across my windows and the woman, or whatever he was with, fell laughing into a bush, I got ready to do something, anything. The male helped her up and began to do an Indian call at the top of his lungs. It was so loud if I hadn't heard them coming, I would have had a heart attack when he made that noise. One of the most offensive disregards for the asleep I have ever seen. So needless to say when I realized it was Harold Smith as he crashed in through the door screaming into some teenage girl's ear about Artaud, waving around the biggest bottle of Jameson I've ever seen in my life, I wanted to kill him. I screamed at him. You and that girl slept through it? I'm sorry. I could have killed him. I know you just got in and—"

All this time William had taken Walter's somewhat vague descriptions and applied them to this mysterious Smith character. How could he have slept through such madness? Where did the man come from and where was he going? He screamed of Artaud at five o'clock in the morning wielding enormous bottles whiskey, arm draped around a temporal teenage love? Hadn't such things existed in films relying on such celebrations of life as antithesis in conveying the message of sterility and mundane acceptance of a meaningless life in order to have the average viewer feel that much luckier to work as much as possible and then beyond that threshold at a certain conscientious perimeter? How could anyone feel such contempt for he bold enough to break the chain that bound they who worked their lives away trying to find good work? William wondered, observing the anger spread across Walter's face, and could not wait to meet this third roommate. He confided also in his residency over in Japantown—he would later call Man Ray.

"He and Isaac are both insane," Walter said. "We can go explore the neighborhood tonight. You won't want to be around for their party. Did you get Harold's note?"

"What?" William asked, baffled and realizing that in less than twenty hours he had been thrown into a game of favorites wherein his favorite was leaving in one week, the other favorite he'd known through tales of varied extremes, and one of the two people he knew in all of San Francisco seemed to let him down each time he opened his mouth, as if his world were but functional in accordance with the gravity of an obtuse, albeit sought-after, infinitesimal negativity.

"He was trying to wake you up even while I screamed at him, reading incomprehensible lines from a notebook he carries around with him now. He tried on your glasses and tried to kiss his date. Then, on the verge of collapse, he wrote out that note to you and taped it to the refrigerator before he crashed through a set of chairs and the girl called a taxicab. I had to escort her down the steps and out to the parking lot. She struck me as a terrible person."

"Look, Walter," William placed his hand upon his tattooed arm, "We'll call your brother this evening and enjoy ourselves. I dislike seeing you get all worked up. When I think of you I think of your brother and I don't want you spoiling your fine day or anything. Just imagine how gorgeous it'll be when you're off work!"

"I needed that," Walter said. "Do you want a drink?"

"I'm fine," William said. "I'm going to go off and explore."

"Here, take this bottle of wine with you."

"You keep it. You're too good. I'll buy a nice bottle of Portuguese wine later for the two of us."

"The owner's rich. There is a taste of San Francisco for you."

"Dinner is on me."

"Could you watch the register? I've got to make change."

"Here," William said. He spread five dollars' worth of quarters, dimes, and nickels on the table. "Now we're all squared up; I'll still buy you dinner."

"I don't even pay rent. Money is nothing."

"We'll have a first-class summer. See you later, bud."

Walter carried on with monotone words to which William replied with casual nods of the head, thinking of nothing but walking all over the city once again until dusk when he would barge forth through the door of the house once more with a jug of wine and meet everyone in the world, and indulge until the end of it, and that Janine! Janine! I'd like to know you well!

Perhaps William could help Isaac and Smith set up the party after meeting Smith along Geary Street at his daylight bar. No, that would be too much. One must remember from time to time to set a splash of coffee into one's whiskey. Instead roam around all day and come back ecstatic talking to everyone about everything. He could not take Nielson's brother's side; that side was a danger to experience. He must care break away from the likes the Walter and Saul, ease in upon Isaac and what was left of his time in San Francisco and Smith, for Isaac spoke of Harold Smith and he had suffered what William had suffered; that, he knew on some unconscious level, was the golden pair; and know their people, and then begin to gather the ranks of some sort of abstract comradeship together, to indulgent wisdom and experience, that incredible clarity San Francisco distills within a young man's lungs and upon his heart.

"I'll be out of here by six," Walter said. He regained William's disintegrating sense of attention. "If you want to meet at the house and take a walk along the ocean out by my girlfriend's house, and explore lesser known parts, more of a nature-side of the Bay. Maybe go out to Berkeley."

Distant lights of that city he'd had a taste of just hours ago were calling his name once more, like eruptive waves rushing, distilling out upon the shoreline of his conscience; when he thought back upon something as simple as the way that bus driver had switched lanes across the Bay Bridge and the sense of awe that had paralyzed William when he looked out for the first time upon the San Francisco skyline. He had never felt such a way upon sight, for he had been born into New York City and had arrived in San Francisco with nothing left but San Francisco.

William shook Walter's hand before he walked back across the short field of shrubbery and into the house, whistling and snapping his fingers. A sense of pity ran through William when he thought of Walter's warnings, disdain; a sense which was cut dead, for he had the bug of life.

"Look at you!" cried Janine, stepping to William just outside of the Fort Mason house. "With—what is this?" She took the bottle of wine in her hands with a smile as William ran his eyes upon her body, her perfect face, the sunlight shining upon her golden earrings. Ah, and to know now that Helena had been but a child—just to think of her small body, her narrow mind. Janine, in the drunken light, seemed at least four years older than him. "2004 Dehlinger, my parents had this once. You have fine taste!"

He led her by the hand, trotted up the old wooden staircase. They sat down to the dining room table with light streaming in through the open window, the open door. William rolled a cigarette and another. Janine pointed to the couch and the arabesque blanket folded upon it.

"I left before sunrise—you kicked me off of the couch!"

"No, I didn't," William said. "Not you."

Janine showed him a black and blue mark on her arm with a frown. William apologized and they had a glass of wine, kissing and laughing between bursts of talk and cautious looks upon one another. Was it cool to enjoy another? Was anything worth effort? In the therapy of desire, amidst Heidegger and the tradition, just who shall teach the Great Architect (Between flesh and force)? Everything and anything seemed natural, at any time, and from beginning to end, when in San Francisco.

"You look great in that," William said, pointing to her gray silken dress stitched from a shirt. "And the black top goes well also. It looks so good I never want to see it again. Is the party tonight?"

"Yes, William; have you plans already? Do we have any glasses?"

"No and no. I just could have sworn it was tomorrow. We ought to do something fun today, something enticing."

"I—you—I've never drank wine from the bottle . . ."

He stood, kissing her on the forehead, got her the finest crystal glass in the cabinet, looking to the note on the refrigerator.

"Remember, William, I have an appointment this afternoon you are welcome to join in on out on Geary Street and 10th Avenue."

"Let's go get you some new clothing and go to Land's End and then go!"

"We'll drink the wine first though, correct?"

"Yes, darling."

Janine blushed for a moment, as if ashamed of something she intended to explain by doing so. William waited, smoking, and inquired.

"We'll wait until tonight for all of that," she said.

"I always side in a much more wholehearted sense with decisions I make during daylight."

"Did you read the note I left you?"

"Yes, it was a fine witticism. You made my day."

"Today is your first day in San Francisco! Come here and kiss me!"

They took to the bed through the doorway and lay in the comfortable bed overlooking the hundreds and thousands of 45 records lining the walls in crates.

"What if this person comes home?"

"He's waiting for me on Geary Street," William said. "Do you ever hold it in at night because you have so many great sequences of ideas in your head and you feel as if you get up to expel anything from your body you'll lose some of the great ideas?"

"Listen," Janine said, having such a state of mind, "Let's call a taxi and go get your black pants, a white button-up, wingtips. A fresh outfit. I'll pay for all of today." She took a thousand dollars in cash from her wallet, "And you get brunch and things tomorrow."

"We'll do that then. I'm exhausted. What time is it?"

"Four-thirty."

"We'll finish this wine first and here, have this, dear." He handed Janine a dandelion he'd taken from the vase atop the piano and made love to her twice.

Walking, forever walking, high-drunk in lust, arms around one another with Janine telling tales, William studying the park around him, across the fields to the streets to meet the cab, he pulling the near inaudible, crumpled note from his pocket and revisiting the general thesis in the long golden field packed with families and lovers, distant harpsichord, through to the fences and to Polk Street: 38 bus to some numbered street below double-digits, breaking through parades mysterious street signs, aligned faces, cafes, past the smells of fresh pastries, coffee, thick nasal décor of bars immense with wet oak and boiling dishes, the homeless people and the boat owners petrified at the overflow of human knowledge, this and that smiling as he, she sang plans of an apartment before families of pelicans taking flight from the sidewalk edge to tips

of towering buildings, delicate middle-afternoon ambiance falling forth
from their spiraling, patterned multi-dozen wings, out toward the never-
ending water. Melancholic fervor gripped William as he clutched his
quarters, languid universal lamentation, thought of his need to get to the
bank, biting his nails a moment, his irreversible strut a refusal to mourn.
It was a moment in his life with Geary Street distant from the cab of open
windows and blue fresh air rushing through their hair when he felt the
blood of words beating within what remained of his heart, that he was
alive, alive, that then his focus and his pride and his dreams more vibrant
and alive than anything and yet O how those families of birds flipped and
flapped to the limitless sky he gripped his coins within his hand and let
life rush through him stopping to lean against Janine at sudden stops. The
cab let out. They drank the wine at Van Ness, laughing through yearning,
wine-dark lips, and a 38 rumbled past, the intensity of repellant, fumi-
gated air knocking William out of his euphoria. Two buses in one, held
together by some sort of creaking accordion, monstrous in sound and
scope. The bus was packed to the brim. Toothless madmen stuck their
jagged tongues out at William through the half-opened window covered
in faded marker still fresh with soaps of rags. Janine leapt onto his lap; he
breathed her black hair, and its loose scent of coconut. He looked on as
the bus began trekking downhill, traffic pressing forth behind and ahead
beneath the concept-sun, its reflection across the peacock ostentation of
skyscrapers, restaurants, apartment buildings, all with a tint and hue just
brighter than any other place in the country—it was unnoticeable right
away, more so something that soaked in with time, yet the unconscious
had long been yearning for, it felt, the city's aesthetic verisimilitude.

Another less crowded bus came to the stop and a basket of characters bolted inside through three, four entranceways.

"Oh they're all just jam packed today—forget, we'll take a bus back,
then, here I'll get another cab."

He saw little through kisses but cathedrals as the Brandeis-blue cab
turned right on Geary and crested uphill.

William looked around half-drunk at the odd layout, an extension of
Geary Street not quite what he had expected in its almost deconstructed
urban albeit near-hamletesque stature in wideness and array of innumerable shops before making out the avenues where traffic broke both ways.

44th Avenue. Between roaring daydream and Janine's long, soft
hands, he had lost himself and was off the mark, a stigma to which he
responded to by seeing just how long the cab driver would continue on

his pace. With his mind on fire, and listening to Janine tell him about her time in Brooklyn, William found himself being transported out to the end of Geary, far beyond where the Hearth should have been.

"I say stop at 10th! You no respond!"

"We can go to Land's End!"

"What is that?"

"We'll go!"

"Go to Land's End," William said to the driver. "And hurry up already."

The driver sped up, groaning down to 48th Avenue; let them out beside a decrepit fence bound by rust-colored ivy scaling the Avenue for the remainder of the block. He was observing his torn bus transfer from Los Angeles when around the quiet block Janine pointed to an enormous opening in the land to their left, the crucial brown of ridged mountains, the eternal green forestry of tree-lain pathways, and the long blue muted sound of the distant oceanic altar-bed.

Janine led him by the hand, her silken skirt fluttering in swift photographic gusts, past the sign which read LANDS END and from an observation deck they overlooked all the immensity of the glittering Pacific Ocean at last, again, drinking wine. The Golden Gate Bridge stood in clear view some miles beyond, clear as day, and William stood alone upon the ledge awestruck and, for the poetic moment, alone. The faint sound of crashing waves prompted his last reflection, his last vision and reflection before diving first into the city life. With all the enormous water and land below him now, his last contemplation of San Francisco, of this accidental journey, of this exiled education in personage and motive vision:

Upon the concrete dock overlooking the Pacific with wind rushing through his body and hair William Fellows had a feeling within him parallel to the last time as if he could remember though he knew it with such clarity just then he had kneeled before God in church and prayed to the Lord. Long ago this became a psychological impossibility for him, to put all forth into the hands of a God he'd known through infancy and childhood which then ruptured upon itself through adolescence into young adulthood though instead at that very moment and with his blue eyes upon the Golden Gate Bridge, William breathed and was filled with the conviction of one who believes in a higher power; he had not felt this sensation since childhood nor did he fathom he would feel it again and toppled over into a coma with the sudden weight of such a feeling; he had rejected the lugubrious absolute, thunderous conviction and faith within no such God, no such other man nor another man's idea, but William Fellows had the capacity of God shrouded within himself; destiny, the thunderous conviction, the accelerated state of mind; O, and let parasites beget parasites, as I transcend Hell, because I was flesh.

He cupped his hands over his mouth and called out to the ocean, singing, relaying his spastic arms, birds racing forth from nests and shrubs, all of his former senses disintegrating into a recaptured self with the immediacy and glow of a lightning rod now overlooking the white crest of water meeting sand and multilayered greens and pathways cascading inward and outward upon itself containing mazes and trails natural as the distant auburn boulders and cliffs he pronounced himself alive through an uncontrollable bliss that had been rushing dually through his conscious and unconscious for a night and a day, a night and a day, in the unreal city where the two come together like the sea to the sky.

Another world had passed over, voices cast within distant limestone recognition.

"Lost loves, lost friends, lost republics, all lost but that then ahead regained," William said, stepping down from the ledge and turning his shoulder with tears in his eyes and sunlight cast upon his worn shoulder and walked back up the road breaking through an unnamable collage, a whirlwind of thought, back to the center of things: 'That Truth is false lest it be motive, pursuit, Responsio haec procul dubio excelsa est, sed adhuc longe abest—et quantum!—a veritate regained. Death to dogma, and death to the mouthing tongues which bark corrupt commandments, for the solitary voice in the world is the voice of the heart, thy self. A Heaven he could believe in was such a vision at Lands End, such a sequence of events as his life had become. Hell, he knew: Consciousness in the modern world. Let me then break through Hell to another side of the volcanic ascension. Lo, and Excelsa timeo.'

William and Janine sat overlooking the land, the field of light. They spoke of candy cigarettes and censorship. Erin called:

"We're going to the party, right?"

William laughed and stood to relieved himself in the direction of the ocean.

"A cab will be here soon; let's walk up!"

"But the Hearth!"

"That's where we're going!"

William walked to Janine and put his hands on her hips, took her around in an evening dance.

"You're beautiful."

The cab drove back past once more the variegated shops, restaurants, cafés, bistros, and the clock broke down to a shattered photogenic hourglass, the driver a welcoming young man in straw fat, carmine-jade feather, golden-brown mustache curled to his rosy cheekbones.

He opened the heavy barn-colored door of chipped plaster, framed by white-brown splinters. The crowd, five around the small bar, none younger than 40. They drank glasses of liquor and ate peanuts from old cocktail glasses surrounded by piles of chipped shells; a plain Spanish woman swung her hips to a jasmine hula-hoop painting the toes of a decorated mannequin at random from a child's watercolor art kit.

"Don't look so enthused," William said to Janine, absorbing the cavernous nature of the bar. "Instead let the splitting of soft shells falling upon marble provide an abstract sort of opening credits to our arrival."

"It's not that!" Janine shouted—"You've brought inside the bottle of wine!"

All the men looked over and laughed; the painter turned, admitted herself as bartender. William finished the bottle at the counter and placed it within a recycling bin. Familiar strums of an electric guitar sounded overhead before giving way to the nostalgic interpretation following drooping, distilled strings: 'Stand—by—your—man—bemp, bemp, bem.' The dignified middle-aged woman turned her attention to Janine and William. The door swung open, closed, the sounds of the street dissolved. The patrons at once mouthed statistics of pony-races from an old-fashioned television set perched upon conjoined ashen nightstands; the bottles of the bar glittered before a string of outdated lightbulbs like the absent eyes of mislaid children in a crowd. William gathered that he, they, must have missed one Harold Smith.

"Take a seat, hun," the woman said to Janine as she leaned over, squinting to the top-shelf stock.

"What is that on top?"

"Jameson aged 16 years."

"We'll have two—William?"

"Dash of ice."

"That all?"

"Two bottles of High Life."

"None of these men are whom you are supposed to meet," Janine said.

"I have fathomed that. We must have missed him. Was there a young man in here earlier?"

"You mean all afternoon?"

"I believe so."

"Harold," hacked Rodney Dangerfield, collapsing.

"Oh, *Harold*! Yes, hun, he just left."

William's face showed disappointment as the bartender got to work, wiggling around as if still within hoola-hoop.

"We can go after this if you want," Janine said. "And stop at the store and get you a new outfit and go to the house later."

"I have such a fun time with you, Janine. Have you ever heard of love at first sight?"

"Oh, stop. Lust at first sight is all."

"But what if that evolves?"

"Then the evolution cannot be contained by the preceding analysis. Cheers, my dear."

"You speak like a surgeon sometimes," William smiled.

"Because I want your heart."

"Do any of you have a razor-blade or a knife?" William asked the patrons.

"Shh!" Janine stutter-laughed, collapsing into William's arms. "You smell so manly and natural. I could breathe you all day."

"Tell me, dear," William said, taking a sip of his whiskey, chasing it with the incoming urine-yellow, perspiration-slicken bottles, "How nice this afternoon was? Couldn't we get a room of our own and do that three or four times a day?"

"Stop it or I just might. Stop it right now, William."

"No."

"Don't be defiant."

"I'll have, no, never-mind."

"What?"

"Nothing. We have a big night ahead."

"Can you imagine sitting here all day with these people? Were they ever young?"

"Doubt," William exhaled.

"Oh, don't be cruel."

"So how do you know Erin?"

"She is my best friend. She thinks you're nice. I told you, we all went to college a few years. She liked you right away, you know, that's the reason why I went for you."

"You are cruel, Janine, just cruel, you modern, modern woman."

"Oh, be quiet."

"Because Erin says, is she from Europe?"

"That's what everybody says!"

"Is Isaac leaving?"

"Don't talk about that!"

"You become so colorful and flushed when you drink, it makes me want to make love to you right here. Let's leave; I want to go to the bank and get money and then go rent a hotel for two hours and then go to the party."

"No! I'm paying today, my treat!"

"I want to take you on a date to the bookstore, though, and then ice cream at a nice café; what about that?"

"Tomorrow," Janine said, kissing William on the cheek, excusing herself for the bathroom.

"Yes," William said.

"You OK, hun?" The bartender approached, "Hungry?"

"I am," said William, "But yes, no, yes I just arrived in the city yesterday from the east! I'm just having such a ball sometimes one forgets one is hungry."

"You looked hungry," she said, smiling. The natural elegance of such a kind-hearted voice submitted itself through the meditative, plaintive gesture of the bartender leading William by his hand around the bar to a faded hallway of smoke-stained wood and exposed pipe hanging overhead beside plaques and posters of famous baseball players and unrecognizable musicians. Limbed tile. Steaming trays of fresh chopped meat smelt of great seasoning stood spread aside small clay bowls of cheese, chili, peppers, lettuce, onion, tomato, beans, rice. Floods burst through William's gums. If he were holding something, he would have dropped it. Janine presented herself behind him and they had a hysterical feast.

"Leave her a 20—this food is too good."

"We ordered a few drinks, babe."

"I'll pay you back. I would rather be outrageous than stingy. She'll always remember us; I'll always remember her."

William studied the map of San Francisco along the wall, ran his index finger through a maze of forming cobweb, dust, donning gracious bow to the bartender for what had been the best meal he'd eaten in weeks, years, decades.

"Ah yes, yes I will, yes I will, yes!"

He rolled four cigarettes, took $200.00 from the ATM.

"What do you feel like when the night begins to fall in San Francisco?"

Janine looked to the sky, to the city streets, to William:

"A taste of honey."

"You, Janine," William said, with his arm draped across her shoulder as the cab pulled to the red-colored curb, "Are a true-coming dream."

She kissed him deep as another 38 tore by and ahead, descending toward the distant twinkling lights of downtown.

"Just please, darling, tell me you're not just drunk, because the night's just not even begun."

"I've never gotten drunk," claimed William at once, stepping to the leather-layered backseat after Janine. "But on the contrary I've gotten quite lucid."

Janine took him through the Vietnamese tarps and live-in hotels of O'Farrell and Larkin, the endless blocks of torn mattresses and needles, lipless mouths and boom-boxes with broken springs, machetes and packets of morphine slipped between wheat buns, lemons, embers breaking off and trailing, disintegrating back to the way of Union Square. He pulled together a silken white dress-shirt, fitted black slacks, black wingtips, mustache wax at the consignment shop, bought a can of Guinness and a glass from the discounted liquor store on Sacramento and walked the streets sipping at the warm froth as the cold winds and fog returned from the coast. They took the shoes down California to a shiner and spoke on the corner looking out along the rising hill of concrete, the waving hands projecting from the ringing trolley-car of indispensable hunger for knowledge and experience, then down Polk Street to a café where a young woman Janine knew stood in a candycane-colored skirt behind the counter. She caught up with her friend as William looked out upon the street once more; it always came back to Polk Street. Janine returned with a tray of Chimay and peanut butter cookies.

"Dessert."

"To better, far more righteous variations on an old theme," William said. The past—now who had said that it was not even past—it seemed, upon reflection—as if a dead zone, as if William had been dead or disillusioned the long time between the winters with Octavia Savonarola—and now Janine, O lost illusions recaptured, methodological San Francisco nocturne!

"We can walk down to the house from here at dusk, it isn't far at all."

"Good."

"We can go by the water again and walk up that back way and stand on the broken-down pier overlooking Alcatraz."

"And never go to work again."

"Never," Janine smiled.

"And then after the party we can go to your neighborhood and do everything."

"Yes, yes," she turned to her friend, "Did I tell you I moved!"

"Where!"

"24th, Valencia."

"We're neighbors!"

"Do you like the drink, honey?"

She wiped froth from his mustache and ran her hand along his leg as patrons began to spill into the café. The serious way in which she touched him, in some strange intoxicated way, William knew suddenly it would be a fleeting affair; and all the better.

"This Chimay is perfect; everytime I drink it I'll always think of you." He thought how strange it was to become close with anyone and always consider the first conscious encounter be it decades past or perhaps a day, it wasn't so much first impressions that intrigued him but the singular image of a man or a woman and how it came to embolden the flower-like blossoming granted, as if an entire relationship pressed forth from collages of images or a singular image. He drank Chimay and broke peanut-butter cookies in half as voices began to break and rush across the contour of the café.

He watched Janine drink in the reflection of the window. She seemed wounded, almost ineffectual by either beauty or something beyond beauty. She seemed to William not quite unattainable but uninterested in becoming obtained or obtaining anyone of her own, or otherwise. William pressed his fingers to lips to his feel his breath and looked ahead, unaware of the street, but breathing and absorbing the universe and such a thing felt fine as artificial light streamed in across the hand-carved wooden table, milk-white porcelain coffee cups clicking against one another in basin-racks.

"When do you your best ideas come to you?"

"I don't know," William said, folding his napkin in half. "Let me think of that."

"Mine come, I think I've just realized, during rain sequences in Kurosawa films."

"Yes, that is a pretty thing."

"My family lives in the countryside in Connecticut. We'll go when it's nice out."

"We'll—"

Janine screamed at once and fell back. William's heart skipped a beat. The café patrons turned to look at the young couple.

She pointed ahead and William saw the homeless man, his face like a funeral, staring down at Janine and grinning, his hand almost down his sweatpants.

"Oh God," from the counter. "Not him again!"

"Get out of here," William said. "I'm going to tell you once, and that's it. No one is derailing my summer."

Goliath looked down and threw a canister of nitrous at the windowpane; William followed an inner urge and took to the streets.

"I said don't bother her," he said.

Swaying, Goliath looked at William, or through him, shifting his crooked jaw, lunging ahead, and missing—his body smelt of rotting cabbage. William gave him a sharp right to the misaligned jaw, to the solar plexus of the temple, and another right hand to the dampened nose, breaking it. He took him by the bubble coat as the streets stood still to watch, the café patrons watching from the doorway with cupped mouths, and threw the beggar into an overflowing pile of garbage cans where his flesh seemed to break away beneath encroaching sirens like deterred cells. William had a feeling that this was one of countless symbols beneath the veneer of an artificial paradise.

The crowd cheered him on. Scarce children clapped their wax crayons together. The barista thanked him with another round of Chimay. William accepted before bandaging his hand and washing up:

"Maybe now he will stop coming by!"

"You were great!" Janine said, blushing, "You're a boxer!"

"There is no way we'll have such an excellent day spoiled." Police took the man to their gated van, waving canisters of obscure sprays in the air, pointing pistols each which way. William loathed them, their hypnotic lights ricocheting through the windows, as a dishwasher filled the microscopic crack with some sort of glue and the crowd returned to its rendezvous. "Is everything still intact? He had me."

"You look perfect. Let's go for a walk when we're finished—this place gets crowded; it'll be night soon."

"I didn't know those types of people left their cardboard bunkers a few blocks that way where we passed the great sandwich shops and dollar stores and frightening bars."

"Seriously they don't leave the Tenderloin but right here we're at the Tender Nob, a cross between Nob Hill and the Tenderloin."

"That is a logical way of putting it. A suggestive portmanteau."

He wondered, reflecting upon alluring texture of her subtle pink lipstick, her middle name, her age, if she had siblings, fears, had voted for such chemical segregations in the tyrannical name of equality, both her perennial luxury of self-imposed grievances and her body's dire accessibility, favorite colors, films, books, records, seasons, if she'd traveled the world, but he knew not to even bother; that he hadn't even contemplated such thus far and in terrible pangs of fleeting sobriety knew in his heart that it didn't matter anyway. Instead, he said aloud as they stood to go, arms interlinked:

"At last: to think and create and breathe for no professor, no God, no parents, no curator, no editor, no director, no nothing, no routine!"

Within the windows of a Russian Hill bookstore Janine insisted they shop the guides, the classics, the discounted calendars, the current works of American writers that everyone praised and bought, those books that no decent person liked at all. But the pilgrim longed rather for a big bowl of lentil soup in some obscure cauldron rather than a look at what dopamine minds paraded.

"It took him eight years to write that, I heard," Janine said. "I used to see him all the time on the Upper East Side. He walks and writes like an idiot. He should be executed."

"Janine, dear," William said, "Don't get worked up. Most modern writers are not writers at all but whining idiots, monosyllabic marketing executives writing lines for people addicted to political theologies, having never read Polybius."

"People read this *crap!*" she cried, throwing her hands to the sky. William took the opportunity to speak, uninterrupted, from the black pit of his heart:

"The problem is that when this sort of writing is 'Hailed' and 'Anticipated' it does nothing but destroy the public's subconscious take on

individuality which is the crux of a prolegomena to toppling any tyrannical, plagued regime of globalism, or international communism, such
as ours, you see. We've lost good art as a nation and now again have reverted to relying on politicians, criminals; thus we vote for politicians
based on looks, jokes, and entertainment value, cheering on their hand
in disintegration and refusing to acknowledge such hypocrisy; we will
continue to ignore such devastation because it is a mirror of our own
unwillingness to look inward once more, to redeem the qualities of a nation of individuals, to rebel intelligently, in that we continue to fight for
ventriloquists. When even the ventriloquists require ventriloquists—it is
time to go. Yet out of such ashes, I believe, shall rise the individuals who
begin any new era, and God knows we need one—We keep thinking the
way we do and our day will come. It will not be the answer to the world,
but it will be in our times worthwhile, and necessary, and will prove the
regimental possibility of cultural reticence to further generations. I have
no intention of ever controlling anybody or any nation's livelihood, and
thus I stand up for the men and women of the world attempting to live
en route to the truth. This man here, in every bookshop window, has
written no masterpiece; instead, he has scribbled in marker some archaic,
grandiloquent diatribe which wields no redemptive qualities nor realities but the exactitude of cliché and sterility. The whole culture's bound
by bands of mental vomit, encircling our psychological planet in vulgar,
lyric-devoid relapses. Polyglossia is a dish best served unabridged. The
man lacks style. Most promoted writers these days do—but then so does
our generation. One feels embarrassed to hear their names mentioned in
elevators. But come on, beautiful, we are young and alive, and our night
will beat the lifetimes of such people, until they realize what eternity is,
here on the streets of San Francisco; for those who grasp deepest the dying light in order to rage against it without ever looking back."

Oceanic wind rushed through Polk Street as Janine pressed her
lips to William's beneath the distant, echoing rapture of cathedral bells.
A light, cleansing mist had begun to fall across their bodies as Janine
dreamt of his golden hair in the sunlight past; or so at least was the look
in her eyes within that salubrious second.

Someday she would allow herself to be loved.

TRANSPOSITION CIPHERS

Through tall, long gates and into the long maze of interweaving concrete slopes and green fields of grass whereupon night had fallen and William, Janine could hear the distant voices growing, nearing, in multitudes. He laughed to himself concerning all the day and with his nihilistic air skipped forth wielding a cane of broken bark, following the irrefutable ardor of pluming chemical voices and sharp, static edges of sounds with Janine at his side.

They stood just past the gates, before the house, William swirling around a portable whiskey sour.

"Ahead!" he cried, as they began to run toward the party, the wavering neon, laughing and between interlocked, swaying hands, the drink tossed over his shoulder, bursting in a stream of whiskey and shattered glass upon the cratered car lot.

Rounding the corner of the ramshackle peach-colored home and tripping over his own feet in excitement, William cut through the shadow-den of wavering, elongated leaves of grass and into a stifling wall of pale gray smoke, Janine exasperated and laughing just behind him. He walked at her side through the smoke, now within the split-second midst of one hundred voices belonging to vocal cords belonging to bodies affronted by the faces of the intractable city night.

"Where are you from?" asked one of the prettiest women, handing him a stained joint. Someone called her name. William stepped away toward Isaac as Janine turned to her friends, to a box of wine.

"I am from Polk Street," William announced, to which the small, gathering crowd garnished zero dismay at his ironic tone of voice—that of peripheral intoxication—but grew more interested. "Before that all up and down California, before that aboard the California Zephyr, before that college in Pennsylvania, before that birth in New York City, beneath this all I don't know, but I believe here is where I'll stay. Ye Old Frisco!"

Smoke blew in a perfect, expanding shot from the very same mouth which spoke such maddened words. Dozens of people, young and alive, streamed to and fro the house in a succession that at once brought a golden aura to the once-still bungalow.

"And you, then where are you from?"

"Norway."

"Jacksonville."

"Oakland."

"London."

And so on, when someone brought up politics to the raving young aesthete who clamored to make the rounds further with Janine. Could this Harold Smith character be inside; wasn't he playing the albums?

"Politics," grieved William, his body gesticulating high. "I have no time, no time for that! Politics are dead!"

He and those closest broke into hysterical laughter as swarms of people turned around smiling and all the conversations of the night grew voluminous, aglow, one specific raving woman breaking bread over her half-shaved head.

"Git drunk!" she shouted, emaciated fist in the air, walking straight through the front door without looking back. William grew conscientious of feeling insane for a moment before realizing that he had been, in the words of another sporadically adequate man, "Thrown to the dogs," and there the dogs had been throughout the land, and here were the angels now across this land, one before him guiding him back to the old house having near fallen off a little cliff while tinkling at the shrouded fount of moon.

Crowds upon crowds of unfamiliar faces encompassed the ranch, all senses overtaken by the sea of voices ruminating throughout, beside oldies music blaring from some invisible corner of which William would investigate sometime later, where arrays of couples and singles did the twist and drank wine. Janine led William to almost familiar faces (As if from discarded dreams), warm introductions with no recollection of names, bottle of IPA, as familiar hands rubbed at William's shoulders; he turned around.

"Isaac!"

The two threw their arms around one another, Isaac introducing William to a group of people, then another group, all of whom seemed down-right interesting. All the jam-packed living room had become tinted with kaleidoscopic rays.

"I must tell you dear Isaac, this H. Smith—whom I still have not meant—sent me on a wild goose chase earlier, I mean well, no, it was one of the best days of my life in recent history, but then well, woman, cafe, drunk, high, drunk-high," William exhaled as Janine turned to a friend. William smoked his seventh cigarette in a row. Isaac burst into hysterical laughter and readjusted his pitch-black blazer, chain-smoking American Spirits. "It is wonderful this party you've got together," shouting over the music, "To see so many people laughing so hard, as if for the first time every time," William observed, draping his arm across Isaac's shoulder, refusing to recall his looming absence.

"The Hearth, Heavens," Janine began, her eyes wild with the Fernet and that felicitously cuckoo sexuality as she turned to kiss William, about to begin a dance.

"The Hearth!" Isaac bellowed, gaining the attention of passersby, "Smith sent William Fellows to the *Hearth*!"

"That woman fed me damned well!"

"Oh William, it took most of us years to find that place, that's all, you'll find all of the real bars, the good bars soon enough, Hell we'll go before I leave, two nights from now we'll go down Columbus Avenue into North Beach for the hell of it, cut out to Market, to Mission and all of those bars, but oh, Hearth, that is the best day-drinking bar—No wait, now we were talking about these books, all of these books, and you the other night—"

"Isaac, brother," said William, "You're going far away soon, far north," sitting down into a chair, pulling one out for Isaac who placed his whiskey-sour upon a coffee ring and sat down, lighting two hashish cigarettes and handing one to William, "Let us save the literary talk for letters, for cafes, for novels, for poems, but now let us drink!"

"When we are older and more worn out and uglier it will be less fun," projected a handsome young woman with flowing brown hair through a hazel labyrinth of smoke, blaring music, and one hundred interweaving, simultaneous voices. William stood at once and took Janine's hand in dance. That woman was his. Isaac handed William a can of beer and shouted at the moon.

"Is it better to love someone, to love yourself, to love life, or two or all three?"

The two swayed with delicious sweat breaking from either forehead, hand in hand, from counter-top to table-top upon the floor of peeling cellophane, their blackened heels clicking in a unified epiphany, an abstract thought process brought aloud, alive, unbuttoning the sweat-streaked silks.

Janine paused for a moment to laugh into the palms of her hands. William stepped back high, drunk, 'Green Onions,' looking over the insane, building crowd, smoking with Booker T his hashish. The beauty of music, he thought, is that it provides structure to the unfolding of the unfolding of our phenomenological ideas—dreams enhanced and interwoven by things such as hashish colliding with whiskey and an armful of Jewish Princess Hipster.

She approached him, this time holding on a little tighter. The more crowded a room became, the less one needed anything save to blow the clock to smithereens. William went to kiss her upon her neck when Janine asked, "What are you talking about?"

"O nothing," William laughed with her. 'Had I just said something? Don't know.'

And when the laughter had then subsided he planted a kiss upon her neck, surrounded by a sea of sound, wherein one moment later after a soft sigh of ecstasy into his ear she did just the same and for some time the two kissed, in the corner of the room, breathing in one another's bodies like the freshest air. Even if for some limited time, a forlorn conceptual abridgement, William now knew what it was like to love another woman. It was possible and it was marvelous. Love was shooting a vile dictator and hanging, drawing, and quartering a rapist at the same time, but even better. It was quitting a job one hated, finding a once-lost wallet, stepping right over a land mine, or peaking on LSD in Death Valley. It was dying of withdrawal and coming across a hidden, miraculous stash. It was everything and more, just to be there. It was the feeling of Janine's mouth opening upon and within his own; that was all William needed then, and everything else in the world could be classified as unnecessary if there was a moment available for clarification. Everything in the world—the past, present, and future—dissolved.

When she had to get back to her friends that too was fine. William took up his perfectly poured Guinness and followed the trail of smoke back out to the patio, Bali-Shag burning between his exercised fingers. The party, the lifestyle was like a parade, the marching band pounding, pounding on.

PER LO MIO CORPO AL TRAPASSAR D'I RAGGI

Upon the deck William stood atop a set of sturdy, broken leather armchairs and observed the multitude of the night through circular hands wrapped around his eyes like binoculars. People came and went through the distant gates, cabs and buses sifting through the winding lot to the front porch, people with their arms wrapped around one another laughing in the distance, onto another wondrous party, bedroom, subway train. Janine stood below, talking and shouting with her friends whose name William would never remember drinking beer or otherwise, smiling and laughing, they looking, waving up at the boy atop the hill. Isaac, somewhere nearer, was raving about the heat death of the universe with a smile on his face, garnished in his fitted black suit. The stars shone and seemed captured within the eyes of each young, passing face, reflective and glittering upon the dark waters, where a foghorn broke across the Pacific, and William gazed out in pursuit of the Bay Bridge. His white shirt was unbuttoned; he began to button it back up and let it go, seeming a more appropriate signal: ragged, destroyed, yet feeling fresh, brand-new. The group William had first stumbled across and the characters Isaac had introduced him to were now getting together, lunging back up the dampened hill, making eyes with William, whose notebook protruded from his breast pocket, pint in one hand, cigarette in the other, displaying the little journal Janine had bought him, knowing all the while that so much was happening already that to keep a journal would be breaking against the current rushing to power in his favor; still, as the fog rolled in, he kept a sentiment for the start with anything pertaining to the advent of arrival, his preemptive strike against fate, against life. From the house came a song William he had always loved: The Vandellas: Nowhere to Run, Nowhere to Hide.

'Who is this man playing music?' he asked himself, 'Who is this Smith? When will he step foot from his station? Also, is he a figment of my imagination? Is this man a symbol for something, rather than an actual being? Cigarettes.'

A chill, shuddering ecstasy, overcame him pertaining to nothing in-particular. He stepped down from the chair and threw his cigarette into an enlarged flower pot filled with old, hardened soil, falling through the door, into the bodily ventriloquies, voluminous music, swaying hips, a presence of stiffened arms and darkness, strange arms extended, twisting around on another and to the ground as if confetti, streamers.

"William," a dim voice exhaled beside him.

He turned around with grand exaggeration, as if a mummy exiting his tomb, and met eyes with Walter. Walter looked out of place in fractured, torn jeans, too-large flannel shirts, mud-streaked sneakers. William looked in place; that much was undeniable. He motioned his index finger to Janine, to Isaac, 'One moment.'

"Long time no see old buddy old pal," smiled William, patting Walter on the shoulder. "The wine was—How shall I say—*Perfecto*." His gesture went unacknowledged, his demented tone of voice discarded, this to which he elided frames of laughter.

"I'm just stopping by to get money—"

"Money? Wouldn't you go to a bank for money!" asked William, rolling another cigarette, offering one to Walter who declined with a plain swipe of the dangling foliage with his hand.

"I don't use the bank. I keep cash in a safe in my room. Also—"

"You lucky dog! How amazing that is! I think I will copy you sometime very soon, unless you've got this all patented!"

Janine approached William, leaning into him. William put his arm around her, meaning to introduce the two and to not introduce the two at once.

"How drunk are you? I have to tell you something."

William lit his cigarette and prepared for the worst by drinking steep from his pint glass, downing shot remnants and shots alike raising Herr K from the tablecloth dead. Perhaps he would stay with Janine if the whole thing collapsed upon itself. In her dark eyes a maze of hidden yearning.

"Please, tell me anything, I feel soberer than God."

"It is not good."

"At this point I've decided there is no such thing as a bad experience for someone like me," admitted William. "Because well, no, go on, and go on. I'm talking too. I apologize."

"It's not about you. It's about Saul."

"Saul! Where is he!"

Walter swallowed. The swiftness of the gesture expounded beyond the roaring sound of music. Still William tried to show a shred of concern. There was something condemned within the soul of Nielsen's brother, one could tell by looking into his glossy slits of eyes set on a holocaust of poetical anarchy. William could not, for the life of him, take it.

"What's happened—Is it your brother?"

"Do you remember his wife? She came by, though you were sleeping."

"I do," William recalled, pulling the image of the young girl from a portion of his mind reserved for dreams. "I do! With the short hair! I thought it had been a dream!"

"His wife is dead. The viewing is tomorrow. I was with them earlier; she overdosed on heroin." Sledgehammer to the stomach, by way of nasal exhalation. "I am going to see him now, at my girlfriend's place." In his leaden voice a tonal agony beyond things morose, that voice of having witnessed—if not having encouraged or enabled—death. "I'll be out in a minute, just wait for me here." He looked around the ecstatic crowd. "I despise all of these people," his voice alleviated once, marching into his room. It rushed through William like a bad dream.

"That is so awful," Janine said. "What is he going to do?"

William rubbed at his eyes and projectile-vomited into that sea of broken glass and orphan beans that was in fact the sink. He knew not what to do. Janine tugged at his shirtsleeve.

"Who was that dope?"

"My friend's brother. I met the man he was speaking of once, his wife never, though I saw her once last night. Did you?" She hoped it was a fleeting notion; it was. "I'm so tired of tragedies—"

William knew the truth was that he was bound to Nielson's brother because he was enabling him sleep on the couch. Walter did not feel like taking the bus across town alone, and did not feel like helping Saul along alone, and wanted to someone to talk to about the incident. It seemed fair and yet incoherent amidst the telescopic casuistry of the party, though nor did William feel like being in an empty room, one of the same serious drugs that had killed this woman. He could put his faith in Isaac, who was to leave, Janine, whom he'd just met, or Walter, excuse himself for the night, and sober up beside two druggists that had just watched a young girl die, but then he could not bring himself to leave the party. He wanted to live; let the dead bury the dead.

"Let's sit for a moment," he said, retracing his steps to the front yard.

Janine sat upon William's lap, the two overlooking the night, the Golden Gate Bridge beyond, sharing a cigarette, swaying upon the rocking chair. He nestled his nose into her shoulder for a moment, refraining, "It is a situation of pity. And there is nothing more heinous than pity. That is all."

"You sound like Spinoza," Janine said, feeling much better.

"Was Spinoza confident?"

"To write that way you must be the most confident of all, more confident than any President or General, and also, you must be smart."

"We are saints," replied William, kissing her lips. She kissed him back with force. He knew a little bit of Spinoza and assumed Janine had just mentioned his name to echo of the Ivy League until she continued through her long, sexual kisses:

"You must come to a point of losing faith in everything before you can attempt to piece the world back together your own way."

He ran his hand through her long, flowing hair, upon her neck, and knew he must share a bed with her that very night. This she knew also. It was the way starlight reflected upon their youthful eyes, exalting primitive beauty and modern elegance at once. "So let us now go back into the kitchen where he won't find us, because, the man's got to turn himself in! I can't go getting involved with overdoses!"

"Wide-open space is not the most inconspicuous," Janine laughed.

William polished off his pint in one sip. The young men and young women sang at the edge of the patio, the edge of the lawn, their body language as if to say:

'If a picture is worth one thousand words, then I am positive an actual scenario in life is worth something like one hundred thousand words: perhaps one million. Our aspect, or rather, our point will be made.' There were even pagans down at water's edge, preparing some type of altar for a band of druids from the East Bay, the altar-builders singing:

It was such a thrill it was hurtin' me
I was sufferin' in ecstasy

With hands interlocked the two squeezed through the living room and into the kitchen. Beneath a watercolor arch William could hear Walter's voice call his name. A tall, thin man who smoked cigarettes between his middle and ring-finger had taken William's seat, he noticed, while at the same time noticing Walter race through the front-door, flushed. William poured two whiskey-sours and thought of how to approach this other man, whose date stood beside him.

"And what is your last name, after all, William?" asked Janine. "I know I know it—I know I must have heard it said."

"Fellows," William said, handing her the strong, wavering drink, approaching the tall, thin man without enquiring of Janine's last name.

THE HARVESTING OF KRONOS

Vapor and fog pressed in. Swatting at smoke with his long, thin hands, the man in the seat made a strange noise at William that removed an irritated look from the latter's face. Through circular glasses intelligent eyes peered into drunken eyes and at once William regained a sort of balance on the evening. And at that instant William knew that he must know this man, but that he must for some docile reason test him first. At times eyes meet as if in pursuit of one another, or any sort of recognition in surrounding, spectacular chaos.

"That is my seat," William susurrated with a whiskey-laden voice, conscious of the hollow observation, taking a step back against the counter-top as Janine galloped off to embrace a flood of friends.

William's words were met with the bawdy, boisterous laughter of a thousand clapping hands, a laugh which roared overhead of the intoxicated montage, which clamored past the roaring intelligentsia and into the glowing white star of the moon, which drew attention from passersby and distant peoples alike, and tore some unwarranted shackles from William's elemental stature. In a split second William thrust his hand forth and broke into a collimate fit of hysterics, the type of actual laughter which can halt tanks and thrash unconscious bodies alive, the type of laughter which confines some men and women to the literal dungeons of ages past, and the figurative dungeons of orange cylindric today, prescription uniforms, prescription cells, prescription lives and prescription deaths, although others break free with such laughter to barge within and throughout the city night of the soul, accelerating beyond the very boundaries of alphabetized existence.

William extended his hand then, which was accepted.

"Thank you. Thank you for laughing in my face. That was the greatest story I have ever been told and it did not contain a letter of a word of a sentence of a paragraph of the avenged world of Spinozistic intercession. What is your name?"

The young man stood a clean half-dozen inches taller than William and wore a hearty expression of Talmudic adolescence on his face, further evident in little locks. William wanted to refer to him as 'Comrade' and go with him to coauthor a Platonic-Sabbatean manifesto, thereafter grab the city by its pearlescent limbs and flip it upside-down, shake the money and wisdom and madness out of its pockets, and swallow the world whole through language.

"Phil Cohen—but oh, why not call me El? Interchangeable."

Phil Cohen, refraining a conversation with the young woman beside him concerning a novel he was at work on which had no actual end, that he would work on his entire life and perhaps serialize if anything (The lack of end he was conscious of; certainly this correlated with the secret intellectual life of William Fellows. The young women then went to smoke, and El removed a crate of Anchor Steam from some unknown portal of the refrigerator, going, "RAH, RAH, RAH, RAH!" At last William had found a city wherein creative projects were the norm, whereupon one might dig ever deeper.

When William had finished telling his story, his entrance into San Francisco, Phil Cohen was having something of a hysterical seizure on the grass in the backyard, lit with flickering old-fashioned lights and the glow of a dozen faces yearning for that which this real world false had denied them of, led them to the spiritual crucifixion of morale, and so now the new generation was unafraid of laughter, and William could laugh at everything: Helena, Home, Hell of the Self. Melancholia: Dead on arrival. Once more he could laugh. And again, everybody now—

It was all laughable because it was all so human; thus simultaneously haloed and purgatorial, they got drunk and regretted nothing, and as Janine later left William Fellows with her phone number he kissed her, opening his eyes for one second to look at her beautiful, perfect face beneath the Estrucan veil of hashish, the concentrated face she made as she kissed him, and then a second sometime later to look out upon the distant glowing Golden Gate Bridge which symbolized to him every dream he'd ever had. Now it stood still before him at the dock's edge as Janine's cab pulled in, the towering orange bridge which embodied that architectural foundation to begin all endings with the past and never vice-versa before the ever-rippling sea and shadowed valleys, mountains beyond, who'd built the bridge, who'd writ the book of love and loss, with cosmogonic soil in cavewomen fingernails.

Isaac, Phil, dozens of other boisterous young men and women whose faces and voices he now knew by heart, never to remember till next time, when there—Lo! Behold!—The fine dame came in, the counter-girl with her candy-colored dress, purse filled with Chimay! William fell back into the bushel as El Phillip swiped through the night with tales of travel and horse-races, self-destruction and the Demiurge. William kept his eye on the barista who knew everyone, her thin figure seeping from the night as words collided with the sound of glass and music, bits and pieces of sentences and songs strewn together by an abstract interior design:

"And disintegrated local poverty, you see, if we can just get this guy, then . . ."

"Then he said they made love in the bathroom for some time, this which they came together, you know? He, man, is like Jean-Pierre, arriving on the American shoreline at last, through the ocean of another, no relation, no, man, of course . . ."

"You know once I lay lusted within your arms, the contextual dual! The heat of the moment—more, and if I never see you again know that it means less than memory for love once thence lost whence I woke alone—"

"Gentile pilgrims and like a prism of lust launched herself into the future. All the hammered city, hers; all her hammered grace, a city. Adrift, the eyes of laughter filled with the tears of life, drink drank drunk with his arms around his memories, drink drank drunk!"

Dawn grew near, the party almost calming down, the volume of the music lessened. Couples spoke with knees touching at the edge of milk-crate seats, the others standing, shouting, drinking rum with wearily narcotized optimism.

"I've postponed the move another few days. That girl isn't moving into my room until then I just found out, so it is not over yet. The voyage does not end here after-all," Isaac said to the barista upon the steps, the latter toasting the former before a moment of wordless reflection passed through them. William thought of last week as Isaac thought of tomorrow as Phil Cohen thought of last year and how offensive the idea of time was, while Harold Smith—Must be him, there, young man in the suit—swayed wide-eyed ready for whatever on Earth came next. He emerged at last in his thin, wiry figure, half a dozen tattoos, pinstripe suit rolled up at the elbows, ragged bowling hat and bottle of whiskey.

"You then," he approached William. "You then who rustled my sheets!"

"What do you mean," William said, combating exhaustion and yet accepting Smith's drink at once, knowing who he was by the elevated tone of his voice, the first and last one that could have spent his days at the Hearth.

"I mean the Hearth! I was there six hours!"

"I arrived as you left!" Again, William experienced that rare, sudden warmth of friendship. Harold laughed and spoke on before him, exuded carefree spirit at the witching hour whereas most people could seldom ever speak of being, or strive to attain a carefree nature, excusing himself for the bathroom and turning around to the side of the deck.

"We will continue the party into tomorrow then, I presume," announced Phil, adding, "And William, any plans?"

He and Isaac sat down upon a long bench, saving room for William and Harold. The record had stopped; William took the needle away and returned, entranced by the allayed chaotic nature of the night. Everyone had left the party and the sun was beginning to rise over the Pacific.

"At some point I'm meeting my mother's friend who owns a restaurant in Japantown and an apartment there whose wife is in Thailand for a few week and he is allowing me to stay with him in that time while I attempt to line up a job, or room, or something to that effect."

"You don't sound so thrilled," Isaac said.

"Please don't mind me, I am just tired, tired."

"Come take a walk to the river!" Harold vociferated, staggering toward the bench. Although William was confident he could not move, the tone of Harold Smith's suggestion banished his doubt as the last of the party-goers waved goodbye.

Such nights, William reflected, brought something to life beyond art, beyond the artless, but never in between. The look in the faces of his memory was the look of concentration lost, in a successful effort to the live the life of art, and have life be the artistic format; words and colors were wonderful but not as wonderful as life, life high and drunk out in a crowd of similar people, studying the stars, breathing in fervent, oceanic air, having been lost now found, lonesome now lusted, alone now surrounded, with never the presence of any overbearing; it was a new foundation to place the idea of life within, for even in the darkest human moments that sometimes last burning fields of years at a time, go on hobbling into the languid night of death like Peter the Hermit, if just for the prospect of feeling young once, and the day of adventure and individualism are the only prudent days at all, the sunlight upon broken columns, desolation angels come not with peace in hand but with swords in mind.

"*Man*, we need more women here," Isaac offered, searching through his phone, rifling messages, his face glowing with the last fragments of energy, "Because well, I, now here, then, William who was that woman in the striped dress? Why'd she leave? What, how did that happen when, do you know?"

"The barista?"

"Who are all of these *women*!" Smith shouted so that he echoed, resounded for seconds across the water thereafter, flocks of birds bolting from their nests.

He stood upon the crumbled concrete ledge and shouted at the top of his lungs, beating his chests, stuttering illegible phraseologies, grabbing William by the tip of his shirt and shaking him about, to which William laughed and began laughing, yelling inaudible phrases himself, old Indian chants of dawn, whence Smith persisted with glowing eyes, "Bring us the women! Swallow the world whole through language like he said—right rather ripped!"

They took off for the docks, William dialogically footnoting something about a Hegelian plant.

"Git drunk!" shouted William, quite high, pontificating, "I just disregard the disdainful and banish all but creative belligerence! I know I am an artist though I do not know what type of artist; all I know is my mind is always reeling, an acceleration which cannot slow down! And now, ladies and germs," climbing the wreckage, arms interlocked with Harold Smith drinking the last of his Old Grand Dad beneath the San Francisco moon, slurred with hysterical drunkenness, the holograms crossing eyesight, "To my dearest Helena C.—Shall I never see you in, even in memory, again! Adieu, and to our love!" He leaned over the edge of a banister and projectile-vomited to the littered litmus weeds. Afterward his body felt much better.

Isaac stood. He ran off to find the women of the night. Phil Cohen was sleeping beneath the grand piano, and Harold Smith, William Fellows, began at once and without declaration to walk down to the hills of grass and concrete from Fort Mason to the edge of the Pacific.

Upon an old, weary splintered dock of the bay with a single red balloon tied to a pillar, swaying in the dawn winds, for a night-cap yelling and singing of the moon and the sun and philosophy and with old Alcatraz before them, speaking as the night had begun for both of them in the straightjacket afternoon, and rippling water passed just beneath their feet and a breeze of perfection cast through the air.

"What is the meaning of anything?" William asked, "And what did Isaac tell you about me?" He skipped a pebble across the water.

"He told me in some strange way that you reminded him of me, and that for some other reason he liked you. He said you were worth doing a favor. You're friends with Walter's brother, right? I assume he is much different. But now I went through what you went through—So hey, stick with me, bud—Walter is bad news, m' boy, just bad news."

"He is. Do you ever feel like an outsider even amidst outsiders sometimes?" William knew he was quite drunk, and yet let it reel.

"Like a novelty item. Even a lot of decent people unwilling to go the extra yard find the committed as novelty items, until you become successful. Then they'll want to wrap their twisted little mouths around your cock." William found it so strange to hear another person say what he had thought, and to say it so succinctly, without a trace of hesitation. "Even at my most orthodox I feel as if in some unconscious way Americans detect something boiling within and retract. But it is always such people, you see, to do such things, that began enthusiastic enough to hear the truth, to face life, themselves, now I'll try to clarify. I find there are none more critical, high-minded than they incapable of creation, you see now—"

In the distance a slow, nocturnal tugboat drifted across the ocean, letting its thunderous horn ring out once. Voices of the night cried out across the pier, somewhere along North Point, or Beach Street, as the aquarium looked as if a long, statuesque face in its temporal emptiness.

"I don't know the reasoning for anything, but damn, there is so much to do, so many songs to be written, photographs to be taken, paintings, films, man, there are so many books to write, so many things to say, so many things to see, to fall in and out of love, man, back and forth and back again up and down the land, and I think that life is the pursuit of the self, so in that case death may come accursed when it happens, and any sort of jumping the gun is just absurd."

"What do you mean?" asked William, with fleeting sobriety. "About death and the last thing you said?"

"Well I just can't believe Walter's friend's wife had an overdose, you see? I knew he was going to kill that girl, but what can you do? What I mean was, then, you hear about these things, and artists indulging themselves to death, and all these wearisome tales, patterns almost, synchronicities that I disavow! My ex-girlfriend just hanged herself and I couldn't make it to the funeral because the room within which her coffin lay was surrounded by the proprietors of her death. Her poor, poor mother," Harold for a moment grinded his teeth in anger before refraining, "It was the minds within the bodies town within the state within the country which drove her and will drive her and innumerable others to mental institutions and youthful graves and *why*? Because this frightened country is disgusting, God-damnit, and that stem with udders that left me in the desert within which I was born; they are all good as dead. Rebellion, exile, and cunning."

William sat dumbfounded. The commonalties set him in a sort of dream state he feared would last until the sun rose. Then he'd know that there were others out there like him, a whole group of them drawn to San Francisco that summer through despair and in pursuit of aesthetic enlightenment. And yet a strange memory of his arrival-night panged him in a lucid moment of suppressed memory that then rose for a moment to its imaginative surface; the words of another hobo, whom William had forgotten on account of the chemicals coinciding with his entrance into the new life: 'Some of these people are blank cartridges, man. Their minds have been wiped out. They walk as though they are alive, but it is an illusion.' Then two ghosted men approached William, Walter and Saul ahead, trying to light cigarettes, the young hobo saying "We're here to see what your condition is in." And while William had walked on, listening to the beggar but giving him nothing more than his transitory ear, he intuited that the money he might offer this condemned soul would go to a self-destruction that would end in either death or recovery, and yet that choice of theirs was neither controllable nor temporal. 'You're new here, ain't ya? So was I! There were others who suffered brutal deaths. Their skulls were crushed with hammers and mallets; the veins of their penises were sliced with Exacto knives; the women's nipples and clitorises were severed with pliers. Human sacrifices, not long ago, on Masonic Avenue right there, in view of the Corporate Goddesses.'

William shuddered to hear this with resounding clarity in the amphitheater of his memory, though not because he believed the story of the hobo, but because it was something of a delayed reaction he had never before experienced. This itself forced him to ponder if it ever happened at all—when, before the Hemlock? Vapor and fog rushed into the scenes of his memory, clogging up what had seemed once clear. These thoughts reduplicated, stacked in pyramidal shards, which lent its force to one pondering a moment if one was oneself going insane. 'Their veins, we heard, were like licorice; and their throats were pierced like hours, but only we had blankets on the floor for bloodying.'

Smith spoke on with rampant incomprehension, keeping an edge of optimism to his voice borne of newspaper solace.

"Nothing matters, but it's a comforting madness to pretend otherwise."

The pair drank whiskey out upon the dock.

"Fate, the whore, does indeed owe me one," William thought aloud, again possessed by ecstatic imaginative awakenings, encroaching sunlight signaled by scattered songs of birds crashing together, and he daydreamt of the films of Larisa Shepitko. Images, gorgeous images—

"For the remaining intuitive, perceptive types like us, and I include you because people like Isaac and I, you can just tell sometimes, you know, for people like us this is the new lost generation unfolding before our eyes, I think I don't exaggerate, lost within the impulse of technology, terrorism that never ends, permanent standby we are on, theocr-cr-cr-atic troglodytes condemning walls from behind walls, an influx of asymmetrical blackouts overrunning the conscious mind. We never awoke to find God in any state at all, but rather slept and sleep through life aware that any God is not of human form; therefore no God had ever been born. Our traits and traditions have fallen dead in fast parallel of the stars that linger above the planet—we've been left to ourselves, to descent, and in some corner of it all souls like ours must break through like prisms in our times and don't bend, never bend, man, you see—"

"So it's not that we weren't made for our times," attempted William, "But that we demand a life of richness absorbed from the ordinary, an acceleration of the senses, as I had been beginning to conjure back east."

"You staying around, buddy? It will be the greatest summer ever. All young men deserve one summer of happiness, one of sixty, I can't tell."

"I intend to," William said. "For me it is either the ecstasy I feel here and have felt here, or life again becomes a joke I am attempting to laugh through."

"The near-future looks fine," Harold said, "As the past is a black and white photograph in mint condition trapped within a three-ringed binder, the future unwritten and nonexistent; thus the prescient hour is upon us to live, the art of life, life as considered the true art-form, and here look, the Pacific Ocean—Let me tell you—"

They looked out at the Golden Gate Bridge as dawn encapsulated in its initium of hazy violet-orange which rippled across the water, passing memories, cigarettes, ideas, the whiskey bottle to and fro with their arms draped across one another's shoulders, throats and chests winded from the laughter of myriad jokes and cries, a lifetime replenished in a day's nocturnal work, and the sun was out in the cold dawn as they walked back up the hill in vague delirium, faint gusts of fog and the rippling waters of passing ships crashing against and through the granite walls beneath the wavering trees, sails invisible before the cool fog, Harold Smith raising a final toast to William Fellows upon the deck which the latter agonizingly accepted, and returning the favor, collapsed, the California sun stretching over his eyelids, both in dreams and out of them a fog and vapor incapacitating one's immediate line of supplemental sight.

6

He bathed before scanning the house for any lingering counterparts from the night prior, to no avail, drinking vile gin and table burgundy before recalling his appointment with Man Ray.

The house was spotless, clean as a whistle. A toast to man, Armorica, land and sea; a toast to life, a toast to death, and another toast to life.

'Lord, I pray in private, never leave me; lead me one day to Augustine, Kempis, Lorenzo. I never leave You, but rather suffer from delusions. I shall never denounce You like so many do these days. Lord, let me live this life until it ends, for I seek You in everything, even if nobody knows it but You, Triune God. I love you Lord, giver of life; I weep to Christ, and the Virgin Mary. My life outside of You is but a rumor. Young once, may all roads lead to Thee. I pray Lord, may you watch over my mother and even Helena below. I shall be reckless, but not unto the point of death. May you bring peace unto Octavia's heart, and all the others who need You more than they know. Hold me steadfast, Lord; John the Baptist, I think of you: bring me to wild honey and then the guillotine in His name. In the name of the Father, Son, Holy Spirit. Amen.'

The beatific wind blew in through half-open windows, blinds rustling like last rites, hidden windows propped up with textbooks and encyclopedias. The clock read four. He reached for his cellphone, did not have one, sat down to a pair of iced Anchor Steam—a cosmopolitan orphanage.

With all of life rushing through him he leant against the iron pillar of a telephone pole and punched in Man Ray. He felt both fortuitous and contingent in calling up a man he'd seen but once some years ago flipping through photographs of his earliest New York youth, overlooking the sundry tugboats of the Marina.

"William?"

"Man Ray, yes—"

And yet he was smiling for once because everything seemed in a sense worth smiling about.

"I'll be there soon!"

You can tell by the tone of a man's voice at times that he is a good man, and before long three beautiful women passed William by en route to the political event that would render their souls and minds so grotesque they would thereafter appear disfigured, annihilated in that long-term they were incapable of comprehending, with flowing blonde hair pointing halfway toward Hell and halfway toward Heaven, a parked buggy automobile halted atop the structuralized shadows of the lot, within which a quick seagull had found a cold, meditative corner in which to gnaw at fresh crumbs of bread.

Bald, stout, adorned with autobiographical bucket hat of felt, and with beaming eyes above strung-together outfit of khaki and button-up (Stream of buses passing by the waterfront, a father holding binoculars aboard sailboat to his young son's eyes for the first time—the sort of moment where memories and present tense collide into the most fragrant introduction to adventure, the magnitude of such enveloped, emotive longings set free) whence with cool, San Franciscan droll Man Ray stepped through the kaleidoscopic surroundings presenting one hand and another around the wind-whipped back of William, Man Ray seemed as if a sort of Buddha with as much, if not more, stored wisdom circulating (Rather than stuck or locked) within his gleaming bald head, which bore widened eyes cast upon all of the land and the sea and the young man before him at once.

"You travel lightly," said Man Ray, stepping back to unlatch the trunk. "I remember when you were the size of that bag." He spoke though in his eyes the older man seemed in awe to have William before him now, a young man, and by Man Ray's casual tone and clarity of mind he seemed to consider William as a proof that time passes far too quickly, although what happens in its midst was most worthwhile, far more than the whole, and what's important is the natural development of the in-between; and as William conducted his abridged examination of his new friend's person, there were another three persons passing through, this time concealed completely in black cloth save their drugged eyes, chanting something foreign, like conductors with an illegible holy book as rectangular batons, prompting William to reflect, as the trunk closed, 'They like so many others strike one, in their confidence, as so detrimental that should one even have to hitherto felt aligned with them, or any such type from any given sect, one would have to admit in the face of such odious confidence that in fact they, like all the rest, are wrong, and that that the horrifying is alone the true.'

"It is great to see you, Man Ray!" They got into the automobile and jumped into conversation, erasing any apprehensions, and William overlooking streets he had not yet crossed as Safeway dissolved in the rearview.

"We will go by the restaurant then, and afterwards go for a drive all throughout the city; my wife is out of town for two weeks. I have a guest-bedroom set up for you two. I think you'll like San Francisco just fine, how long have you been here," drifting through Fillmore Street, shedding glimpses upon the innumerable cafes and shops, overhead cables clacking while on the streets lighters lit, music cutting in and out of auditory scope, buses turning exhausted around one windblown corner or another which had no visible underside.

"I've been here two days or so," William explained, elated at the natural warmth generated from his mother's college friend and of the secured two weeks and all it implied. "I've already made some friends!"

"This is that type of place," Man Ray concurred, pointing out various past living spaces and streets of interest. "Better than southern California, right?"

"What strikes me most is that everywhere I go everyone seems to know what I'm saying—have you ever felt that way here?"

"I never visit home because of it," he laughed, with an undertone of seriousness, "You already know, your mother told you, I've lived here for thirty years. Nothing else seems to work, for me. Oh, and here, take these—I made you a set of keys—oh you've got to watch out—" He swerved past a creature dragging shopping carts filled with crushed aluminum back from the black lagoon of Larkin Street.

He snickered with Man Ray, approving him, and they took to Bush and Buchanan through the long shadows of fresh trees, Japanese architecture cutting in through the spaces of buildings and elongated, sloping hills of San Francisco as the sky expanded above them and within the wondrous eyes of passersby. The car became a ship, Rimbaud's drunken boat, and Man Ray steered the wheel, William looking out along the culminated wonder, streets to know soon by heart, to live upon. He and the captain barged out again along Geary Street. This time the sights of the dissolving city into wide-open lanes of shops and picturesque, multicolored collages of approaching and fleeting shops with widened doors and glistening overhead panels, down and off of Geary whence Man Ray turned at 6th Avenue into Clement Street, ducking thereafter into the grocery store and guiding William up to Green Apple book-shop, the food stands of broken-teethed saints gargling illegible psalmodies, enraptured, dense smell of bagged fish filling the traveled air through psychological vagabondage and symphonic, beating hearts within each passerby clad in the rags of arrival, the late-afternoon bars of summer where women sit outside reading foreign magazine in millennial dresses, flowers flowing amidst streams of dirty-blonde hair. William walked past the shops and out upon unfamiliar streets observing signs, shop windows, textures of voices, sounds of skin, and the smells barreling forth from one café, restaurant into the next. He sat down upon a shabby red wooden bench and thought at length to himself of his comfort. Exhaustion crept upon him, and contentedness encroached in the quickened, delirious moments until he fell asleep sitting up, fighting the urge to go seek out Harold Smith in the Hearth. Within a café he ordered coffee and walked back up the street in a forlorn state of mind, perching himself upon the edge of Man Ray's Toyota. Through one side-street it seemed as if the Hearth was in looming, a hypothetical scenario which brought a smile and dozens of fresh faces and voices to his mind. His dream had involved the east, he recognized, but could not recall further specificities. Nielson, bless his soul, was still escorting Carson from one drug den to another, or one city to another, from the end of one wit into the next and final wit, all of which made no difference in the world to Carson, the ruined artiste, and that poor girl with long hair he dragged around with him in and out of yardbird wisdom and torturous irrelevancies. All of Jerusalem, if not all the country save this furthest end of western civilization, seemed as if incinerated. All the bars stuffed to the brim with desperation and longing, and the households which one had left which contained parallel resolutions, of what origins and of what ends? It was a modern tragedy, William decided gazing out from the beginning down towards the blurred edge of Clement Street and its subtle perfection, that state of which so many friends lost had sundered amidst, within; to agree with nothing but misery and to refute nothing but individual responsibility—for comfort had grown out of hand like the stream which at another related edge of the aquatic world housed typhoons, tsunamis, tidal waves to swallow all of the land whole—and thus chemical alteration became thence no celebration, no advent of the psyche, but rather an unconscious tribute to the sheer collapsing of dreams whose seeds had never been planted, of lives ruptured and disfigured by slogans propagating nothing but freedom and opportunity, of retinal singes thrust forth from the violet mandatory donation of television screens, and this, all of this, was the damned generation, he clenched his fist within his hand and knew that Smith had been correct, the midst of an aesthetic exactitude; the art of life. He would first master the art of life before he began any serious effort at conveying the wrath that boiled within him, that brain-breaking wrath bound not in futility and spite but in an irremediable actualization of the truth, and a longing for durability, or tradition, in the generation lost to pocket-sized Technicolor absolution.

Before the world would listen, he would listen to himself and those wild-eyed ones around him, the kingdom of exile, and breathe that oceanic air, and by some hook or crook shape the desolation before desperation before acclamation before rejuvenation. He felt afraid to call home; things came to the surface in San Francisco that were elsewhere condemned to the anchor-dimmed depths of the psychic sea.

For a moment Walter, Saul crossed his mind. He stepped back in, ordered a pint. Even in their madness some sort of colorful erudition presented itself, tainted nonetheless, to William's aesthetic perception, again a sort of cultural fluorescence. San Francisco seemed to contain indescribable compounds and solutions of hope, of sense, of clarity. Even though his wife had died, William had a hard time believing that if Saul stayed in San Francisco the situation would not in time take care of itself, whereas back East such a scenario to coincide amidst the severity of seasons and behavioral patterns seemed haunted by an unsung strain. San Francisco, then, contained qualities of Heaven, and William felt angelic in the virgin days along her street, for Heaven must be a fine place in life—conscious eternity in any form was Hell—had not anyone thought of this in time sitting beside a hot tin bumper streaked with the misguided feces of seagulls, drinking your beer on dear old Clement Street with a headful of ideas that were driving you insane beginning to work themselves out at last?

Deep within his soul William was, in earnest, unaware of the grandiose, specious state of this consideration of any such place. Was anywhere so fine? He did not give a damn. The global, that dream of mutants, had died, become fossilized and buried. On the third day everyone was still sleepwalking through the decadent millennium.

For he had nothing to lose, and even wrote the first sentence of a book never to see the light of daywhile in line at Green Apple, within the cover of Bruno Schulz's *Street of Crocodiles*:

> *It would have been the year 2070 A.D., but time was no longer recorded by Christ; instead, then, it was Abortion Day, Year of Alphabet Inc., and not even a digital mouse did click within the camps.*

In such a case one may put all of himself into life, and such cases happen seldom if at all. On top of that thought, conscious consideration unto action was the even rarer rebellion. Today's newspapers justified that which yesterday's had railed against, and the world was a mess which would in time turn disastrous once again. Rebellion, then, seemed as if an encyclopedic entry for the most real definition of beauty and love in such a circumstance. The finest rebellion seemed procured in the mere enjoyment of life, having first relentlessly examined and reexamined just what is worthwhile.

Still what interested him most in the fire of his mind upon the subtle beauty of Clement Street was an acutely calculated exactitude pertaining to the art of life's non-existent present moment caught, the near future always now, now, *now*.

As Man Ray hurled himself through an automatic doorway bearing immense packages, William was then thinking with perfunctory gaudiness of that Janine, of that woman in the candy-cane dress, as with Man Ray loading the restaurant's groceries into the trunk, driving into the sunset back down Geary Street. William shed a vague smile to some glistening scarecrow of a man out playing withered black tambourines in traffic.

Within his new bed, his temporary, kept-together two bedroom apartment of silence and freedom, he slipped into a sleep which lasted something like twenty-four hours, for when he awoke a note explaining Man Ray's running of errands for the evening, across the bridge, was being carried out, and a number to call if need-be.

Outside of the fourth-story window, Bush and Buchanan, William observed San Francisco. Hunger had passed him by, and he began to sample imported Thailand beers out along the counter and within the refrigerator. He turned to the laptop at the desk.

E-mails: Two professors, Nielsen Benveniste, Octavia Savonarola, Helena Caravan.

He discarded Octavia's enthusiasm for the play, which had now served as nothing more than the catalyst for William's internal doubts he went on unable to say aloud. Nielsen's was a lengthy enquiry filled with updates from the world and his own life—'I told you being in San Francisco is like being in another country, I'll keep you updated on the happenings of the world'—Ober and another professor seeing if the references had been of any use, and Helena calling to say she was bitter that William had arrived in San Francisco and had been staying awake at night crying. He read her message once, twice, and deleted it.

It was true that William, in his heart, would always love her in some way, yet it was truer that an adolescent portion of his life had passed over; he put a filter on Helena's e-mails and would never speak with her again. The sadness of this necessary gesture brought a tear to his eye as he overlooked Japantown just before sunset, families and lovers passing through a closing-down parade, carnival of sorts, the last streamers bursting through sparklers and fresh rushes of steam from immense, outdoor pots of food he could smell from his high window. Before arrays of foxglove, jasmine, and pinkish white geraniums, quaint pots of impatiens, where sunlight wavered between an orange emblem with black etchings, a pillar encircled by shuttered discs, the pilgrim contemplated his next series of movements.

He thought of Helena for some time, visions of ouroboros. She'd go on and live, blossom into some sort of woman, run through the nights as if nobody cared, screaming and loving and crying, ignoring all the stares—she'd long for William to come, but he would never go back there. For now he had before him dense, raving crowds, barbiturate praises of folly and precocious revelry—and through the intoxicated throngs of crowd, he could see Octavia as a light between truth and intellect, the one back east worth saving, who'd written, "Our bones are buried half in Redhook, half in Jerusalem, sure; but did not Moses himself refuse to budge until Joseph's were retrieved? Can these bones, then as now, *live*?" Nay, ne'er beautiful save in myth all Graves's goddesses, he slurred through his fingertips, all temporal things are, at their core, Bacchic whores. "Search, wretched one, the waters around your shores; and then look into your bosom, whether any part of you enjoys peace." Meanwhile a lady with stockings and umbrella was translating something to her friend from a tablet ringed in rubber, saying, "Come and see how they love each other in the parade! Every day a parade!"

Wandering the Bay Area at sunset, he contemplated that these are no persons one met every day but people who knew something extra about the fragility of consciousness and the rest, elsewhere, deluded, plunged into the abyss of moral propaganda, their minds rotted out by a concept they live by and yet know deep down is untenable by volition of its sheer Utopian nausea, housed within the deontological mausoleum of manufactured public opinion. Athens and Lacedaemon be damned; take thine own unto contemplation—and he saw a woman scratching herself bloody on a mattress with neither sheet nor blanket, a crushed shoebox for pillow, and fecal smearing around the snipped handles of ovular white rope. She could shield her pain from nothing but more pain, screaming into the diseased mattress, as remnants of parades, like human confetti offcuts, staggered by.

He tilted the last of his first drink to her, to sunset, and wiped a tear from his eye, then another, then back ahead again, through the hallway of framed rocks and mountain kings, and after two drinks and a list of books to buy from Green Apple come tomorrow, he felt much better.

7

"We need to restore the faith of our generation. I don't know in what. But in a sea of faces glued to cell phone screens, I fear the future. Maybe to create a new world of real feelings. Computers and internet social networks have numbed human interaction to the point of a glossy 1–2 sentence comment. That is how we summarize our feelings these days. If for just once someone would reach into this cesspool and save us from drowning in our own shit."

—OVERHEARD COMMENT ON THE L TRAIN

HE COULD NOT GET ahold of Janine—in fact, the number did not work at all but went to some automatic static—either he'd misheard the numbers or . . .

He contemplated the daylight's last hour and thought of Phil Cohen.

"Yo-ho-ho," slurred an exhausted voice within the second ring.

"El, William here, William Fellows," concealing excitement, drinking in the nude with his legs crossed upon a butterfly chair, his feet dangling from the balcony.

"William, ye bard! I was just talking about you. What's up?"

"I'm sitting at the apartment in Japantown drinking imported beer. Do you live in San Francisco—My memory's not so hot these days." He closed his eyes and stood up, summoning energy. "I was thinking of a long lost love, Octavia, the woman who buried my bones in Jerusalem; would it not be fitting if she, too, mosaically retrieved them? Tell me, great hero, if you come from Hell, and if there are nunneries or hermitages there; cloisters, monasteries, what have you? Ah, like a burning foundation in my throat. But anyhow, you should come over comrade and we will hit the town and have even more a ball than the other night.

I've got your number written on a sheet of paper. My cellphone is long-gone. This is the house phone. Let us get moving on the dictatorship of the proletariat!"

Stark laughter broke through across the line prompting William to shed an instantaneous roar of laughter through his window, prompting paused bodies to turn arched heads upward, handfuls of designed fans blinding eyes from the looming sun to look about.

"I must break through this total lethargy I have been dwelling amidst here in Oakland. East Bay. And have off from work tonight—I have been napping all day," the voice channeled. It was as if two old friends were homing in on their Wednesday coffee-talk. William felt so comfortable he sat back down daydreaming of the brilliant corners of nocturnal San Francisco to turn into and around in the anarchic night. Three sheets to the wind on a trolley car, condemned to mystical visions of burning the tree of life to the Machiavellian ground. He gazed about the guest room: the desk, the mattress; a fortress. Studies, work, school soon enough, once life died down. "Have you been to the Mission, or North Beach?"

"No, though I've heard of it. North Beach and Mission I have not been to. Isaac says we should stop by," William tossed into the conversation, "And the three of us will hit North Beach in commemoration of my arrival, his departure, and your sanctifying tome."

The pair again laughed. Neither had ever met anyone at a party that seemed suited, indelible, for comradeship beyond another three drinks and half as many hours of moonlight.

"I believe my night is set," as a woman's gentle voice spoke in the backdrop, Phil Cohen responding with an enthusiastic, 'Mm-hmph,' "You've saved the best of San Francisco for last. Atta boy."

"Janine wants to take me all over the Mission, her neighborhood soon, so let's meet at the Fort Mason house and head downtown. No women allowed tonight is all I say. Just the men go out. No apprehensions unless it is concerning a batch of women or heated discussion or physical altercation." He cut himself off. William stood up and wanted to scream with happiness. "Please understand, El, I don't mean any of this heat of the moment epigrams. I have no idea what I just said. The Thailand beer is nice—" Flustered, 'twas called. Phil Cohen cut him off:

"I'll be at the Fort Mason compound in two hours wielding a six-pack of Simpler Times. See you on the porch."

"What is Simpler Times?" asked William. He lit his fortieth cigarette of the day, breaking into a coughing fit.

"Oh, a nice standard beer—We'll make a voyage out of the night; I'll take off in a while. Tonight!"

William put the phone down, threw the empty bottles into the trash and grabbed another three. It seemed as if there was a purposeful synchronicity in life, or some immaterial, unquestionable happiness, changing into the outfit Janine had bought him, wetting his hair and polishing his wing-tips with polish bought at the corner market.

He took off into night heading back down Fillmore, contemplating the idea of bookstores or libraries having membership plans for late-night hours at prices the serious would pay in a way to encourage self-teaching scholars or otherwise. He made it down Fillmore in drunken daydream, and once again stepped past the black, towering gates of Fort Mason.

Isaac was carrying a bundle of laundry across the grass field as William approached him, their heels clicking, synchronized along the winding lot. In his eyes the fuse burned that had burned since Hemlock, one of physical frailty and looming departure. When at last Isaac noticed William, he could do nothing but smile, place his basket down upon the old moss-strapped staircase.

"We have good timing."

William leant in to shake hands, helping him load the basket inside. The door swung open. Smith burst into the kitchen fresh out of breath, red-faced, wielding a bowie-knife in one tattooed hand and fuliginous coconut in the other.

"Ode to the rings of Saturn! To chaos and night!" he cried, "I was looking for you yesterday!"

"I've been in Japantown, I'm staying there on and off!" William ejaculated.

"Oh, right, damn, well I'll be in later! I have to go run some errands!" He drank the coconut juice in one sip, tore a handful of flesh from inside, and rode his bicycle straight out through the well-lighted pebble pathways.

"He doesn't stop," Isaac said. "I mean he does not stop; I've never seen anyone like him." William laughed, noticing not a single outfit thus far had been changed since the party. Everyone had a ragged summer charm about them and smelled halfway between dried sweat and inexpensive deodorant. "Let's take a seat bud, what have you been doing all day?"

"Had a drink earlier, lounged about, got situated there just yesterday."

"And how is Janine, you lucky devil?"

Isaac spoke on, a distant sort of woe on his face as he looked down at his reddish knuckles, rattling upon the table as to intercept the temporal silence; William took two bottles from his coat pockets and set them upon a pile of San Francisco Chronicles.

"I'll see her soon."

"Hear from anyone in San Diego?"

"Helena."

"That all?"

"Yep. For the first and last time. You've shown me too much already just by being yourself. I shall not leave San Francisco for a very long time. Bottle opener?"

Isaac took a lighter from his pocket, popped both open with an innocent grin.

"I think I might take off tomorrow morning," he said. "Just worked my last shift over at the café."

William felt almost intrusive and knew not what to say; Isaac stood up and seized a bottle of Convento from the cabinet.

"I wasn't going to do anything tonight, but now we might have to." He looked over messages, concluding, "I'll know at some point tonight."

"It's a shame you're going so soon," William began. "What I'll do, or think I'm doing—no, not for doing, but for not doing—such is my prerogative, my maxim and my salvation—I shall be sighing lamentations in your absence, comrade." He bit off the end of a spliff. He spit it into rich grass fences before flowerbeds at the foot of the holographic mountain, there where souls were singing in the nest of the sun, something concerning a life that was imperceptible outside of the hashish valley.

"The night is young! I'm just going to Portland anyway," Isaac said, changing his mood as if he were going for lunch across the street. "And the sole way to leave anywhere is to do it like it's the last raucous night on wormhole earth! And ah, El is on his way. Did you meet El? Yes, yes, you did. I've known him for years. He's another type, like what Harold was saying."

"What did he say?"

Isaac poured two glasses of wine, tilting his to William's:

"You know just meeting certain people, and you just get along right away. This wine isn't bad, is it?"

"It is very good," William agreed. Light reflected from the cracked piano keys as becalming wind rustled upon the old pale-green blinds.

"It's hard to imagine leaving this place. I won't understand it until I'm a few miles into the highway, reflecting on all the lost days when I was never so moved by the flow of life. Broke up with Erin. Sad, sad, sad."

Two children walked by the window and sang along the sidewalk, swinging upon their parents' hands.

"I'm glad I decided to turn down Hemlock Alley."

"I'm glad you arrived. Also, because that girl I was with was beginning to drive me nuts. The inferior sex . . . paying her honor is ridiculous."

"What'd she do?"

"Oh, just nagging about everything, and then nothing personal but that Janine is nothing but a cunt, well not so much a cunt, but just dissatisfied with any position we're in, but she liked you. I had never seen her smile like that."

"I don't know what any of them want. I think the best thing to do is not care. It takes good discipline to not care in the literal sense, and you cannot do it without consideration, but I think you can get yourself to not care at a certain point. You must long to do it is all. You must have no faith in telling people how careless you are, or putting winsome dye in your hair, spikes in your flesh, and repugnant, deplorable tattoos across your body. You must show them you do not care by living it. Otherwise you are just another bondservant full of predetermined suggestions with an onerous, meaningless job."

"That's true. I'm moving in with an ex-girlfriend in Portland. That's part of the reason I'm leaving."

"Why else?"

"I just can't stay still anymore," Isaac laughed, loading up a corncob pipe with loose tobacco. "And I think if I stay here any longer, I'll die. I'll be back, but if I don't get out soon, I'll die or go insane. Look around you on the streets. I doubt all those people were born ill. There is no greater city I know, nor city more difficult to be productive in—you walk outside around here and the last thing you want to do is worry, or work. I wake up in the morning and brush my teeth, contemplate if I should start drinking. I long to be drunk when I am in San Francisco, and when I'm anywhere else I wish I was having a drink in San Francisco; much follows, but you get my drift. Any artistic pursuit I had has just sort of fallen away. Be careful—for now I'll get down to business as the rain falls down."

"I understand," William belched. "Have you seen Walter around?"

"Not in days."

At that moment Phil Cohen appeared, towering in the doorway, a six-pack balanced on his head. Isaac's eye lit up. El came to the table as Isaac took the beer to the refrigerator, the general mood elevating, El dropping a battered edition of *Life and Fate* on the table.

"Oh no, damn," Isaac cried from the kitchen, returning, "Forget that woman I spoke of, let's just go out all night! How can I ever be sad when after all, the sun sets!"

They recalled the party with contagious, photographic memory as the beer and wine went around, the music coming on, and then the three of them bolted forth from the rickshaw home, voices bursting with ideas, vigor, and the reaffirmation of life, straight to Columbus Avenue.

Along the Avenue endless, glorious streams of passersby spoke familiar, foreign tongue together over the smells of fresh food from rows of Italian restaurants and quaint, ancient bakeries—there was a street whereupon one could stand for a moment, stoned and drunk and in love with life, and condemn oneself for thinking at any point that all this was anything short of miraculous. And as was the case for William, such a formulating thought was cut off by something of an actor's group, dressed in clothing from a century back, flouted by persons who'd even manage to bring by old-fashioned, albeit apparently functioning, cameras. These camera bulbs exploded at intervals while trolley-cars crossed up and down the tilting street, nightfall again upon the city. El pointed ahead to the hundred distant lights glowing upon Broadway as lit matches exploded in passing palms, the scent of weed and wine rushing through misty air, accentuated wands of ember running, dissolving to the tune of lungs, voices.

William stood outside of the bodega overlooking a beautiful group of Australian women passing him by; one with blonde hair in a blue skirt turned to him, smiling the way one sees in rare memories. He broke away from the door to approach her.

"Good evening," he said, smiling at the girl, marveling her—unnoticeable freckles which at once added a specific tenderness to her body, and looking past her blonde hair to the rest of her whispering group.

"Good evening to you," she smiled in an accent, she and her friends laughing, showing a full smile of milk-white teeth between red lips. They started to walk away at once.

William walked confusedly to the doorway and listened to Isaac speak at the counter to El:

"I was considering earlier the ontological value of the way hearts are drawn." He drew a simple gray heart upon a napkin, sliding his money ahead.

"What have you gathered?"

"It makes me think—Thank you, sir, goodnight!—That the purpose of life lies somewhere between a teardrop and a big, flapping ass."

El walked ahead, propping the brown paper satchel within his arms, pointing to the streets:

"Look at all of the beautiful young women out tonight!"

"I spoke with some just now who seemed quite interested, heading that a-way."

"Ah," Isaac said, "Good thing I know where they're going, then. It's a matter of five or so bars. We'll hit them all. If no one is going to tell me the meaning of life, then I will have to create and recreate it each night until I die, and it never mattered anyway."

"Let's go get those girls," William said, adding a nihilistic manner to his stride, waxing his mustache within the window of The Stinking Rose, keeping up with the quickened pace of El as Isaac leaped once, spinning around, his eyes vibrant, his rosy nose bulbous and distended.

"Not yet!" he cried, catching glances of wonder and curiosity at once, "First we go, we begin the night upon the concrete bench of Joe DiMaggio Park! Come on, men!"

They hooked left seconds later on a discreet, one-way street corner and took seats upon an elongated concrete bench before a narrow, wire-wrapped maze of crisp ivy strands. Phil Cohen removed a pint of whiskey from his bag and passed it around, lighting a cigarette and sighing. Isaac cleared his throat, rubbed his acne-torn nose with an intoxicated smile. William drank his Anchor Steam from the brown paper bag, took a pull of hashish and exhaled a triumphant cloud at the fluorescent bulb bound by microscopic moths.

They discussed the best types of women, the best ways to have them, through laughter of spit-split beer. William gargled beer listening to Isaac tell his tale of Arabian Nights that could have made Pasolini blush, or given him a poem, the end result being fumes of fire-hydrant cracked alcohol fuming out upon the deserted sidewalk of the tranquil street. Lazy crickets. The tipped glass became a glint of stolid ritual as stories macerated and evaporated through a perpetual process of imbrued dialectics.

"Walking that solitary road. The road's remote if one is willing to reject that which is false, that which one tears himself from in this life if the innocent shall divide the silver," raising his triumphant turn of whiskey, a tap unlatched in a blinding passing headlight. "Wistful elongation: deliverance dissolved."

For an hour they drank and spoke upon the concrete row laughing, singing, and crying at once. No one brought up Isaac's departure save for the occasional solemn look of the eyes.

"I knew a man," he laughed, "Who drank a bottle of brandy before he got out of bed, requiring a pint to get a comb to his head; he said life's nothing more than hallucination, talk nothing more than recitation. What does this mean, O dreamy dream?"

A bum approached out of the shadows, thin as a scarecrow, pouring a jug of wine across his body, making sounds and motions as if being and electrocuted. He went to sing, clapping his hands and showing off a set of three golden teeth in the spotlight, beating his fist across his shirtless chest of abdomens and torn flesh:

> *Bring me, more wine!*
> *(Sing it)!*
> *Bring me, bamboo!*
> *(You got it!)*
> *Smoke black twist and you might get pissed*
> *And when your luck runs out just reminisce!*
> *You know!*

> *Bring me, that envelope!*
> *Bring me, the code!*
> *Burn that bridge up past the ridge*
> *And afterward we'll have port a la mode!*
> *Come on!*

William threw his arms around Phil's shoulders, Isaac's, as they stood swaying with the man out on the street, shouting to drunken Columbus Avenue:

> *Bring me, more wine!*
> *Bring me, bamboo!*
> *Smoke black twist and you might get pissed!*
> *And when your luck runs out just buy some bliss!*

"Night, fella, night," the man danced off, clicking the bells on his torn slippers together, marching diagonal and away from the mob. He fell against the fence once, twice, straightened himself out and turned around as if within a duel:

"Da name Charlie Hustle."

The trio passed through alleyways wherein the drugged and drunken of all ages passed by in a silvery light; the distant charge of North Beach rushed on, its taciturn neon flood encompassing every which multihued way. Heat pressed forth from the carnival lights even at its distance, enormous naked cowboys and neon women flickering on and off like tattooed lightning, heat emerging from the outdoor sidewalk cafés.

"Ah boys," Isaac swayed between El and William, drinking whiskey in the midnight hour, slurring his frail frame and torn velvet eyes, weaving in and out of hundreds of fleeting faces aglow, "Ah you know, in my life! I've forgotten what to say! Here, here we are along Broadway!"

He ran a miraculous hand across his face and seemed to sober up at once, parting his disheveled hair aside in one motion as if before some unseen mirror. San Francisco seemed, amidst William's recurrent formalistic perceptivity, to possess the kind-heartedness akin to a mother's memory of cradling her first-born child. The beauty of the night moved him to new experiential heights as the crowd rushed on; they took to an alleyway beyond the bend of liquor and sex shops and sat upon a long stair out of perhaps hundreds which rose like a simultaneously horizontal and vertical high-rise in the drugged night to the unforeseeable top of the concrete alleyway—Romolo Place.

"You know I was out walking down Fillmore today looking upon each shop window with the core of earth burning somewhere below my feet, the sky clad in its torn blue overcoat, inhaling the fumes of passing bakeries and afternoon barrels of rum and crates of cracking crawfish, new born children passing wide-eyed cooing in strollers with fleeting eyes more piercing than any harpoon, any bullet, for life is life I realized in my lonesomeness of walking down the crowded street a stranger, I saw fractions of myself in every living thing around me, eyes met mine, electric cables cracked above buses, bodies broken down and bodies being born like an immense symphony of life, it sang to me, conducted itself from darkness and death the rumor, I heard music coming down from the sky of my mind, I thought of beyond either sky, chaos on earth as it is otherwise and I knew then looking to fleeting yellow eyes of some ancient vagabond crutched against bolted automatic doors, rubber mats stained with sentinel newspaper ink, an undescriptive doorway dealt the epiphany of the self, and anxious as a burning Hell I took a sip of apple cider, wise beyond granular years by centennial groans, utterances, deleterious stabs in the dark, splintered forest green leaves my lungs willing lungs inhalant, all two of them, while someone spoke of the revolution of everyday life, another said 'I hate this life,' but till the body breaks down I remember today as I'll rise tomorrow, I'll live tonight as I'll know of nothing else, purgatorial mutations rushing through my blood, overgrown paths cannot contain me, the town cannot contain me, till our blue eyes turn a poisonous yellow thy ought to defy the infernal machine of mass-psychosis, mass-paranoia, and ah, so I thought today of thought," William exhaled, shouting to the barreling fog as if attempting to traverse nearing, imaginative galaxies. Isaac and El cried vivacious to the street below, to the fog of smoke, southern, arrays of fractal glass. Though just some years older than William the two had come to embrace and partake in such sudden actualizations along such grand streets. What stopped anyone from anything but another's opinion, and if the idea in the first place had nothing to with the latter save aftermath? William contemplated his breathing, his eyes, did they glow in the dark that would look into another's before downward, upward, then again ahead, in nocturnal hours we know the daylight does not exist, so when and if it comes around you know it is a liar, just look into its eyes before returning and to the ceaseless and rushing bodies breaking through manhole steam ahead, just around midnight and a foghorn, aye, the ghost of John Bunyan opening that window there, blasting Canned Heat—

"When we say we see we don't see but still we see, so we see after all but what do I see? The eye of God, gentlemen; the eye of God."

Neon reflected in the innumerable windows blasting through jam-packed street after street, towering collages of flickering color several stories north before further arrays of sex clubs, syringes split in chipped charcoal gray curb-ends, distant voices traversing through polychromatic mirrors.

"So straight to Buddha Bar!" Isaac shouted. He lit a cigarette of success and turned, marching to Chinatown knocking the tilted head clean off a transgender mannequin adorning torn nametag ('Tenis') spun her pearl necklace around, spitting vindictive foam to the shadowy ground of needles. El outstretched his hand, taking a drink with the other.

"Not yet Sonny Bono," he broke his silence, "Let's get one drink at Vesuvio's upstairs first."

"Oh come on," Isaac said, crossing the street of car horns, encroaching buses, and vocal lanterns ignoring crosstown traffic, "Vesuvio's is so old-hat. I'm going to get a little bottle of bootleg gin at this video-store and meet you there."

William tagged along with El to the wooden-gold door of swimming porcelain art and noticed the bookshop just beside him.

"How interesting," he marveled aloud. "Although now is not the time for books at all."

The seasick doorman tucked his flashlight away and waved them in with resolution; a drunken chorus of voices crashed through the alleyway's fleeting stillness.

Inside—roaring. William's merit of a good bar, no television, was in accordance. Bodies collided into one another with near-grace. If one thought twice one could fall into some other daylight world which seemed worth knowing, so instead he or she thought once, and pushed ahead.

Isaac appeared and ordered a tonic water for his bootleg gin as El broke through the mob behind a waitress handling a tray of cranberry vodkas, tilting her head of hair held together by white ribbons to the steps, her glass lenses reflecting off the overhead chandelierand the solemn waxen frame of a woodcut Grecian urn.

"Brethren," said William beside the windowpane as Isaac pulled a seat in, "To arrival, departure; to movement, and to San Francisco!"

Peoples from all directions propelled their heads round to lift their glasses high; William raised his as far as his arm would reach as a splash of whiskey fell upon his hair. Groups clicked glasses together crying out in foreign languages and English, words breaking together like waves:

"Git drunk!" someone shouted, "Get drink, get—drunk!"

Suddenly an estranged chant began as he tapped shot-glasses with El before turning to Isaac whereupon each young man put forth such an effort into the toast that their shot-glasses imploded together upon impact. Shattered glass rushed through streaming whiskey and steaming Irish coffees, descending to the floor below. Witnesses broke into concealed hysterics before a colossal fit of laughter broke free at once, raising high as the rooftops and beyond, as a cartwheeling dwarf collided with the piano man, and the odd couple fell screaming down the narrow staircase with the rumble of some distant fireworks in a dream.

Then as William was about to veer his head from the guard-rail, a boisterous man with British accent whom William almost assumed Christopher Hitchens ordered two more shots up to the gentlemen.

"Fernet!" El shouted below—"Two Fernet!"

At that moment the fine Australian girl placed her hand upon William's shoulder; his instincts took it in his, kissing her palm with absurd dedication and with the harmony of the faculties, shouting to her over the crowd, "So you have refound me from the earlier corner where you left me behind! And now your soft palm beneath my upper shirt sleeve warming me up in greeting; oh, you've done such a thing that plucks the soul out of, out of something I forget, and turns religion into just a bunch of words! I would marry thee, O synchronicity of San Francisco, and old hairy dumb head and his containing multitudes was starting to make sense after all, though knew somewhere embedded within thou wouldst returneth!"

She had her friends conjoin their table as everyone introduced themselves, William thinking of all his collegiate years. He knew not if it had been a waste. He knew where the country was going, however, and looked around at the party roaring about him. He knew not what to think; the fine young woman sat beside him and shouted to his ear over the roaring crowd as they introduced themselves to one another; he pronounced her last name as she placed a fleeting, exasperated hand to his chest. He excused himself for the restroom to part his hair, and to return to her eyes and to the enraptured, unreal city. Voices rushed together unbeknownst, some like a thousand canons on the eve of warfare, others the redemptive pipe organ through pluming incense eyes, and the anonymous annihilations breaking apart the structure of routine like choruses of choral music which began to soar across window panes, across the sky. One could be so heartbroken and sober one instant that one couldn't bear the sound of his voice even within his mind, the next so drunk that he could not fathom speaking; that was life, and it wasn't cruel but lopsided, like all those years praying in church, what did one even pray for? "Perhaps," Hitchens barked at William, "there was one prayer outside of peace: to love Him so much one proved oneself in being crucified or beheaded. Forget tootsie rolls, capes, and unwise beads: somebody hand me my shotgun and one last tumbler of wine—Amen, Amen, Hosanna in the Highest. Give me no Odysseus's scar, nor his warhorse, but a poor ass, for Mother Nature is nothing more than prostitute-landlady of a haunted house. Amen I say to you, rabbi, language and death, reality is mythology, some contagious disease of victimhood in need of abolition." Mortars took off in the streets below, the scent of gunpowder and burning fuses rushing through the raucous bar.

When William returned upstairs everyone took a Fernet to Australia, to America, health, and in a flash the group was up and dancing through broken crunching glass beneath polished shoes and high heels, a slated mosaic to absorb, silken collegiate dresses and accents brushed against the young men as William stepped to the young woman dancing his way, guitars and pianos crashing through overhead speakers to the percussive smash of clinking pint glasses and trays of mugs.

"I'll come visit you someday," William smiled with his hand in hers, sharing the remains of a bead-dripping beer, white foam swimming across his mustache, the engraved wooden tabletop.

"But tonight," she exclaimed, her face angelic and rosy, her voice foreign and familiar, "My friends and I want to do something *tonight*, we go home, back to school, in two *days!*"

"You can all come to our place," William smiled—first to her, then to El and Isaac, waltzing through the rows of girls shaking their hips, hair breaking to and fro, "Out, right on the Pacific Ocean!" He pointed through a brilliant corner of the window, past youthful passersby pissing in the idyllic wind beside single-file lines of head-hung monks of torn brown silk capes, ancient loincloth-strapped beggars, didactic toothpick models on phones, the last bohemians streaming by in vivid counter-balances of one another, "Or you know, dear, it's his place there, my friend Isaac's place," hands upon hips, pressing together, away, physical synchronicity, falling into the mesmerizing stories of one another's lives, nearing lips toward one another's when Phil Cohen twirled one of the women around, kissed her hands upon his knee at close of song, breaking through the emerging applause to announce through cupped hands:

"Another round!"

He stood up, smashed his head on the wooden channel streaked with flattened black foreheads of nails, the phantom navigator of heroin-percussive night pressing on through unseen speakers. Isaac slipped him a 20, William doing the same, as everyone took to dancing so insanely that partners were crashing into chairs, others clutching at the trammeled ground as if attempting to hold tight, till most of the bar was dancing with the hushed light of the cool night in their sparkling eyes, rising and dissolving amplification—

"We get the next!" cried one of the little women, names exchanged to no avail, the Australians trading Isaac and William in spastic incre-ments to scream at the greatness of life, the young night, bodies pressed against one another and twisting to the music, sweat breaking through their matching white shirts, sleeves rolled up, sweat streaking through the hair, those elevating musky scents one turns away from when within new proximities to reconsider, to let one's self become engulfed by the fire, as a transgender Berkeley post-grad repeated to anyone who would or would not listen, "My dissertation is against the patriarchy, and more specifically is on the historiographical ontology of clitoris in aesthetic theory, or really just ontology of clitoris", but then William cast a black magick spell upon it and, poof, it turned into a rabbinical hat.

El returned as William spoke with the former's dance partner, the fine plump redhead of the batch, spotted in freckles and straight from Dublin, had been studying down under, two waitresses behind him with ten whiskey shots on one tray, ten on another, matching pints of Anchor Steam, Sierra Nevada, "And Old Crow, Jameson, Grand Dad, it's a mixed Goddamn bag—I threw the bartender 90 bucks and he said he'd concoct a party-bag Ding-Dally-Da Da" and Phil Cohen had such a fine look in his eyes, one of a man who'd rob banks to give to the poor if he felt so inclined, or just indulge pleasant and never pretend that the cities sober weren't stiff, the way out became the way in, "Wahoo!"

Jessica returned dowsed in sweat, breathless having laughed so hard as she and William sat down beside one another at the window seat overlooking the streets, conversations continuing to break through and within one another as the dancing and music purged on, hashish smoke, opium fumes pressing across the aisleways. She placed her leg upon his and pulled her chair up to kiss.

"Let's go!" she pulled away, "To your friend's house! And get drinks on the way!" Jessica pointed to Isaac and El, removing their shirts and dancing in a sea of women, their uplifted, flailing hands smashing against wavering portraits of some artist or another—she had a tone of sudden love in her voice, the love of night, of Joyce reading a newspaper with headline of Joyce reading newspaper to the seventh power. William looked over her fine body, his mind spinning, refraining to a cosmogenic nonchalance, working on his pint. He pecked her on the forehead:

"We'll go soon!"

"We'll go drink some absinthe!" She removed a small purple bottle from her purse. William looked into her eyes for a moment. He had an idea of what the sort of woman he could marry looked like. He broke away from the thought, although she did look not unlike Yvonne Strahovski but some years younger, years equal William's. "Let's leave them!" she shouted. "We'll meet them there!"

William took her ahead through the roaring crowd, everyone ecstatic to meet in time, out into the first taxicab, limbs flailing just over the shoulder of a rushing waitress as seen through the window above.

"To Fort Mason," William said, "And take the long way, without the timed lights." He smilingly overpaid the driver.

He rolled down the windows as they pressed back across and through the warm night, the volume dwindling to the background as the driver swept through Chinatown, through the tunnel. William placed his arm around Jessica to kiss at once, the warmth of her flesh against his palm filling his body with hot rushes, streams of light flashing across his eyelids soaring through the vacant tunnel, her warm body in his arms, the cool wind fluttering through their hair like sails of a ship.

Smoke hung in the abandoned household. Jessica coughed, stepping outside to hack. William perceived a note alongside the couch cushions stacked upon the floor:

S, W: Will be back late. Late night smoke session on porch? Sausalito at dawn; bicycles I've got an extra, there, behind you to the left. See? Went book shopping. Need talk. Where R?

HS

William smiled and tucked the note into a compartment of his wallet he had begun to save such notes as Jessica inquired of its author with her arms, from behind, wrapped around his chest. William leaned one way, tripped over laptop cables, and Jessica's buttocks struck a tune, a high note, on the piano.

"Oh just a note from an old friend," William said, as they broke away from piano, humming in synchronicity, waltzing about the Fort Mason home and into the kitchen.

Jessica marveled at the drawings along the wall with her delicate accent. Beneath the archway connecting the living room with the kitchen William wrapped his arms around her, explaining Isaac's longing to plant an orchard just there through the window though he'd have to go, their faces pressing in turns against one another's necks, noses cold from the night wind, removing one another's coats which fell to the uncarpeted ground in a parallel swoosh.

"Come here," Jessica said, giving William a long, laughing Eskimo kiss. She seemed so innocent he could have sung her lullabies swaying in his arms, tucked her into bed. He took her by the hand to Harold's room, pretending it were his own. The moonlight streamed in over the bedspread as she flipped through the countless records, William pouring two glittering absinthes cut with Perrier into octagonal glasses. She ran her hands along his chest and ribs, unbuttoning his shirt at its center.

Lightning rods broke across the sky as they lay together upon the couch drinking absinthe. He ran his hands along her pale chest.

"How will I find you? Do you have Facebook?"

"No, no."

"Why?" The look in her eyes was that of a mother having lost her child.

"I have no cell phone either. I ran into the ocean with it."

"I could never!"

"Everything in moderation," William said. "Excluding moderation."

"You," Jessica laughed, "Are crazy."

"Is it better than normalcy?"

She kissed him as they looked out through the window, tracing patterns amongst the stars. How could he ever speak to a girl without accent ever again!

"I leave tomorrow," Jessica broke away, "And back across the ocean." He ran his hand through her hair, unsure of what to say.

"Otherwise we could fall in love," he sighed, rolling another cigarette with his free hand.

"Life is always this way. Doesn't it taste like black licorice?"

"I never thought of it like that," William said.

"No, puerile—the absinthe—doesn't the absinthe taste like licorice?"

"Otherwise we could fall in love on Columbus Avenue!"

Her eyes twinkled as the ice cube crackled within her glass, the mixture dissolving, popping away into a sort of greenish fog.

"Falling in love in San Francisco!" she whispered, pressing her hands to William's; outside a distant car could be heard coming through the gates. "But what is the meaning of this *life*!"

"I do not know," conceded William, "But we'll always have a piece of our hearts in this city—"

He stood to dress and felt her smile upon him as she dressed beneath the blanket, taking a half-emptied bottle of Dante from the counter.

The cab pulled in, dropped off an older couple at their bunk entrance. They sat outside on the bench, readjusting Velcro shoes.

"Did you hear about the looters," said the old man in a southern drawl. He touched his face, stood beside the door. His wife fumbled for their keys.

"No, what looters?"

William lay down beside Jessica as they listened on, squinting at one another in concentration.

"Threw bricks through the new Starbucks window in downtown just after we walked by!"

"Good," his wife said. Her voice was that of a boot stomping on a fresh-cut flag. "They should have bricks thrown through their windows every single night across the country."

Another set of headlights swam across the wall; the clamoring voices again crashed into heightened recognition. Jessica and William held one another as the giggling, crate-carrying saints stumbled in through the front door kicking and screaming.

"Oh," William said. "And I just wanted once more-"

On his head Phil Cohen balanced a carved crate of bottled ale. The women leapt to the couch, dancing and tumbling, drinking champagne from paper cups, singing at the top of their lungs with a drunken harpist's entrancing precision a song William could not recognize in a language he thought he recognized.

Then, with both a bang and whimper, Isaac fell through the doorway with Harold Smith on his back, with his flailing, free single hand compressing clay opium into a ceramic pipe—and as soon as the women had risen to speak with Jessica of their tales and bottle caps clicking hit the floor, Harold leapt off of Isaac's back, and in one motion shouted 'William!' while leaping atop the couch telling three stories concerning the nothing in particular, his hands wavering at a dizzying, contagious speed.

"Now listen!" he cried, William holding his hand, bolting up and dancing across the room to the record play. He touched the needle down atop the Chamber Brothers, unlatched his beer—"Time, my boy, has come today!"

"And in the morning, bud, sunrise, we cycle past Sausa*lito*!"

And he meant it; William felt gladder at that then he ever had to be alive.

For some hours they sat around the front yard drinking beer, absinthe, smoking weed, opium, cigars, hashish, and even a jug of Carlo Rossi appeared out of literal thin air. The women struck chords upon the piano as El disentangled a mighty tale concerning 'The Man Named Mustard.'

"But ye brethren," he began in baritone, "We shall save that for later, for another impenetrable time and place."

At sunrise Jessica held William and did not want to go; the cab was waiting.

"Meet me here on this exact date next summer—if it's meant to be, we'll do it!"

"No, no," protested Jessica in a whisper, her precious accent softer than the hand with his own, touched by the light mist falling across the Bay. "Out on Columbus Avenue—right where the street begins to turn," she pouted." "Where I first saw you."

She had a tear in her eye as they waved from the cab, veering around the field and through back to downtown beneath the forming red sky.

Harold and William watched the sun ascend and ripple across the Pacific from the dock, the Golden Gate standing before the distant sun. William could not help but weep.

"You're safe here buddy!" Harold Smith shouted, awakening the same nest of songbirds. He patted William on the back as he stamped out the last of a spliff. "And that girl was beau-ti-*ful*! I'm impressed!"

"True beauty can but vanish," William said, gallant exhaustion approaching a complete demise of vocal equipoise. El and Isaac lay strewn, distant, beneath the piano. "Though I suppose that is what must be most beautiful," he refrained, concluding, "That which can never stay."

"Stop it, man! Today is the first day of summer! Now get ready! You'll need a real tragedy, boy, before you keep talking like that!"

William excused himself to bed as Harold embroidered a distressing look of inquisition; William wondered if he had some insect upon his face or had developed a third eye.

"What?" he asked, leaning against the chipped, engraved pillar. He took out his butterfly knife and carved his initials. Smith followed suit. William carried on carving as Harold said nothing as to keep him occupied, awake.

"Well!" he shouted, polishing off the coffee and the wine. "Let's go!"

They took off at dawn for the Golden Gate Bridge.

～

At a café in Tiburon they had an Italian lunch and reminisced of childhood; in Sausalito they ate wild berries and contemplated who would take Isaac's room.

"A girl I hear," Harold said, "Which could prove interesting. Now listen: I'm going to make out a list of the best bars, record stores, cafes, et cetera in San Francisco and we're going to hit them all this weekend. You haven't even seen a quarter of the city!"

The condonation knocked William dead as he dipped toasty bread into oil with bicycle chain-stained hand.

"The Mission, Golden Gate Park, Sunset, Lower/Upper Haight, I mean man, I'll give you the *real* tour of the Tenderloin also!"

Stares came from all around as William, Harold looked to their bicycles, reflections in the mirror. Either man's shirt was torn in half, soaked with sweat, matted hair composed of grease, battered shoes, blue jeans tearing at intervals: an axiological conundrum there in the inveterately restive edifice.

"I feel like a king," exclaimed Harold, finishing the wine—"Now let's go!"

"You ever think this life," William attempted to say. He shook his head as if the unattainable words would fall from inside of it.

"Think what, buddy," Smith said.

"We ought to slow down, living this way?"

"What way? What do you mean?"

"This lifestyle."

Harold let out a roar of laughter that reared juridical eyes his way once more. Silver knives set down upon porcelain plates via veined, sagging hands.

"Man," he said furiously, in a way that banished doubt, "I will drink all I damn well please until this world seems something other than a catastrophe, you see," his young eyes bolting open, "Until—damnit—Until the sun breaks down!"

"Fair enough," William Fellows said, his eyes fixed through upon the moss-wrapped patio's edge, upon the entrance to the misty bicycle path.

The late-Saturday afternoon house was curiously quiet. Smith knocked at Isaac's door before opening it. He turned back to William, whispering:

"You see he'll never *believe* we just did all that! He'll just never believe it! Google-Maps—Fort Mason to Tiburon—In our state! His rosy red face is going to let up and then, William and then—"

He walked inside. Less than five seconds later he gasped.

"What is—"

The room was bare. Isaac's bed alone was left, which was also bare, save a slip of paper:

"I decided it'd be better to get north as soon as possible so I left this morning. I am no good at goodbyes but last night, for me, was a fine enough farewell party. Miss you all already. Next time you're having a drink in the city or reading a good book think of me, give me a call—To beginnings, to endurance—I am off to pursue my art more ; I have the energy to begin in solitude recalling the art of life that is San Francisco and I'll be in Portland if you ever want to call on me. I will be back someday and will call soon—A time it was, and what a time it was. I raise my glass to the city, tilt my brain toward its beauty—Recaptured, recaptured, and we will all meet again!

"Isaac Muir."

William thought for a long minute of the suddenness with which everything in his life had begun to take place. Two, three, four days. Harold could not place the note aside nor let his eyes come from its contents; his stillness was for William a heartbreaking sight in the vacant white room, where funnels of light preserved hovering particles of dust.

"Another one bites the dust, Monsieur Fellows. Long live the queen, the king, mothlight, and cetera. Brothers Quay, Stan Brakhage, we all fall down."

"No emperor shall save you, nor shall you save yourself. Only the One can save you; there, in silence, where the angels sing."

The single window stood with its view of the bark of an ancient, towering tree. Past it, seagulls sifted through the fresh air, a delivery truck turning out of sight at the gates. Green fields of light pressed on across the land, and William turned back to fall asleep before he could do anything else. He heard Harold slouch down upon the mattress, and thought he heard his face fall to his palms.

8

SEVEN DAYS TILL WILLIAM returned to Fort Mason, during which hours he explored the length of the city by foot and train using the advice of Janine (Who'd managed to get through to William an e-mail with plans for a later date—'In Prague—Can u believe!?'), Harold Smith's handwritten maps ("New girl's moving in and we all got to be on our best behavior at the Fort—See you in a week?"), Man Ray via topless Toyota.

Upon Valencia Street he dreamt of Janine, of Octavia, drifting in and out of innumerable bars and bookshops, loading his bags up and his mind before reclining amongst the hills of Dolores Park, wandering about the sand at the edge of the Sunset, dabbling with the miniature subway trains, napping in the Buena Vista Gardens.

Octavia, Skype, and a bottle of wine in the quiet evenings, restaurants and Giants games with Man Ray. Octavia, he knew, was all he missed on the east coast.

Things undeviatingly decayed, as things are wont to do, all across the country, down and into Jerusalem. Each week an increasing number of jobs were being shipped overseas or exterminated. Depression, Ms. Fellows explained in her quiet way, rather than the desire of gain, swept across the land and the voices of the living; the local and continental economy had commenced to dive rather than fall just days after William had departed. Even the hours at her latest temp job, a queer co-mixture of scrubbing toilets and the digital acclivity of a cremation company's advertisements, were shortened, though Ms. Fellows had kept security-money tucked away for William, depositing a final $500.00 into his account at a time when he'd not dare investigate his balance, and so the parade, or procession of Saturnalia, was back on.

In a night of peril he e-mailed Janine to say he would not make it; but Janine's finances, she reassured William, were indispensable, and

William took to eating each meal at Thai Restaurant on Buchanan Street with fresh ice cream desserts and beer just before his cash advance.

Something, some sort of epiphany, overcame him in his wanderings alone. The feeling of drifting in and out of the Mission's bars, listening to the conversations, walking out to the Gold-Dust Lounge at midnight, walking through Chinatown in the morning, out along the Avenues on a misty day; there was much inner richness to absorb in solitude, a sensical transcription of the short days and long nights. There was the thought of a new phone, though it felt so fine without one.

It was an immaculate, rejuvenating feeling to walk out into the summer day with a fresh sleep had, an attaché filled with resumes and cover letters, and to hand none of them out at all. There was the whimsicality of applying for the random waiter position, or in a lucid moment some car dealership out on Market Street, but otherwise it was much better to use the resumes as a coaster at an outdoor café or dimmed tavern over cocktails listening to tales of earthquakes, sex parades, the great artists, the next festival, and to take down notes on the city's layout and language in the crevasses of dog-eared pages. There seemed always a parade happening. Distant drums could be heard always, and it was much better to partake in none of the parades, but to instead let them soundtrack one's afternoon and evening from a fair distance.

Man Ray was the most amiable of hosts. He spoke at night of San Francisco Giants games with descriptive eye, took William on long tours of ancient war bunkers and lighthouses, beaches with enormous black boulders covered in strange shades of mist.

"I hate to say it is not so mystical," he admitted one day while readjusted his Taiwanese straw hat. "And to the contrary that boulder is key destination, for reasons unknown, for the pellets of passing pelicans."

Memories of concerts and people, the city over the decades, his phenomenal adventure tales from the Orient. In some obscure, nonchalant way, he made William feel as if it were his apartment, the restaurant his enterprise, the city his own. And each day at sundown, having stopped in to wash his face and have dinner, William stepped out along Bush, christened by the bells of St. Dominic's; the bells pierced the pilgrim with new, implosive love; gone were the days of small towns and smaller minds, and makeshift philosopher-kings. For now William dreamt each sunset of two angels swooping down with fiery swords, more like luminescent rods in a revealed aesthetic proximity that was both clearly visible and imperceptible, with theirs tips missing albeit aflame, guiding him along his strolls, expenditures in beatific asceticism.

On a cool night William sat beside his window overlooking the streets, contemplating his next move and what was happening at Fort Mason, when Man Ray entered the room with an optimistic look on his face; he'd found William work at a good magazine, or work at a high-paying record shop within walking distance, or even he had struck the lottery; the look on his face emanated a contagious glow.

"My wife arrives in three days!"

"Wonderful!" William stood dumbfounded to shake Man Ray's extended hand. "She home earlier than planned?"

Man Ray responded negative, and continued into a tale of the orient (Pierced bulls the size of elephants . . . The red-light district . . .), unlatching a jug of imported wine that had arrived earlier in the mail.

After the wine William began to wonder what he would do. The live-in hotels were just more than he could afford with his spending habits. He kicked himself for having lost touch with Walter so quickly and feared his new friends—gratified as he felt to have met and known them—were neither obliged nor in any position to support him. He gave up looking for rooms; he could not afford the security deposit nor the psychological strain to tell his mother he'd profligate cash the way he'd once summoned monkish verisimilitude. Yet he still had no desire to give in.

Ms. Fellows called again to announce that some universities had been calling about scholarship acceptances on file—perhaps the pilgrim ought to come home, and treat his journey as a summer fling? Each school, each professor, each letter in the mail relayed to William's ear like a kick to his stomach.

"I'll let you know," he explained on the second day, the room put-together and his blinds drawn. He had no intention of working for a newspaper or going back to school. The country had proven to him that one could no longer put faith into anything; everything the state had was stolen, and everything it said was a lie, some psychotic mutant babble. Thus one moved from being-in-society to being-in-death, the call to existence, the philosopher's stone and all its abounding grace, William surmised, a matter of interior refinement. Rather than by Pythagorean natural philosophy or physics, one adduced that the interior measure of being is as vast as the exterior. Time and space were simultaneously likewise internal; the tautological end of technological enslavement was nothing more than the eschatological equivalent of premature ejaculation. The kingdom of God was, yes, in you; but the internality of alchemical expedition was itself the apprehended cognition of phenomenological spirit that must be pitilessly transformed from the base metal of collective memory into the golden crucifix of vision. Thus the tarnished globe worked in the mass production of morons; the thinker therein stood alone: 'Diogenes was looking for an honest man, and I am simply finishing off his work in my lifelong pursuit of a single honest woman.' His mother's words terrifyingly turned from disappointment to fury; her son seemed demented, as if set upon ruining all that functioned in his life, if just to return home penniless. She slammed the phone down on him.

On the third day he thanked Man Ray with a stolen bottle of rum, and as Man Ray never drank liquor he declined with best wishes, thus rendering William Fellows some rum richer as he walked back out onto the crisp dusk streets.

At a payphone he called Janine, hanging up, walking down Buchanan to Fillmore, to Fort Mason. He found anomalous delight in the way anxiety seemed to no longer to travel within him. And on the rare occasion no one was at the little house and the café was closed, William walked back out to Dolores Park to read and rest, at a time when the park hadn't yet taken on a magical aura for him.

On one such afternoon he awakened from a dreamless sleep, a full, lukewarm bottle of Anchor Steam cradled under his arm in paper bag, tobacco leaves sprinkled across his chest. Then glancing over his shoulder, he was cast in the approaching shadows of ascending and descending blondes in the middle of sloping Dolores Park, strangers breathless with visions of excess: "Meet Nina. She was a federal judge, but now lives for heroin and pills. I would say they made the right choice; wouldn't thou, William?"

"Do I know you?"

"I see you've traveled some. Is it so, O bard? Come to the beer garden!"

At the beer garden he took a cocktail and accepted a shot of whiskey from a man with one arm who had met George Bush, Sr. The women from the park had vanished.

"He was so ugly," the amputee explained, "That after a while he became beautiful. Some people, even the richest, have teeth so mangled they caint get dem fixed. I love Brian Eno and once translated a biography of Edmund Husserl. Then I smoked crack." The tales circulated, including a 'whoroscope': "You see, a full moon's a-coming!"

Three hours later he began that great, rowdy walk down to Bay Street, stopping for a bodega beer. The Fort Mason house lights turned on as he cracked it at the open gate.

9

As the thing we call the moon appeared he sat upon the front porch drinking Rockport, chain-smoking Bali Shag, eyeing his feculent tennis shoes (Wingtips broken in half from miles of walking), thumbing through *Moby Dick* amidst a perfect circle of cigarette ends. A new, crisp beard grew in along with his hair, which was now again light blonde and parted to the side. For an hour he sat beside the locked door drinking wine contemplative, beginning to wonder. He had Harold Smith, Phil Cohen on his side, he knew—and Janine, that Janine _____.

Tourists passed through the scattered doorways of the building below. One waved; in such an instance a sense of humanity retained itself.

God help thee, old man, thy thoughts have created a creature in thee; and he whose intense thinking thus makes him a Prometheus; a vulture feeds upon that heart for ever; that vulture the very creature he creates.

He slammed the book shut and tossed it atop his torn bag, crossing one leg over the other, drinking the wine and beer.

An aquamarine taxi-van curled up beside the stairwell, its headlights cast across and through the field. Through the sliding door exited a beautiful young woman with long blonde hair, giggling as she waved goodbye to the driver. Passersby stopped and stared before carrying on in fear of being caught; she glanced their way and they returned to business, cursed matches, just to turn around all over and whisper of her beauty. William studied her movements—as he had studied the movements of innumerable passersby—this time out of less operatic desire to move than out of complimentary intrigue. She wore a sleeveless black dress and curled hair to the length of her back which rushed in the wind like golden-yellow flowers within one of either Strabo's or, say, Didymus Mountain's good gardens.

"The fact that nobody reads *Purgatory* or *Paradise* of Dante's *Divine Comedy* says more about the disgraceful human race than him," fumed William, bringing his conversation with a most patient stray feline to an end, "And I'm taking it to heart. These lambasted, godless plebs make me sick with their television ideologies while I wrestle with the problems of Dostoyevsky's poetics and drink burning rum and think about making babies with my sexy woman," &c., and it began with that incisive element, that vivacious innocence contained within her brief outburst of laughter, that caught one's eye. The mahogany trunk thrust over her shoulder shone beneath a fluorescent streetlamp like fresh polish before an ardent flame in those initial subterranean hours.

She ran an affirmative look across stapled sheets of paper, glanced upward once with wide, watery eyes, and ascended the stairs. William rubbed at his temples, hiding the wine behind his feet, throwing a stamped-out cigarette into the distant aluminum bucket of sand. At once she set her suitcase down before him and with that obscure innocence— though she seemed older than him till chorus night-drunk emerged victorious and all doubts passed painlessly of natural causes—William in his drunkenness grew ashamed, cast within the shadow of such presence,vis-à-vis the despairing reality which had submerged him, and he looked into her watery eyes like some sort of wounded prisoner.

"Walter?" she asked, with a smile that could encompass and shatter dreams.

"No, no."

"Oh—Um, Harold Smith?"

"They went out, I think."

She looked to the Golden Gate Bridge once and away, scratched soundless at her scalp.

"Do *you* live here?"

"I'm staying here for a few weeks," he blurted out, wiping burgundy sketches from his lips. He straightened his shoulders, regained his composure. His fantasy had become relayed fact by way of poetic memory multiplied by impulse; ethereal beauty will do such things.

"Who *are* you, then?" She dragged her suitcase across the porch to sit beside him. He looked down the front of her dress. For a second her nipples shone, as the top of her dress fell beady and dark. He could respond with some deep nasal inhale, some swallow of untraceable saliva. Without taking her eyes from his side-profile, she hiked the front of her dress back up. "And may I—if you don't mind—have a sip?" She pointed to the wine, letting out that girlish laugh which from there forth could always veer William back toward veracity.

He handed her the wine, extending his right hand.

"Thou doth not know where the left has been. Signed: I, William."

"William what?"

"Fellows."

"I dislike shaking hands. I'm no germaphobe but I dislike things I don't know the reason for."

"What is the difference between Eve and Mary, thou viper? What *is* providence?"

"Everything and nothing. I studied theology at Princeton Divinity. You can't impress me like that."

"So you are against shaking hands, against discussing the Blessed Virgin, and I assume you want to come inside and make yourself at home and drink my wine, and smoke my cigarettes?"

"Precisely, in a sense."

"Well I do like you, at least little, for seldom does one hear aloud 'dislike;' it's oftener something one reads in books. But anyfuck, you don't know the whole story behind shaking hands?"

"No. Who does, anyhow?" She drank from the bottle and removed a wiry pair of glasses from her purse and put them on. "William Fellows. Are you going to let me inside? Don't you see it is getting frigid." She rubbed her sandwhite upper arms with her palms, some concomitantly calculated drama, the drama of agnostical humanism.

"I have no key. I've been locked out."

"Figures. I'm Heather." She giggled again, each time a voluminous subtlety recaptured, increased. His foggy oceanic eyes met hers.

"I believe we have the exact same color eyes."

"A few people have blue eyes."

"Oh," said William. "Well anyway, I am drunk."

"A lot of people are drunk. Hmph—Do you believe in astrology?"

"No."

"Good. I can't trust anyone who believes in astrology." She ran her eyes along the exterior of the house. "This will be much different than Brooklyn. Much more innocent, I think," beginning an aimless, orchestral whistling.

"I can't trust anyone who whistles aimless."

"It is not aimless." The innocence dissolved from her face.

"Where in Brooklyn?" William cut her off. She picked the wine back up and drank with haughty vigor.

"A little place you may have never heard of called Greenpoint."

"In fact I've spent quite some time there," he explained, drinking more of the wine, rubbing at his temples, crossing one leg back over the other.

"Well that is nice," she said, as describing instead the current of wind rushing through the porch. "Strawberries, cherries, and an angel's kiss in spring," she sang angelically. Against his will, William's heart fluttered with delight.

"Along Franklin Avenue where—"

"And where did you spend the best of your time in Greenpoint?"

This William could not specify. What would he say?—The Bar with Free Pizza—Manhattan Avenue—McCarren Park—Pencil Bar—Blackout—Veronica Club of The People or Whatever in God's Name It Was Called—

Instead he watched Heather wipe a spot of wine from her lips and imagined the beauty of her clad in black peacoat, stockings and beige wingtips trotting from café to train to bar, from their future Manhattan lover's bed back to Brooklyn morning with an iridescent glow about her, and just enough brutal ardor contained in her eyes upon inspection to make her impossible.

She seemingly expected no answer to the question.

"Are you a friend of the guys that live here?"

"One is the brother of my friend back East, the other a new friend. They—"

"Are you from the East also?"

"Yes. I just finished school there, in Pennsylvania. Then I took a train to Los Angeles—"

"A train! *Me too!*" William sighed with relief as her face lit up like a pinball machine, the revolutionary connection of wine.

Ms. Daily threw her arms around Mr. Fellows, who at once inhaled her perfumes placing his tired hands upon her exposed, soft back. With his grizzled chin upon her neck, his hand sliding for one second one inch along her back, a silent tide had rushed in through him, one which both one of them ignored, returning to coy posture. William laconically snared, right leg crossed at the knee.

She retracted as beyond her shoulder some debauched, Spanish picnic grew out of hand (Sombrero rope as noose, m-80, rumored face tattoo, etc.). There was a catatonic blink in her eye that signaled some sort of deficiency that would have ruined another woman; for Ms. Daily it seemed to enhance her irrefutable presence. William would have inquired had he not felt magnetized. "But Los Angeles, why—"

With that her tone reverted to a calming, maternal stature.

"Well my friend and I rolled into Los Angeles, caught a ride down the Pacific Coast Highway to San Diego, and I failed to grow accustomed there, so I caught a train up here."

"I didn't know anyone else was making as random decisions, such adventure-stories of reality at this point in time also. They say on the news it is dangerous, or as if the prerequisite is being a filthy punk rocker with awful tattoos dragging a dog around and yelling at people for cans of Budweiser. But no, I did about the same thing as you. Left the east—just had to leave. Brooklyn is not the world; it is the illusion of the world. Everyone is ending up in San Francisco this summer. Where next summer, New Orleans? Do you have a job?"

"No."

This the pair, admitted by body language, found frivolous as anything to speak of.

"I took the train from Penn Station to the Embarcadero," she began with a nostalgia William felt fine to hear, then looking down for the wine and noticing his book and his bag. "What's in the bag?"

"My belongings. I was staying with another friend for some time. His wife was in Thailand."

"O," she crooned. "That sounds nice."

"There was an eagle in my dream," sang William, "And a multicolored door. And beside the towering door, steps: the first step, I remember, was marble white, polished and shining in such a way that I was for a moment struck blind. But I retained sight, and uplifting my weary, wincing eyes, beheld rough, cracked stone of a shade darker than purple. And the third was fragmentarily distended, in parts more like a ledge; and on the ledge was Porphyry, who lit himself on fire, blood spurting from his slit veins. And behold, then all was still and he stood there drenched with soot and smoke, before flames shot out of his veins like fire, and then I awoke. Why are you looking at me like that?"

"Oh no, your shoes!"

Heather and William looked down, shocked to catch his big toe protruding through both the sock and sneaker of his right foot. Heather gave him a testy, severe look.

"Are you sure you're not some rich kid bumbling around, enjoying himself with a nice bank account in Montana, or where did you say—"

"Pennsylvania."

"Oh right, well there are a lot of types but, hmph, I bet you're not one of them. You would be in a bar drinking something nice and not sitting out on a porch drinking wine by yourself. I don't mean to be cruel."

Again, she seemed elsewhere, as if reciting poetry to the engraved pillar between them, her watery eyes filled with the memory of Brooklyn bars, night and madness, cacophony, epiphany, and the phenomenology of being given.

"Somehow that did not seem cruel. Keep talking." He drank more wine, pleased with this Heather 's sensical fragrance.

"Well anyway, you're not like everyone else I can tell. But wait. What if I am staying across the street and just felt like torturing you? It was an instant response, say, to the sight of you when I saw you from the street all alone, reading *Moby Dick*!" Somehow this, also, did not sound cruel but untrue; even her dark entries seemed less like shades of vehemence than, well, erroneous ghosts in the prehistoric happy hour of implosion.

"Then fate is a fool," William said, drinking from the glowing dark-green bottle with slight savagery, which for a split-second occupied Heather's blue eyes in the way of widened pause. She could at once say nothing, opting to interlock her hands upon her silken knees looking to the floor panels.

"What brings you to Son-Fron-Sisco, Ms.?"

"Don't be so nervous."

William looked at her, squinting.

"I'm not—what do you mean? You don't even know me."

"I'm a fine sensibility," Heather said, "And I bet you're nervous. Oh, well, it is a long story."

"I have no idea when anyone is getting back here. We may be out here awhile."

"I talked to oh, what's his name though, he'd be here he said," cutting herself off. The pair looked at the locked door, the lightless windows. "Well if worst comes to worst let's have them down there hold our bags and go explore the city and drink coffee in cafes and talk about philosophy, the futility of man," she exclaimed, as if she had grown sick and tired of the problematic planet. "How does that sound?"

William spit wine out across the nocturnal lawn in laughter, causing some sort of rabbit-pack or another to scurry off in a stream of shadows through swaying weeds of distant porch-bottoms as Heather shrieked.

"Why did I move?" she seemed to ask herself rather than William, refraining for a nervous moment to carry on without looking his way as he studied the lipstick red as a rose upon her moving lips. "After a few months I just, I don't know, felt as if I'd been to the sort of depths of consciousness our generation stomps out of twelve-dollar movies over, waiting forty weeks on return-lines while everyone around me nibbled their fingernails and cursed talking on the computer of the future and the past at the same time but you know, it wasn't New York's fault, it was no one's fault, per say, I just needed a new scene. Someone recommended I apply for a job here where rent was free, so I did, and got in right away. San Francisco always seems like the best place to return to—"

"Here," William said, attempting to hear no more. "Have some wine."

"You'll get me drunk! I'll show you a fun time tonight!"

"You can show me all of the great spots sometime, perhaps."

"Let's go now!"

Heather leapt from her chair at once, throwing her hands to the sky.

In another psychological split-second, two things happened:

First, the sound of her holy voice awoke William from his looming confusion, depression. It mattered not what she said, nor how often she spoke, but rather that these things were icing on an existential cake; sheer existence, side by side, filled his soul where for so long despair had come knocking. And so he squirmed backwards where, Isaac had said, the winter rain got in, through the window behind his head in order to let this Heather inside, and begin a family right then and there, publish in the spirit of Novalis divided by *Paris Spleen* his journalistic magnum opus— even greater a spectacle, for he had never written poetry nor would he in his life—while she; what did she even do? Secondly, he realized that she made him feel poetic; that one could feel particularly poetic, in as real a sense as one felt horny or hungry, as a thought is as real a thing, the notebook-keeper said, as a cannonball. Something like James Agee. The way her lips moved up, down, and that laugh! Well, she could do anything she pleased with that brown-blonde hair, that body, that mahogany trunk, and that laughter which trickled down at all the right moments! Then, having leapt up with a childlike energy, her black and white dress soared as a parachute, tapping her on the forehead, as another gust of Bay wind ran throughout the contour of the porch. Within that second an image burned into William's insatiable mind which would later go on unable to define itself until he read the words of a friend who'd died all too young: Meet me here, nothing can satisfy me.

Gripped with the paralysis of instant memory, a reflection of the present, William halted to structuralize what he had seen, to hold onto the spark of that image as if he were nearing in on the culmination of a long laboratory labor:

He had eyed the rose-red, statuesque lips, carved for her tender, near-tan face which stood out with an unmatched sexuality and spoke in parts calm, others maddened. There must have been, as William had foreseen, a warmth contained within such a mouth to break every single heart in the world. Adoration poured forth from the excitement released from within her, an adoration for everything available to her, which nonetheless made one feel quite important, moment by moment, in Ms. Daily's presence, an accidental amorous context contained within each word she spoke. With that mouth she'd struck the chord which re-capitulated, in an hour of physiological shipwreck that not even Aloysius Bertrand could mollify, San Francisco, and William's personal illumina-tions, to life: The immediacy of the individual's need to thwart boredom. Boredom, which some might argue, solidifies the meaningless nature of life, in pursuit of multichemical indulgence. He'd seen it in Isaac, Phil Cohen, the Shroud, back home in Nielson, Manheim, and even Carson when he wasn't too close to the sociopathic edge damned to the past. Now Heather wielded this sensual casual tone about, and William prayed that such a fine woman would be his new roommate, if all went well. Perhaps the most difficult element of this actualization was in the way he would have to play his cards right that evening; in some abstract way he knew Walter could not care less about him, and that in a way, more so than Nielson, he almost enjoyed and encouraged the idea of suffering. He'd warned William against the very men he went on to think the most of. It was a matter of time before visual evidence of developing relationships ensued. Saint Smith, at least drunk, though everyone was and always will be drunk, had promised William sanctuary—still at dawn, the dawn of the soul, he could be held to nothing, though William in his negated turn could not care less for the summoned strength of such arms. So then the most difficult part of that evening, for William, was not the solitude of Fillmore, nor the way he told Man Ray he was all set with another friend and had a few potential jobs lined up, nor the way Man Ray's wife recalled William as a young child and seemed so saddened by the rapidity of time which struck a chord frail even through deliberate drunkenness, nor was it the way lovers and friends seemed to laugh all around him more than usual, that night of prior loneliness, from restaurant windows to the long quilts of dusk stretched across the fields of Fort Mason roaming the unknown streets with Ishmael; no, the most difficult thing of all was with circumstances thin as ice when Heather leapt into the air and her dress bolted up like a flock of doves and William laid eyes upon those long legs of cream, those plain, silken underwear which concealed a thing at all which just above—as far the dress had flown north—was the tip of the slightest belly he had ever seen, which in its own right offered a further, strange indescribable attraction applicable perhaps to if anything, then the current fashion-trend of emaciation—but then back down, the long legs he could almost taste, warm wine running through their blood like his own—his biggest problem now, his single concern, was to go about Heather the proper way—with restraint; in control; a perfect casual pitch.

"First, I have to use the bathroom," he said, standing and stepping to the door. The door-handle would not budge. Her sweet laughter resounded once more, as her dress had fallen back down, straightened by the palms of her hands.

"Looks like you'll have to go outside!"

William tucked down his pants and waddled to the side of the porch.

"William the penguin!" she laughed, curling a lock of her hair, rolling him a cigarette.

He held his erection in his hand, cast by shadows and unable to go, zipped and turned back around.

"The damned thing won't work!"

She said nothing but shrugged and finished the wine with a quick sip.

"And now my wine is gone!"

William raised his arms to her, holding an invisible object to crash down upon his innocent culprit, who following his lead of slow motion raised her arms, an astonished look developing upon her face. He placed his hands within hers for a moment. With an edge of desperation he wanted nothing more than to then sit beside her, kiss her lips fully, open mouths at once, let their tongues meet slow and long, and with hands interlocked the two—with the intentions of sincere friends—set off, returned for their luggage, tucked it beneath the porch in the backyard and took off for the city which twinkled with the lights of wandering stars. They took off through a maze of concrete which led to the main streets. Nothing seemed to matter but that moment, as Heather blushed, skipping instead of pacing, with each external agreement gripping hands for half a minute. People passing of every last location, situation, credence, gave some sort of acknowledged, affirmative look their way. Admiring eyes crossed along the entranceway to the gates like fireflies. William felt as if he were understanding discipline, that he was growing up somehow. It felt good.

"I've been reading Raymond Carver," Heather said upon Bay Street. "Have you ever heard of him?"

"He is a bit callow for my standards," said William.

"What do you mean?"

Heather swallowed and touched her ear.

"I mean his books are sort of apish is all," William explained. "If I believed in sympathy at some vast rate, I would appreciate him, though I don't, and even if I appreciated him as a person it would be some regrettable off-handed way of discarding his ideologies."

"What are his ideologies?"

"I don't know. All I know is that I just don't know."

"Have you even read him," Heather defended. "Have you even read him."

"No. I just felt like going against the grain. Forgive me."

"Don't joke around like that," she said. "It is not funny at all. I knew a publisher in Manhattan—"

"We're out of wine," William said. "It looks like I'll be going downtown. Goodnight."

Each off-handed comment they made to one another was enhanced by emerging, automated light revealing teasing smiles and sinister twirls of golden locks, auburn mustaches.

"Where will you sleep?"

"That is no longer my decision."

"I'll forgive you for that strange arrogant remark and go with you," suggested Heather, removing a silver flask from her purse and taking a sip with her pinky extended to the Milky Way. "Mm, a gin and tonic. Here!"

From there they walked to Polk Street and the outside world seemed again to dissolve. It was the way she blushed instead of nodding, the way she skipped instead of pacing ahead. Who else could get away with this, considered William. It's like Empson and that neck beard, but even on him it was imprudent. She lives in a time of her own.

Walking up Polk Street the gang of two struck upon a string of agreements in topics ranging from Carlos the Jackal to the Women of Manhattan:

"They're just the worst," Heather laughed, "Thinking that women should be that way!"

She made a daunting impression and William laughed, drinking the gin as if it were water from a fountain.

"Storming down the street with their big flapping asses and legs of veins and wires, their heels clicking like hooves of a horse, interlinked with that grotesque poverty of the streets. I do not miss Manhattan at all. Beyond Manhattan. Going through it and coming up for air in Brooklyn is always the greatest feeling. Tranquility meets some fresh elemental contour. But almost all my family is from Kent Avenue, so it's old hat to me, and I am Dionysus."

Fog came in and the tops of the buildings went invisible. William again began chain-smoking. He smoked seventeen cigarettes in a row, Heather rolling them intermittent and laughing along Polk, across the obstacle course of democrats and dung.

"God," said Heather, "Sometimes I'm just so happy I could cry!"

"This gin and tonic is powerful."

Heather stopped him and explained that he would act as her husband if any strange men tried anything; she was hit on a lot.

"If anyone tries anything, I'll knock him out clean with this," William said, patting his leather-bound edition of *Moby Dick*.

"We'll pretend we're married!"

"But Dame Fellows, of *course* we are married." They danced through the fog. "Our ring is in the shop is all. That shop there. See, that man's going to leave a message on our answering machine in no time. He's polishing our rings as we speak."

"How could we be married without rings?"

"Stranger things have happened," William said.

"Everyone is crazy these days. I saw a video online of two Cornell— was it Cornell? I don't know, don't care—robots having a conversation—"

Heather Daily shrugged her shoulders with a vague satisfaction, and they walked ahead. She sent him a naked, serious look that William ignored. He cared less to get the least bit serious. Life had done him in and he would emerge victorious. When you've walked the streets of the desert with blistered feet quite sure you will commit suicide at the next bridge, have grown up without a family and for a while it seemed fine because no one else did either, and your line of working is going under, you are either going to take the paranoiac route—being on the verge of understanding the universe while acknowledging the paradoxical flaw of the misapprehension of becoming inclined to hidden meanings—or you can throw caution to the wind, take your body for a body, your mind for a mind, and sharpen the two to a ready point and set flight into the dawn of the flesh that is life; implicative is not an unwillingness to go, but one can go out swinging, burning down the machinery of life, and burn your own philosophy into the times, the times without such thought are as interesting as ash and as memorable as birth and sheer rejection from every corner of life can become the amplification of the individual soul if one is unwilling to go down; at eternity's gates real life begins where the keys to the locks evaporate.

"Let's stop into a bar, that one over there," said Heather. Polk Street flattened out as the array of shops and restaurants became clear. "Do you want to stop into one?"

"Not really," said William, "Because in all of them I'll be looking for someone like you and I've already got you by my side!"

Ahead some sort of parade was dispersing. Tambourines crashed against gongs and horn arrangements and bright-colored costumes and streamers blended well. It was a sight one could almost taste.

"Revolution always fails because one cannot advocate disorder who has experienced it. Revolution is a mental institution, where the doors are best locked, and sanity man's security, in Pelikan's vindication of tradition."

"There's always a parade beginning or ending in San Francisco these days," Heather said. Troupes of drunken foreigners passed William and Heather by as she took his arm, bringing an experimental silence to their lips.

A lanky man with acne-torn scars across the beak of his nose appeared abruptly, streamers tangled within his gelled hair. He screamed in William's face:

"Jestesmy najilepsze, jestesmy najilepsze!"

William attempted to weave around the man peacefully and industriously although it was clear at once that this wouldn't go. The man's breath smelt of sardines and his eyes were glazed over with a filmic waste. The man pressed himself against William as Heather cried out, falling against newspaper displays, and he screamed in her face at an even more abrasive volume as the band neared in, now coinciding with streams of laughter:

"Jestesmy najilepsze, Jestesmy najilepsze, gringo!" He extended his hands toward Heather; she glanced at William with frightened eyes.

"Be gone, relinquish, thou and thy goyim, before I put a spell on thee," William thundered, albeit ridiculously outsized and outnumbered, "Before I knock your teeth out." He was quite positive he could not take all of them. The man pressed past him, turning around:

"JEST—"

William struck him once in the face with the edition of *Moby Dick*. Pieces of the dust jacket tore off and fluttered away, spiraling through the brace-grated gutter. The riotously base imbecile tumbled forth into an idle moving truck spray-painted with a crowned pig by broken chariot, less hurt than insulted. Crowds did not gather; the music and the streamers pressed on with collages of interjecting, twisting faces.

Then suddenly the formerly inconsequential apes of wrath lunged at William as a young girl in the crowd cried out. William punched one in the mouth with such vigor his knuckles were bruised, cut open. It was an all-out fight for a few seconds, the man getting a left on William's chest, a childish kick at his ankles; William socked him again the mouth, crashed the book against his face, and punched him clean out in the street. The nugatory alien fell away, spitting a broken tooth and pulpy spit to the aluminum linings, the ponds of cigarette ends. Heather stood still with her mouth ovular, an unseen forehead vein emerging to pound twice, thrice.

Relatives were being rushed in. William hailed a cab.

"16th and Mission!" Heather shouted to the driver. Heather wrapped a handkerchief around William's knuckles as the parade pressed on into the fog. Through rearview mirrors they watched them running, pointing, staring. Before William could celebrate his victory, he let the absurdity of random violence run through him. It made sense. He was proud to have struck the man with the edition of Melville and thought as little as possible of Heather—this beautiful stranger—and her proximity to him, wrapping bandages around his hands and whispering doctoral inquiries in that fantastical way.

At 16th and Mission the party continued. Swift scents, bursts of food-stands, taquerias fumes sifting through the evening air, a man in sombrero playing mandolin through speakers, bottles of tequila clinking in the air, margaritas poured on the multicolored, tile-reflective subway steps. William stepped into its vivid, cultural sense of life dumbfounded in a constructive way. The streets were jam-packed. Children with cowboy hats ran by pepper stands and crates of fruit firing off cap guns beside beautiful young women walking hand in hand with their mothers in identical hand-woven blue ball dresses. Mustached men in blue jeans drew from crackling wicker pipes upon crates and barrels, scattered benches, barstools, the distorted-mirror sides of food carts. Fumes burst forth from the taco trucks as great steaks sizzled before open windows of apartments, the silken blinds rushing in the wind as enormous chefs sprinkled extra cilantro to paper dishes. The dozens of old-fashioned storefronts became alive with wide-open doorways from which salsa music discharged out into the streets, clapping hands, readmitting the nocturnal party of purgative reconciliation. William turned to Heather who was looked fixedly ahead with the light of the night in her eyes.

"How is it San Francisco becomes a different world five minutes any which way in a cab, a twenty-minute walk and you'll see—"

"Let's walk!"

Dark bars lined the streets between Mission and Valencia, lit by obscure, fading neon signs, not quite yet crowded beyond their velvet sheeted entranceways. Young people drank beer out on the street and hookers marched ahead to Mission. War veterans drank rubbing alcohol at crumbling bus stations and an array of live-in hotels gathered endless batches of arms torn by needles. All of this was becoming something William was getting used to though; on the west coast, or in the Bay Area, poverty seemed far less conjoined with violence than in a place like Baltimore or Philadelphia; in those places a man looking for a cigarette could look for one with a butcher knife; in a place like the Mission anyone desperate enough to ask the young for anything on the streets seemed far too debilitated by drug intake to move, or put together the rest of the sentence. Obscure inquiries broke in like shadows along the street and one just walked on aware, focused on opacity and pleasures. William thought of Janine for a moment; didn't she live just around here?

The crowds synchronously lit up opium and hashish, bystanders looking out to the gleaming full moon interlaced with passing clouds amidst the gate of the sky. He felt comfortable and was glad to have arrived, and fell behind, enamored by the array of interesting shops, theaters, bars, cafes.

"William Fellows!" Heather cried, "Come!"

He ran ahead, placing his warm hands along her bare, cold arms. They took off down Valencia contemplating the first stop ('City, drunken city').

"You saved my life," cooed Heather, taking up William's hand. "I owe you!" Her nipples came through her dress like little rocks. William noticed them in accordance with Heather as she blushed, and the pair looked straight ahead through a silent pact of ambiguity. William removed his coat and placed it upon her; it was far too large, ill-fitting with her immaculate dress.

"We're not in Brooklyn anymore—the nights are cold. Let's go back to Mission and get you a coat. I saw a place."

Heather wrapped her arm around his and they took off down 17th, stopping at shop windows to polish off the gin and do their hair. She studied his profile, placing the book into her purse with a giggle.

"Of course you'll stay with us! We're going to be good friends, William! Do you like me?"

"I like you; we will indeed become good friends."

"Why do you like me?"

"Because you don't care," said William at once. They walked ahead, crossed the street, stood before the windows of the outlet store. "You have those who care, those that claim to not care, and then that rare breed of people that don't care. You exude it. It is attractive, a—attractive quality as a person. You have a mystical nihilism about the way you walk down the street."

"We're going to get drunk tonight."

Streams of passersby poured through the gridded chaos, gaudy berets, essays and aphorisms, the sphere of day a burning vault. Bacon-wrapped hotdogs sizzled upon small tin grills; they took two and ate outside of the store.

"You look like a soldier from the civil war with your bandage. You've got sauerkraut on your lip!"

"Thank you."

"And then at the end of the night we'll go to Dolores Park and watch the sun rise. Do you think our bags are safe?"

The synchronized radios stopped playing songs and an update rang out upon the street; more troops to another foreign country—the bill had just been signed. Police rushed through Mission Street in a sea of sirens and glass bottles smashed along the ground.

"What do you think of the war," Heather said, "Of all of this happening today."

"I don't think of it," William said. "I think so detached of the whole thing that if I appeared shocked any longer at the state of the world I would be acting. Dying doesn't seem too big of a deal, for it is living I'm much more interested in."

"Me too."

"America doesn't exist to me. There is water and there is land and there is space. Anything in life becomes simple if one just faces the facts that there are no answers but suggestions. I am interested in art. Art is a suggestion, great art is a great suggestion, a corner of a street in the city of the mind that one might want to consider taking a turn down in order to find a much happier life for themselves. Paintings, films, photographs; these things enhance people's lives. Speeches, wars, weapons; these things ruin people's lives. The vomitous media can go on with its chants of inanity, the newspapers can regurgitate their surveys and death tolls; count me out. Politics is the assumption that people are dead and alive, that the world is a simultaneous slaughterhouse. This, my dear, is the subject of my rebellion. I've just got to find the proper vehicle."

If the world had a fixed structure, it was one of beauty in the arcaded windows upon nocturnal Mission Street. Flamenco music returned and the children began to laugh and sing again as Heather and William strode into the outlet shop, its ornamental clothing strewn across ropes of clothespin and masking tapes. The meditative, robust cashier smoked cigarillos. The speakers resembled satellites and they danced through the cramped aisles, singing and laughing aloud, spinning one another in circles past party favors wrapped in cellophane, holiday cards without envelopes, generic bags of expired potato chips, crates and cases of fruit-punch soda, bootleg movies, household appliances without boxes, a basket of batteries, until a long wall lined with raincoats left William, Heather mesmerized. She rushed forth to the chartreuse-yellow raincoat and began her uncontrollable laughter; William laughed with her as she pulled the hood over her head, looking cute, like a baby duck.

He at once loved her and acknowledged her madness, an ideal woman to revolve around in his equatorial state, and a woman that would take time to attain. Was there any end to San Francisco?

It was nice to know he might live with her, though, for in that case he would not attain her at all for the sake of his own well-being but be around her and feel young and good about everything, the way he felt watching her dance alone in the raincoat which came down to her knees. She took a pair of scissors and cut the dress above her knees where the coat passed over, prompting William's heart to break in admiration of how endearing Heather Daily was in everything that she did in a sort of awful bliss. Her hair flailed before a fan like multilateral masts of a lithographic ship, mimicking overhead music with her rose-red lips.

"You know my parents live out east in a broken-down cabin," Heather said, out of breath.

"Let's get your coat and go! We will dance somewhere!"

"We'll go have whiskey!"

"Whiskey with ale; it is a good combination. Absinthe and black twist afterward."

"What is black twist?"

"Weed barreled into an emptied Dutch outlined with pencil-thin snakes of opium."

"My friend might meet up with us."

"Bring every friend," William said at once, taking her hands for a final dance, moving from thought to speech act: "Diogenes was looking for an honest man, and I am simply finishing off his work in my lifelong pursuit of a single honest woman."

He paid for the coat and they took off back to 24th, Valencia, Guerrero. The streets had become more rampant. A young man smashed in the windshield of a Mercedes-Benz with a cinder block and ran off before a rushing cameraman. The music poured forth into the streets like heavy liquid. The voices of the street echoed fell and rose.

"The last time I walked down this street there were tears in my eyes," said Heather, walking along 24th and Valencia. William admired the beauty of her side-profile and waited for her to speak again. "And what were you doing in Brooklyn, monsieur?"

"An old friend lives there," William said yearningly. He longed to say more though fell at once enraptured by the city. "The muse of this cocooning mask, a guiding light of mine, a best friend from school years."

"A love and a friend are the best kinds," smiled Heather.

He wearily peered into his forever-emptying wallet; had to hit an ATM. The roaring scene around him subsided until Heather was back at his side laughing, pulling him forth back up to Valencia Street. The great frayed rubber raincoat! The looks on passersby's faces were the physical decoding of William's thoughts.

Again, in a matter of minutes, or more-so a sudden flash for the high ones, the two were catapulted into another scene. The Flamenco music had given way to choruses of drunken voices, leading all the young men and women across the roaring streets smoking something or another and waiting for love or otherwise to fall into their laps from the sky. Drunken women with foreign complexions walked arm-in-arm with one another, their eyes bright with the full moon glowing snow-white, teenage girls with ostrich voices and slit skirts of fleeting, true longing, a solitary hashish-high old man wielding fractured ashplant whose slit eyes apologized for nothing amidst the long-gone lights of sirens ricocheting mothlight in a dream, the discarded dreams and memories and words lost and sought belligerent in the eyes or passing faces or downcast young men marching ahead into the void.

With the lure of magnets the couple caught a dozen visual stamps of approval before catching the closing door to Casanova. The most embittered passersby, wheezing lumberjacks and genius American Apparel catalogue cut outs, appeared embarrassed of their inability to keep their eyes off of Heather, walking in her raincoat, for she had outwitted them all in not caring, instead paying nominal sums to play dead-serious games of dress up.

"Let's go in!"

They weaved through the condensed crowd, he and Heather pulling up adjacent stools to the free jukebox. At once she began punching in numbers at random. It was impossible to hear a sound from the speakers over the collage of voices anyway.

One haughty, out of place cougar—perhaps from the Marina—shot a look at Heather. William watched her disdain for the free spirit with a caustic eye. He knew not what to do as she approached, placing a hand of jewel upon the neon-yellow raincoat. William and Heather turned to the older woman and laughed in her egregious face.

"What are you doing, going to ruin the thing like that?"

Heather looked up:

"I'm just playing with the jukebox. Is it yours? Never mind, lady. You're drunk and an old hag. Get lost."

"Don't talk to me!" the woman screamed. She dropped her purse to the ground; William retrieved it, handed it back. The woman snatched it and broke away.

The natural beauty magnified by near-proximity was enough to stunt any progressive aggressor into at least retraction, if not total submission. The cougar, however, was quite drunk. Where did she come from, where would she go, and what did it matter?

She returned, shook her glass with barreling contempt, ice cubes creating the sound of little broken bells. William could hear such music, the shaking glass inches from his face. The woman's rage shifted from the raincoat to the random selection of the jukebox to the undeniable joie de vivre of this Heather. The woman looked to need a fight before she went home, so she chose a bar full of fun young people. People did these sorts of things when something happened to them in life sometimes, William guessed. She fell back, the long wrinkled flesh beneath her too-tanned upper arm jingling like awful bells amongst the crowd, the inadvertent retrieval, oblivion, her exhausted face within drunken hands as if a reputational guillotine.

Heather pulled her stool closer to William.

"What was wrong with her?"

"We're all in the gutter," cried Heather, "But some of us are reaching for the stars! Nothing can faze me any longer! What will we drink!"

She took a handful of money from her pocket and stood to go walk to the bar. William extended his hand, drawing her nearer. She sat upon his lap. He lifted the last rubber edge of her coat as to have his jeans pressed against her skirt, refrained. He smelt the strawberry-scent of her flowing dirty-blonde hair through the dense smell of stale beer and barrels of rum; he caved into her shoulder at once, rubbing his nose upon the sticky nylon.

"What do you want to drink, Mr. Fellows?" looking over the side of his face. She kissed him on the temple.

"She didn't get away safe," smiled William, extending a $100.00 bill from his pocket. Heather's laugh hit a height of precision he could not have fathomed. Nor had he had fathomed he'd ever do such criminal things.

"Tuck that away somewhere," Heather shouted, "First I'm buying us two whiskeys. Then we'll go off!"

After four whiskeys, life digressions, vague kisses, art, sexual tales, politics, the sounds and the furies of San Franciscan nocturne, 2:30 AM Heather and William and a couple dozen others stumbled back out onto the cool heat of Valencia. Everyone was to meet by some hook or crook at the 500 Club over on Guerrero for after-hours. First, though, William and Heather walked on further down 16th Street packed with all the shattered glass, the insane, the rich, the war veterans, the beautiful, the damned, the artistes, the druggists, straight ahead up that long sloping hill of Dolores Park to talk all night beside one another overlooking all of the glittering city, thoughts and expressions falling photographic from memorized ideals lost, of unrequited premeditation, toward a new consciousness either had read about in books no one had ever heard of.

"We went to an insane party, there were people having a threesome in a walk-in closet, this guy with two women, and he had the letter 'p' tattooed across his forehead seven times, in a half circle."

Heather and William lay in the grass all night talking and laughing, giving the stars names and discussing the future till the first signs of dawn, when they made it back down the hill through all the sprinkler-streaked green mass of Dolores, and into another taxicab. Heather at once fell asleep upon William's shoulder. He had the driver go around awhile as he reflected upon his life as lights passed over his body, over Heather. Time had begun to pass, and such is the unconscious motif of external travel. After the ride throughout Mission's disjointed renegades calling out for battered solace, Downtown's troubadours, butlers, limousine-men smoking cigars, North Beach's sudden silence, shops closed down for time, Chinatown's sneaking garbage-pickers, fish deliveries, crackling wooden crates of food and drink, Fisherman's Wharf's rustling distant boats, seagulls crying out to the red sky, after all of it William felt fine about life, for life would beat on but in that moment he knew he was the happiest young man on Earth. He pressed his nose to Heather 's hair, inhaling and breaking away. The colors and sounds of the city poured in through the open window, rushed over his face and through his hair. That, then, was life everlasting, and anything else anyone had ever told him was true had been false.

The door was unlocked. He placed Heather upon the couch, removed the neon-yellow coat and tucked her in with it. She spoke inaudible phrases amid her sleep, her return to San Francisco.

William brought their belongings in from the backyard. He curled up with his long coat as blanket, his stained shirt folded into a pillow, wondering for a moment whatever had become of his rabbinical hat; and meanwhile across the living room floor sunlight crept in through the wide window; thus the pilgrim dreamt of Octavia Savonarola, of tomorrow, and fell into a long, peaceful sleep. Down by the water a marching band was warming up. Two dozen drums beat and echoed, synchronicity, that last sight of a hummingbird balanced upon telephone wire, this that, and the northern winds.

He could not sleep. He instead dumped Jameson into half a bottle of crisp ginger ale and made his way toward Columbus Ave., 'in search of the Lord.'

In and out of consciousness, the deveined, bleary-eyed boy pilgrim stood outside of a Latin Mass. He tilted his cupped ear to the entranceway, listening: *'Te Deum laudamus'*—'sing, O door hinges: sing unto thy ten-ant a new song!'

He was afraid of the bliss that burned inside his heart. He felt his heart was on fire. It was the whiskey. But was it just the whiskey?

He recalled *The Way of the Pilgrim*, that obscure little book both his mother and Octavia of all people both loved. He walked back to Fort Mason smiling and distributing money to the homeless.

10

But then the door was violently swung open by some godforsaken force. Nielsen's brother? Another dream? William awoke to the hand shaking his shoulder restlessly and for a moment did not recognize Walter. He'd cut his hair short and appeared morose with a sobriety out of his control.

William awoke with a cough, readjusted his glasses, and understood he'd be most drunk for another hour. Then everyone would have to start taking it easy.

"Hello, man," he feigned sullen; "Fancy meeting you here!"

"Where you have you been? Everything alright? I was visiting home; me and Nielsen tried calling you."

"Phone's dead," William explained, stretching his arms and legs. He looked over to the couch as to introduce Walter to Heather though she had gone into her room.

Walter had taken to a severe, bad-looking half-beard. It looked like he'd gone to castrate himself but instead like cut off some pubic hair and stick-glued it to his chin. Six or seven curled, misaligned hairs grew from his chin, offsetting anything he said, or any object he'd place his eyes upon. He stood before William as if to imply something. William stood to squirm past him and invite him to lunch, explain of his last two weeks, till the pilgrim dizzily fell over and clean through the coffee table.

He pulled a splinter from his arm and re-administered his conversation.

"Isaac left in the wee hours for Portland and it was so abrupt, you know and I was down in Japantown for some weeks before," as William's voice trailed off in a severe look coming from Walter. He assumed morphine withdrawal was the crux of it but its severity made one unable to speak at all. Vulgar moments of silence broke apart the attempt at talk.

"Don't look at me that way," said William, pathetically attempting to reassemble the table.

The war had begun.

"You can't just show up and freeload! And these people you go out with," he reverted to whispering, "That I told you are awful! You went to the party and even from there you let me go back out to see Saul alone! Then I don't hear from you for weeks, my brother is exasperated! You don't even call him or anyone!"

"Calm down, man, good God!"

It was a perfect summer day, and its brilliant hue reassured William much more than any voice at all that he would be alright. Some people were just grouches and had to get thrown under the wagon, others were outside drinking wine in the park. He scratched at his greasy hair and re-administering beard and felt good, Jesuitical, garnished in poverty. Ode to Gerard Manley Hopkins! Looked to his pockets, roaring boisterous—still had the hag's one hundred.

"My manager saw you on the porch the other day," Walter said, "And she said no one can live here that doesn't work here. I'm sorry, man."

William removed the lengthiest splinter from the ground and leaned upon it as a cane, looking over the house contemplative and daydreaming of Columbus Avenue. Or better yet, Clement, Green Apple Books! He marched to the hallway and took an open bottle of Dante from the kitchen and took a swig.

"Alright," he said, "That is alright. I understand. Alright." He knew that this was bad, quite bad, but still he did not believe Walter. He felt that Walter felt betrayed and now would betray William—this was understandable. Still it alleviated William somewhat to consider he was not being thrust out by force, but rather by some incoherent punishment posed, sounded via the ineffectual.

As Walter spoke, half to himself and about half to his cat, leaving whatever dialogic crumbs were left over for the pilgrim, confusion of the senses slipped within the gates of Fort Mason, beneath a hollow moon. He recalled last evening's nearly stepping on a neat pile of needles for the third time since first stepping out; and as his heart skipped a beat, flirting with the dual of aspect of microbiological infection and losing his borrowed dwelling place, the mountain seemed to move, and with this conceptual movement it became a thing that had been made, rather than an immovable structure that had always been there and always would be. No, it had come into being, the pilgrim conjured, this makeshift bungalow no longer a little larger than the entire universe; William envisioned what that looked like, this idea of mountains coming into themselves, its authorial origins and structure; and it appeared as though things were no longer made by what men had theorized as invisible accumulations borne of nothingness and temporarily host to mammalian enterprise geological principles just another prostitute in the physiology of language games. Perhaps there appeared a cosmic war at hand, waged and raging, modeled on cognitive adherence to a poetic structure to the conceptual universe. The pilgrim reflected that human hands were nothing but emblems of the divine; William could see the voice of procession and form, and it sounded like softly falling snow, there in the late autumn of unreason.

"It wasn't my choice."

"It is alright," William repeated.

He snapped out of his thought.

"Yes, Walter—whatever I can do to help."

"And you will need to replace the table."

"Did I say I wouldn't? Did I ever ask for anything else? Don't take advantage of me, exploit me because I'm staying with you, it's like turning life into a line of work. I don't know why this is all so negative. I thought we were going to have fun."

"My life has turned upside down in the last two weeks," Walter said.

"So stand on your head," began William, feeling as if halfway suffocated.

Harold Smith burst through his bedroom door wielding a bottle of Jameson, bilingual Benedict, morning erection through underwear there in the deranged dwelling place of Latinity, William's leather jacket, rubbing his eyes through the doorway and into the living room, talking to himself:

"Welp I need a smoke damn proper, a little he-hay and a bicycle ride across ye old Golden Gate nor now, then when, cash this check, dobba-de, dee-doe, diddle diddle dee-dong-dow, go to the record shop, clip m' toe nails, bang on the drum all day, yep welp," and paused, noticing William and Walter standing in the morning light with nothing between them but the remains of a second-hand coffee table. He overlooked William, and noticing his cane began to break out uncontrollably into a waterfall of ecstatic, hysterical laughter.

He took an old eye-patch from his coat pocket and put it on as a necklace which jotted as he passed Walter to clink bottles with William.

"Yes," he said, elbowing the air, "Yes, you're back—Life in the afternoon, say, where the Hell you been! And you, Walter, you too!"

"I flew home some days after Saul's wife died," Walter admitted, pretending to not notice Harold's wiry, extended hand. The energy and sense of life Harold brought to a room just standing still broke down any negativity and made the least-bit miserable man feel worse than foolish.

"Darn," he said, "So I heard. Have some apple juice."

A painting that had been hanging on the wall unlatched, crashing to the tile floor, its clay frame cracking in half. They stared at it until Harold relayed about how beautiful the day was to be. "Oh—oh you see!" He flung open the windows. Physiological despair appeared to fill Walter's gray eyes as he appeared contemplative and eager to deliver bad news. He turned to William:

"What are you going to do, just drink until you run out of money? Just a constant party all summer long? Pretending the whole thing isn't—"

Smith cut in, seemingly wounded:

"Oh Walter," he began, stringing an outfit together from clothing strewn across the piano seat, "You're just a miserable old dog with the emotional capacity of a nine-year old. Don't go bugging my buddy here! We got big summer plans! You've made it clear that you're uninterested in living, so just go on to wherever you intend on going! Go back home! You look antsy!"

"I do have somewhere to be!" Walter screamed, kicking the air. He shot frantic looks in all directions. William yawned at extravagant length:

"Merde."

"I'm going to the office!" He kicked the broken table. "My brother's on prescription drugs, my parents are getting laid off from their jobs, my job is being threatened, the damned country is doomed, and I'm just sick of it! Sick of it!"

"Nielsen is on prescription drugs?" This bit of information disturbed William, although by that point pharmaceutical drugs were commoner than toothpaste in the average American medicine cabinet. "What happened?"

"What does it matter," Walter spat.

"Don't get that way," William said, getting serious. "What happened?"

"Mind your business—why did you even *come* to California?"

He had tried but it would not work. William decided it would be more interesting to roam the streets on such a day overlooking the live-in hotels for a room of his own and decided to go out harvesting depression's brainchild, the lyrical wielding of a machete:

"Some people are grammatical errors, others misplaced apostrophes; I'm beginning to think you're of the latter," William said, stretching his legs across the shattered coffee table, soaked in glass-enhanced streams of sunlight, and took a glass of wine.

Harold cut in with his attempt at politeness:

"If this whole thing is about the coffee table then I'm doing downtown to get a new one right now!" Walter spit at the ground in reply, glaring at Harold. "There is a parade that's going to last all summer; either you're marching along or you're going to get trampled! That's it! So stop ruining everyone's fun, you junkie!"

Walter screamed so that his voice cracked; he turned around at the door, foaming from his mouth:

"Enough! You're both getting thrown out!"

He stood still for a moment, as if to relay he would accept one reply, his hand on the doorknob.

Harold Smith halted hysterical laughter for a moment, tilting his head back to make clear that such a possibility had been disabled weeks earlier.

"Welp, bud, the ornamental conundrum to your crumbling solution is that Isaac and I already secured William's stay here a while ago. Knew he couldn't just rely on you, so he's at least got the couch—we may fix up the attic for 'im till gets his sore feet on the ground!" The look in his eyes was of an ambiguous fever; neither Walter nor William knew if this proclamation was truthful at all, each taking to polar-opposite anticipations.

Walter opened his mouth with an accompaniment of cringed eyebrows when Harold's reopened and Heather laughed, emerging in the enormous yellow raincoat from her bedroom, jogging to the bathroom.

The door slammed behind him on his way out. The first fresh, oceanic gust of afternoon air burst it back open.

"Hell!" Harold shouted, wrapping his arms around William and sauntering around the living room barefooted while playing swing music on the grand piano, "Let the summer begin God-damnit, let the parade begin!"

But meanwhile, as Harold fell back asleep and there was the question of replacement furniture, income, and whether the pilgrim was officially returned to sleeping outdoors again, he returned to a place he had not been in many moons: the sickness unto death of metaphysical doubt, impending doom, and the sense that one's bliss, now interrupted, has or had been a matter of delusion. Walking down to Joe DiMaggio park, sitting down for a shot and beer again defused the existential dread, the thrownness of having come suddenly to ponder if one was, in fact, *wrong*. About what? Well the sun became a flashlight, and delirium was the taste in one's mouth; the last thing one wanted was to face one's mind in clarity, and yet the opposite was itself repugnant futility; but again the pilgrim's frame of mind was broken up, as another distant parade neared in, and he found himself south of Market:

Wagons and oxen, both flesh and not, carvings in sacred gilt, suspended in space, caged men in leather and a horror framed by language; William could see through memory a voice, and touch the texture of a song; and nature and art were lovingly at odds, like two puppies or kittens.

He cleaned off his tin can ashtray, genuflected, and sat back down to Polyclitus's *The Canon*, feet well set on a drained crate of ale—there is nothing new under the sun, save for occasionally visible speech. But again his peace was broken up, and again familiar faces were uplifting his exhausted arms and taking him down the street.

William did not entirely understand why his friends, who he again had trouble recalling either name or place of origin, sought to witness a parade concerning bondage and pride, although they were more fitting themes than anyone present seemed to comprehend. He was the first and last young man there standing still, in his cape with olive branch and book, looking on as men beat each other's breasts, backs with whips, chains, and fists. Blood spilled; booths brought in men to have their bodies tattooed and pierced; tents provided shade wherein one could, out of sight, inject heroin, meth, cocaine, speed.

And encircling all the festivities were naked men, of various build and shade, overburdened, with boulders strapped to their backs. Others, in the ring outside of them, wore dog costumes made of leather, and ran on all fours, leashed; others burned themselves with cigarettes and cigars, swallowed urine and had their genitals pierced before a dozen cameras. Bruised men congregated on yet another exterior circle to speak in coded languages, beneath masks, while around them men signed up to have themselves genitally injected with diseased semen; men dressed as security guards were pushed down further and further upon lubricated traffic cones; men and women alike climbed stepladders to leather swings, their bodies covered in rubber except for their exposed anuses and vaginas, where once situated, police horses were brought forth—

If man had been a worm who, despite being slated for dust, had a chance to go through the cocoon to become a butterfly, here that possibility had been destroyed.

He was neither perturbed nor shocked, and at the same time this was no longer a matter of acceptance, embracing, or the unheeded idea to forgive them; they knew precisely what they did, and what came of it, and sought nothing but encouragement: such was the angel of decay, the breakdown of empire, Maltese knights driven to firing infidel heads out of canons. Sexual liberation was, at last, enslavement; its wage was, is death. Liberation, yes; but not on its enactors' terms.

William felt nothing but the insect poverty of ideological decomposition; he would now have to begin living a double life, one in which everything was perfectly fine, of lower level thinking, and another in which he took care to furnish his perceptive apparatus, and perceive everything around him with a blend of material phenomenology, secular metaphysics, Gnostic political religions, and the Christ who everyone had forgotten about, who had flipped tables, brandished a whip, and screamed at people.

These were not things William, preparing to turn around and depart, longed for. The pilgrim had no Christological bent about him. He was just, in moving from shadow to reality, beginning to understand the complexity of things he had been led to believe were rather cut and dry, when indeed nothing was cut and dry; indeed the crisis of the modern world was predicated upon the severe hope that technological saturation could maintain its barrier between concept and reality when it came to redefining what is and what could never be. And it came close to doing so, ensuring that it would be psychologically impossible for persons to come to their senses, let alone revolt—but he was beginning to understand the hitherto imperceptible: for this the pilgrim would take up his olive branch and book and spend some further nights sleeping on the bed of earth, wandering exilic throughout the poetical day.

11

BEFORE ANY SORT OF replaced coffee table the objective was to set up the enormous sound system in the dining room, share the Jameson, and have William hand-select a hundred or so records he'd like to hear. Such a number was difficult in the fresh afternoon, for each of Smith's thousand records were of high quality. Heather appeared at his side, delicate sip and sour face of the concoction, mute, flipping through the albums with him in her tank-top and short-shorts as Smith sang at the top of his lungs from the living room over cans of beer, cleaning the house spotless, twinkle:

"Summer's arrived—Dressed as a Dream—San Francisco Summer it is, it seems!"

Heather stood, danced a number.

"Damn!" he shouted to himself from down the hallway, as Heather and William laughed in secret and together as Smith's proclamations meshed with recollections of the night. "Damn, damn it's Heaven outside! Oh my God! Now come on kids, well, not quite kids, I understand you two yes, well, we're the new threesome of great things, led by fate, united by the Bay, no now don't get all tangled up, I'm a straight man, but I mean frontiers! Adventures! So get dressed, we're taking Muni downtown!" Excitement thrust itself from that voice, each syllable unanimous with the impact of an orchestral machine gun, contagious as wildfire. "It all is so great!"

Heather took an old blues album in her hands and overlooked the inner sleeves.

"I like the sort of people that conduct ships, drink by the sea, scrub dishes, and cook falafel at 3:45 A.M.—don't you?"

It was that San Francisco way of waking up beside a half-drained bottle, feeling lousy, and just walking outside to the porch where the amplification of anxiety, disorder dissolved into the drunkenness of oceanic air. Everyone was out along the summer streets and park in a celebration of climate, exile, life. There was no city in America one could remain so guiltless and grooving high, and in fact it seemed suspicious to go on otherwise. ("Heard Bob quit drinking, smoking." *What?*")

While the television-voices of the general public went on across the land in fear of everything at once, glorifying propaganda and gladiators, those at the other end of the coin who hated that two-headed whore of media and Pentagon and loathed the law seemed to all arrive in San Francisco that summer. Types such as Isaac with art on their minds left, seeing it coming, to get down to business. For the rest of them, those unsure of how to rebel against their generation and not quite ready yet to subtract themselves from life in order to immerse themselves in art, there was an immense group of people with whom to enjoy oneself with that summer.

As William watched Heather latch her sandals, Smith fell around the room into everything at once, a candelabra's silver light shined on everyone, borne of innocence and solitude, an imperishable harmony of reflexive light, and rooted thus in salvation. Harold poured out highballs creating a map of the plans for the day and each suggestion, each street to walk upon seemed like a profound discovery.

"You can't trust anyone that doesn't shop at thrift stores!"

Everyone was pounding their fists on the table in a percussive cross-fire, taking a drink and pouring another, and it was a miracle anyone got anywhere at all.

"Just before you two got here I was down, real down, in the dumps."

"What happened," William said.

"With Isaac leaving and all I just felt lost, was having a drinking contest by myself."

"Don't do all of that," said Heather. "That's so sad."

"Enough!" Harold threw a set of dice upon the table which rolled off and out to the kitchen. He downed his drink. "We got to move! Let's go!" He was possessed by some sort of miraculous fever and led the way to the bus stop explaining of the night's enormous stew dinner concerning a rare Chinese spice he would have to find, lighting a pipe of hash out on Bay Street. It was seventy-eight degrees outside with no breeze.

William walked between them looking upon the holographic city, wondering what would come in the next minute, the next month, the next season, and knowing in his well-weighed heart it did not matter, for the parade, or Saturnalia, was in comprehensive swing. Smith made frenetic gestures with his arms, hands, as if electrocuted, spouting off various epigrams and fractions of wisdom in a shroud of pluming smoke:

"Look, look, you'd better love life, babe, because dying is something else!"

"And, and, you, you now!" He grabbed William by the shoulder as the bus began up the hill. "We all need to damnit, *damn it*! I feel it, it is a telepathic vehemence! Sake!"

The 30 pulled in and they arrived at Chinatown having snickered and told jokes in the back of the bus all the way. For a half hour Smith ran in and out of dozens of shops, at last finding his spice as William and Heather took bubble tea in an appealing, old-fashioned shop with imported spice barrels for seats, discussing everything and finishing one another's sentences.

"You know how some people live day to day, hour to hour? Others far more serious, living childhood to death caustic, convinced that with death life begins?"

"Oh and aside, yes, the thing is I've begun to feel as if I'm living minute to minute!"

City Lights Bookstore appeared on the right; William recognized where he was again and thought of the Australian women, of Janine, before looking at Heather and forgetting either.

"We'll have a Fernet Afternoon," Smith reappeared.

"All of the houses have been built."

"Let's go to Lust Lady first."

Heather giggled, leading ahead to a secluded doorway. Passersby glanced her way, Smith looking at her hair rustling in the cool wind.

"I remember now!" he shouted, his eye lighting up as if the fingers of some God had just snapped together, procuring a colossal vibration, "Yes, Lusty Lady—I—damn—I!"

After the live show the sun had gone down. A dollar a minute was not bad, faces lining the distant mirrors surrounding the stage. William contemplated the aurora-borealis while watching a plump woman have tokens of demonic magic inserted by another frail woman, each quite kind and interested in their activities. The slot for dollar bills reeked of Jerusalem trees at spring's end.

Buddha Bar was empty. Harold ordered three dishes of Sake, six glasses of Fernet, and a dozen imported Japanese bottles of beer. He knew the bartender and beat him in dice, then was defeated, and they shook hands. The bartender was a young card-shark and amiable as a host in the dim bar. He charged less than half-price for the rounds of drinks and told long stories concerning his childhood upstairs, gang warfare and riots in Oakland and he too took down enormous glasses of brutal imported wines that smelt of cleaner and spewed bartender anecdotes:

"The older you get, you know, living my life, you develop a fair tolerance for booze; it is absorbed from the lost tolerance for nonsense, because for any good man or woman an affinity for the prior coincides with a violent disdain for the latter."

Hours passed. The conversation turned chaotic, the bar crowded, the spirits high. Harold left for the bathroom downstairs to roll hash into a spliff. William looked at his reflection in the mirror; he grew more confident in himself every day, more content with life. Nothing superb was ever accomplished by adhering to the standards of one's day. He observed Heather's eyes upon him in the darkened mirror and felt innocent and yet possessed by passion. He combated and embraced her proximity. Disco lights ran across their arms and faces in a slow-motion multicolored stream.

"What'll we do tonight?"

"We could go to Mission again."

"Yes!" Heather draped her arms around William, pecking him on the cheek. "What about after all of *that*?"

"Then we'll go to the zoo."

"The zoo won't be open then, though."

"We'll go to the airport and watch airplanes take off and hope no one brings a box-cutter onto any of them," William said.

"That is a terrible thing to say. We can go to the airport and watch the airplanes disappear into the sky at dawn."

"You want to do that?" William looked into her hazel eyes and in a flash he knew he ought to call Janine soon for he still hadn't returned her e-mail and he knew that one should never place his hand upon a beautiful roommate's thigh; but then again, in the name of parsimony, nor should one encouragingly let him keep his hand there.

"Let's dance for now," Heather said, taking William by the hand.

She, that Heather, was an excellent dancer. Jazz came on overhead and went well with the voices crammed together and breaking through the small, compact bar. They took to a slow dance, William pressing himself closer to her neck and inhaling.

"Oh, why can't we just dance, and just always enjoy ourselves."

"We can, though," William explained, "Or at least we will try to."

"?"

She rested her pale cheek upon his shoulder, running her hands through the buttons of William's shirt, unbuttoning one, two, and placing her hand along his ribs and down. He placed his hand over her back and felt the slick, warm flesh as she squeezed her hand within his. She turned around and pressed herself against him, moaning, and dancing that way.

"We have so much time, though, and that is all is," William ponderously denoted through encroaching slurs, "It is just so much time."

"Oh, stop *talking*—we never have so much time. The present and the future and the past are the same hallucination, don't you ever think about that?"

William listened to her speak, taking dampened strands of hair from her forehead as if readjusting petals and leaves of a fine autumnal tree. Heather closed her eyes. He placed his thumb upon her lips and held her, lost in the dimmed room of distant jukeboxes, the crack of dice barrels breaking forth past chips, and marble glistening with spilt tequila. She took his forefinger within the warmth of her mouth, circulating the warmth of her tongue upon it, and laughing extinguished she and William's parallel blush to lead him back to their seats.

"Two champagne," William ordered, taking them to the table.

"How could you know someone as evil as Walter! He looks so *evil*!"

"Does he?"

"I don't like him. But what Harold—Harold's his name, right?—said was true. He made sure you could stay long before this morning."

"Good."

"So you don't have to worry about anything!"

"How do you know?

"He told me last night!"

William paused for a moment reflecting, realizing through a peculiar melting sensation within him that his body had connoted something his mind had as of yet to recognize, let alone process.

"What was that all about?"

"We stayed up all morning telling ghost stories!"

Just then Smith leapt out of the crowd and back onto his seat. He juggled the spliff he'd rolled from aerial palm to aerial palm before Heather snatched it from thin air. William realized that it was from within his bedroom that Heather had reemerged that afternoon.

"The voice of treason: Da-ba-ba."

"La-la-lalalalala-la. La."

"Now listen up, see that torn turtleneck belonged to great meaning you know, you just know when it's time to well, turn off the, no—a toast! A toast!"

"Fernet!"

"Fernet!"

The music grew louder and roared through the bar.

"A friend of mine who goes by the name of Remy Martin is coming to town soon, William, I want you to meet him. This isn't a drinking pun, but that is his name—Remy Martin. He reminds me of you, kind of, at least the things you like."

"He sounds like a damned good man so far," William admitted.

"Oh God," began Heather.

"He is!" shouted Harold, banging his fists on the booth table. "He is!"

"WE'LL see him soon!"

"Tonight is like Christmas."

"Abstraction," Heather said, "Begin again."

"'twas the night after the night before Christmas, and I was drunk and stoned—"

"When my woman got in beside me, and into big brass bed we tucked—"

Someone in the crowd lit a coaster on fire and smashed their cell phone against the ground. The bar took a violent olfactory turn. The scent snapped one out of a full-on trance. Harold Smith, William Fellows marveled, overlooking Heather through the alcoholic haze: That lucky, or crazy—

Candles were placed around the table. Dozens of faces lit up about the cramped bar with a cast-orange glow. Heather placed her chin within her hands, sighing and beginning to tell a long, sad story from her childhood concerning a maternity ward and nine stages of the history of the language paralleling the nine months of birth. Solemn music played overhead, throwing off the prior pitch of voices and string arrangements.

"Who wants another Fernet," Harold said after the completion of the tale.

They took three more Fernets each and a couple of beers remained. Heather gave her Fernet away. Smith took it down.

"They don't have much of this on the east."

"Doth?"

Heather giggled and admitted she was losing track of what was going on, taking hot tea with ice water.

"Let's move the parade. Adorable Heather decides."

"Let's go to Zeitgeist!"

"Over-rated," interjected Harold. "That is place is overrated. It sucks. It was good in 2006 but please, I'm begging you, no more. That damn place!"

"You seem more offended by the bar than anything," William suggested.

"It is a good bar for desperate people. Overall its better days are long-gone in an area of much more interesting bars. Zeitgeist is a fine place for a fake ID. Let's begin at the Ace Café."

Heather looked half interested and half hurt as she inquired.

"It's over on 14th or something, yeah, you can smoke inside, IPA drafts, great filthy kitchen in the back. Yes! We'll start off there, there. Someone was just saying in the bathroom that external disintegration is sometimes the unseen byproduct in the affirmation of productivity. You believe that! But I'd rather be—No, I thought to myself, I, I'd just, I'll well, be signified . . . and with the undermined, the, the," Harold stood up abruptly, knocking over his stool, "Let's get out of here!"

Harold led Heather and William by the hands as they stepped out back into the resurrected night cutting through light-streaked alleyways, the new triangle amongst crumbling streets where the sound of distant gongs resounded, laughter and songs through clouds of fog and smoke. The lights of the strip clubs shined so one could not tell midnight from noon. Strange broken-brick buildings hovered overhead, towers before the entranced maze of steaming food, unfamiliar voices, screaming children of night playing in abandoned lots and glowing playgrounds which seemed almost nonexistent but as a metaphorical summoning brought on by the prolonged drunkenness and hashish.

"To the Chinatown tunnel!"

You could see it, rumbling buses and succinct, gleaming cars sweeping within, without the tunnel of maltreated dust-walls and ovular light, rounded ceramic lined with spray-paint and exhaust. Harold pointed to enormous letters outlined through the dust: CLIMATEGATE

"Who the Hell did that!" he shouted, "And what the Hell does—does it *mean*?"

William pondered, felt the Fernet burn within his chest, the hashish microbes rewiring his once-plain sensory map of the city, and all the world seemed as if turned upside-down and best yet, all of the neuroses of modern living had been tipped into some lethargic black hole or another, and out of his life. Circuitry clicked and shone vivid within his mind, a fleeting notion to which he responded with a raucous cry and half a marathon of matchbooks exploding like gunpowder to his death march of cigarettes.

Heather and Harold talked just ahead as William reflected it were as if the tunnel itself weren't real one bit and each passing automotive emblemized a day, a month, a year past, none but the wind made sense of such innocent captivation, announcements and laughter and drunken passersby less real than part of a static lattice. William looked to Heather, tossing his cigarette to the floor whereupon it imploded, a fresh neon series of microscopic embers as she smiled, Smith hiking up his sailor-pants and leaping, reaching for an untouchable ceiling, crying out with all of the lost time and paradises at once caught in a living haze, reclaimed, regained, golden, as he shouted aloud an Indian-cry that resounded through the tunnel embodied nearing Union Square, and so the weeks of summer roaring marched on right then, as the voices of smiling summer night resounded true and near to the wild at heart, with all their little screens and Eric Gill impressions both in private life and across signs designed to draw forth cash.

And for two weeks or so such was the routine: Awaken in the early afternoon, scrape together breakfast, meet at the kitchen table, laughingly reminiscence the night, recite journal entries, tell childhood stories over a mimosa or Bloody Mary, reconnect the puzzle pieces, evaluate peoples met, peoples seen, peoples perhaps worth pursuing, before taking off down any street in one glorious direction or another.

Brandy by the water, whiskey at the start of special hours or evenings, iced coffee in Dolores Park, long, deranged evenings of live music at Gold Dust Lounge before passing midnight and stumbling back to Mission, Valencia, Guerrero, a hundred bars open all night where everyone had a drink in one hand and something of substantial value in the other; be it a work in progress, a portfolio, a tilted foreign hip, a drink, a burning stick of something, directions to the next living quarters to sit within and yell, or observe, or beget white rabbits, or to become something not unlike oneself.

Janine came around a handful of times but felt put off by the presence of Heather and Smith aside William.

"Harold seems—just—I don't know—I don't know if I can handle it."

It was unlike anything she had ever seen, and so William spent most of his romantic time with Janine just the two of them and some of the nights William slept at her apartment.

Walter, Saul, and anyone interrelated had moved out of the house. None save friends of Harold, William, at odd hours Phil Cohen, or Heather was ever around. The dictatorship of the philosopher-kings was under hedonistic way, with a caveat: all of the noise of the world, all of the asinine barbaric yawps, was revealed but a bagged breath of wind, which, it was revealed at midnight, changes names because it changes directions, but is beyond the technological façade nothing more than a skeleton who changes names because it changes directions, though its destination and methodology is permanently fixed, with two ideas available—sense of egomania and recognition: and when you think about it, argued the pilgrim, our desire to measure the planet or space is less wise than it is indictive of our futility to assess our cognitive limitations. Now it was the time of the assassins, the time to overthrow the overthrowers.

"As that fly over there has no idea it is in a bar, within a building, upon a block, within a neighborhood, within a city, within a state, within a country, within a continent, within a world, our most brilliant scientists offer nothing beyond that fly that is buzzing around the bar, destined to die in a glass of whisky."

Somehow William always had money in his pocket also; each time he got down to his last hundred or so, a quick move-in job or some lawn-mowing gig would pop up. He got a medical card on Geary Street in a gated café and sold his share of weed and hashish and made good money. Some mornings he would think aloud before falling back asleep in the arms of someone or another, 'Someday I'll wonder how the money kept coming in, where it came from, where it went, and how it always rushed back like the sea. But even in this moment I've no idea of anything but seventy dollars in my pocket which is fair enough for later today.'

If there were signs for hesitation, they went on ignored because there was neither persuasive nor foreseeable reason not to proceed unchanged. To the contrary, each new cast of people and places seemed to take the prior week to another level of indulgence. Green lights shined at dawn and emerged in the afternoon. The reason Smith referred to it as a parade was quite simple, although he may have referred to it as a stampede if there was the slightest violence involved, for often enough anyone involved in the revelry of that summer did not make it through the night, nor through their lives unchanged. Hard drugs increasingly around and were increasingly ignored, on that fatalistic road entitled Taboo. William ignored all of this, as did Harold and Heather, for there seemed no reason to get so involved in drugs being shipped in from the Middle East, or some cockroach Nevada bathtub. Big books and studies were proving this information correct with the hardest drugs; even if one despised himself enough to do heroin, he ought to have despised the current government enough to not support their real objectives, should not have despised the potential of his, her own mind and imagination so as to shut it down; one turned blue in the face making sense, only to vanish in order to go turn blue in the face on drugs that ensured what contradiction could be dealt with emotionally but never logically.

William stuck with his senses deranged and never paralyzed with such memories through initiation into the San Francisco underworld as he walked along the streets at dusk:

The night Heather danced atop a slick table at the Knockout on Valencia and fell clean off, into the arms of an observant William—Two more Hamm's, bud!; the night Harold grabbed on to the back of a garbage truck roaring down Market Street at dawn, holding on with one hand, drinking from a half-pint of Old Grand Dad with the other, making it all the way to Twin Peaks before falling into shrubbery and sleeping through all day to return home to the worried pair of Heather and William laughing more than he ever had in his life; the time William stood up after a dozen whiskeys in the upper-level of Vesuvio's, creaked the long window open, and jumped down to the street below thus to meet with a round of maddening applause—from passersby, the doorman, and a police officer alike—then to crawl back upstairs, finish his beer, and take off for Noe Valley for 36 hours with a student he had met to engage in a two-person neo-renaissance and listen to her recite her bad poetry in interims—William would read Pasolini and make love to her over wine, but the extent of that relationship began and ended in a week; the night William and Heather walked home from the thrift store at sunset reflecting upon all of life to make a detour and sit along the sloping hill and fields of Dolores Park and cried with their arms around one another at dawn promising to never take anything for granted every again; William and Harold down at the waterfront for the first time since the beginning of it all after a long day of laughter at the Hearth, talking of infinite warfare, the crippling technological neuroses born upon their generation's psyche, pondering, 'And if the best instance of life may be that afterward there is another eternal life, a Heaven, would it not indeed be by default a Hell, to be conscious of that which could never end? The principle of serenity pales in comparison to the advent of recognition in the never-ending. Man created God for God to recreate Man. If this is not the truth, what is?' while distant boats crawled toward and beneath and past the Golden Gate Bridge, that figurine as if carved into the mountains, the sky, the ocean beyond; the night William asked Harold , 'Did you reassure my stay here with Isaac, or did this all begin in an effort to get Walter out of the picture?' to which he said in earnest, 'Are—are you kidding me? We knew as you knew that this is, was, IS just the right time and seldom in life does the right time for anything announce itself proper without trembling anxiety, hesitation. Isaac told me that your story was so similar to mine he held back sadness when he first met you, how dirty and skinny you were at a distance wandering around with wine-lips, old Bill! Those women he was with liked you, he said. The emergence of Jerusalem's Rimbaud! One said you seemed as if an angel. Now I, I don't know about all that because bud one of the first times I seen you you was drinking whiskey at the edge of a bar by yourself ignoring everyone and looking through them, but we made damned sure to let you lay down and get comfortable, and now look at us, man, look at us now! We're God-damn k-kings, kings I tell you! March on!' wherein the excitement grew so out of hand upon bicycles the two rode back and forth over the Bridge, past the Marina, past Sausalito again, vanished for twelve hours, ate wild berries and laughed , ecstatic words and wisdom of life spilling forth from the beautiful days of the young men which raced to the end of day, to the night to start anew, where and whence some of William's reflections seemed harmless in content, then it was the emotional context with which he at times considered with nostalgia for the present, weary though never worn out, and always Heather Daily there, near and far, who watched the boys of summer in their ruin, standing still and maternal, smiling watery eyes, with her old yellow raincoat.

No one worked beyond the Fort Mason residents-proper a couple of hours per week across the street, and the weather was only perfect. More happened in a week than in the preceding decade. At last, at last, the summer William had foreseen along Avenue B, the Brooklyn Bridge, the flashing chimes of used bookstores and nocturne's straw for the fire, and habanero lunch with mahogany hummingbird.

12

During the first week of August Heather and Harold were at work as William sat on the back porch in shorts and tennis sneakers attempting a tan, drinking iced tea with brandy, filling in crossword puzzles with alternative words which correlated to his current euphoric situation, reading *Roman Poems*, while seagulls flocked overhead beneath the cloudless blue sky, and he listened to nothing but baroque classical music on discs borrowed from the SFPL at volume levels ranging from the contiguously intimate to the community-wide, aimed devoutly at the high distant gates. Mornings of extinguished guilt, a gravity disburdened—a second book out on the table, Girard's *I See Satan Fall Like Lightning*—the air beneath one's feet, like the craft of thought, work of a master craftsman. The ones who'd vanished, Saul and the others, legends in their own minds, might as well be called Mars, Niobe, Nimrod. Now each day commenced with a thrift-store-found Troy in ashes and ruin framed on the wall, Heather Daily out of the blue, beige dresses without underwear, offering to rub every muscle, then vanishing as another sick crew stopped in:

"We long for death like marble index; give me your best vein, and let me show you how it's done and delayed at once: you seek both virgin and whore in one, you who, caught within eternity, are temporal."

Nielsen sent an e-mail on his brother's behalf earlier in the week, had just made it to a flea-bitten apartment north of Philadelphia. Octavia kept in touch with packages of photographs, booklists, and a shared—albeit for the pilgrim sanctimoniously rejected—Netflix password. She was the one he longed to see; for Ms. Fellows was in a depression and would not speak to William and seemed almost spiteful when he told her that all was going well. She found him a failure. William repressed on a near basis his desire to see Octavia Savonarola, to speak with her for hours at a time, to invite her to San Francisco. Someday, he thought—some fine day.

He tried to forget all of it as distant dogs and children ran gloriously about the expansive fields, en masse across the elongated, shimmering grass fields of Fort Mason when Phil Cohen was on the other line. His voice alone made William feel elysian:

"It's alright, all is well. I've been nearing the end of the line at this job. They're going to lay me off; been saving money, reading, not doing much. Where are you now?"

"We've become something of an exploration-driven threesome over here," said William, "In the friendliest sense of the term. Going out, sleeping on the couch. Have you met Heather?"

"No, no," El laughed. "Should I meet her?"

"She is fun. She is like a great sister. Nothing incestuous has happened thus far, except I believe the first night she moved in, with Harold. I guess it's none of my business."

"What about that girl?"

"Janine?"

"Yeah."

"We're through."

"What happened?"

"We just stopped talking one day," William admitted. "I didn't want to meet her mother in Walnut Creek, and she began to ridicule me and I stormed out of her apartment. Then we got back together, and she ended up having to get labiaplasty. Then I ditched her one night for Harold Smith and she tried to throw me in front of a bus. Those 71 buses don't mess around."

"Were you alright, man?"

"I made it out untouched. Helena visited also."

"Oh?"

"Yep."

"*Why?*"

This, for one reason or another, was true. It was a brief, irresponsible encounter that could not have occurred without harm unless Helena was on her end narcotized by pills and scientism, William seemingly permanently hammered on Bay air, fountains of booze, and armfuls of literature.

But to begin, William had phoned down to the restaurant to visit Man Ray and his wife and to arrange a feast for nine, ten people; they were hiking in the Muir Woods all day. William had been unsure if he had hallucinated Helena Caravan calling days prior and erased the fragmented memory from his mind. He was stepping into the café at Fort Mason when Harold handed him the slip of paper:

"She's been calling all day. She sounds furious. Don't worry buddy, we're still going to the party in the Sunset later—No matter what the Hell happens! Women are crazy!"

Nostalgia came dead on arrival.

He met Helena down on Beach Street. She had discontinued birth control, gained some weight, and was doing her best to shed her adolescent qualities, she confessed (She had taken to wearing a bold tan and flannel shirts, walking like a sodomized ballerina). Disoriented William walked the streets with her and felt less disgusted than bothered by her presence. She spoke of the most irrelevant, trite topics as if to bother William with some onerously cinematic endgame in mind, and even quite hammered he could not withstand her company. He feared after an hour and several drinks that the girl was not out to exasperate him, but that some meteoric shift had overtaken her consciousness—Dread plagued him; had it always been this way?

Her voice had acquired a sulking, absent quality to it and her life with Randall Kant and Co., Helena explained, involved a routine of nothing whatsoever delaying institutional registration, parlaying dating websites in an effort to meet, apparently, as many men possible all equally striving, from the feculent sound her polluted music, for first place in the contest for the most obtuse addlepate then living, and an apparent full-time unpaid internship on shrines of mental degeneration such as Facebook. She pouted as they walked down Fillmore Street to Buchanan and William had nowhere to take her. People stared. She spoke of a nervous breakdown she'd had in William's absence and something about Judith Butler. It was difficult to tell whether the once-precious girl had turned out helpless beyond measure or if she was just a standard case for the times. Either way, William repeated to himself that she would return home to San Diego. That seemed like a fair enough punishment.

They caught a cab to Buchanan, inside of which she told William that he drank far too much; the pilgrim simply contended that she, Caravan the Younger, accused too much; and that it was much more enjoyable, from the cosmological point of view, to imbibe than it was to accuse. Both she and the turbaned driver smiled; but only the latter's did lift William's spirits.

William still had his key. He knocked several times and took her inside, made love to her, and again, and they slept for an hour. Afterward

William showed off every restaurant and bar to her that he had been to, explaining how exceptional it was, seldom sharing his drinks, and when she grew angry enough at last he had a cab take her to the Marriott in Union Square. She stood in shock as he dialed the number and arranged the ride.

He refused to accompany Helena. The simplicity with which he left her behind filled him with such joy that William threw a party that night, and he felt for sure that he'd never see the girl again. Some years down the line he would go on to cherish her love, but that summer her memory was far too engulfed in some black American cloud, and if she were to drift away he no longer felt that a part of himself would follow, but rather his heart would become emboldened and move on. He relayed such information to El and took down a shot of bourbon, plucking hairs from the extensive patch upon his chest, waving to a group of Spanish men and women and flipping through his stack of books from Green Apple.

"I left the old lady too," El sighed. In the background a woman yelled, mocking, for him to shut up. "I've been bored. Unproductive."

"You ought to come see me," William said. "It's been too long."

"Do you work?"

"No. I haven't thought much of that. It's like—hmph—like, I suppose, San Francisco as a whole grows bored with me if I begin to worry about anything. You're right, though. A part-time job would be a fair deal."

"Indeed."

William thought about this for a moment and although he could not imagine himself working, he began to contemplate the idea of taking up some undemanding job for a blanket of security money.

"Why don't you come to the city, El? We'll go on a big walk." He stood up, outstretching his arms to the sun. "We'll get lunch, hit the town. I'm getting drunk over here."

"I could use a break from the old lady," yawned El. In the background William could hear a gasping sleepy voice, the sound of a smack on his shoulder.

"I'll be down that a-way in an hour," William said, "Down near Powell. Don't get yourself hurt over there. We got a big day ahead of us."

"See you soon!"

He dressed up in a plain outfit of white t-shirt and blue jeans with hair parted to the side, a clean shave, and got together a bundle of resumes before walking out, to, and down that entire sloping, mid-afternoon Polk

Street ramble with the light of August glowing behind him, stopping into this gin mill and that for a pint where he'd become chums with the bartenders, and then ahead.

The two met at Union Square on a bustling summer afternoon. En route to a café El knew of which would also be the first destination in William's job hunt the two passed by a large, gleaming aluminum hot dog cart. There was, though, one key difference William noticed as he approached the vendor for a drink: A cute girl was working, perched upon a cooler listening to music and reading from a lengthy book. Making a mental note of the book, Pound's *Cantos*, formulating memories of *Cantos* LII. El spoke as William fell entranced by the scene.

"I've never seen it this way. In New York it's much different."

"Oh?"

He bought a seltzer water, dumped a tumbler of whiskey into it, and they walked away catching up, discussing what to eat.

William could not get this idea out of his mind, however: That sitting about beneath an umbrella over-charging tourists and eating potato chips, listening to music and people-watching. Plus, how fine was that girl! How would one get *that* job!

El and William walked on discussing life and love, liquor and literature, although William was visibly periodically preoccupied. On the opposite side of Union Square it was another parallel scenario; beautiful young woman relaxing beneath an umbrella, lifting the scalding tin lid of a boiler, appearing indifferent to the world around her.

"Is this the norm?" asked William, eyeing the next bright-red cart.

"I never thought of it that way. But it is. Why?"

"In New York it is old men standing about—and don't get me wrong, they are wonderful men—but I just never imagined this, this is sort of like a Brooklyn boy's dream, or perhaps I am feeling fine; just give me one second before we go to the café."

William approached the cart and introduced himself. In a lucid moment he missed the young woman's name.

"Are you hiring at the moment?"

"I don't know," the girl said. Her beauty was breathtaking, began and ended with her light-green eyes. "But I can take one of your resumes." She flipped a hotdog upside down.

He handed her the resume, turning back to El.

"Let's carve through the park once more; I want to give another one to that woman over there."

El laughed as William cut through fumbling lines of incompetent tourists with hideous garments, hair gel and unwieldy sports watches, with his maddened eyes fixed across Post Street, just outside the Great Wall of Macy's.

"Yes, so I'm going in for a career, revolutionary at that, as hotdog vendor," said William. "Let's hit the café then, and then carry out our day. That will signal the end of my applicable day. We've got a big day ahead of us, and I've got my eye on the prize," approaching the next hot-dog cart. A sort of madness had come over him. El felt it and smiled through gusts of cigarette smoke. Life seemed innocent enough for just another moment.

"I remember they cut rocks beyond that little window there, I used to swing by. All is well; to the hand-carved staircase!"

Out on the steps the young men laughed as so many persons, in so many different ways, went to and fro work! One could no longer remember what it was like to work, staggering from staircase to Columbus Café, recalling stoned days past.

"I saw the guy from that orgy all bandaged up on the train. He said he injected his forehead with something to numb it and then carved off the tattoo that, he claimed, he did not even remember ever getting. The spherical ring of the letter 'p', seven times. His eyes were like tomb slabs. Then a dozen other persons, women and men alike, all got on with their heads equally wrapped up. So I got off the train six stops early and just booked it."

A light dawned on William in the afternoon where chaos reigned.

"Phil, just give me a moment. I hate—I truly hate to say it, but I must at some point develop a sort of income. I have had a revelation—watch me."

The pilgrim washed his face in the public fountain, dried off with napkins borrowed from one vendor, and returned refreshed to the hot dog stand.

"Excuse me, I forgot to give this to you. I'm the one who bought the seltzer water. I believe I'd fit it on the staff quite well." He turned to a tall, blonde woman beside him, a friend of the vendor's. She wore a short maroon dress with long legs and a bowl haircut. She looked disdainfully out upon the crowds of people as the vendor overlooked William's resume.

She said something to her friend in French, pointing to Jerusalem University. William arched his elbow along the countertop. A battered white van pulled up behind them. A youngish woman came out and spoke, or croaked, in a frog voice:

"How are things?"

She took the resume into her hands as a response and gave William a perplexed look, croaking:

"You know we get about a hundred of these a day."

He sensed a mechanical falsity in her voice and edged in while all the frenzy of life rushed around them, the shadow of the Macy's wall keeping them in a constant, casual tint:

"I've been made well aware. But that is why I stuck around, to let you know that I am more qualified and ready than any of them. I'll start right now if you'd like. I intend to be a top-notch vendor." He began a speech concerning his American odyssey being somewhere interwoven with the hot dog business in San Francisco but knew not have another drink of soda.

"Well," her voice alleviated at once, "That'll be unnecessary, but," she tapped a pencil along the resume, William made eyes with the French girl for a fleeting moment, winking to Phil Cohen in the next. "Aw, heck, can you come by tomorrow morning for an interview?"

"Of course," William gesticulated. "When and where, Madame?"

"We'll meet in the park at noon? How about—Wait, what did you call me?"

"Who, me?"

"Yes."

"I said of course," William lifted his arms once more, "Tomorrow morning—what time and when, ye frog?"

"How about 9:00—At those benches there."

William met Sheila in Union Square the following day at noon, having fallen asleep at seven in the morning upon an old sneaker for twelve minutes after screaming about unions and smashing bottles with Harold, El, and varied strangers of the Mission Night until 6:00 am. The parade continued, world without end, and no job would stop it for a breath. Sheila had his resume within a pastel-pink trapper-keeper and had certain sections marked with highlighter.

"I'm impressed you were, let's see here, key member of the Pennsylvania Collegiate Journalism Society. This means you deal with people good, right?"

She croaked of the history of the company, Franklin's Franks, with pomp and gusto. William listened to the ten-minute speech, transfixed.

"This is not just about hot dogs, but about inclusion, tolerance, and smashing racism. LGBT people deserve equal rights. I'm not even 40-years old, and I'm mad horny. We must dismantle the system that allows to proclaim that we must dismantle the system. We're a no-nonsense business." She cut the speech short with a growl, adding, "And we've been known to fire past employees who cannot comply with the rules. What do you think?" Wide-eyed tourists dispensed to further benches, their heads bobbing to and fro landmarks like birds without wings.

"I'm fond of rules, regulations also," William said, boasting, "To boot, I've been known to hold jobs upwards of three years, even at my young age, based on such disciplinary passions. What good is the world without rules? Better to sleep beside a drunken socialist than a sober anarchist."

"That's what we like to hear," she smiled with crooked affirmation, nodding her head, ignoring the last bit, and making a note.

The two swapped life stories. William gave her his signature and was set to start the next day.

At nightfall the threesome had fewer drinks than usual. Wine, at that. El came by and they had a big barbeque in the back. Rain fell through the misty night, and everyone stayed in to get sleep. The pilgrim fell asleep at once and for some time could not tell if he had dreamt or seen Heather and Harold kissing beside candlelight in the wee hours of morning. Then they stood for one bed or the other, pausing to kiss at length beneath the kitchen light. It all made sense in a fragmented way if it were anything but a dream: ah! Fatalistic as he felt come morning—As one reeling from the effects of undecipherable dream/reality may well feel—El and William condemned a strange blend of environmental prolixity ad ecological proclivity apparently speaking for an audience of none outside the hostel, walked to the bus and headed downtown, to the Union Square parking garage, where he and El parted ways, making plans for the near-future.

"That was all I needed, bud," El said, "Now back to work at the old house—San Francisco has jostled me out of my prior slumber."

William arrived on time, absorbing the fate that he was to sell hot dogs, exhaling cold air as if it were smoke down Geary Street. He began to turn around and walk home. That croaking voice called his name; he could not go on, he went on.

Two women, aside from Sheila, were already there: Honda, who clocked in at 5'1, 200 lbs. and wielding a phenomenal grunt-laugh at the end of each sentence she spoke. The other was the first of the girls he'd seen with El: Alison. She had a nice haircut and wore a small yellow skirt.

They introduced themselves before wheeling a massive steel cart out into the awakening city upon an uphill concrete ramp. Alison's buttocks shone through to William's face. He would never see it again, but it seemed to stamp an immense glow upon that day of initiation, his beginning as a worker, a hot-dog revolutionary, in San Francisco.

Alison trained him that day for some hours, beginning by unveiling the reddish tent, which was quite like unraveling an enormous condom, the lighting of the burners, the icing of the soda, quarter arrangements and paper-money stacks. William said nothing all the while, for he was in love—With the city at dawn, with the psychotic revolution at hand as temporal trade in meat mogul, with Alison– Regardless if William loved ten women at once, he loved them all in earnest; he did that much, he would often console himself at night.

The sun seemed larger, closer than usual, pulsating as if the neon heart of a cold, uninteresting universe, and nocturnal tidbits of Grotius and Filmer intensified through rising of exhaustion from mounting traffic along Geary St. He listened to the traffic and Alison's voice, perforating a conjoined, elemental tone.

Macy unveiled, to the delight of present paparazzi and swirling lines for double decker buses, their 100th Anniversary billboard, which covered half of the building before them. Towering tactile legs, bells 'round a harness, lips like sugar and backdrop like shifting tic-tac-toe boards. Thousands of busy bodies weaved in and out of subways and doorways as if alive for the first time.

William at once admired Alison's nastiness in regard to the customers, their worn eyes set somewhere along the neat chintz of her skirt as she took money from each of their hands (One, reflected the pilgrim, would be astounded as to the innumerable amounts of patrons who: A. Eat hotdogs before noon—B. Count incorrect change, and thank walking away—C. Who do not count their change but ask for receipt, as in an effort to return the frankfurter some fine day?). The two were friends in no time over a bond unmatched as learning to cook and serve The Original Steamer, The Daly City Dawg, The Jouncing Jumbo, The Chicken-Apple Sausage, The Rajun Cajun, The Polish Paddleboard, and The Punjabi Panorama in record times with the agility of a percussionist on speed, leaping to and fro, stirring around like spastic wires as the hours of the clock beat on. Hot dog vending seemed in variations like dancing, or like a cramped performance space set within some metallic, curtainless cube.

"The owner will later explain to you, William, that the intended action time for vendors was seven seconds, for opening the lid, fetching the hot dog, putting it in wax paper, grabbing a bun, sliding in, dishing out."

"No kidding," William said, stunned. He fell over the soda cooler, and Alison took him by the hand.

"You alright? You're very pale."

"Oh, I'm fine."

"We're about ready to close. You can leave now, I'm good here; just know that closing down is the opposite of setting up."

"That seems applicable to the theory of relativity. Thank you for everything, Alison. See you in two days." He had his eyes on the clear container packed with at least a hundred dollars in tips. He put it together: everyone tipped, there was a Wednesday paycheck, and you pocket (concoct?) your own tips at will! When in doubt, Plato. She reached her delicate hand in, counted out fifty dollars, and handed the stack to William.

"The bank will take the singles if you can find one that's open."

"No—no—I like didn't do anything!"

"William," whispered Alison. "I made two hundred dollars in cash today. It is no problem, silly goose."

"How about I stay around and we go to the Gold Dust Lounge," said William, wiping sweat from his brow.

"Truth be known, the truth remains unknown. But regardless: I'm twenty and have no idea where my ID went."

"Half of life is looking confident. How old do you think I am?"

"Oh, I don't know," she laughed, "But you are crazy."

"Oh," said William.

"That is a good thing."

Walking home to Fort Mason was the grandest thing on Earth. Up to Post, westward, stop at the café, people-watch, then all the way home with a case of Anchor Steam beneath one's arm, a little spending money in one pocket before out all night with the bright threesome. Rejuvenation cast itself upon the coming nights and William then knew that his incestuous dream had been just that, a dream.

"A want, no, yes, a whiskey! Come on! Turn it up!"

The house was a mess 'til tomorrow, but its heart aglow with forthcoming chaos all fixed and fresh as little kisses, just a little more, with everybody happy.

On the second day downtown William was given a verbal warning for a book he found in Hemlock Alley but no one else appeared to recognize, entitled *Because I was Flesh*:

"We do not pay you to read."

Although reading such books make life worth living, considered William, still yet between pages I conjured that the childish cataclysm of micromanagerial ethics is not so bad in the beginning as it is recognizable. The furor would grow, one knew, but that day will come some other time. Sheila went away to let William run the cart alone. He made his money but sat still and listened to KUFM.

'A great day,' William sketched into the diary he'd begun again, 'Out on Geary Street. At noon I took a break, read my book in the park, wished I'd brought a hand grenade instead. It's as if they ship boat upon boat of the planet's worst over here with some magnetic lure for Union Square. Contemplating wearing a bandana sometime soon. Heather visited today. We spoke at length, I gave her a soda, we are going to Berkeley tonight for some sort of reading. Harold has gone to Southern CA for a few days. Poor man.

'In other news: the chicken apple sausage was the last hot dog I tried. After that, I will never eat another hot dog, perhaps a pretzel-diet. We are allowed up to $7.50 total value in food per day although it has just struck me that from now on, I will just pocket a ten-dollar bill each day and see what happens. The best hotdog I've had thus far has been the Punjabi Panorama. I am unsure of its ingredients and unwilling to investigate, although with the aid of sauerkraut, relish, and onions, I enjoyed myself. Also on my break I had a glass of Racer 5 (breath concealed by butterscotch candies) at this little bar in Maiden Lane where Harold is going to play music soon. Sometimes I wonder what everyone east is doing before I realize it is beyond irrelevant, picking up a library card tomorrow, Augustine's death and Goethe's birth 'round bend, regular correspondence with Octavia, who I now must write at length on—Our feelings for another—'

Sheila's disturbingly abrupt ribbit cut him off.

"How's things?"

"Perfect," William said, tucking away his notebook. "Pristine!"

"Good. Be back later." Her phone rang as William took an order and turned back around.

"Your training shift is over here, which is a good thing. You're doing good, well. And you're going to head down the street to the Grant cart, to work with Honda. When Alison returns she'll send you over there."

"OK."

Alison arrived and scribbled down directions for William. A cheerless feeling came over his stomach either from the food, the beer, or the fact that other carts were stationed at stranger intersections of downtown. The domination of the absurd squalor at the core of this fleeting notion evaporated whence he reached down to his pocket and knew today he had made something of a hundred dollars already, readjusting his mustard-streaked smock, striding through clouds of smoke down the sunny side of the street.

The pattern of work wore on, work in that the actual dullness, and its mechanical nature, of the job became exhausting. He had foreseen all sorts of madmen, pilled out conmen, daylight strangers and a good leap back into the journalistic underbelly, or undertow, but instead spent most of his weary days down on Grant Street, little tip money equalized by the mathematical con of his own.

If no one were home by night he hopped back onto Columbus Ave. from Bay Street recalling sweet moments beneath bright lights of Italian restaurants, walking along their heated sidewalks at midnight, $1.50 IPA drafts at the café, returned a book to the library, waved into the bodega he bought drinks from every night in August, watched the 30 barrel downtown, once taken to work every morning from Fort Mason at 8:30 am, roared by on those first solemn nights of San Francisco, to sit by a window-sill alone ruminating upon asceticism, order, parataxis, a multi-volume literary history of farting, the anatomy of melancholy, and a book-length study on Klemperer displaying how what passes as progressive media is today identical, if accelerated, to Third Reich propaganda.

Harold burst through the front door one quiet afternoon as William rummaged through his journals. Heather had gone out of town, back to Brooklyn, and for unspoken reason William had been in solitary-adventurous moods. He knew where to find who but instead walked the streets alone letting his mind reticulate everything with fish oil tablets and black coffee.

"Man, man, I—Damn, where have you *been*! Cab, cab out front, help me load these crates, c'mon, Union Square, records, tonight, Otis!"

William reeled. He'd had an afternoon beer there earlier and overlooking the passersby through Maiden Lane vowed to find another daylight drinking spot within walking distance from the hot-dog cart that wasn't the Gold Dust. No one lonesome ever ought to sit upon a velvet couch and what is purposeful, O Pacific, what is purposeful?

Without hesitation he jumped up and helped hobble the crates down front steps, through the fields of weeds, into the cab. Harold latched the trunk of records closed and catapulted into the cab through William's open window, prompting the cab driver to scream in foreign tongue.

"Bale-o! Wah-hah! GAH!" situating himself proper, responding with a yearning, "GO, damn-it, GO! No, now, Van Ness! Timed lights, Sir, you see—!"

"Step up on it!" William piped in, with some cruel air of cliché, tapping at plastic walling between him and the driver with an index finger.

They took off through the late afternoon of downtown San Francisco and made every green light.

"There is this, well look we'll all, now, see go out afterward and catch up, I know it's been just some two nights of mistrial, of bad timing, no phone's dead mine I mean, but this girl is in town, this sophisticated lady, this one a while ago I met at Otis, a bar in Maiden Lane, when her boyfriend was out of town, think still is, O, that's her! Here, buddy!"

A lonesome dark-haired plain beauty came through the entranceway, lighting a cigarette out along the sidewalk. She smiled at Harold and the two spoke.

"Go on, get set up," she said.

William helped get the crates in fair order. Harold approached him and pointed to a table beside the window.

"You see now, those guys there I don't know if you met, but you want to know them. Musicians that tour the world, literary scholars, voracious readers they are; I am glad they came. Never seem them altogether. Here!" He handed William a Red Stripe. William approached the table and a hand, swooping, fell upon his shoulder.

"El, whoa! Now everybody—"

"Good day, captain."

"Just one moment, going to have a smoke—"

El pulled a chair to the table, igniting conversation with the well-dressed scholars.

"BEETHOVEN WAS DEAF—"

William walked outside into the crystalline, forming night as she removed another cigarette from her purse.

"Excuse me," he said, leaning up against a gate. "May I borrow one of those? Then when I get cigarettes, I'll give you one."

Voices swam overhead through open windows, traffic jams purged forth, music played even further back, minute, echoing and resounding between inhalations, exhalations. She had, within some minutes, revealed to William that her husband was overseas, that she had multiple grains of morphine. He drank his beer down out on the street. With the cigarettes' simultaneous end came an anxious silence, a dreaming moon.

'What was that phrase rushing through my mind as I ran back down the stairs and out here because I liked the way this woman looked so much, she in turtleneck and foreign sweater and tights and concealed you cannot imagine her body beneath it all—Oh yes now it's come back: Meet me here—nothing can satisfy me.'

"I am out of cigarettes," she announced.

"Let's go take the morphine instead of this. This will always be here."

Instead of asking him his name or he hers, the two leapt into a taxi-cab and William, instinctual, reached to turn his long-gone phone off. His nihilistic reflexivity had rushed back into him, with the oceanic air rushing rosily across his temples; and for a horrifying moment he pondered in earnest if he were not losing control.

Haight Street to Stanyan and into the little well-lighted apartment. They drank vodka at the kitchen table. On the third glass she removed the grain from her purse. All the while William studied her lips feeling well-nigh damned, well-nigh riotous in the compulsory madness of everything, eyeing the color arrangements of her small library rather than its titles.

"This is strong," she smiled, "So we will start with a light dose. A friend of Harold is a friend of mine—I'll stop by soon enough!"

"Have much of it have you done at once thus far?" William asked. The northern rattling fan spun out of control. She pulled the chord shut, removing a long-sleeved white shirt. The kitchenette grew warm at once. Still through white tank-top her breasts shone. William's fourth vodka had an adverse effect. The analytical rejoinder of his mind began to pace as he watched the delicate hands cut dark pellets of powder in half with a long, gleaming knife.

"I mean in the literal sense," she said with concentration, her reflected face sifting in and out of distorted view, "I just picked up an hour or two ago. My intention was to have drinks, dance with some of those people, come home and try a taste of this. But I haven't made a new friend in a long time. The city will do that to you. Everyone has their own city because everyone belongs to the city at once. You have specific places, routes, apartments you venture to and fro from, and then the city becomes more-so an internal thing, you know? And with Malachi in New York I get so bored—"

William drank his vodka and said nothing. He looked over at the bed across the hallway and thought of her husband, or boyfriend, wherever and whatever he was. One thing worse than being cheated on was having it done within the very bed where one would sleep upon returning. At that point it matters not if men are on the moon, for a man scorned as such is transported right back to the cave. Upon an elbow he drank, nodding to patches of words he channeled incoherently, returning the tightly wound bill, swallowing a tablet, though his anxiety began to dissolve at last. She placed residual morphine on her tongue, on his.

"To the Holy Spirit."

There was something infantile, atypical about this pronouncement, William thought; soundtrack that tap of plastic cups, that swallowing of the seed. For the first time since arriving surface-level appearances gave way; he less hated the woman before him, the drugs entering his poisoned bloodstream, but rather despised himself for entering this situation, as though he were being dragged along by some invisible chain whose decimating required as prerequisite, expeditionary rejoinder by way of desiccating taboo en route to even subtle, albeit intuitively prolonged, acknowledgment. Furthermore, while he had grown used to the pathological desecration of Christendom, now he sat personally violated; and thus he made a mental note to soon thereafter return to the fury within him, what it meant, and what it might say about the path he was heading down, and if it were not, at least in a traditional-philosophical sense, satanic. Was it right to be reminded of genealogical faith, sacrifice, and sacrament in an unthinkingly ironical, narcotized sense, whereby it was when placing morphine upon another's tongue? Gulp, me lad, and figure it out later:

"And silence becomes this grave."

William made himself another screwdriver.

"I'm fine."

He did not want to jump the gun but felt within minutes waves of pleasure rush through his legs. He did not want to seem as if inexperienced so he continued to drink, to kill an undying pleasure, until she before him began to exhibit unhinged effects, to which he would rather observe than succumb to himself. She let her head make slow, circular moments, her eyes glossy and thinned, grinning through parted lips.

She packed a pipe of weed and passed it to, fro.

'Drugs,' thought William, 'The world of drugs.' He caught his reflection in a television screen.

"Let's to go out," he maundered. "Let's go to a bar."

"I'm broke," she bent sinister, laughing for some extended seconds. "We can drink for free here. We won't want to walk soon I bet anyway."

The effects of the weed wore into the microbes of his brain with the electrical consistency of live cables. This also seemed intrusive, unpleasant. The room seemed much smaller, and much darker, as if projecting his state of mind. He felt the dry tongue within his mouth move, the vodka within his chest burn, and smoked several cigarettes, each successive self-inflicted singing of his fingers bringing him awake. What was everyone doing getting drugged and drunk at a point like this in American history? Escaping, ignoring, for the truth was too much, the armies too large, historical full-circles too cryptic and ah, it was just nice to justify sitting still, doing nothing in an overdriven world, where some sought four symbolic years of illusory bliss or illusory sorrow, others the Fourth Reich, others still the primordial solitude of quatrains.

"What time is it?"

"We have not even been here an hour. Well, maybe one hour," she smiled.

Warm, entrancing ecstasy of body and mind, building like winter frost upon railing, overtook him. It felt fine although he did not want to admit it. Then he admitted it and relaxed his body along the couch, seduced and surrounded. Cars, their shadows, hissed, stretched past and through the gated window.

"Don't drink so much."

"But how do you feel?"

"I feel fine," she sighed. She stepped over, laughing, coldly placed her hand upon his.

"A friend of mine's sister's boyfriend has a loft on 24/Mission, he is a lawyer," William thought aloud almost unaware of her proximity. "His apartment is my favorite, yours second-favorite."

The way she stood to adjust an alarm clock filled William with abject pain. Her glistening eyes and her rose-red, late-twenties lips—so many men and women looked and acted the same any longer in that there was nothing to look to but the night, if but in order to wipe clean the slate of the day away.

"My birthday is tomorrow night."

"At midnight?"

"Yes."

"How will we celebrate?"

"We won't."

"Why not?"

"Because I cannot move." His body wanted to smile; his mind refrained from such remittance. "What do those people think of us that we left at the bar?"

"I don't know." She sat beside him, took his hand again in hers. "The suddenness, I don't know if they even noticed, left them speechless. I turned my phone off. Has anyone called you?"

"My phone died. Rest in peace."

"You're white as a ghost." She placed a cold hand upon William's forehead. He lifted the plastic cup of orange juice and vodka. "No," she said. "You are too pale. Come here."

Vague images, decomposed sentences filtered through the circuitry of his mind. Hannibal's elephants o'er mountains and breaking to and fro on the streets of an unknown city. She took him up from his seat as he slouched ahead to the table, leant up and regained his composure.

He straightened her out beneath a glowing fluorescent bulb and pulled her shirt up over her head. She bared a look of shock. He looked at her full breasts, spacious nipples, curled hair protruding from her underarms.

"Are you a feminist?" he asked.

"No," she pressed against him.

"Good," said William. "Because I hate feminists." A surge of energy rushed through him.

The two sat along the edge of the long bed entranced, saying one thing or another, the memory dissolving, her open mouth placed to the side of his bare neck. She kissed him for a long time.

"I am a horrible girlfriend."

"Don't worry about that. Don't worry about anything. It will give you gray hair."

He felt detached from the universe of sex and death, staring ahead to a print of "Les Demoiselles d'Avignon" long atrophied by pens and markers, signatures and drawings.

Their mouths mended with the violet taste of vodka.

∾

William read over accursed scribbling in his journal some nights later upon the porch of Fort Mason. Summer was coming to an end. Autumn was on its way, and his birthday had just passed:

'Dear Reader, or Heather Daily, Queen of the Savages: My first actual surprise birthday party was the next night. I'd never had one of those before. The day started off all right, riding the bus downtown for a part-time shift. I worked on Geary Street and wore skin-tight white jeans and a bandana. I don't know why. I never wore a bandana before, and I never will again. Throughout the day I vomited thirteen times. I suppose in some sort of withdrawal. Last night, which night? I did not know her name. Last Tango in Frisco. We all look so angelic upon the streets and we are all so depraved. Other news, other news:

'That Friday was the second time I saw that French girl by the parking deck. She walked by at noon and I met her that afternoon because Alison was there and wanted directions to Fort Mason because my slight plan was perhaps to have some people over.

'I was whipped with delirious exhaustion bracing myself for the 5 o'clock ride through Chinatown, and the party, my birthday—Knew not whether anyone remembered it was my birthday, or if I'd drink whiskey by the river and begin looking for an apartment thereafter. Had over $1,000 to my name at that point. I should have more, don't. Someone else has it now and is trading it in for the same things I did.

'Surprised no one in the Frisco-Franks world is catching onto my thievery. Perhaps they do not care. Perhaps, though, they are tallying up all sorts of evidence against me, if to unleash some sort of Pandora's Box upon me when I least expect it. I suspect, though, that little but several littered packets of sauerkraut would emerge from such a box; I never return to the scene of a crime, for if I do, I wear fresh sets of gloves.

'Meeting that French gal was brief, I tell you, but I hope to see her again. Alison knows little about her. She just comes by in a low-cut dress and drinks Coca-Cola. My trembling hands smelt like a banquet hall composed of Rajun Cajuns, dear reader, and I do not know what to do. It'll begin with a warm bath, and end with another profession. I wonder at times if I've given up journalism.

'I got in, night of B-Day, and Heather had made me a big cake. I vomited the rest of the morphine out of me, got down a piece. It was delicious. She came back a day early from Powers Street just to be around for my party which Harold was going to DJ. He didn't mind at all what had happened. 'Go on young man, roam the streets more like a comet than, than, sifting cellophane, get loaded, get loaded, be smart always, happy birthday sonny old pal. Knew you'd like that gal. Wild woman.'

'Knew a handful of people at the party and a handful of them knew me. The band couldn't go on due to Fort Mason policies; some strange authority alluded to Harold and I getting thrown out of there for in about a week although due to peripheral intoxication this did not register but as a stiff joke. The Ghost of Walter? Where has he been, anyway? Strange bird.

'Things were wild regardless, as I am sure at this point is not surprising. I hit on a lesbian and a cold, bespectacled girl (Her partner? Never found out) beside her for two hours straight and by that time of course, guess who arrived! The damned woman from the night before! Yes, morphine gal 101! No Alisson, no Frenchwoman, no Janine, but God! By the time she arrived I was a wreck, mumbling and singing and swaying, attempting to forget all about work in the approaching daylight hours, the night prior, the planet, self-destruction, et cetera., dawn-awoken anyway to the computer signaling some popping sound as a newsletter from the Film Forum was sent my way. Happy Birthday to Me! Gordon's Vodka—

"Time went by fast that night, and to prove so I smashed a clock outside on the porch, set ablaze an (sic—forgive me, my Blackwing Matte was it seems at some point decapitated) book entitled, 'Life's Book of Questions' in the backyard (You should have seen how people cheered this quaint, metaphysical action of mine—I suppose we are all nuts) and came back inside disheveled, incomprehensible, covered in ash and soot laughing and indulging, etc. But something strange, I believe strange could be the term, no—let's try surreal, yes, it was surreal when the gal arrived in her foreign rags and I was still able to feel desolation as I realized it was now already as if nothing had happened the night before. We made feeble attempts at discussion though it was apparent I was more so butting into her conversations I was uninterested in though jealous of nonetheless, looking back on it is so painful, loving an unlovable woman whence other forces arrive, economical umbilical-cords, speak over cigarettes, butting into her conversations at my birthday party, how foolish of me!

'The sad task grew weary as ever and I ended up drinking on the couch with some men discussing M. Heidegger, old Plato, Coleridge, Wagner, a wind-bag named Bataille for the 17,000th time but gone as I was, she was all I'd wanted in her sudden detachment, the thing was too much. Stepped outside for a final cigarette. She'd gone. With another man? I stumbled out into the parking lot as she pulled up, headlights crippling my delicate retinas—She had a car! What! All dizzy Earth spinning, she said:

'"I had a lot of fun."

'"Oh, oh yeah, yeah it was, where ya headed?" I asked ridiculous and bewildered.

'She smiled and extending her delicate hands said, 'Over towards my neck of the woods, another party.' I yawned and looked up at the half moon, which looked like a neon boomerang flipping through walls of fog. I asked her if she were sure she could drive. 'I'm fine . . . Stop by again sometime, you should meet Malachi . . . You guys would get along I think . . . ' adjusting her stereo volume up a little big, glancing at me lifting her thin eyebrows, drifting away into the winding night. Malachi was all I could remember. What is this life? Malachi? Seventy people screamed and yelled outside of and within the house. Meet Malachi? A voluminous mass of smoke and bodies crowded the doorway and porch, but I had exhausted myself. Hello, Malachi—Heard we'd get along. I stared at the scene for a while devastated, no one recognized me as I weaved through and straight to Heather 's bed for rest as the wind had swept the ashes from my body, and somehow everybody let me be. I awoke in fine condition to an empty house of morning one year older, alone, to the sound of that e-mail received—

'I can hear you, Heather, laughing distantly from the cab out front! Sorry 'bout the rush, pal, but that's the city for you. Call OS. Goodnight!'

William awoke to the elongated rumbling of a motorcycle outside. He stepped outside in his underwear and made binoculars with his eyes, scanning each which way of the perimeter, feeling again like he'd been mugged last night, caught in the crossfire of some chemical gang warfare or another.

"Down here!" cried the young man with his waxed mustache curled at the ends, wiry glasses, above the knee forest-green shorts and a flamboyant striped, candy-colored tank-top. William felt delirious and turned around.

Another young man with a flowing black beard tip-toed out of Heather's room as the motor subsided outside. The man approached William, hacking oysters:

"Happy belated birthday, sir!" They shook hands as the other man bolted inside. William recognized him at once from the taxicab coming back from Lands End.

"Man, wow, let's go, we got to go to Santa Cruz, then LA, then all of that!"

"Lucky dogs," said William. "I wish I were going with you."

"Well you're coming by this week, right?"

"Ah yes, yes of course," he slurred, ashamed of his intoxicated arrangements. These two did seem quite interesting, though. It was the look in their dark eyes. He knew not where he was going that week

They exchanged information. Daniel and Aaron took off. William took a shower and caught the bus downtown.

"That's the thing is later we go to—to Clement Street!" shouted Harold—"And that's the thing, you see, about gin—"

He recalled he was due at work in the late afternoon and ran out to the bus.

There, in the heat of it all, kicked in a physical condition he knew not of. He was quite late, his body dry like plaster, filmic eyes bloodshot, cough broken with mucus, bones sore as if disintegrating, cells writhing, gums discolored, vile, a sore jaw of chattering teeth. The vibrancy of the city seemed as if, for the first time, a hallucinated joke. Sheila came storming , croaking through the death throes fog; Honda ran for cover to the Macy's bathroom.

"You're an hour late!" she croaked, dropping multiple lime-green dozen pamphlets and crying out. Proposition 8.

"There was a surprise birthday party thrown for me last night," William said, "So please do pardon my condition."

"We're running a business!" she mustered, in a voice of fingertips to plastic buttons. "And you were four dollars short the other day! We're putting you on Grant!"

13

A NOTE ON THE locations as written by *Anonymous*:

> Memoirs of a Hot Dog Vendor: The Revolutionary Hour
> *For all the Oppressed, From Vegan to Carnivore*
> 'Geary: Out front of Macy's. The money-making spot often taken by the more attractive female members of the revolution as well as I. Sheer, illegible madness. Attempt: Ideal for hustling.
> 'Post: Out front of Levi's, across U. Square. Parallel to above in all ways but windier.
> 'Grant: Something like an abandoned ship out on some concrete island. One man referred to this location as an outdoor jail, outside of the Gap store on Geary/Grant. They say this place is great because of the regulars, but I met a regular or two, and they were quite irregular. The management crew always finds a reason to scream over perpetual low income at Grant, including the vendor's hat color, posture, eye contact, but the truth is otherwise—Location. This street corner is dull. The micro-managerial barbarisms play out like a tape loop in a cancerous purgatory. Still my time for these memos has been accumulated along Grant Street.'

Honda sat atop the cooler picking dirt from her fingernails with plastic, light-charcoal toothpicks. Plasticity, with its mask of sweat, seeped from her waxen face.

The pounding at William's temples peaked in severity. He realized not one of his co-vendors, none of his hotdog comrades, had made it to the party and this reoccurring thought bothered him, for now there was no one to sympathize with concerning the total chaos of the evening. They laughed and wish they could have made it. He could not wait to get home to Heather and Harold.

He felt burnt out on obligations the rottenest bits of his soul seeped through him for some hours, telling himself to rest, rest, rest after work, the entire day was automatic and memory could be bothered with none of it. Faces, voices, familiar and otherwise wove in and out of sight and sound though nothing registered until the close of day.

William stood beside the closed-up cart as the evening truck rushed in, recalling a fragment of something Honda had said:

"... And of course you know the one, right, he-he, he's got a mansion out in the East Bay so I been here oh my, oh my a good, oh, almost three years! Do you—You have to see his mansion—"

"What do you think," William proposed proposing to the driver, running out of breath, "Of the metaphorical value of the mansion? Of the end-sum being to attain more than is useful? I want to do things like write collections of essays on the psychological dementia of mansions; their implication, their illusionary necessity, their potential genius, etc."

William reached into the money pouch and treated himself to forty dollars, plus the nine in the tip jar. Heather had invited him to a post-birthday coffee talk at a café. On the way home William ducked into Gold Dust Lounge. The band was just warming up.

The bartender placed a napkin before him.

"What'll it be, kid?"

"Do me a favor, sir," William said. "Ask me for identification."

"Let's see it." He examined it beneath a strike-anywhere match, struck off the oak countertop. "Well!" he cried out, "A birthday drink is in order!" The bar sang Happy Birthday as William ordered a Fernet and an Anchor Steam, polished them off in two minutes and placing one of the twenties on the counter threw on his jean jacket.

"I wasn't joking, kid," said the bartender. Gray hair ran greased, pulled back atop his balding head.

"Well that's a belated birthday present for you, then, because I don't care about money!" and hit the marvelous streets back home, stopping once to absorb the voices from below, in chaos: "I am Orestes! I am Ovid! Son: behold your mother! Forgive her!"

"We make soundtracks for the blind here, brail sheet music. Last summer I adorned a hair-shirt for 90 days. It is as though I was wrapped up in thorns; my flesh is scarred at every part"—interrupted by carnivalesque festivities.

∾

Heather was sprawled along the couch reading Dostoyevsky's *The Possessed*, when William arrived home an hour or two late. He had stopped in for three Pabst at Hemlock. Heather placed the book upon her chest and tucked another beneath the covers.

"I thought you weren't going to come," Heather laughed. William smiled and settled down beside her.

"I try to always come," he said. As if her newborn son he nestled into her bare shoulder calmed by whiskey, intoxicated by the indescribable scent of desire that was Heather's body.

"You are not from Jerusalem, I decided; you are a pilgrim whose being there was temporally incidental, but truly preordained."

"None prayed for me save an old man who sold combs and harmonicas, and he said to me, 'I've been made homeless after working for the city 40 years. Those who have the least give the most.' That was on the way here—his hobo friend, one who carved toy trains for abandoned children, was disfigured from having last year run into a house on fire to save the woman screaming inside. He had himself been orphaned, and thereafter joined the military. He opened a bookstore for a short period of time out in the Sunset, but suffered from a vision that led him to break down, mentally and physically, in remorseless, unfortunately public, repentance—"I see a sign that God loves you. Please pray for me, from time to time, to help me.""

Heather knew not what to say; she seemed both perfectly sane and absolutely convinced. "May your reason take up arms," said William, "And smite impulse!"

"How was your day?"

"Pale face, sore body, an inability to look into one's eyes, sidewalks lined with disgusting garments, and consecutive persons with teeth that were in places spotted with circuitous rust, elsewhere gone. Then a group comes by from the Arts Institute. A little of everything."

"It was a long day, William, and not in a good way."

He swallowed: a reminder that another life, one of schedules, problems, and predicaments predominated. He went to light a cigarette; but there would be no more smoking inside. It both made sense and seemed to indicate something more horrifying to him: the force he had rode in on in was indeed, aspect by aspect, slipping away.

"Did you feel bad also? I felt very bad. Crippling anxiety all day. Couldn't tell if I was dreaming or not—still can't."

"But beyond that I mean there was a fight, William, Walter and Harold had a fight."

"What sort of fight?"

"I don't know but it's bad. There was a knife."

William sat right up: "Really?"

"Across the street they said that you and Harold have to find new living quarters."

"Why me?" William asked in disbelief.

"I don't know. Let's walk and talk, I've been inside all day drinking wine."

But as they were walking with arms interlocked across the nocturnal field William realized he had dressed too lightly and ran home to grab his heavier cape, and palm-wreathed staff. When the laptop rang and it was Harold and there were voices projecting in the background he thought of all of the women he'd made eyes with the night before and that he had blown with negative glares, defensive and bent on his other inoperable woman.

"And I'll explain all this other stuff in person. We'll be OK, m'boy, just get here already, I bin calling all day! Call any vegetable!"

William ditched Heather and caught the bus to Page/Stanyon at Fillmore's 22 stop. At the party Harold was so drunk he could not speak but through inaudible bursts of recognition, rectification, and William drank alone at some nameless table for three hours. No one approached him. All of the women had boyfriends somewhere down the hallway, across the statelines and the seas, and he wondered how alone he was in his observations, if isolation seeped from his body, the look in his eyes, the way it very well may have. All his nails were bitten down, and something sudden and new and ferocious was burning inside of him: No one had any solid answers, the room spinning around at an unpleasant rate. What was everyone celebrating? He excused himself for the bathroom and walked home and felt much better to be out and walking alone in the tranquil night down the concrete slope of Haight Street, to the rags of Market Street where singers resounded, disturbed by the unspoken turn things were taking, and his unconscious—or unpreventable—part in the movement of caustic veneer unto phenomenological perception.

When he arrived home no one was in. He slept well upon the dreamless couch and awoke at dawn.

In the morning he washed up for work, checked his e-mail:

Discards—Please   Read—EMPLOYEE   EYES—DISCARDS
REPORT—etc.

Reply |————@aol.com to————————————

————————————————

Show details————

The Original Steamer, The Daly City Dawg, The Jouncing
Jumbo, The Chicken-Apple Sausage, The Rajun Cajun, The Pol-
ish Paddleboard, and The Punjabi Panorama
Hi everyone,
Yesterday, one of the vendors had the following discard
amounts:

13 buns
14 Jouncing
8 Paddleboard
5 P. Panorama
4 R.C.
1 D.C. Dawg

Cost of these discards: over $50
I'm not meaning to single out this vendor, but discards
have become an increasing problem at all the carts and I need
to address the issue. With the reduced business levels we are
experiencing in this scary economy, we will go bankrupt if our
discarded food costs are 60percent of our payroll costs.
About an hour before closing, you should have TWO kinds
of hot dogs in your cooking water– O.S., D.C.D. Please note the
following:
1. Polish Paddleboards and Punjabi Panoramas are our
smallest diameter dogs; therefore they heat up the fastest;
2. As the end of the day approaches, you should keep your
water in the 180 degree range so you can put in small quanti-
ties of Paddleboards and Panoramas which will heat as you
need them;
3. The other dogs (Jouncing Jumbos, Polish Paradox(sic),
Rah-Hoon Ca-Hoon, Chicken-Sausage) are PRIME CON-
TENDER dogs with a limited following that take a long long
(sic) time to cook. You need to SELL OUT of these dogs as the
day goes on and NOT put any more in. Instead, as the evening
approaches, direct customers to the dogs you have left: "I'm

sorry, I sold out of Punjabi Panorama, would you like a Daly City Dawg instead?"

4. Like vanilla and chocolate, Originals and D.C. Dawgs are UNIVERAL—MOST popular and people will order them if you have nothing else to offer. Please let people know you've SOLD OUT of the other items, as that speaks to their popularity. Please DO NOT go into a long explanation that you have the dogs in your cooler and can put them in if people will wait 5 minutes for them. You've SOLD OUT of that item . . . direct people to the gourmet dogs you have remaining to sell, or if all gourmets are gone (good job), offer them an (Note: Message cuts out, several lines of code)

These are very, very scary times. We have no idea what next year will be like with banks tightening credit, homes being foreclosed, and almost a million people having lost their jobs in the past 6 months. Some economists think we are heading into a depression with 25 percent unemployment. Please be sensitive to how hard it is to keep a business profitable these days, and let's not be reckless and throw dollars away into the garbage can. No. Support LGBT rights with your extra cash. Read a copy of Donald Trump's the Art of the Deal if you want to sell hotdogs like a dignified master craftsman, and tap into the mind of a genius. We must sell wieners as though we had guns to our heads; nothing less than perfection.

Please RSVP so I know you've received this email.
Thanks, all . . .

———

Before William could react, Harold Smith stumbled in through the door with a black eye, his autographed cast of an arm trapped within slings:

"Get your things, all, well you don't much, have much, put, put them in a pile in my room and damn, the whole thing is awful! I'm going home for a day or two, I pulled a knife on Walter! He's returned!" His face turned white with an unspeakable exasperation. "Quick, give me your belongings to stow away, and stay with some good gal, man, or someone, for some days!"

Harold accepted a single bag from William.

"I have to run, that's all I got. Explain when you get back."

"I'm so, so damned sorry man but we'll be alright, we will, just think of all the good times!"

"Relax, Harold. It is time to move on. That is always a good thing; wayward, my son, wayward."

"You got it all! You got, I'm keeping my window open, sneak in if you need your bag! Meantime sleep with some women 'til you get fixed up proper with an apartment!"

"I will," said William, stepping through the doorway to the sawdust morning, absorbing Harold's fragmented, purgatorial dispensation:

"Wisdom and goodness to the abhorrent seem abhorrent, filth begets nothing but itself! There, man—there, I've said it all!"

On a late lunch break somewhere between Market and Mission William still felt unaffected by his sudden need to relocate. There was something about San Francisco which sort of emblemized calling on anyone for a favor with all intentions of at some point returning that favor. Even calling Janine, with whom his one-night stands had dissolved, seemed applicable. It seemed proper to give heed to things whimsical; in fact, it was the way William felt each block of each street he walked that summer, ducking in and out of doorways at his choosing.

Still, rather than call Janine or Phil Cohen who had been rifling through his latest revolutionary poems, or even those young men he'd just met departing on motorcycles with whom he had made plans, William hit the Apple Store—Internet—and brought up a list of single-occupancy hotel rooms for rent. His smile widened increasingly as a thousand foreign people and spliced images burst, rushed around him, at his august findings:

The host of rooms were on either Polk Street or Mission Street. He made a list of three prospective hotels and returned to the hot-dog cart late assuming the end was near since having received that morning's memorandum, being its anonymous target, with plans still yet to distribute at least 100 more wieners to the woebegone, and at least twice as many dollars unto himself, in order to procure a week's deposit at one of the weekly lodgings he planned on exacting his next austere encampment.

Something of a mob had formulated around the gleaming metallic box. Sheila, Honda, and a man quite akin to a human walrus in dewdrop-green suit stood stately before the cooler. Sheila bantered a rugged arm William's way, the six sets of eyes traversing toward his solitary march.

"William," croaked Sheila, "Meet Franklin, your boss."

"Good morning Franklin," smiled William, studying the short, fat stool of a man just past middle age whose fluctuating stomach protruded like a fine camel's hump inflated, deflated with air.

"Bill, well, sorry it took so long," he extended his hand with gleaming, suspicious enthusiasm. "I was down in Dublin visiting with my wife's family!"

"Well lucky you, lucky you, sir. I've longed to meet you. Your suit, may I add, is a work of art. Good morning Honda."

"It is mid-afternoon," Honda explained, snuffing.

"But Billy I must tell you, the reason I'm even around at all," Franklin exclaimed, turned tomato-red, "Is because sales at this location, just, well, they just *aren't* up to *par*. It's not your fault. Rather, you see, it is a long-standing issue." He removed aviator sunglasses from his breast pocket, wiped the lenses clean with his cuff links, and continued. "We're going to shut down an hour or two earlier today, as you can see," pointing to a nameless immigrant who thrust cans of soda into the back of a lacerated white van, "And we're going to have this cart up and running maybe twice a week from now on."

"It was the best of times, it was the best of times," William sighed, adjusting his belt. "Though I understand, Franklin." The short man's eyes leapt this way and that like grasshoppers, till he lit a thin cigar. His suit broke a hundred passing conversations in half. William observed the towering architecture around them, distilled with cool, overcast sunlight, the nervous nature of fleeting passersby relinquished by the fragrant late-summer breeze before fishing in his pocket to make sure he'd already taken his $7.50 allowance for lunch: trolley fare.

"We're going to open up shop on Kearny Street," Franklin coughed through an evaporating gray-white picket fence of smoke, "Starting in two days. How that sound?"

"The word traversing through my mind at this very second, Sir Franklin, would be: 'Majestic.'"

Sheila cut in from the cauldron where her throat once was:

"I got to go check up on Post, Geary. See ya'll soon. Talk to you tonight, Franklin."

"Ye," his teeth grinded, "Ye."

"What about me?" Honda inquired. She stood displaying her artificial smile, sweating between William and a billboard marked by lightning rods. Rated PG-13. Select Theatres.

William shook Franklin's hand, pressing his thumb between the unresponsive second and third knuckle.

"Clean up shop, darling," said Franklin through clenched yellowish teeth. "Me and Bill are gon' take a walk around the block."

With that, Franklin putted around the corner in a shroud of smoke. William collapsed while concealing withheld laughter between the wavering litmus green and figurative, impending doom that blooming cigar smoke, those signals walks with a stranger so often imply. Laugh, and laugh aloud, for whence and once the city is one's easel there is no such thing as canvassed problems but painted portals of entry. William accepted his fate as a thief, caught red-handed, and pretended he were en route to some guillotine as he stepped upon Sir Franklin's shadow.

"I ain't got much to say but keep up the good work, kid." Franklin handed William a soiled fifty-dollar bill.

"Are you sure about this, sir?"

"You're new once to the city; embrace it! You're mad chill, my nigga."

"Um, what?"

"Well you know," Franklin relit his cigar, "You know I felt bad but I know it ain't you, it's that Honda. She's been here three years, I feel bad for her always, see, so I can't let her go. Know her mom too. Way out in the Richmond. Used to live there myself. Ha. Can't count right. Damn anyway," Franklin stopped in his tracks, "Glad to have you aboard, William, cause see Sheila and Alison, they all like you too, and I trust their judgment. You'll go far in this business, kid. You're a natural. Ha. Damn run this enterprise. It's no easy work being a mogul around here." Franklin took a bite of his cigar, nibbled leaves, and spit out a blackened gob along the gumstruck sidewalk. "Lotta crooks in town. Gotta have the right one on your side. Nigga knew I was coming back to Oakland with mad cash years ago, tried to hit me with a wrench and I shot him dead. Law are for peasants, and we Kings. Well I mean I am, but you still with me, Bill— yeah. But there, there's a little cash to hold you over the next couple of days till we get situated on Kearny Street. Bing, bang, boom, going to be big, big sales. People got to have they dog; they damn hot dogs."

"Are you from New York?" William investigated. "I mean, also, are you . . . like a rapper, or something? I have never learned much of you outside of the website biography and the great things your subjects say of thee. But I did not know about . . . all of this."

Franklin had just stood straight up, flapping his green arms like wings of a pregnant hawk, strident and drawing even more attention of the most peculiar sort from flocks of shopping bag-branded passersby. It were as if he could ascend with rockets to the moon, that hotdog inhaling fiend, or somewhere close to the moon, beyond the clouds; that was the look in his jotting, starry eyes, as he took to shuffling alongside a shadow, taking a stab at boombox, whispering rhymes into an imaginary microphone. He then cleared his throat, tucked back under his shirt two golden necklaces: the Star of David and, oddly, the letter G.

"No, no, I just get excited," admitted Franklin. "Well kid, I got to split. What you reading?"

William handed him Octavia's mystical chapbook. Franklin flared a hairy nostril, tilted his head as if a speedometer to the right, the left, shouting, "Take this instead!"

From his back pocket a packet was presented: *The (Abridged) Story of Franklin's Franks.*

"The condensed version," he added. "Vital, nonetheless."

"Thank you," said William. "Thank you."

"And for the love of God, kid—they says you don't have a phone—here, take this little thing. I'll be in touch!"

The two parted ways. William took Post all the way up, activated the phone at the shop. Standby once again was a strange notion; still he felt sane reading the first line of the packet:

> *What you, pioneer, hold in your hands; this is my version, my branch, in the ephemeral history of America; this is my rise to power from Telegraph Avenue to prison for lacking permits, to the riots and dismay of vending on the streets of California, from hard knocks to hot dogs, the true, shocking tale of—*

William threw the packet into the trash, a notion which within half an hour he'd come to regret through hysterical tears of laughter, but by then he was out front of his first living-destination perched upon the corner of Polk and Sacramento: The Scenic Route (Hotel). William recognized the proximity of the place to Hemlock and thought of Isaac, and everything before Isaac and after Isaac. Discolored, slanting walls. He stood on the corner of Polk and Sacramento for a moment and watched the world go by concealing his smile. His phone rang; apparently Franklin had loaded it with co-workers' numbers, having thereby given them William's.

"William! Come to our party tomorrow night in Dolores Park!"

"I will, Allison," William said.

"Yes! Tomorrow I will call you and tell you what time!"

He threw his coffee cup into a trash can, striking a legless bum in wheelchair on the tip of his maroon beanie:

"What about I sit at the top of the hill with a jug of wine and read European poetry until I see a group formulating like an aurora borealis below me, at which I will be pulled forth toward, for my will, from there to provoke a geomagnetic storm?" Drunkenness captivated his verbal relay as he had his eye on the first option of a room of his own. This he had never known before; he was on his own again, and without problematic catch or fear, for people who cannot suffer can never grow up and can never discover who they are. "Forgive me, I have not slept well, and when I sleep unwell I confuse my thoughts with my words."

"What?"

"I am too excited to talk. I am about to go move into a hotel room."

"OK!"

William hung up the phone, swung open the heavy door, marched up the torn discolored rug-clad steps of the Scenic Route.

Photographs of Arizona and bodybuilders lined the walls. Coffee steamed somewhere and its scent ran down the thin hallway. William noticed a short man at the end of the hallway, speaking with an accentuated lisp, his earring shining beneath the rustic hallway murals, tinsel chandeliers. William stepped over a squeaking baby mouse as the man finished up his sentence:

"One's called, see, Local Color and was a bath-house for some time until you know a decade or something ago that was raided by some bourgeois fascist pigs and you know the rest of the story, while over by Spielberg's set, yes they're still, I *was*—"

The man of average height and middle age turned a pleasant face to William. He resembled a healthier consideration of Frankenstein. The other man stood up, adjusting himself upon an unseen stool. Up close, William was taller than him.

"Hello/May I help you?" the odd pair's words clashed at once.

"I read an advertisement concerning a room for rent," William said. "I just got into town from the East. Have got the money on me now, ID—"

"Have we even *got* a room for rent?" the short man asked himself. He walked through the barn door and propped himself upon another stool, opening the small office window. The plastic window stayed tilted at such an angle as to reflect the framed postcard photography of wild horses and movie stars. The tall man flipped over a tin, rectangular sign which had read, CLOSED, and the short man cracked his knuckles.

Observant of the seeming-landlord's flipping through a notebook with cringed eyebrows, William grew weary. The day was young, there were almost too many options, and yet there was some strange comfort within the Scenic Route Hotel. Polk Street, in its subtle way, had rambled and etched itself into the cell of his tin heart. Some minutes passed by of nail-biting and negative shakes of the head, uproarious sighs, flailing of ashen lips.

"I wonder who posted that," the giant admitted, chewing on a ball-point pen. He placed a quarter into a vintage gum ball machine, sent a discolored circle racing down the winding chute through a maze of dead bulbs. William further observed the smoke-stained walls around him, the cool breeze running in through the single window beside him. Rusted fire escapes ran up and down, interwoven with wisps of plastic ivy.

"I may have misread the whole thing," William broke the silence. "But anyway, I've got to move on. Take my phone number down if anything happens. I'm off to Mission Street."

"What you doing on Mission Street?"

"Finding a room."

"A hotel room on *Mission Street*?"

William grew defensive at the man's almost-critical interrogation and yet something in his lisp expelled the option of complete nastiness. The man outside of the office scratched at his scalp, chewing on grape bubblegum.

From behind the office the man spoke: "You don't want to do that. You know who rents those rooms out?"

"Who?"

"Drug addicts, drugs dealers, whores, transsexuals, the diseased, pimps, undercover cops. That's it."

William found this difficult to believe and stuck around another moment to argue.

"I've been there for some weeks and have seen nothing of the sort but thank you for your optimism."

"You've been on Valencia, Guerrero, upper Mission past midnight sure, now, but have *been* to or past the hotel district past midnight?"

"I don't know," William admitted. Arnold Schwarzenegger stared him down through a thin sheet of glass. Was he the governor of California?

"Then you haven't. They're always posting advertisements you don't want to bother with." He flipped through his log once more. "You know there is one room for rent down the hallway, although it's not quite the most spacious."

"Take me to it!" said William.

With his crownlike hoop of jangling keys, the waddling man led William down the short, plain hallway. Paint peeled from doors, light-bulbs buzzed overhead, savage coughs broke through doors open an inch by old-fashioned chained upper doorway locks; was that, even, Charlie Parker playing "Anthropology"? And had the modern world existed? There was something alluring about the Scenic Route's beautiful obscurity, there all along, hidden in plain sight and hidden in Nob Hill's shade. William looked about with perverse delight.

The door to room Apt. 12 swung open. A large, clean bed with fresh sheets in one corner, a window through which for a moment something like gunfire went off; but it was not quite gunfire, or at least not the type William had grown to know so well back in the paths and forests of Jerusalem.

"Hear that?"

Sink and mirror at the foot of the bed with some feet between to stand. An ancient hutch for clothing, a desk for anything—the desk, William knew—that was the desk at which to begin again! Lamp beside the bed; small bathroom and shower outside of the doorway. The room was about the size of the storage room he'd spent some adolescent Pennsylvanian years in. To some the room may have been insignificant to the point of hilarity; to William Fellows it was that indescribable feeling within him, the recognition of a room of one's own, which combined with the dresser that could have indeed convincingly been set in an Etruscan branch of any given museum, rendered William surprised by joy; and at that moment as the landlord lit a cigarette and shrugged:

"But hey, you're a young guy, not home much. This might work out."

He winked to William as ash fell to a flattened cardboard shoe box.

William stepped inside and looked around, sat at the edge of the bed and peered through the window. To him this was the actual mansion, that symbol stripped of its skin, the mansion of the self, solace below not gunfire, it seemed, but children with fireworks; and the mansion of America was some dwarfed, figurative nightmare, as growing old must be Hell in big houses.

"I'll take it right now, without question!" William said in earnest.

"The first week is $150.00. If you stay, sign papers, it is $120.00 a week."

"I can run to the bank." The landlord pointed to a smoke alarm and they resumed chain-smoking at the edge of the hallway.

"Well how about instead you let me make a copy of your ID and I'll stick around an extra half-hour, get you a key made. I have rehearsal this evening. Small role in *Milk*. That Harvey Milk movie. Sean Penn—"

But already William was jogging down the hallway out into the street, hailing a cab.

The landlord walked back to his friend, dug out the extra key, photocopied his ID.

"He's even younger than I thought. He's just a baby."

"Something about him."

"You think in a good way?"

"I don't know."

"That's a good thing," lisped the landlord.

William marched past the greeter, white teeth and two bowls of lollipops, and straight ahead to the waxed, polished desk.

"How may I help you?"

"I want all of the money in my account, down to the last penny," William said. "Thank you, ma'am."

Strange looks were shot his way, formless and rustled, grocery-bag customers rubbed at their temples, and four dozen surveillance cameras stretched their necks around.

"Have you considered—"

"No, no nothing. I know how much money I've got and I need all of it now. It's my money, not yours. Sometimes we forget these things."

Within a minute the young woman slid forth an envelope containing $1,364.98 through the mouse-hole beneath the elongated sheet of bullet-proof glass which ran halfway across the plastic interior of the bank, plastic down to the last muscular movements of replaying commercials on three dozen interwoven flat-screen television sets.

"And close the account out also," William said, tucking the envelope into his coat. "Just close the entire damned thing down for good. When they ask why, tell them that it was time to shake the dust from my boots."

If he could not shake the sense of dread that was so often heightened by sights of the demented homeless or dialogical reminders of finite precarity more generally, a room of his own quenched a great deal of such an anxious thirst. He did not miss Fort Mason nearly as long as he had envisioned; indeed his melancholic farewell lasted about as long as his taxicab departure, up to and through the gates.

THE LANGUAGE OF THE GRAMOPHONE RECORD

Polk and Sacramento it was. He lay back in bed, looking at the ceiling. He drank from a bottle of Rockport at close of day, tore the smoke alarm from the wall.

At once he realized in his absolute rejuvenation that he must call Walter. The East could have the East, but now that William needed nothing but the grace of good luck's (against the pilgrim's nebulous will, he could not suppress the notion of this synthesizing as a collision of God and Fate) embodied continuum he knew it well and proper to extend his hand to Walter regardless of the calamities that had passed through Fort Mason, which went unknown in looming at that vicious minute's distant hour. William found it amazing to consider indulgence over the course of months, that many people—millions, even—were also in bed across the globe with their bottles of wine. It was the one consecrated thing anyone could have in common besides approaching death. Yet if you were not there you could never understand it—that much was true. If you had not driven across the Bay Bridge with Phil Cohen at dawn drinking whiskey and stamping your feet upon cinder blocks—If you hadn't stood atop the Muir Woods, plucked a flower, and held it within your wallet where some keep pictures of their family—How could one anticipate the darkest hours within such indiscriminate ecstasies?

With detached signification William called him, Nielsen's brother; to his surprise Walter responded at once, to boot. In fact, he, his girlfriend, and Saul were at Napoli's on Polk, the pizza restaurant which accepted food stamps. William ran down the few blocks to meet them. He had neither tied his shoes nor even placed the opened, uncorked bottle of red in a paper bag.

He sat down at the tilting aluminum table and passed around the bottle of wine. Saul seemed to have recovered and spoke, or rambled on, of any which current event crossed the radar of the overhead news broadcast. Walter and his girlfriend listened to William and Saul speak while the looming acknowledgement of whatever had happened at Fort Mason drifted to a halt overhead like shadowy clouds. Everyone was friends again, eyes glazed, till dawn. It begins and ends at Napoli's.

~

Out of a lucid dream, the contents of which evaporated with sudden consciousness, William awoke with his eyes bolted open to a endless mirage of sirens passing through the street below. Through his window he could see little but afternoon sunlight. On his phone a message and the time: 2:25 pm.

He paced about the free five feet of his room nursing a glass of warm water, observing that he'd shaved at some point the night prior and had managed to stain his set of courtesy towels with wine and blood. William swore a musty smell arose from his clothing in spurts, which he had for some putrid reason that made about as much sense as Napoleon's upon exiting the pyramid, adorned the last half dozen days.

"Remember," Harold's voice came back to him from last time in North Beach, "When you want to save $20.00 on laundry just throw your old clothes out, go to Macy's, and in the fitting room double or triple layer clothes that don't have the plastic thing on them. That's all there is to it."

Two hours later, emerging in three layers of Levi's long-sleeved shirts and jeans, William took an elevator down to the food court. There he took some reusable shopping bags and unloaded his clothing into them in the confines of a bathroom stall.

Back in his room, clean shaven and drinking ice-cold Rogue Dead Guy Ale, the pilgrim remembered to remember to retrieve his bag from Fort Mason, to check up on things with Heather, Harold! Harold! How could they have—

Beneath his bed an empty bottle of wine; a mysterious, empty can of Heineken alongside the shoebox containing his savings. The money was intact as he set off for Fort Mason, coins and keys jangling in his wallet.

The door was open though no one was home. No one was outside of the building across the street, featherless bipeds sprawled upon neither the fields nor the canopies.

The interior of the house was spotless. William wished there was some way he could find out what was happening with Harold Smith and if he could help him out in any way, and what was true and what was false concerning the whole debauched circumstance, the whole shady business. The refrigerator was empty save four cans of Tecate that had been in the vegetable bin since William's first night in San Francisco. In a sort of commemoration of everything in his chaotic near-past unto his kaleidoscopic near-future he cracked a beer open, sliding open the still kitchen window, letting all the slight breeze of Indian Summer drift in. He stood beside the window drinking, awaiting Harold Smith. He did not come. He sat down upon the couch.

Ms. Heather Daily Dearest: *I don't know what is happening nor what will regarding here, now, things, although I hope to hear from you soon. Here is my number. I moved into a room on Polk/ Sacramento yesterday. A handful of days without our adventuring seems like an eternity (As soundless and as meaningless). You have my number, call me soon. I saw R. last night. We got drunk and high and still I know little of what's happened. Stopped by to pick up my belongings, or rather, my bag. In the corner of Harold's room, no one home, I'm drinking beer by myself—How can this be so fitting and so sad at once? Earth's core burns beneath our imported rubber bottom shoes. I peeked in your room just now hoping to find you sitting about listening to headphones or something, or at least the yellow raincoat on a hanger; alas, there is nothing here this afternoon but quiet desperation. Remember us on the beach? Someday there will be a movie. It will save people's lives, as you've saved mine. May have witnessed Walter's friend overdose through a pizzeria window on Polk Street last night. Call soon. How melancholic I feel just now but why, why, Heather, God Almighty, I am engulfed, period, in despair, period. You wouldn't know it if you saw me—If you saw me now, I'd be smiling out on the sunny side of the street. But inside, of course, ah, I have no company without you! Soon!*

Love,

Fellow (sic), William

The nearing rumble before the gradual subduing of an encroaching, roaring motorcycle broke the silence. Light footsteps jogged up the front stairs to the tune of dangling keys and he pushed, breathless, through the half-closed door.

"Hey you!" Daniel shouted, "Ah-ha; the voyage that never end—a boy and his wine!" He pointed to William's beer. The curled mustache, the dazzling persona lifted William's spirits. He did not know why but he was glad to see Daniel again, this being confirmed by the warm, proper handshake Daniel made with William. It was that theoretical polygamous matriarch, Janine, William knew, Janine—and that William had made plans to travel with Daniel the night of his birthday, plans which would never be realized or instigated or acknowledged, thank, and yet plans which could be explored in a more tranquil afternoon.

"There are a few more in the refrigerator," William encouraged him.

Daniel placed his motorcycle helmet upon the table, opened a beer, and sat across the table from William.

"Cheers," said William, lifting his can to Daniel's, "Although please remind me your name—we met at my birthday party, didn't we?"

"What a night, Daniel I am, yes, now do you still stay here? How are things?"

"I moved into an apartment yesterday in Nob Hill. All is well; exhausted but working on that. Working part-time for the revolution."

"Which revolution?"

"The Franklin's Franks revolution downtown," William said. "I couldn't have smuggled in more money with a proper master's degree at this point in time."

This passed by Daniel, who just a second or two later let it register that William had a room of his own.

"You already found a room! Yes!"

For some time, the two sat talking, discussing life without consequence in San Francisco, Manhattan, Brooklyn, Daniel's overseas travels, William's American travels, motorcycles, literature, whiskey, women.

"See that picture, there, I cannot understand who that beautiful ballerina *is*."

"Oh," Daniel said, "That's Anna Pavlova, man."

Daniel had stopped by to have sex with Heather, William learned, who had for some time dated Daniel's bandmate. That was long gone, and Heather was to have been home already.

An hour and four beers passed. The discussion had grown phenomenal, lengthy, Daniel announcing: "Well look, I've got another date over in your neighborhood about now also. Heather must, something must have happened. Let's go to this other girl's apartment and have soup. But first, why are we alive?"

"I don't know," William said, feeling good. "But I can recite you a note I wrote earlier today upon waking up if you would like to hear it—a sort of purgatorial dispensation."

"Yes!"

William got into clean clothes as fog, mist swept across the vacant fields through the old bathroom window. He returned.

"Critical," he announced, "Is a metaphor for unproductive; lack of productivity is a metaphor for emptiness of the mind and body; God is a metaphor for the unfathomable, developed memory borne into this present moment having never existed before amongst never-ending never-beginning existence; Heaven is a metaphor for Hell; Purgatory is a metaphor for alphabetical delirium; Hell is a metaphor for a wasted life prolonged; futility is slang for he too nervous to admit paralysis moving none but his pupils; and metaphors are ash in the ephemeral fire of gravitational synthesis. That is my way."

Daniel stared with entranced eyes into the sawdust of sundown till he fell over to the floor kicking and screaming. William left the note upon Heather's bed and walked with Daniel down to the motorcycle.

"Certain friendships are eminent in the way one's hand is shaken, an unspoken wonder such as changing seasons, wandering stars, photographic memories," Daniel said beside the motorcycle. "I've got two sips left in this can of beer." He took a sip. "Here you go."

William raised the can, announcing, "To the death of one generation and to the birth of another." He held tight the leather strap and racing through midday downtown San Francisco at 90 MPH to Polk and Post, the wind of summer gone rushing through their unkempt brown hair, laughing, the birth of yet another gilded comradeship. And to think all the while Daniel's twirling mustache retained its slanted balance.

"Tell us who you are, from where and whence you come."

"You do not know my name, and thus where I come from is nowhere—or perhaps more fittingly, the name of that land is Hell."

"O Caesar, why does William not tell us? He let slip something of a river, out east. I thought he was from New York. No? I for my part thought he said something about a valley, a valley whose name perishes."

Five floors up an ancient Otis elevator and into the long, old-fashioned room where Sasha's voice was at once like a quilt, occasional and soft; its presence reminded one of youthful things as she spoke readjusting her long dark brown hair, some type of foreign complexion, wore clothing from that vintage store on Van Ness where she sold clothing, went to college somewhere, and in San Francisco one could catch up on things having met just one moment ago.

The three spoke at once of love:

"The first time I ever had my heart broken," said Daniel, "God . . . I was so young, maybe sixteen, but through that devastation I knew that it hung so heavy because the precluding sense of phenomena that existed first was important. I was reading Joshua Slocum, and since then I've decided that at one point in my life, I will sail the seas, for, oh, say six months," he added, curling his golden-brown mustache. Sasha leaned in closer. "Oh, and didn't I *tell* you?" he stood exhaling a deep breath of bedroom air and sat back down smiling, rubbed his thighs, feverish, "I'm getting my taxi-cab license next weekend!"

William nodded in approval of multiple things but before any response turned to study Sasha. The contrast of her tone and facial appearance from one moment to the next was intact with Daniel's. She seemed a charming little girl whence blushes of red came to her whitish-tan face, the way she held her hands at her knees in a clenched grip, polite, eager grin, concealed widening. Such transformations are noticeable in most people, but the most triumphant to watch are those who light up over an undying passion that exists within the proximity of a potent body parallel, observing the photographs of docks, basket of ripe bananas, little blue stickers and mint tins, before again within the wall of flesh where it was Sasha's emotional body that existed within her, that fresh gust of wind in the desert of telepathic relay as she looked to Daniel's eyes, the interlocked hands at the knees of her torn stockings constituting cities of the human spirit under-populated, sightings of magnetized Fraxinus nigra.

"WAHOO!" William yelled, feeling overcome with carelessness and random triumph, his hands cupped over his mouth in a sort of insane yodel as he dashed to the open window tipping over a ceramic ashtray, and once again yelled out of the window, "WAAAHHHOOO!" his garments akin to a scarecrow's which just then flickered in the wind of traffic. Daniel leant over his shoulder, crying out to the Polk Street, to Divas.

"My roommate is sleeping," laughed Sasha. "She is depressed."

"Always, friggin, sleeeeeping," Daniel moaned, blowing air through compacted vibrating lips, sounds of a sighing kazoo.

"What, why! Doesn't she know we could fall in love or eat lunch?"

"She is depressed."

"Everyone is depressed. It's a matter of interpreting it as a lightning bolt or a crutch."

Daniel sang a lyric of a song he'd written in falsetto.

Sasha responded: "I don't know about her."

"God," William said, accepting a sudden glass of tea, "There will be so much more time to be depressed when we are older and uglier. Obligations are the drug I am most burnt out on."

The apartment, the room gave off a majestic quality with its high ceilings, long hallways, grand piano, modern kitchenette, bathrooms within bedrooms, sparkling silverware within open black-marble drawers with engraved, untouched silver handles.

"What are you two doing today?"

"Oh I don't know. Maybe linner somewhere."

"And afterward?"

Sasha shrugged. Outside a siren wailed: now *there* were some authentic gunshots.

"Anything I guess," checking a text message, sending one.

"There is a party."

"Where?"

"Berkeley, a lady friend of mine who studies film and knows everything about music who is a DJ."

"Beauty Bar?"

"Yes on Tuesdays and weekend sometimes."

"I'm broke," Sasha admitted.

"I've a party in Dolores Park which reminds me, well, of good feelings. I had a vision in Dolores Park."

"I'll make soup, tomato soup for you boys," closing the window. "How does that sound?"

"Yes!" Daniel winked his way. Sasha stepped out to boil water, whistling.

"I've been trying to stick to wine because I don't get uncreative-drunk on wine. But then I don't get drunk enough. Then I mix it with some beer, or a gin, and get destroyed. William what shall I do?"

"I don't know much about these things. I just do what seems good for the present. I may be tortured as the best of them at times, but I know such torture's an illusion, a lost illusion, as lost an illusion as Brooklyn. I am never bored; I am trying to say: I tell you that much."

"Memoirs of a Cab Driver!"

"Yes, the book is waiting to be written! The book is you, I, alive, God when he was young, the Advent of thought!"

"Damn those who differ."

"I'll be your agent."

"OK."

William barged over toward the open window before glancing through to the kitchen and noticed Sasha grinning his, Daniel's way, she knew of madmen together, the city must know their enthusiasm and embrace it like birth, the colossal vibration spun from such glistening webs of minds, thoughts—Daniel draped William's shoulder to yell out of the window: "Bulkington! There, bearded!"

"The advent of thought," William recited.

"Listen though," Daniel whispered, staring at the wall. "That's the sound of a woman opening a can for her two favorite men, two men she'll never forget."

"What goes through her mind now?" William asked.

"All that races through my mind in attempting to unravel hers through the heat of a mechanical can opener, oh and there's a pot hissing with water on stove also, a coterie of sounds sweeps through my mind now, the direct essence of fragility and its colors."

"They leaned over the edge of the soft bed, studying wooden gloss floor; one can always sense the solemnity of a young woman's first city apartment, it is a beautiful thing to be inside of, perhaps more beautiful than being inside of the woman, though the apartment contains scattered books and magazines and magnets of mothers still stuck to the refrigerator and things you can pick up off the floor. In love you can all but pick yourself up off the floor," William said.

"We have not yet learned enough because we have not made enough mistakes, a listening to the soup plop into the pan, brief sizzle. Listen," Daniel insisted. "Listen to the water boil." William found him insane, but then again, the insane possess that rare quality of friendship where you can always be yourself around them.

William agreed, memories of nights ago returning with steam, of sunrise raving with Daniel and others of cosmopolitan mirage, aware of the principles and situational tranquilities of one's own life there forth to stamp out bad eggs, for here comes everybody—

Sasha opened the refrigerator, extracted a container and shook it; Daniel tapped William's shoulder with his knuckles pointing to the doorway blushing—

"Is water OK?" Sasha asked, displaying a plastic container of filtered water.

"OF COURSE!"

Daniel exclaimed something further inaudibly, falling from the bed. "That's what I was hoping for," thought William. The pan hissed again. He pondered the strange reality that it would be his first San Franciscan meal without alcohol.

"Do you need any help?"

"No," she smiled.

"Who is throwing this party on Haight?"

"Oh you know a long a story this girl Vynessa but you met her—"

"The one who was crying when we picked up the motorcycle?"

"Yes, you may have met her William, she's been depressed, the damn weather or something I guess, to be vague, but yes so many people seem sloth-like, and depressed, like."

"Why don't we hop on a boat and go to France? I know a mother who would finance a trip for the three of us, this girl's mother."

"What. Where do I fit in?"

"I will tell her . . . I will suggest to her . . . Something like buy one get one free. It will never work but there is a translucent quality of daydreams I often obsess over, for the sake of daydreaming, living in another world of words wherein nothing goes wrong, beyond even Sumer, into that bicameral breakdown of mind that even old de Maistre himself would gush over. The most dangerous safety-net of all."

Daniel curled his mustache, asking, "Is any of this possible?"

"She told me something, the two of us could go, and I know a fair bit of the language and an encyclopedic amount of French literature. I'd stay inside the whole time and just write postcards to Americans and eat French fries," William said, "Because who cares anymore. Oh who am I kidding, I no longer talk to the girl."

For some time Daniel and William rocked back and forth on the floor emulating delayed effects of a pushing match, that fresh scent of tomato soup beginning to boil, smiling in the summer afternoon, squirmed, kicking legs to and fro as Sasha peered her head around the corner of the kitchen entrance where on the wall there was a tapestry, gold and red, of Jesus Christ, frayed. Milton in a corduroy handbag.

"I had to stop recording my dreams," Daniel said as William resituated himself on the edge of the bed, "I end up getting bothered, bothered sometimes, by the whole thing, and it's all your goddamn fault!" He pointed to the mirror. "I can't help it man! My subconscious began collecting details so dense it began to alter my present, or waking, conscious. I'd do the dishes in my dreams, pay rent, make dates, record music, paint, buy household items, and damn, to then have to do it all over again after realizing that that was just a dream! Ugh! Déjà vu got to me, felt as if I could express myself in waking life through fragmented terms and things panicky that threw people into an anxious fit just hearing about it, like nothing is worse when you just want another beer than this maniac who's making sense—because the maniacs who make no sense are laughable—but then the others ah you have to be in the mood—like over coffee talking about one dream for twenty minutes and about the literal physical exhaustion I was being driven to through unconscious rendezvous such as eighty-mile bike rides past Sausalito, and ah you know already all of this though," he blurted out, exhausted having just recited these words within the time-frame of a single breath.

"Even the description of this strange process made me exhausted," William said, shedding an inadvertent yawn, "Although you make absolute sense."

"God," Daniel sighed, adjusting the neck of his sweater. "I um, yeah I know, it is like I, ugh, man, oh wait, SOUP! I SMELL SOUP!" He sang at the top of his voice the rhythm of 'Summer Wine,' Hazelwood/Sinatra, adding, "The death of art, this general notion brought on by neocapitalistic mass-production of subculture, viruses man, this whole ideological tabula rasa is nothing but a canvas, O blind masses of willing self-induced degeneration! Pawns! I have a phobia of pawns!" He leaped up, jumping on the bed, touching the tall ceilings with the aid of springs, the tips of his hands, "O life!"

They leant in on an imaginary, or auditory, peephole, could hear cabinets opening, closing, quick subtle clank of porcelain plates, Sasha's sensitive motions—"This is what I mean," Daniel whispered, "When I speak of the beauty of moderate daydreamt experience. We can't even see what she's doing but we can feel it, yes, this is a beautiful moment, oh my God, she's put on soft country music, Tammy Wynette, is this happening? It is I know! I is!"

Sasha placed the plates upon the table as Daniel began marching around the apartment, the room, stomping his feet, singing:

"Get up me lad, young William, follow me now!"

The pair about the house, William chanting in a baritone voice, the rhythm of lead, "YEE-OO-O, YO-EE-O, YEEOO-O, YO-EE-O, YO-O, YO-E-O, YEE-OO-O, YO-EE-O!" clapping his hands thunderous as Daniel sang, to the beat of a drum—Daniel's Song:

"As long as the acknowledged depression does not fill you! For we acknowledge and never ignore the interrupted and experienced potential and happening horrors of life, we sabotage ourselves the way this television set will and says to discredit the evil of the world is to be wrong, for he who challenges nothing has no accurate opinion, you know? Fear eats the soul and rejection's what we're fearful of. Technological rejection turns a chance opportunity into that false, permanent, television discouragement, lingers in the musky air like blood, but I say rejection's not so bad as it is temporal. And so you get rejected by a town, a man, a woman, a professor, a parent, a job, a screen, a country, but you know what man, it's everything to acknowledge and nothing to absorb that piddling satanic fear. The mind wanders and so must the man, the woman, in order to know what is happening. The song of Daniel, the chant embryonic."

William took a good look around as Daniel took a breath, a golden aura formulated around him as in that moment this near-stranger seemed the physical form of art, for he did not (attempt to) blow William's mind as much as he articulated what all modern men knew somewhere in the recess of their ignored minds, souls, in a clearer way. Drawers opened and closed; silverware set upon the embroidered mahogany table.

"The propaganda will grow ever more colorful," Daniel sang through a new march even more fierce, throwing empty cans and cassette-tapes through the window like Frisbees as the people of the street shouted in unison, "As we say it can't happen here until it does happen here, the way it always does, no one stops buying gasoline, you spend less money, the protest of huffing about the obvious in small groups and see for me it's either a bomb or a book, the truth is more violent than the political suicides and the reasoning behind the subliminal wars, ah God, I can't get it out of my head but no one I know can either, there's got to be something to do, SOMETHING-TO-DO, but no, there isn't, there isn't! Ye chant, William—Ye Chant Embryonic—"

Sasha cried in:

"The soup is on the table!"

The tribal dance came to a halt. In the silence William's stomach growled its vociferous message.

"Aw man let's eat in bed!" Daniel shouted, reverting to a vague youth untying his shoes, blinking, cutting himself off. "Man no that's pushy, I hate, or, disavow pushy, it's so unattractive and I'm digging a verbal hole, I'm sorry, Sasha!" He hobbled forth to hug her wearing one shoe.

William jumped up, kicked his decrepit white sneakers together in mid-air and waved over, trotted toward a big triangular hug; they rubbed their heads together, groaning, laughing in an uproarious pattern before sitting down for hot tomato soup, salt crackers, and a pitcher of water.

"A toast," Sasha said, tilting at last the carafe of chilled white wine. "To San Francisco!"

"Daniel, Sasha, I must be on my way. You two ought to open a restaurant."

"Hear that!" cried Daniel.

"Aw, thank you!"

"Let us hit the beach or the highway sometime soon and be good friends," William said, extending his hand. "And I'll see you around, neighbor," he smiled to Sasha, hopping back into the elevator and down to the pre-evening out to the discounted wine shop on Van Ness where the word of the day was always buy one get one for a nickel.

As the building door clicked closed behind him, the pilgrim was again reabsorbed in the brutal contradiction of the streets, the endless procession of the rich and the homeless; he thought to himself, 'It is no wonder the gentrifiers are always so hollow in their apparent morality; for they are, in their way, colonizers of invisible violence; they were pastured by Circe, those ugly swine, falling and swelling into the abyss of futility, so consumed by fraud that they can no longer even fathom the state of things, cornered in by a disastrous system whose earth shall not be recognizable in even a thousand years . . . so walked the police officers and their subjects, collectively damned, through the ever-increasingly hazardous streets of plague and waste.'

"Their rallies for the "climate" are mere symbols of their herd stupidity," scoffed a passerby, which shocked William. "And every decade they need to call their fraud a new name, all for poisonous sin and object-culture, the accumulation of objects . . . you see even the corpses you step over on your way home, and that one there, knows that their memory perished before the earth even before they did; their names would never be renown in the streets"—meanwhile in the Tenderloin the voices hushed as William shudderingly walked through the infernal debris, taped off piles of needles, excrement, and corpse, aberrantly aglow in a bath of siren light.

But then suddenly a man dressed as a gypsy queen dropped a mini refrigerator he'd been waddling with, cradled between his arms, which was smashed on the ground right beside some developing crime scene; police car doors slamming, voices ordering, the gypsy screaming through glass pipe inhalations:

"They gon' find me an' kill me!"

"Alright—I think this is where I exit."

William walked on.

The summer was over and had been for several weeks, and yet it did not hit William until that specific evening along Van Ness Street when the winds began to pierce his soul straight through his coat. An exhausted mailman barreled by with a click-rolling crate of mail, the racket of deformed black plastic wheels. He dragged the rectangular pouch as if it were an anchor, rattling and scraping down the street as an overweight cop jaywalked past a small group of transsexuals over toward a mural of human waste along the front window of a darkened Edinburgh Castle, gun drawn, tiptoeing to the destroyed refrigerator and all it entailed. William looked one way, another, held the keys to Apt. 12 in his hand, and walked bout the autumnal city of death and fog for hours, to the outer limits of the Sunset and back cutting through Irving and Judah, Lincoln and Taraval, through Golden Gate Park to the Tender-Nob.

The next morning the pilgrim picked up a used copy of Augustine's *City of God* from a sidewalk sale; a bright spot in the city of death and woe, or molecular ritornello.

Moving toward Market, he saw a familiar face, one of the regular damned, crawling from its cardboard box:

"Dis stone! Dis stone use t' be a man! I knew dis stone when he was a man, an' a boy!"

Two choices when dealing with invisible vipers and their bait, the impalpable entrails of the city of man, noted William in his Augustine: see the hook and apprehend it, or submit to the culture industry, its codependent taboos, and perish.

He celebrated this insight at Columbus Café.

14

WITH FORT MASON OFF-LIMITS and phone service cut out, the centripetal parade went on unmarred save the absence of Harold Smith and Heather and everyone in between. Soon Smith would be having to find another apartment, Nielsen had mentioned Walter had already moved back east, and the details of everything would have been interesting although there was no easy way to attain them and the hard thing was to get one's self situated, at the drop of a hat, in San Francisco.

The room at the Scenic Route was just larger than a walk-in closet, William came to accept, intact with sink, bathroom, window, dresser, and desk. It was a minimal way to live, and the pilgrim arrived with simply a small radio, half a dozen garments, and a shaving kit. He christened the room with Rachmaninov's *All Night Vigil*, accompanied by a memory of midnight vespers, having borrowed the disc from SFPL in a haze, yet pleasantly surprised to find the recording among his belongings in a sober state of mind, serene yet depressed.

The room was old-fashioned, perhaps outdated and claustrophobic, but much more interesting than any loft back along Kent Avenue in that in such a simple atmosphere would disallow one from getting comfortable until one was willing to accept time slowed down. Even among the modern apartments of relatively young persons who often flock to certain cities for certain reasons, the unspoken reality was that most of them did not need to work; there was no threat if their work was to cease; their parents were not poor, and such was reflected in both their strange sort of limp when walking down the earphones street in pre-torn clothing and lenless glasses, or simply their apartments, decked out with a systematic array of meaningless objects.

The pilgrim was much more interested in the ancient monastic cells of friars: a bed, a book, and perhaps some straw. Living quarters that were not designed to intoxicate but encourage one to temporarily rest with no pretense whatsoever of mechanical grandeur. There was no television set nor computer nor telephone; Franklin's phone ceased working about the time William ceased showing up to work, as a combination of wine, beer, A.B. Cook, and Henry Vaughan rendered him blissfully unemployable. William adapted to this lifestyle with fondness. At the end of the day one could use his food-stamps for organic cheese and crackers, spend two dollars on a bottle of wine, take a walk down Polk to the discounted liquor store and buy six pints of Guinness for six dollars, and at the root of it be faced with one's self, an open window, and summer's end streaming down Polk Street, pillars and fortresses of overdue books from the SFPL, from Green Apple.

It was there, after a long night along Valencia Street, that William spoke at length with Octavia and began to feel useless, panged with an incomparably abrupt sort of desolation that was not simply a matter of being reminded of the past, or a distant figure, but that in speaking with Octavia that the pillar found himself pitilessly dissecting himself. It took many hours to accept the sudden loss of Heather, of Harold, of Fort Mason and all that he came to understand of its symbolic qualities after having left.

"But don't worry so much," she said, "I wish I were not here, and there with you just having *fun*. I remember, I don't know, months ago, the last time we spoke or around then, mentioning the winter of my soul, William; but that too also dissolved, just like the season. I have been drowned in depression, but always brought up for air even when I was convinced that no one was coming to save me. To that end each day is a miracle; and it is not a miracle because one has survived, but in surviving one has come to see what life was all along, and what the occult forces of the world demand one neglect: that life, and each day therein, is a miracle. And thus began my new life, when at last I was flooded with joy."

"There has to be more than fun, with you and your success!"

"Nothing is definite yet, William."

"Still, you stick to your guns. I miss you dear. Someday the streets of New York will be alive again, dowsed and flooded in colors."

"Are you drunk?"

"Halfway."

"What about your play," she inquired, "Why not touch it up, have it performed?"

"I've got no computer."

"Make edits on the hard-copy."

"I lost it."

"Write another one."

"After all that journalism and having decided I quit the whole thing, I can't get myself to do much at all. Modern theatre is putrid. They wouldn't let me in."

"Don't look at it that way. Oh, have you heard from that, what's her name?"

Ah, Octavia—Could even make God himself seem a 'What's his name!'

"Don't talk about her. Not since last time when she came to visit."

"I understand. I've got to get on the train soon. What is it, 5:45 over there?"

"My clock is broken also."

"William, come on! Get it together!"

"I've got it, I've got it. There's a party I'm going to tomorrow night and a good number of friends out here. Everything is wondrous; I suppose I just miss those two, the situation I had, that I told you all about, you see." He lit the last smoke of a pack of a carton of American Spirits and tried in vain to convince himself that he had bought it much longer ago than he had.

"You'll see them again. You've got to occupy yourself with *something*. I thought you were going back to school."

"Down in the air."

"What does your mother think of all this?"

A sense of reality came through him, a sense of life beyond San Francisco, for the first time in months. He bit his nails, flipped through newspapers, and knew now what to say.

"We don't talk now," he said. "She was furious about the college thing."

"That's terrible!"

William knew, then, or could at least admit, that it was terrible. He felt as if walls were closing in around him, or as if he were going underwater as the sun began to rise over the Pacific.

"I have it under control."

"Why don't you come visit New York for a few days?"

"I can't."

"I'll pay half. For God's sakes you sound bad!"

"It is just exhaustion."

"What is holding you back?"

"Work. Creative work and professional work."

"At the hot dog stand?"

"Yes," William said. "I have been taking notes on the experience, and now it is my gateway to a social life. Party in Dolores Park the other day, tomorrow night. It is not just vending, you see, but it is the art of thievery, the revolution of stealing from the rich and giving to the poor, in which I partake."

"You're telling me that you can't go into a bar and strike up conversation and meet people that way, at least? Or in a café?"

"Doesn't work that way in San Francisco," William admitted. "New York bartenders are the greatest bartenders on the planet, hands down. A number of the bartenders in San Francisco, alas, seem legends within their own minds, and the bars are uncomfortable to go in alone. One of my favorite pastimes in New York, Brooklyn, was drinking alone when I waited for you to get off work and class. Damn, I miss New York."

"Come back!"

William contemplated this and realized he longed for Octavia at that moment more than any city; within rare, true love, any city in the world becomes what it is: The backdrop. Out of love, or in loveless states, the city becomes obsession, one's sense of identity, and that is not just icon-worship, illusionary, but it is false and in bad taste. That was the unfortunate thing about Brooklyn, or at least having grown up there: It was a fine place to be, but it was much more interesting from a distance. Very few people would admit this upon arrival, and as many would find themselves unable to leave or to feel contended. Brooklyn was, from a contextual point of view, the place to experience. Alas, the context did not hold up, and the scene played out like a censored film adaptation of Manhattan in the fifties, and that was that. So it was the beauty of Brooklyn one must absorb, and never the symbolism. Just look into the eyes of any bakery owners, of the young men with silver teeth who make sandwiches for the alcoholic populous till dawn. Still, when you knew what you were doing these people were easy enough to avoid, save strange darting eyes drugged with coffee upon cold subway trains in the morning. Ah, how he longed for everything!

"I put it this way, Octavia: When you want to get to New York nothing will stop you—You'll consider robbing a bank, reconnecting with worthless relatives, changing your last name, and all sorts of things to get there and get down to business. And yet when you do not want to be there at all you will do whatever it takes not to go back—Most often people who have not lived in the city do not understand this, the people there do not understand this, and that is fine. When your work is done in a place like New York—"

"Oh, come on!" shouted Octavia. "You're talking nonsense! I said consider visiting—God—what's gotten into you! All your e-mails are somewhere between happiness and sadness, sometimes sentence to sentence. *You're* the one who's been indicating you haven't been getting anything done in the creative sense, no assignments, no further education—Nothing! Out of nowhere!"

"That, Octavia, that is what I have no problem doing. I have two primary occupations these days: Exhibit A: Thinking to the point of despair and coming up with notes to jot down that appear watered-down on paper which some day will become a string of essays in the Chronicle. Exhibit B: Saturnalia, the harvest of Kronos, or more simply, the parade."

"What par*ade*?"

"It's an old term Harold Smith started using at the beginning of summer. We refer to our lives in San Francisco as 'The Parade.'"

"What does that even mean?"

"Well," began William, "There's a parade of some kind happening every day here on the streets, and while that is fine and festive and nice and all we've begun a parade of our own. Several people are involved, a number have been trampled, and now the frontiers have been divided up. I feel as if things will get under way, to an order of sorts soon enough and we'll be back together. I'll have to explain it to you in person, or *you* come out and visit."

"So it is like a big party is what you're saying?"

"More than that; I don't know, I'll have to explain it to you in person. We like to smoke expensive pipes, cigarettes, weed, drink absinthe, whiskey, beer, wine, read good literature, ride bicycles."

"I have to go," Octavia said. William took a deep breath, stamped out his last cigarette. He felt something bad in her voice; it seemed a reflection and a lost tolerance for his lofty nihilism. "William, sometimes I worry about you. You seem to have lost track of what's happening anymore in the world. You never say anything any longer of that which you once executed so well, journalism. You ought to get online and research old Jerusalem—The town is disintegrating and so is most of the country. This recession, this collapse is no longer some timorous rumor, William, and your silence on the whole thing is sort of disturbing. The most vocal boy I ever knew—Think of what I said and call me soon. I'm late to the train—"

He started writing a novel concerning people of the street, writing imaginary biographies of each person that passed by his window and hoping that by the end of it some sentimental melody would hold the collage together. By late afternoon he had a dozen pages of extra notes, twenty handwritten pages. He edited the writing as it went along as if writing by hand weren't a slow enough process; the simultaneous editing weighed the ideas down and the process remained anchor-like amidst instinctual schools of thought.

Octavia appeared, somehow, within each person: An aging woman would have been a phenomenal painter as a gorgeous young woman; passing businessmen and blue-collar men had, somehow, fine felicitous wives at home with exquisite taste whose aesthetic theories were drawn from Octavia's latest emails; a young woman passing by had a good journalist friend at school whom she was just now going to meet for coffee; a beautiful middle-aged woman speaking in a foreign language on the corner of Sacramento was catching up with her artistic daughter in New York, hearing all of the great, productive news; a hunchbacked man in polka-dotted suit was making his last calls for the upcoming art gallery— he knew just the girl out east to showcase—he'd read an impressive string of articles on her. William was to dedicate his book to Octavia and began to realize that the novel was a man at his window coming down from a long night and morning, heartbroken and seeing his true love everywhere on Polk Street. No dedication necessary. William did not know if this were true and could no longer go on with it. He decided to remain idle until the party and discarded any artistic output. In the evening he rummaged through the pages, decided them insubstantial, threw them into a dumpster, and turned back to buy wine out on Van Ness for the party. Homeless men approached, rummaging through garbage for food. Potential audience.

Out on Mission Street thick steam alleviated through metallic capsules to the sidewalks intertwined with the fog through explosions of salsa music, children running 'round with their dollar-bills across the suffused mosaics. The singularity of alcohol cast aglow within passing eyes of dancing bodies, brows streaked with glistening sweat beneath the blinking lights of vendor-carts and ice cream trucks, cannonball breasts and enormous asses tap-dancing to the music, distant grins highlighted by handlebar mustaches. William weaved through the nocturnal stanza feeling fresh in the breeze, enhanced by speeding automotive bullets, foreign chants, the endless pulse of weed smoke, maracas, rattling gongs, the sanctuary of steady, beating drums. Thousands of voices crashed together in the course of three blocks, the most important conversations on Earth, an Amsterdam of the senses.

William had a quart of beer back on 16th and Valencia unaware if he'd be late and set down his bag watching the montage of people pass before him.

Environmentalists dressed in orange capes were screaming at someone for dropping a can. Brawls broke out. All of it ended with a young man blowing ringlets of smoke into the eye of the speaker as she broke away in horror.

At the top of Dolores Park, near the subway, he sat down with his wine beneath a bright light and began to drink. He overlooked the park below as the remains of the day's crowd dispersed in opposite directions. The lights of downtown San Francisco glittered distant and if one squinted enough there was the Bay Bridge, automobiles pressing beneath the quilt of stars, the maze of iron and cables.

William found it stimulating to imagine everyone outside of work; that was one thing all jobs had in common. A group of two men and a girl below: He thought of Harold, Nielsen, Heather, Octavia. He recognized a voice in the darkness, speaking French—it was the girl from Union Square in her maroon dress. William hid behind a bush and watched them pass by, one of them carrying a case of Corona.

After a while they were at the other end of the park and William returned to his lounge, his crossed shoes pointed like a trigger at the half-moon shining through the distorted green brushed with the blood of the wine. The group sat down on the playground ship down near the woodchips and William listened to them laugh, echoing through in little ruptures across the immense landscape of the park. After half an hour had passed and still no one whose voice he recognized had arrived, he grew weary and convinced that the party had been altered or canceled. The trains rushed to and fro behind him as William hypothesized alternate plans in a cloud of flickering headlights.

Yet all his plans returned, attached in some way, to Fort Mason. He would wait it out, tonight, antsy as he was for the night to begin, if for the sake of meeting another group of San Franciscans on his own. He watched people come and go through Dolores Park by night for an hour, marveling the prospect of making acquaintances with his own, unraveling another

San Franciscan reality. He looked out to the Bay Bridge, uplifted his wine to Phil Cohen, and the pilgrim emerged from the bushes in which he had camouflaged himself, the importuned cosmos silent as ever, supposing that, perhaps, he would not make any new friends without Fort Mason in his life. And this was rather wistful to consider, as Walter was tied to Nielsen, thus in a sense rendering William to uncomfortably consider how capable he really was in severing himself from geographical Jerusalem, now that the Jerusalem of the soul had been extinguished; he had mistaken the part for the whole.

Then suddenly all fifteen employees or so arrived at once. Laughter and voices rushed together and spread across the dim, sloping hills of the park. He grew afraid to stand and time pressed further on, to be recognized as the strange loner, the outsider, arriving and leaving alone, and could not move. 'You exaggerate,' he told his mind. 'Cease your Scientifics!'

When the wine was out, he tucked it into a hole in the ground and uncorked the second bottle. Twenty serene minutes passed.

He listened to the distant, cascading summer voices, and felt content to experience the party from a distance. For the first time in San Francisco he felt as if on the other side of the window looking in; it was the plague of anxiety as he recalled having never driven a car, having never attended a prom, having never completed his graduate, doctoral applications, having never played sports well, having never even obtained a high school yearbook. All of these things, these ingredients for the ordinary American youth which he had passed by rushed through his memory once more as he watched the crowd congregate and shout and sing below—he felt at last and again a part of something, and yet his old ways taught him to not rush into the party at once but to let it soak in, to know now that there were places and crowds in the world William could belong to, to arrive and to leave in the morning hours, for the pre-sunrise hour was for contemplation and composition what pre-Socratic thought was to the history of the world: necessity in breakthrough. Insight.

Wind swept in with cold dewdrops as airplanes soared through the black sky; there was no longer any point in waiting around to die, he knew, with another dent in the bottle standing up, looking to the distant lighthouse and to the wooden boat. He could feel the wine shining in his beard beneath the moonlight, that damp carnivalesque September by the Bay.

"Hey!" a charming voice resounded from below.

He set out for the drunken boat, the sounds of laughter coming together like music. He walked down the pathway parting his hair to the side, half-drunken and half-aroused, disheveled and poor, feeling beautiful within. He thought of lighthouses, to have a shift end and march back down to land and share wine with friends and the gravitational retirement of smoke, clinking glass, the colorful interior harmonies of Walt Whitman, turning eyes aglow, and then women, men embracing one another. He made the rounds and it all began again, the minds on fire guiding the eyes of prisms.

"William! Yes! Did you receive the memo? Oh!"

Blunts burned down in a vapor of thick blue smoke twisting through fog and whist out to Dolores Street. Voices moved through refreshing pellets of rain. William eyed all the familiar faces, caught up, and one of the van drivers called him over for scotch.

"You have good taste," said William. "You never see any young people like us walking around with a bottle Talisker Scotch."

"Good taste is the first step in living a good life," Jacob said. He had just quit Franklin's to take up an internship at a popular magazine in the East Bay. Weightless bodies crashed together beneath detailed voices laden with uninhibited enthusiasm as fragments of embers and labels spinning sifted to the ground. It was amazing to imagine everyone at work, sitting upon coolers half-reading electronic newspapers and magazines in neurotic silence, and here they were dancing in the park, falling over with laughter, briefing Thomistic metaphysics learned at USF with fresh ecumenical obstinacy, and unyielding parenthetical insight.

All the while, William noticed, that French girl weaved in and out of sight. If William felt her eyes upon him, he delayed a moment before turning to see she had not been observing him or had just turned away to another conversation.

"Alison," William said, shouting over a dozen voices. "Now how could you not have bothered inviting Honda! What is wrong with you— How paradoxical, this panorama!"

At last she approached and spoke in her way which defied specific grandeur and yet seemed disengaged from the archaic, the trite. For instance, William could tell by looking into her eyes in the darkness of shadows and intoxication that to even mention the weather could be a death-sentence; this attracted him.

"I've quit smoking," she exclaimed, "But I still like to roll them. Keep talking. I'll roll you cigarettes."

She rolled thin cigarettes as William expounded upon topics breaking through his mind at random, tales of the summer.

Yet at her side reappeared throughout the evening just the sort of absent-minded, forgettable type of person that she seemed to feel such disdain for. Wonderful women seemed to have a knack for village idiots, William gathered, and in that case one could never lose control nor get hurt—Men, of course, were not much better.

William therefore did not reveal himself too vulgarly, choosing instead to mention French films of value and further tales of his traveling. She explained France to him, life there today in both the country and the town. He listened on to what she said, losing memory of it in blue hazes of smoke some seconds later, and understood in bursts, or a look in her dark impenetrable eyes, he might have something in common with the girl. When she wanted to come off as so, she had a fun European attitude about her. She seemed wealthy, if her brands of purse, clothing, and phone meant, indicated anything, as William felt his own interior rhetorical grammar dissolving like quicksand to the thorough blend of extremely potent smoke and spirits.

The man beside her, fetid and named something like Chip, spoke ('The hella worst combo') of his ironic argyle vest, sifting in and out of a mundane recitation concerning fashion magazines and the liberal political movement. He readjusted his patriotic button several times. William blew smoke in his face.

After the eighth or ninth drink he felt the girl falling away from him. Morose stupidity can outbid handsome indifference, but it cannot hold a flame to authenticity en route.

She took away to the bathroom as William made the rounds.

"William you've got to hear this story," Alison began through drunken laughter, and William listened on.

The argyle vest returned.

"Let me tell you," he said, interrupting tales of thieves, of falling leaves. "Of my cabin in Vermont."

Alison gave him a severe look as William made his way to a group huddled around the bottle of scotch, jotting down phone numbers and inhaling deep the perfect, dampened air, overlooking the jets of sprinklers projecting across the lawn, trains rushing across tracks, voices at random breaking out across the park.

The vested man stood atop the boat, the curling hairs upon the back of his neck aglow.

"A toast!" he shouted. "A toast to everything!"

The crowd in part disdainfully lifted their drinks; the French gal was back at William's side looking on in embarrassment. Her hand curled into a fist.

"To nothing whatsoever," William said, tilting his glass of wine to hers. It was hard to believe she could be even friends with the man let alone the other thing. Reality seemed sad for some people; whoever the lanky vested man was, the pilgrim reflected, it was terribly obvious that no one in attendance looked at him with any sort of loving mesmerism, but that he was the boyfriend no one approved of. Did she, though, with her bowl haircut and short maroon dress, rolling all those perfect cigarettes, reciting Prevert, Sand, Colette, and Baudelaire in French from memory—did she really call this man her boyfriend? Ah, fortuna! William did not enquire further.

At 1:00 the last of the party turned to go home. The girl—he still didn't know her name nor she his unless she'd overheard it—had taken off with her man although some sort of spark had been lit to a fuse; it was the way she smiled at William, and how it dissolved anytime the man wrapped his arms around her.

"Who is that girl," William inquired.

No one was quite positive. She a friend of a girl who hadn't made it that night who had quit weeks prior.

"Something European," someone recalled.

William bid his farewells and felt satisfied walking along the quiet streets alone.

The bars and late-night cafes, restaurants were packed. He turned off Guerrero and began to walk up to El Farolito on 24th. The street grew hushed as he walked ahead, drinking one of the last Corona bottles. He stopped in the bodega for a loose cigarette and made small talk with an amiable Spanish man whose face was covered in violet patches of veins which resembled vines. He was there every night and loved to speak in earnest of the Giants. William stopped in when he was in the area to discuss the game, have a cigarette and farewell.

On the way he out he walked straight into a woman, whose drink fell from her hand and rolled out into the street.

"Bonjour, mon ami."

Somehow it did not surprise him in the least to see her again.

"What are you doing here?" He looked over her long legs and arms, her ample breasts and cute haircut, feeling confident she had followed him down and not caring at all.

"Just out on a walk," said William.

"Alone?"

They began up Mission to 24th catching one another in the reflection of mirrors and vacant shop windows divided by a dozen iron bars.

"I hadn't walked alone in a long time."

"Aren't you tired?"

"No. Are you?"

"I guess not," she said, opening a can of ale and walking ahead, handing it over to William. "Don't you find it sad to walk alone?"

"Not at all."

"I do."

"If you walk alone and feel alone it's natural. It's much better than walking in a crowd and feeling alone."

"So you feel alone a lot, monsieur?"

She seemed strained to have been beside him once more, as if he had awoken her from a nap to insist she walk the streets with him. Still he felt no desire to push her away. It seemed far more worthwhile to walk the streets on a Saturday night with someone and see what would happen.

"I'm turning around here," he said. "I was going to eat up there but I'm going to walk around instead. I'm not hungry. You can come if you'd like."

"I don't want to hassle you," she said.

"I don't mind if you hassle me. Let's walk together. I might hassle you. Where is that other guy?"

"I ditched him at the subway." Mariachi bands poured through the alleyways beside vendors rolling tin carts along before the closed shop windows. "He went in through the turnstile as the last train pulled in and I turned around and ran off without him. He was on his phone and didn't notice, I assume, until it was too late! Aren't I cruel?"

"He seemed like he deserved it."

"No one deserves that, though," she refuted. "Comment t'appelles-tu?"

William knew what she was asking when his mind ventured toward Janine and plans to visit her apartment all the while knowing it would be hopeless. He had waited too long. That vile, low down, extension that served for so many years as an uninvited guidepost, had almost teamed up with the smoke of drink to persuade him otherwise.

"It will be good to sleep tonight."

"Then why don't you go home?"

"Bad memories."

"I asked you what your name was," she said, overlooking the side of his face.

"Oh, I didn't know," William began.

"Well I—"

"I don't want to know your name," he said.

She stopped in the middle of the sidewalk; noticing he'd slowed his pace but would not stop walking altogether, she returned to his side.

"Why wouldn't you, if we're going to walk together?"

"We don't need names—I am tired of remembering. I don't want to know anything about you."

"I want to know about you, though."

"That's fine."

"Let's turn in here," taking William into a dark bar. They sat at the dim counter alongside a dozen other couples. Red lights ran across the dark velvet interior and minimalistic tapping beats interwoven with dark synthesizer ran down from the ceiling.

He indulged one last memory of Janine, if he were to see her that night at all, and he longed to fall ill in front of her apartment, for that might attract her attention.

"Do you know that you can walk around naked in San Francisco?"

"Someone told me that."

The bartender brought their Fernet out with Anchor Steam and William was pleasantly surprised. He asked the girl to tell him more, sensing a philosophical bone within her body.

"I don't know what I was going to say—oh—I think that we are less ashamed, you see, ashamed, like, of nudi*ty* than we are our unending need for that which we come from, pun intended, see, out of, through, the mutual/sexual and embarrassed wheel of life."

"I see what you mean. It is dim. You're the type of person who likes these bars."

"What's wrong with darkness," she said. "We're all going to die. That's all we know."

"I know more than that," William said.

"No you don't."

"Yes, I do."

"Then what is there?"

"There is no use in thinking that way. It's like misinterpreted existentialism. I'm over it. I'm going to enjoy myself."

"So am I, though."

"Good. You have nice taste with these drinks. You're a pretty girl. Did anyone ever tell you that?"

"Everyone tells me that."

"Good."

The bartender took William's five-dollar bill from the counter and sent an enormous, rosy smile his way, guided by a hitchhiker's thumbs-up.

"What do you think of love? I heard you talking with those boys with the scotch about women."

"Love?"

"Yes, love."

"Sometimes it's happening and nothing else matters in the world, then sometimes it's not happening and everything else matters in the world. It is uncomplicated."

"What else matters?"

"Everything."

"You're so vague," she said, taking her Fernet at once.

"That's a lie."

"No, it's my opinion."

"No, it's a lie, because you didn't follow me here because I seemed vague. You followed me because you like me."

"You seemed much more interesting at the park. You were just trying to sound appealing in front of all of those girls, weren't you?"

William finished the Fernet and then the Anchor Steam.

"Goodnight."

He began to walk back down the street, listening to the music and feeling like a million dollars. She came up right beside him.

"I didn't mean to be rude."

The next bar was packed.

"Let's go in there."

They stood in line, William opting to buy the next round.

One table was left in the back; she secured it, smiling, and William brought over frozen margaritas, cherry on top, the size of measuring cups.

"What do you think of love, then," he said.

"Love? I see it everywhere and yet I never feel it."

"That's what you think of it?"

"Yes," she stated, "On advertisements and scripts—on a park bench, always in a song."

"You see songs?"

"Yes! Of course! One *must* see music! And if love doesn't work you can fix it up, or destroy it, like a collection of stamps!" She leapt up and ran through the doorway, returning with a middle-aged man; she whispered to him before he sat down, his tattooed arms muscular through cut-off denim jacket speckled with peeling patches, his dark face of clear, hardened sober eyes offsetting his limp handshake.

"Luis runs the anarchist bookshop on Haight Street."

"I guess I'm not supposed to say your name and not supposed to ask yours," Luis said. "I don't understand. You kids are bizarre. Did you hear about the teenager that was shot on the tracks in Oakland? We're driving over to join the riots in the streets now. We're bringing police brutality to an end. You two in or do you have work tomorrow? We've had enough of the regime. We're taking them down tonight! Smash the police!"

He screamed at the ceiling and bolted through the doorway, hopping into a pickup truck double-parked on Mission Street.

"I used to work with him," she said. "That man's filled with theories. We started a book on the Spanish Civil War together. Margaritas always get me in the end; make sure I'm all right."

"And you do the same."

"We're all lazy bums," she said. William observed her black lace stockings while someone repeated another's demand for Herbsaint. Aromatic black licorice wafted through the aisle way. "No one's working or looking for work, just a party."

"What is the reason?"

"I don't know, do you? Also, wait—I don't care if you don't want to know my name, I want you to know my name. It is Melody; Melody Nelson. But go on: do you know the reason?"

"It is, in my mind," William said, summoning an obscure wisdom as if to prove her wrong, as if to admit that he found what she had said earlier offensive, "Basic if not elementary philosophical anecdote: Those in power without prior experience must spread falsehoods, blatant lies concerning those 'Below' them—often times the aforementioned being much more experienced on the specific topic at hand and co-dependents—in order to implement an authority which does not exist (Default); then for us, concerning capitalistic schizophrenia, technological fascism, ethical decay. So, a man in our disintegrating society with any sense of decency must move on and let fate have its way, for fate concerns one's impulses (A culmination of life lived, equalization by actualized individual-standards, divided by rationale). In such a case the next road, or plateau, is not at all empty but, precious—iridescent. Capitalism is schizophrenic. Do you understand?"

"You mean that one cannot even rebel against the source any longer?"

"What is the point? A man can live if he does not prescribe a thing to anyone. He is best off keeping to himself and his loved ones and his friends and to just not bother with much but sharpening the blade edge of his mind's eye. What revolution is there tonight? Men with guns going to Oakland? An anarchist bookstore that pays taxes? I have nothing against anyone—I've learned to not give anyone such credit—and I appreciate spirit and recourse, but are we still turning to the past in the face of a technological fascist police state? A crumb of the culture is set on a revolution that takes place upon a permanent tomorrow, the majority of it Hell-bent, obsessed, addicted to telling the world of its meanderings, convinced they are special having been brought up such a way, when in reality no one is special at all, addicted to the media of the insane. Corporate media is mental illness. The world is in flames and there is no revolution; the revolutionaries are as loathsome and paranoid as the politicians. The ascension of the individual is all that matters. For I am the atom-crusher of lukewarm coils, the cattle who believe anything, let alone everything, they read in digital corporate newspapers. I am the atom-crusher of lukewarm coils, the cattle who believe anything, let alone everything, they read in digital corporate newspapers. You'll see in time that your beloved social justice will itself end in the identical genocide and slavery its proponents ferociously claimed to disavow . . . They are convinced they know what they are doing, and thus have not the slightest clue. All of this genealogical morality leads exclusively to the holocaust of western civilization . . .

"Weep not at my tomb, but in the empty mirror of global technological feudalism that is to come, at humanity's hatred of reality!

"It is said that my forefathers go back to Josephus," continued William, a mysterious foot tenderly rubbing at his, "But then some terrible mishap transpired in a Hebraic theatrical response to Steinbeck some decades back, from which my poor father never recovered. His response to my poor mother's pregnancy was to promote his response to of mice and men; "Of Kikes and Cucks"; subsequently he went the way of Kate Croy's old man."

"Have you spoken to him recently?"

"The last time I had anything to do with him I was soaring head first out of his penis at the speed of light and into the arms of one of my mother's eggy weggs. Does that count?"

Melody smiled into her drink, making a little halo of salt atop an ice cube.

"Tomorrow we should go listen to the gospel singers at Union Square: 'Rejoice, you who overcome!' I mean, it could be fun."

But William started nodding off, thinking of Octavia, and the overhead music quieted. The bar was not closing, but a moment had come about all at once whereby the last ten patrons were indeed five hypothetically monogamous couples, each party involving a person three or four sheets to the wind, but surmounting a comeback. Thus William awoke:

"When your mind is set on earthly things alone, so it shall be singularly crushed."

"You said, in your sleep, to 'ask your beloved Octavia about the accord of love's measure, and its eternal Worth;' her name escaped your lips as you slept."

"I apologize. Today has been a long year." He retrieved a newspaper upon which to roll cigarettes, first looking down at the cover. "A violent weekend in Oakland, eh?"

"Yeah, I guess."

"You guess? Four innocents were beheaded, three people walking by the mosque shot to death, nine in critical condition, and a concert for young adults plowed through with a stolen eighteen-wheeler; eight total dead thus far."

"Don't be a bigot. That's not all of them. We don't have all the details yet."

But Melody's eyes were veiled by subconscious knowledge that she was regurgitating propaganda rather than making a point; if her body was a mind, its legs were now stumbling drunk, like Verlaine, Baudelaire, Huysmans; ground down at the mill of posthumous animalism, eyeless in Gaza. "Never mind. Let's get back to what we were talking about." She drank her margarita, savoring the taste, as if to express her process of absorbing the philosophies of William Fellows.

"Then what is your vehicle?"

"I am working on it."

"And in the mean-time?"

"Anarchy of the imagination."

He curtailed the political banter, that which comes about amidst forming relations over drinks when one person is trying hard to come off a way they are not, and the other person acknowledges this and sets out, egotistically, to destroy arguments he sees coming from all possible angles in one blow, as Eric Dolphy came on and everyone cheered up and decided to stay out all night.

"Well I had better get going after this drink."

"You are not even halfway done."

"But if I don't say it now then I'll want another after this."

"Do neither," William said.

"What do you mean?"

"When the bartender isn't looking, we'll take our margaritas and catch a cab to your place or my place."

"I live all the way out by the Sunset, by S.F. State."

"I've never been there."

"Where do you live?"

"Polk and Sacramento."

"How do you afford *that*—Well, alright then—Sure, we'll go to my apartment. We'll split the cab. Cheers, cheers," she smiled at last, pressing a folded piece of paper into his hand. William unfolded it, glossed in the light of a cupped pair of matches, *Les soleils mouillés/De ces ciels brouillés/ Pour mon esprit ont les charmes/Si mystérieux/De tes traîtres yeux/Brillant à travers leurs larmes.*

"Tomorrow we journey out to the waters of peace, walking toward the sunset, a cloud of smoke coming toward us. And even if we don't, it is at the least a fine thought."

William's eyes were inadvertently upon the sticky ground as Heaven called—a tender hand around, upon one's upper arm, beneath the shirt sleeve, encircling incantations and the discernment of aesthetic beauty.

15

BLINDING SMOKE IN NIGHTS deprived of every planet; mornings whereby clouds blended into fog atop the cliff, outstretched in the wood-shadowed haze of wine and hashish smoke forested days to rustic nights beyond the city limits, days bending together like the words of a lengthily brilliant conversation.

William met Heather in the Tenderloin for drinks. The reunited pair caught up at once and sat outside at a tin table reading the newspapers, zines, and John Keats. She'd run into El at Dolores Park who'd obtained William's address and left him the return letter beneath his door. Still, she explained to William, not even through familiar faces for whom the reign on intoxicated philosopher-kings had simply rerouted rather than upended, there was no word of Harold Smith and she awaited new room-mates at the house, which had been on strict watch since the incident, itself still veiled in some obtuse ambiguity which William decided he would give up on until running into Harold Smith again.

"No friends but best friends can go out and read together," Heather smiled, William looking into her eyes, outlining and underlining the best words, phrases, wisdom, leaning over one another's shoulders observing varied poetical treasures.

At dusk the words, like co-heirs to imaginative resurrection, melted aesthetically together. He ran his eyes along the fine print to no avail. In moments he could do nothing more than observe Heather out of the corner of his eye and recall looking down from the forestry of Muir Woods at noon some weeks back, the sun breaking through the microscopic city below between spaces of trees alongside trickling creeks. Each time he looked to Heather in her peacoat and leggings he wondered if he were in love. Each page of each magazine he read did not register. The sentences and paragraphs were not accumulating, surmounting, but slipping away. He gave up reading, looking to the sea, and recalled the way the formulaic Pacific mended with the clouds at a point, an image he could never forget, one he would always associate with Heather.

The shortest absence had made his heart grow fond; he should have said or done something upon the mountains, upon the midnight avenues and barstools.

With her he knew it was most difficult, however, because William could see himself staying with her a long time each time she laughed or told a tale. Hers was a voice one longed to hear for decades, for it was wrought by fond memories; it was just too unobtainable in its potential to lead to something constructive. He'd developed a dreadful fear of handing himself over to any woman and thought to begin combating such a disadvantage for the notion of bliss; he would be frank with her. She spoke first, through insatiable laughter, covering her mouth with one hand and pointing with the other to a group of senile men on Segways.

"Frivolity," she laughed, "Is an inheritance like no other."

Overcast, people-watching, several heated discussions concerning screens, or extended minds.

"I met this girl last night," William exhaled, "With whom I may carry on a strange, anonymous affair with. We don't even know one another's names."

Heather closed her book and leaned over the table:

"Oh! What is *she* like?"

It hurt him that she showed no sign whatsoever of jealousy.

"She speaks French and English, was born in France, and agrees we'll see one another and not have mutual friends for the sake of identity."

"Lucky!"

"I left her at sunrise as the fog was rushing through the Sunset," leaving out that he'd slept beside her in Dolores Park, also. "She lives somewhere around there."

"That is so excit*ing*!" She gripped William's shoulder. "I wish!"

Heather Daily, Heather Daily, were you not supposed to readjust the drawstrings of your yellow raincoat, let the hollow wooden handles click together, and tell William that that road went nowhere?

Heather reopened her book and skimmed through pages, inquired no further into the matter. William watched the crowds of people and the trolley cars pass along the street. The rain let up.

"Do you ever think," Heather said, tracing her long fingers across the grated black table-top, "That perhaps in this city people indulge a little too much? Just in other places it's not like this." The look in her watery eyes was that of having reflected upon autumn in New York City, a contagious idea that at once set alight some dormant memories within William's heart. "I mean, you know there's just, for the most part, that sort of disciplinary ethic there that incorporates itself into the daylight."

She looked around the terrace. Everyone was young and rosy and had a drink in hand amidst a cloud of smoke, waiters outpouring through side-entrances with steaming trays, strange liquid concoctions, fresh cakes interlaced with astounding hashish. Trolley bells rang out and children passing through sang indistinct songs with their blissful mothers, fathers, often one or the other, both.

"The Bay just doesn't seem like the type of place one comes to restore the cells of the memory bank," William announced. "Everything here is just simple and beautiful. It's not the sort of place to get much done but know that, and breathe, which is perhaps more important than anything. An elegant distortion sings like chimes in the air for me and I can't see much of a reason to bother with sobriety. The craziest people I've ever met in my life have been disciples of sobriety. Till I get back down to business I see no other way."

"It's all been so beautiful already," Heather sighed with a tint of triumph. William wiped a tear from her eye as the distant foghorn resounded once and again. She began to laugh. "I just don't remember all that much of it, the specifics. And we are so young!"

"It's OK," William said.

"Sometimes it worries me, though."

"Why?"

"Sometimes it all just seems so unreal."

"It is."

"And is that OK?"

"Of course. What is the other option, the idea of a sure grip on reality? That is impossible anyway."

"I knew it. I don't mind though."

"You could always slow down, of course, but then in a place like San Francisco one might be better off taking up photography than slowing down."

"How do you mean?" Heather scooted her chair closer to William in two metallic thrusts.

"All of the best things worth remembering are impossible to remember."

William leaned on her shoulder, memories falling through the bitter, filthy air, untying lace when back at home, thereafter untying ideological verticality, knots of wrath in the sense of a casing that death uncloaks, alcoholic afternoons and vagabonds blinded by smoke, seemingly far from the residential ruins of broken families, cultural destruction, stale style, animal violence and excoriating rejection, the types one who grew up on Lombard's *Sentences* seem to have glossed over in realizing, perhaps, that this geographical psychosis was less overcome than put off:

"The technological world is barren of every virtue, but not because it is the technological world; technological acceleration is simply bold underlining on the paragraph structure of life, pregnant with malice—we are all in the gutter, but never mind the stars; give us instead the cause of all this destruction, just the cause, so we can at least begin to fathom living in anything other than shadowy stupefaction. Yes, my dear Heather, they know Aristotle and Aquinas, and the litany of atheists, yes. But there are two types of philosophers, and the one that is inauthentic is also the one that is erected and finished in classrooms."

"Yeah," said a nearby drunk, "I was thrown outta SF State. It lacks both hunger and offers hollow theories where a firing squad would do much better! Yeah, yeah, you even read Deleuze and Guattari, and have recalled the cosmic foundations of city-building, of the archaic core of all technology, of the path upon which, for once, Rome and Augustine converge—swelling and enclosure is no longer your bedroom, and a poem no longer a naked person! The poem that is called the world is itself a swelling enclosure deserved of what is coming, which is desecration— you see where the road of pathological altruism leads, for all its political religion: excrement, disease, and needles!"

William sat astonished. Yet he did not want to get to know this man. He could not even bring himself to look at him. Identification of crisis is nothing, thought the pilgrim, if one does not follow that ever-present epistemological origin: *know thyself.*

"I don't know," said Heather, repeating herself, ordering two IPA.

Sunset was approaching; the disgraced academic returned to his cavernous corner, pulling at his graying beard and flipping through an indecipherable text. It seemed swell a time as any to profess his love. His heart rate rose, overlooking the couples come and go, and he took a last

good luck at Heather, with vivid recollection, and thus contradicting himself, the first night he met her. Even then he had seemed so much younger.

The waiter returned with their drinks. William looked into the suddenly tired eyes that met his own.

"I've got to get going after these," Heather said.

"Where to?"

"An old friend across town—I haven't seen him in years!"

He thought of his chance having been blown, or better yet, having
never existed. He erased the thought from his mind as if it were lead from
a sheet of paper.

"You've—you're not being yourself—didn't even—touched your
drink!"

"I'm going along," William said, placing an amiable hand upon his
chest.

"Lunch on Friday," she reminded him, before embracing and waving, disappearing into a cab. William drank his beer, leaving a dollar
bill on the table, and found it odd that she never spoke of Harold Smith
anymore.

He felt himself succumbing to an interiority of blinding smoke, and
retired home for bed.

16

GRANT STREET WAS AN extensive day each Friday although time passed
when one expected an anonymous French mistress to arrive, or appear, at
any moment. William changed from his cloak into peacoat, and now had
his hair trimmed at the barber shop on Hayes and Octavia, there where
the moist, thick vapors begin to thin out, the sphere of the sun shines
weakly through them, and the city of orgies lies ahead afresh with all the
potency and act of a summer weekend in the Bay.

Alas, she did not arrive. William began to wonder if he'd dreamt the
whole nocturnal reemergence out on Mission Street.

"No, no," Alison laughed on break at the Gold Dust Lounge. William bought two rounds of afternoon screwdrivers to compliment Alison's Fernet. "She was there alright, she comes around, but isn't she so
mischievous!"

There was little to do but listen to KUSF, con each foreign customer
for amounts of money so audacious the customer felt foolish to argue
and make out with a hundred dollars at most before cashing the Wednesday check and walk home, or anywhere in the pale afternoon sunlight
of Stockton Street with five-hundred dollars in your pocket. Rain was
rumored to arrive but not until much later as he set off from the Union
Square garage for another free three days. First, however, the lunch that
had become an after-work cocktail in Soma.

"I need a break from the Mission," Heather had explained earlier,
paying William a visit in a brand-new aquamarine dress which caused
near-pain in its subtle beauty beneath winter coat. For the first time in
years the pilgrim found himself forced to lean in ways that covered up his
second standing; only now that he was a little older and wiser it seemed
less anonymous than obvious. "I find the same people in the same bars
doing and talking about the exact same thing: Nothing."

Such was recognition of that earlier allure, she went on to explain, of the christening-process of their last duchess on the wall, the lost city. After some months, however, this realization of agonizing, almost sad repetition drained itself of prior convenient, wondrous qualities of vintage disco lights and graying DJs. All at once, she explained, the Mission had come to garnish itself in despair akin to meeting a major politician or celebrity in person, but without the redemptive value afterward of an autograph.

"You know that boy I met the other night?"

"You had mentioned," William offered, concealing his pain.

"We went to a party where it was made clear no one was in it to make it big. That was the topic of conversation. Then you get any of them alone, and guess what! It's enough to make Spinal Tap seem as if a serious film!"

"Oh, come on. That's hideous. How was the show?" William took a Punjabi Panorama and threw it at a flock of seagulls while traffic police blew silver whistles in the reflection of turning double-decker buses. Exhaust shot into the afternoon air.

"It was fair. I should have invited you."

"I don't do live music. I never understood the point."

"You had mentioned."

"I had?"

"Earlier in the summer one night."

"Oh," William said, looking away. "I must have forgotten."

Heather laughed, extracting sunlight from the grayest skies, her image coy and precious. William concluded:

"I suppose at the end of the day I would rather go in the shower than watch live music. I've just never been interested in the concept."

On the long, cool back porch just off Howard Street they drank and discussed recent, past days. Someone had carved "Nilsson Schmilsson" into the wooden post. William smiled.

"I've got El and Daniel coming by the apartment for a moving-in party tomorrow night, but not much else. Of course, later on—"

At once Heather seemed despondent and did not touch her drink. Her precious face seemed caught between an emotional breakthrough and an emotional breakdown. She spoke of how her old friends had let her down, and how she missed Harold Smith and worried about him.

"I try not to think of it all that much—he'll be fine. If anyone would be!"

"But William you don't walk by his empty bedroom every day. The house is so sad and you're not even allowed to come around because then I'll get thrown out."

She explained that sadder still was the mechanical nature with which her old friends spoke and lived, and saddest of all was she knew she could never live such a way again. Some sort of psychological barrier had been crossed within her mind, and unless she found a way to deconstruct her intellect, she would remain on the permanent other side of the psychological fence and consider herself different than most people, or as if nothing could satisfy her any longer.

"Of course," she added ruefully, "This is because I want what I cannot have; I have no interest in things such as discussing sports and the sneakers of passersby! Wanting what you can't have—Life's one true consistency!"

"I agree with the prior though not the latter," William said. "You must admit that if you can't judge a person by their shoes then you cannot judge them at all."

"I'm not always so confident!" Her eyes lit up. "The possibility of moments—for life is at its finest when we are unconscious of it!"

She pressed her hands across her dress, flattening any rumpled area. William looked away from her legs wearing a false smile, bad childhood memories entering his mind.

"What do you think of when you look away like that?"

"Not always the same thing, though not anything, I suppose. What happened to Harold?"

He knew by now through Nielsen that Walter had brought heroin to the house, spilled some near old Harold Smith's bedroom door, and happened to be walking in through the front door as Saul bent down to sniff it from the ground. Harold pulled a knife on him and there was a drugged, drunken brawl.

He inhaled her apricot perfume, its distinctive scent the one to render William useless.

"He'll be fine," she said, changing the subject. "You must be thinking of something!" She placed her cold index finger to his temple and rubbed for a moment; he felt as if he were being touched by a girl for the first time.

"It's just a shame that human principles seem to shatter universal realities and vice-versa. Everything is a mess when you start thinking that way." Memories of autumn walks with his poor old mother whom he had not spoken to in months rushed through him and he found solace in that Heather could detect budding melancholia at once, for if he were to act unnatural around her she knew at once whereas with almost everyone else in the world a flowing naturalism was, pondered the pilgrim, impossible to attain, for it is detected with fear and cut down with the self-turned switchblade of useless dialogue. He had returned so intensely to thought that when her voice pried him back again, she was at the bar, the robust leather-coated man pouring three shots of whiskey, shouting:

"One's on me! You two together?"

The bearded man placed the bottle of Powers back on display, its dampened glass reflecting colorless across aluminum kegs and trash cans.

"We're married!" Heather laughed, throwing her arm around William's shoulder.

"Well hey," said the bartender, casting his small, beady eyes and goatee upon the hands: "Where the damn ring is?"

"We don't believe in that sort of thing—isn't marriage just the truth that you'd rather be around one person more than anyone else in the world?"

"Then to both of you!"

All the madmen and madwomen from dimmed booths and urinals chanted behind their tilting heads:

"Ay!"

They roamed through downtown streets, alleys, cafes and bars all through the beatific night, stumbling into Market Street, still at 2:00 in the morning. Thin layers of mist hissed upon the gravel beneath passing buses and taxis. A streetcleaner hosed down the sidewalks as William and Heather ducked beneath the high, long marble entranceway of the Orpheum Theatre.

"We ought to get a cab—there's one—"

"I've changed my mind, I don't want to go home yet," yearned Heather, watching sheets of soaps water rush past the streetlamps. "Let's let this pass and keep walking, it's so nice outside."

"Where?"

"Oh I know," she said, "You don't have to come along. Are your bones tired?"

"Just everything around here is closed down now," William said. "It's been too pleasant, mellow an evening for me to even fathom hitting an after-hours place."

"We don't have to buy anything—I mean just stay outside and enjoy the end of summer." She pulled back her dampened hair and stood beside William, looking up at him, "I just get so cold standing here."

"I know," he said, opening his jacket with his pocketed hands and letting her cave in. He felt her uncovered breasts upon his chest, his ribs, his steady-beating heart. He closed his eyes and leant back against the doorway. A distant mob screamed and laughed, breaking the silence of the night, laden car horns railed on, either one dissolving, like smoke from a shaken match.

Heather sighed, setting her hands across William's chest, then beneath his shirt, as he wrapped her in his coat.

"Let's go now," she said, pulling away and taking William by the hand to the streets of evaporated rain, of transparent steam. "I have to show you something." Her voice took on that sort of tone which ex-lovers can but ever hear in memory, as she began to gain momentum, jogging ahead with William racing just behind her, his fleeting mind bewildered and wandering as he held her hand and looked amongst the dozens of towering buildings in absolute silence around them.

She let go of his hand as William asked where they would go, racing up the gleaming desolate stretch of Market Street's rows of bricks beneath dim chains rattling with sudden bursts of wind like field recordings of an arctic, transitory spasm.

Vague clouds traced the autumn sky and through the glowing, crescent moon as Heather stepped in and out of a closing bodega. She returned spinning through the doorway, a half-pint of brown-bagged Old Grand Dad in her hand.

All the way to marvelous Dolores Park their eyes did not meet, she one, two steps ahead, racing to some unknown horizon. The night seemed hallucinatory in its dampened stillness, the park ahead containing cloaked and captive means and ends of channeling fog and detonating sprinklers. There was no sound at all for curving blocks but that of dampened leaves rustling upon one another, the quickening clicks of heels upon the slick brick ground, as William pondered whether this was the summer's end in earnest, an event beyond calendrical invectives, or Heather Daily was rather too high to care, or legitimately lost, but then the thought was released like a receipt from seven months ago out into the garbage can of the past, and all the seasons save the instant were but consecrated urns in concept-being.

At the peak of Dolores Park William lay down his coat. They sat beside one another in the cold near-morning and watched distant, microscopic cars cross the Bay Bridge beyond spectral-arrays of lights of downtown's skyscrapers and fluorescent bulbs. William began to hiccup.

He looked ahead holding in his breath and felt Heather's eyes upon him once more. He knew now, at last, the near future held the long-awaited golden aura of passion he had always dreamt concealed within her love. He would either make love to her and never see her again or make love to her and stay beside one another always. All the poppies in Afghanistan couldn't slow his heart.

She laughed at his hiccups as he looked ahead over the city, the darkened sloping hills of the park and interjecting sprinklers, thinking, 'All of lust begins this way; with this unreal moment,' and at last turned his mouth to Heather's, hand upon her yellow raincoat.

Only when he turned inward, he found, upon opening his eyes, Heather gazing ahead, unconscious of his proximity. If she had not looked so serious as mercurial clouds raced past at expeditious rates, as though Ms. Daily was literally hypnotized, he would have touched her face.

"Did you ever notice," she said, "That I don't do drugs?" She took a long sip from the bag and wiped her lips dry with her wrist, with an expressionless gesture passing the bottle to William. She pulled the front of her dress down to reveal tattooed, luminous flames upon a familiar-looking plate, a familiar script, a familiar archangel figurine. The detail of the drawing, the inscription, was astonishing, and William studied it.

"Have you ever read William Blake?"

"No."

"This is a poem of his, a plate he'd drawn. My parents read him to me as a child." She wiped mist from her forehead, upraising her dress, looking ahead, somewhere between reflective and focused, swallowing, as the moonlight bathed her blonde hair. William felt caught within a lucid dream, sensing white shapes around him, conscious of galaxies burning beyond that tranquil moon, colossal shadows spilled and frozen beneath them amidst the shades of San Franciscan night.

The veiled anxiety within her voice was that which prompted William's and he tried to switch the subject for fear of further panic and destruction of the moment:

"How about Harold, any—"

"William," Heather said, "Cannot we focus on our conscience, our own actions? Isn't that enough? I'm trying to tell you something."

She seemed to drink herself into sobriety, refusing to look any which way but to the city skyline. Her lips trembled:

"But they're in prison now, my parents. I never told you that. They threw drug parties when I was a child—the morning of the last one I woke up from a bad dream and there was a man I never saw before, his face blue and white, hanging from a noose. I was so scared I could not scream, nor move, nor close my eyes. His body was a blur as I fainted. The police told me later on that he had taken some hallucinogen but I remember screaming, the image of his hanging body, and nothing else."

Her words were like fragmented memories of a dream in the morning as a tear fell from William's eye to think of her as a child, and to think of a child in such a way; he felt as if such a child, and could neither move nor say anything; his hiccups stopped, and the tone of Heather's voice became trembling and sorrowful, resonant of a life altered and destroyed by one distinct memory, and William took a leaf from his pants-cuff—leaves, scattered like some Homeric children unto men.

"And do you remember what you said the night we met out on the porch? The idea concerning life, modern life? You spoke of always knowing emptiness and in past years beginning to grasp, to breathe the everyday life of hopelessness—emptiness, of course, provoking difficulties while hopelessness, of course, provokes madness. Emptiness will keep you moving, will make you unable to sit still. Hopelessness will subtract you from life and deliver you to either complete artistry or complete despair. You either do God's will, however brutal, or you spend your days knowing you're not doing so, and die from it. There are no longer results but equations. The hopelessness of location becomes then, in turn, the hopelessness of the universe. In which case we either crack, die, or create another universe of our own. That art which everyone shouts about in bars and basements, that art is nothing but bars and smoky basements. Real art, I'm coming to find, is beyond a matter of convincing, of conviction—it is a matter of ethereality. There are no classroom lectures but infinite futilities." She lost track of her words, drank more, appeared as if unwilling to detest or acknowledge her last comment, drank again, and spoke over the sprinklers. "It begins with traveling until you realize that the soul doesn't care where it is, for the soul is always inside of the body, the hallucination of the mind. So we either turn on the TV, join the army, of let the internal fire come out of us, you know! That's what this tattoo means—it's not a compliment from some drunken man when he takes me, it's not some appealing picture, William! It is an imitation of life and the impossibilities of the transitions.

"There aren't any small pleasures in life, William, just the blind circuitry of chaos. So, while you're a wonderful boy," she draped her arm across his shoulder once more as he listened, offended and entranced,

"You'll always be a bit too young for me, and besides, where do you think all of this life is going to get you, anyway? You're all just racing to breaking away from the real, and I've had enough—I want to indulge in the real." She smashed the bottle of whiskey against a pillar; they descended the grassy slope.

"But I came forth from that cloud into its rays, already extinguished on the lowest shore," said William, as they stopped mid-street. Before them a sort of installation: a wooden staircase that a dozen of so steps rose no further, nor even had a platform to reach.

"I don't get it."

"Maybe it's the artist's idea of love."

"How so?" asked Heather.

"Natural love is always unerring, but the other can err with an evil object or with too much or too little vigor. Hence, a staircase in the middle of the road."

"I still don't get it. I was thinking something about evil pleasure. It says evil on one step and pleasure right there."

"Perhaps it means that because love can never turn its face away from the well-being of its subject, all things are safe from self-hatred."

"No, I see a love born in Aurelian slime, or even old crossed-eyed Sartre at the end of narcotized rampage: subjugation, grips of power, injured and insulted—that which flows after the good with a corrupted order."

"But then it is too an abrupt emblem of object-culture, and the eternal recurrence of goods that do not make one happy; if they did," concluded William, "brainwash would be unnecessary, addicted to that chemical compound of stupidity and exaggeration."

"Perhaps their hearts are restless, till they rest in Him."

Heather and William sat on a nearby bench until the sun rose red across the dreaming Bay. The birds came out. All that made sense was that sense not asked to be defined. Trains rushed through.

The pilgrim's eyes were exhausted, burning when he fell asleep upon the floor, Heather sound asleep in the bed.

She was gone in the afternoon when he awoke, and it was such a shame to end things so that were never to happen by saying them aloud. As if to further explain herself, and her need to move on, she left the raincoat upon his coat rack. A part of William wanted to thrash it, another part wear it himself, but he felt unable to do either and let it dry out, slanted, upon the windowsill.

He found her thoughts fascinating, her body precious, but it was too human to have to sever things off in such awkward movements. He knew he would never see her again and began to look ahead, his mind as transient as the lost souls he had encountered out west, and those who had encountered him.

He remained astonished for a long time that she had recited Augustine like that.

17

HALF A CASE OF Three Thieves wine, a crate of Bass, crushed grains of morphine piled upon a distant mirror, the open window of a tranquil Saturday night as the air brushed through William's new Venetian blinds.

"This includes everything," Daniel explained with a twirl of his mustache, "From oral sex received to strange requests from the taxi-cab to the old regular heave-ho. Few, quite few of the encounters I regret, because regret is a vice worse than all others." William felt high just listening to Daniel speak while overlooking the collection of good books, records, bottles, empty orange cylinders and half a carton of American Spirits. His little radio relayed nearly inaudible baroque music. Blue smoke turned to the whistling wind from between Phil's middle and ring fingers; he too grinned, captivating by Daniel's thoughtful vocal tone regarding his completed list of sexual conquests. "But at the end of the day love, trust, relationship is the key. That is what I long for in my masquerades, I believe. But good God, that Heather today, that woman is gonna wind up dead."

William sat upright in shock:

"What do you mean?"

"Just ripping through cocaine."

"Oh."

"She said she hadn't slept in days. Well at least she seemed that way when I saw her at the cafe today. Maybe she's not actually on drugs. Maybe she is just insane."

"She was filled with wisdom last night," William said, then realizing he could not convince himself to care enough to continue.

"There must be a new philosophy, a new something to believe in," El said. "Sometimes I laugh just when my tears have been exhausted. No," he shook his head, "Never-mind that. I don't believe that at all. It has been a long few weeks is all."

"How so?"

"I don't know. I've got to snap out of it though."

"Here is how you do it," said William, stamping out a Cuban cigar.

He stood tall and poured himself a tumbler of Powers; dropping an ice-cube into the cocktail glass he stirred the mixture with an unsharpened pencil. Placing the drink down upon the windowsill he filled a small mason-jar with wine. He poured a bottle of Bass into a tilted pint glass and let it settle. First—in two gulps—he took the whiskey. He took the red wine in as a shot. Then in a few synchronized gulps he took down the ale, replacing the glasses alongside the others upon the desk, wiping his beard clean, unbuttoning all but the last button of his denim shirt.

"That is how it's done," he said.

El and Daniel followed suit once, then twice, and the three were engaged in a warm banter of recent passive tales and philosophies. At some point in the collage of brilliant conversation El crossed his left leg over the right; and a fire burned in his eyes.

"Now may appear to you, my brothers, how hidden the truth is from those who claim every form of love to be itself a noteworthy, praiseworthy thing, and how this disease has—among other things—decimated our heritage. I met a lady like a waxen seal, who said to me, 'I am two decades pregnant with doubt'—such is the crooked timber of humanity.

"Yes," said El, "But that is not all. Indeed I have myself as of late partaken in a most potent form of self-reflexivity."

"What is it?" asked Daniel.

"Have I ever mentioned 'Mustard' to either one of you?" Cohen spoke through tusks of smoke.

"We have not spoken at any length of mustard, I believe," said William, "Although perhaps at an earlier, violent hour as brethren of the common life you did mention this Mustard; in fact, just in recent years I've adapted—"

"No, no, comrade; I mean the man called 'Mustard.'"

"I know not a man called 'Mustard.'"

"Nor I."

"Do you mind if I engage, or," relighting a cigarette as William smoked from Daniel's pipe, reminiscent of the last of some morphine-laced blend, "Or shift the conversation in another way? He may be no Walter Benjamin, no Robert Walser, but this Mustard is an obscure worthy philosopher in his own right. And he is much more important than any charlatans and all their degenerate precepts being glorified now based less on intellectual innovation than proximity to genetic or genital defect in our recalcitrant institutions, or in a word the unfathomable depths of that ill-cloaked synagogue of Satan being plumbed, being pathologically dodged in global academic circles at this very moment."

"This 'Mustard' seems as if an uncanny fellow. Who is he? Where does he reside?"

"He resides in the memory of my mind," El hankered. Daniel and William leaned in to listen to the ominous tale. A foghorn resounded through the street. El cleared his throat.

"Now let me bless this room, in the name of my rabbinical father, and the rabbis who taught us. First, William, with Octavia thou shalt move from concept to union. You told me, beyond midnight, when my phone had passed away, that that which is substantial is distinguished from the base metal of matter albeit joined to it; it is both recognizable and imperceptible."

"That I said," stood the pilgrim. "That within each of us . . . within you is the power of counsel, itself capable of guarding against the threshold of assent. Though I've got my Plotinian partiality, let us acknowledge that Plato, Aristotle, and the pre-Socratic pagans penetrated basic moral principles," he said, pointing downward, El up, Daniel crouching together with the boy sages. "As through one window you see some withered old man in a tub beside them, hallucinating Alexander the Great, you see another to whom it is known that your base desires deserve neither praise nor blame but discredit—convergence and repetition as love arises alongside both necessity and your power to restrain it. That reality is shaped like a copper bucket still on fire, atop a cemented hill, while the great crowd below transforms from a single-file lunge to the disorienting breakup of sudden running—ye make grace grow green!"

"There are still monasteries?" Daniel said.

"I have officially lost track of what I am saying," said William. "I meant to render a prolegomenon to Mustard; I suppose until the sun itself breaks down that all this is just transmuted thinking into dream. Please, now I shall smoke my pipe in peace."

"Well, William, thee I thank—even if I grasped ten percent of what thou hast said, it'll have been worth it. But yes, let us return for a change to mysticism, my brethren: more in Woodside, Queens is where I began to reflect at length upon the man. It was a time I'd been out East with my sister some years back in the dead of winter. It was the first time I'd ever been to New York, to Manhattan.

"While there I took up volunteering in a used bookstore on Crosby Street. We were there to see my sister's high school love, a designer in SoHo, and because the two of us had had enough of the world at that point in time. We got in her car and began driving, driving as fast as we could. While one slept the other drove and vice-versa throughout all the American landscape. In four days of steaming black coffee and the piercing chill of the land we arrived in New York.

"I speak little of the land itself because it would be erroneous of me to claim I remember much of it. I was so absorbed in disappearing, breaking away from the complacencies of warfare, two bars in town, jobs which led to nowhere, stability and wealth which had both turned out to be grandiose optical illusions routed in fear, fixed in death. We opted for life and were given life, in the baron winter of ye old Manhattan."

El crossed his right leg over the left, inhaling. William dimmed the old triangle lamp to add effect.

"Manhattan took us by storm. It was no northern California suburb; of that I was sure. My sister met up with her high school love; I was assigned to his sister's apartment in the ghetto of Queens. She was a kind-hearted obese gal with peg-leg and mustache and ate pastrami sandwiches. I fell in love with her, yea, though alas, it did not happen. I roamed the streets at night against her warning, taking in that ancient scent of oil-laden abandoned lots and mountains of garbage bags torn apart by the hands of famine. I awoke the first morning feeling ill at ease, listening to rigatoni music—or whatever it is called—breaking through the walls, a woman moaning with pleasure for hours. The man grunted as the bedpost smashed against paper-thin walls and after lacerated, sleepless hours I still could not fall asleep. Manhattan seemed so far away; I tell thou.

"Ye Daniel, ye Bill, I tell you now of this tale, this pursuit, in acknowledgement of our current friendship amidst Saint Francisco and I exaggerate none; one who must exaggerate will never preface his tales, and let them run rampant with sheer disregard for respect. Here now I profess to relay thee the simple tale of Mustard, a tale which I always found accordance with the oceanic wind of summer's end in beauty and in simplistic scope, as the air is everything at once and unseen. Now, without asking, I may assume I've made myself clear; thus I shall bring thy tale; east, west; vice, versa.

"It was a quiet day in Manhattan by the time I got out of the subway, quiet and still as bronze. I'd eaten a knish at Yonah Schimmel on Houston

Street and from there I intended on a long, solitary walk of thought up to the Mid-Manhattan library, a good five avenues and 49 blocks to the northeast, nay, northwest.

"But just at the other side of the street I stepped through a mountain of snow onto cold, black liquid which had been so still I tell ye I thought it was a patch of sidewalk! Alas, with one foot frozen and soaked and surrounded by a hundred lunatics passing each which way through blanketed mazes of oral vapor, I took to hopping upon me left foot just out of sight—lo and behold, ye cruel city, yea, capital of the universe of death—I made it through the stampede of Europeans, students, hobos, models, and plop! Me hobbling, hopping left foot surmised in a patch of cement in the snow and went down and beneath black, frozen waters again, as I limped south amongst railings and frozen posts at once fearing that mischievous, harrowing merchant of hypothermia.

"Stark laughter broke through unseen mouths, passing in high-pitched radio-program giggles. For a fuming moment I reached for my blade and was going to end it all over one or two of them along Houston Street as my feet froze to the bone; an incensed rage overcame me when I turned back to witness the parallel grotesqueness of the voices and the faces from which they fell. Then I thought of a tinsel discount store I'd passed on Ludlow Street and limped through the cold, ashen-wet winds through shadows of buildings dragging one boot along, then the other, straight through to Delancey.

"For a dollar I bought two pairs of thick, wool socks. I pulled one of the other as the fabric strands intersected through my dampened, peeling skin, creating a violent itch cast off by numbness. The tenement sky stood still before me, blackened by years of cast-iron sequences of lost illusions, my fingers stretching through the holes in my gloves.

"To my left stood the Williamsburg Bridge, its red divided grid looming over frozen waters, its entranceway held by the clouds and appearing as if one passed over the bridge en route to some invisible world. Dim, blinking lights pressed on to the beat of one thousand constant automobiles, cyclists, walkers, the distant rumbling of the JMZ which just had cut underground. The American flag waved above the vast Axelrod; as if magnetized I felt myself drawn to the structure.

"But as thou hath heard thus far, 'twas no day of easy succession, nor success of any type save my fleeting, candid observations of lower Manhattan. Brooklyn had called my name though, alas, nay did I make it to her widened arms although that isn't to say I did not try to cross the bridge on that brutal, wintry day.

"Yea, beyond the waters below which thrashed savage beneath the sky's unexpected splitting in half, revealing a duplicated gray sheet of infinite silence. At the tip of the first ramp I placed my fleeting hand to the red rods and reflected upon the ceaseless soundtrack rumbling above, beneath, around me, that consistent rumbling of Manhattan—and I realized, dear friends, just making out the Domino Sugar Factory, that in my walk of miles, thousands of sets of eyes, I had made eye contact with my detractors. A profound sense of futility gripped me upon the bridge. The women were built either like hippopotamuses or tacks! The men staggered and strutted past studying the void of the ragged sidewalk entrenched with ice. The city around me seemed as if the Inferno; the rumbling of a passing train reminded me of fissures in the earth, of the ground opening wide and swallowing my conscious observation of life whole! Skeletons pushed strollers as portentous angular chrome towered overhead! Ye inhuman maze of skyscrapers, what karmic furor!

"I, gentlemen, was still neither in awe nor fear. 'Twas the strangest of notions, one just beyond alphabetical delirium, linked to that occasional sleep paralysis—for I could not move nor admit I was awake, and yet I wanted nothing more than departure as the fierce winds sucked tears clean from my reddened eyes, like vultures plucking at the heads of wild game!

"Heat surged through me blood! No one around I was not dead! Ye faces had absorbed the unfathomable horrors of sensical lead, of mental vomit, ye brain city rioting! To look healthy upon that day, that momentary grip of madness was to appear engaged within some evil masquerade! I stood overlooking the architecturally coal-gray matrimony as hail felt to the land, clicking off the concrete and the windshields at once. I felt the color flush away from my face like nameless water down a rotted well!

"Thus, I broke free from my horror at last, the sobering clicks of hail breaking my arm from the iron of the bridge. I began walking faster and faster down the ramp, my eyes fixed upon nothing but the chaotic void in front of me; human beings became plasticine barriers to either ram shoulders with or carve around and nothing more. I forged ahead spitting out the sweat that dropped to my dried lips from my forehead. My feet ached but were coming to terms with it. I longed to have such a nonissue as slight pain, an itch, on my mind at that point, ye brethren! I raised my battered hands to haunted brow, my somnambulistic stride of sore shoulder-blades blanketed nigh, ye brethren, nigh! The hour was nigh I say as I stepped—"

"Phil!" shouted William, as by this point in the tale Phil had taken to smashing the smoke alarm with a hammer, crying out in choruses on the streets below, stomping his feet in a stampede, "Please, please, relax!"

"No, no!" he shouted, before sitting down in the chair once more, sighing, crossing his leg over the other.

"I thought this was a tale about a man, about ye mustard man!"

"'TIS!"

"One must be virtuous," Daniel recited with his hand over his heart. "Now, El, continue on, please; whenever you are ready, sing thy allegorical song!"

El crossed his leg over the other, cleared his throat, parted his hair to the side, and through a filter of swaying smoke refrained, while William and Daniel leaned in even closer than before, William closing his window halfway as outside the night became wild:

"Smokestacks, diamonds, the black heavens, champagne; morphine, embers, lemon peels. Though battery-ram iron, Manhattan, and death to the happy face, someday we shall all no longer exist! No city, no I, no thee; as I am of my own death, I am positive of that, of the death of everything! We come from nothing and crumble beneath the flames of disassociation!

"Now, now, now as I stepped forth past the broken teeth of passersby, limousines carving through ash-pools of puddles, cross-eyed men ruined with the weight of loneliness, their bald unwrapped heads banging against aluminum gutters while the savage winds of ye frozen Hudson river water barrels forth some condemned frost of the shattered milky-way; one by one any beauty in the city—it all fell from my sight; pale horror ran its course. All of life was unfathomable, or the essence of manifestation, and what little was fathomable on this planet was but varietized prostitution.

"Buildings began to go up in choking, roaring flames. Children screamed in the street. The young and the wealthy and prosperous could find no cabs. Cars ran off the road and through fences. Helicopters commanded action, the navy was on its way. Spasms of sun-orange, gas-blue fire wavered in the brutal ardor of the wind. I turned my cap down past my eyes and walked through the Inferno; I no longer had control of myself; a hallucinatory panic-attack that would not lessen. I said a silent prayer, O brothers, the damned foxholes! Eternity shown its deconstructed face through muted tiers of a savage, physiological Armageddon; glass panes burst like bombs, shards sparkling across the excoriated sidewalk. All the snow had been melted to puddles, the puddles lacerated to thickened, tasteless wreckage.

"Overridden with delirium, hallucination, I stopped into a bamboo storefront for a dish of sake. I was met with a savage skeleton whose teeth bled green light, whose body smelt, wreaked of copper. My memory underwent blackout.

"I cavaliered out onto Canal Street and Eldridge, and the hail had ceased. The quiet, rundown part of Eldridge stood still. I attained levels of calmness. Solace overcame me. All was well, for seconds—

"Then a hand gripped my shoulder. I cannot convey the terror I felt at that moment in any justifiable language. I felt as if a demon, or some sort of possessed form had its hand on me; I looked down, discreet—half a thumb was missing. The hand was human, its plump thumb cork-like. I then turned around, my brethren, expecting the climax of a nightmare to unfold; instead I turned around to see a patron saint in the abstract descent of it all: Mustard. He stood at a powerful 5'3, the body of a brick. He wore a stained smock and his black hair was caught in disarray, comparable to the spokes of a wheel.

'lo, he said. Hi you now. Me Muhstd.

Who?

I Mustard. Hi you now. 'lo, 'lo!

O, said I, with the relief of money, A pleasure to meet thee.

You loo' nerv. You OK.

I been thinking a lot. Me head spinning with thought.

La-la-la, laughed Mustard. His smock was covered in sauces and sweat, his trousers torn at boot-end to shreds. His trunk-like arms came together triangular to light a bent cigarette. He was balding, I noticed, his face filled with an accidental wisdom. He smiled with yellow-cracked teeth. The Inferno began to subside. Sweat broke less, less from my brow.

I make big dumping now. You no tink too much. Get belly full. We go be OK. You look at ground I see. Nothing on ground.

May I ask thee a question?

Ya-ha, exhaling a thick stream of smoke.

What is meaning? And what is your meaning to life?

He grinned and began to send his half-thumb back and forth like a speedometer.

He-he-he, Mustard laughed. Hoo-hoo-hihi. Mean! Look at tum! We live! Eat fooh, mah fine wife, ha, I know-know! May go to when I die, he said, extending an arrow of an to the forming blue sky. Life mean live; more ask questions less you know, he-he-he, you muss lih, seize day, seize t'day!

I have been depressed. I left me heart in San Francisco. My sister expects me to stay here but I'm depressed.

New Yaw awways be he! Go see!

I shan't leave my sister behind, though, man!

Yun man, lissen me, en lissen goo.

Yes, said I.

Children ran through the streets, screaming as the sun stretched out across the city, reflecting once more upon each bit of chrome, glass, aluminum, water, memory.

You cann do, you caann' pease er'one. Follow heart. Me? I go home on boat thih weekenn. No'ne know but me and my wife. She China.

Why you go, man, why you leave me so soon?

I come lass yea' f' mun-ay! Da money ain dah good! Why stay depress! Da worl' is da worl'! Fo you, me! He! Ha-ha-ha! Hoo-hoo! La-da-da! He-he-he! We eat big now, sad man! You big sad man! Ha-ha-he!

My sorrows are not a game! I cried out, pushing away his hand.

You big dumb! I know one to know one! Ha! No see wife in year! What you do! He-he-he-he!

"The feast, gentlemen, was beyond memorable, beyond epic proportions. We spoke of our lives over sake and dumplings until midnight. Mustard told folklore tales and waved his half-thumb in the light of the moon. His brother got him the job at a little tin shack, and my favorite dumpling joint bar-none, Prosperity Dumpling. It is a place of saints.

We walked out to the subway train.

Wa now, said he. Big poo poo n seep. He-he-he-he-he.

Going back to Queens, said I, woefully.

He smiled, walking backwards, descending the stairs.

He! Ha-ha-ha! He-he-he-he-he! Sleep night! Hoo-hoo-hoo! La-la-la! Ha-ho! Sleepy night! He-he!

"But herein lies the strangest part of this advent, dear sirs. The last two weeks of my most metropolitan February advent consisted of mornings in Woodside, afternoons in the Village (East, West, the Heavens through), and every so often an evening in SoHo. Often, I'd get a candy bar and a pint of bootleg rum from ye olde Woodside bodega, Happy Happy—ye know the name, the place, the element?"

"Yes," William nodded, smoking through the lamp-light, "Yes indeed I do." William lost his mind with excitement.

"Nay," decried Daniel, "Nay."

"Railroad tracks rumble overhead the bodega. Fireworks burst through the streets in streams of sparks crackling across the icicle-granite sheets in the dead of night. Crumbling factories bellow smoke like compressed chimneys, down white smoke from a grated plastic. Distant sirens crackle and dissolve, like wood clad in old-fashioned brick furnaces.

"In the midst of my long nights within the big woman's guest bedroom I listened to her carve pastrami as the lovebirds had their way above, yea, and no less than two-dozen times did I fear the ceiling fan would break down and lacerate my worn jugular! Men, 'twas oblivion in a townhouse! Men, 'twas anyway the circumspective circumstances of which ye narrator began at last to contemplate our hero, ye Saint Mustard!

"But first, a question—What is that feeling in the night, brethren, when one feels defeated before a search engine, and the relentless wind howls through, and one is feeling defeated and yet, yet! Once the sound of rain had that beatific quality, that sobriety which pours down on one serene and yet depressant, and ah, no, no avail! Such a mind was I whence I undertook recollection, and such a mind was I whence I stepped forth to the light of the revered.

"From there I experienced two weeks of New York bliss. I felt intoxicated just walking upon the streets I'd once found unfathomable once I'd grown accustomed to them. Even as I dashed off postcards, I felt pity for those not with me, in my lonesome hour, in Manhattan! Where else could one be! Broadway, Columbus, 14th Street in the morning! I took my coffee, my tea, my whiskey. I laid three prostitutes with borrowed money! Whom could be happy with a job, none near happy as I to roam the Brooklyn streets in love with life, snowfall and barroom intermissions, breaking up the game of life like sand through an hourglass! Ye worked for the filthy rich, in the overture of some agonizing year to obtain a fifty-cent raise and new television sets within the paradoxical gambit! Not I! I walked penniless and fell in love at each corner.

"When times grew tough, I smoked arrowhead tobacco and auburn weed along Allen Street, Front Street in that dam of frost, hiking through slush. Wise I, me bought goulashes, hunter's boots! He and ha! No season to stop me now! Each conscious New York City moment the internal, external observatory! Each conscious parade of lucidity of oh, brethren pardon I! I done me in a moment and yet I'm just at the climax of ye tale! Let me pause, please and pardon, let a man bow out of life!"

Phil Cohen relit his cigarette and overlooked the city below, beyond. Daniel and William tilted their head to the window, all the while observing Phil's fierce concentration; comradeship sifted through the air of the room like the breaking news of some strenuous mammalian sin having been absolved.

"Truth of the matter, ye gentle folk, is I met Mustard quite in a peeping-tom matter. When all grew lousy with my sister and the young woman I'd been staying with, I had sayeth to myself, 'Tally-Ho,' and began to awaken from the crooked couch at dawn. It was a tad bit lighter on the ears, you see, to sleep away from the honeymoon.

"Incoherent, I at once began my extensive, baron-cold walking through Queens, through Brooklyn, across that Williamsburg Bridge as a saint and again through the late-afternoon snowcrest barracks of ye Delancey, deep within that familiar looming of Eldridge of beyond, yet back.

"So, as I spoke earlier of the death of everything—here, then, on a fine New York Friday afternoon, was the *life* of everything! I spent my days counting the seconds and still time had flown. I give up and turn down Eldridge in the rain!

"There—lo and behold, me temporal captives, saints amidst the satin night—through that physical litany of observant, hear-say explorations, I stumbled at last upon that ramshackle dumpling shop—Yes, comrades, I am all aware of the vagueness of that understatement concerning Manhattan's Chinatown, though men, men; hear me out! One shop, that which I spoke of just earlier, drew me in once more! And thus I stepped forth magnanimous step by magnanimous step through the barren street with me hair in disarray, me coat punched out with tobacco holes; begotten all fragmented distant seas of thy self-past a-wreckage! And whoa, Mustard, he whose half-thumb encapsulated the witless moon! Had he missed his boat! O, ye dumpling house!

"Chipped cardboard posts with scratched out prices struck me fast, succumbed to thy retinal preoccupation. Where hath he gone! No canned soda, hath I proclaimed indignant—where is my brother! May one place his—knit gray flannel cap upon of thy five wooden benches in order to restore sanctity, disquietude! Step away, man, and get your jangling car keys out of my eardrums! I'm on the lookout, cannot you see! Where is he, that Mustard!

"No one spoke a word, then. Not ye chef, not ye cashier, not ye sesame pancake, not ye four patrons stumbling in past the heater-hummed matchbox countertops, not ye oil tycoon, not I. Whitesmock pork-stained of pastel steel, withered countertop of copper! The rooster! The rooster sauce! O, ye dumpling hound dog!

"She explained that Mustard had run away. He would be back any moment.

"Art though prices prehistoric, asked I.

"What want! cried ye counter-keep. She had the look of latch-gold watches in her eyes and yet it vanished! What of goldmines! Now what want!

"I stepped back, brethren, before lunging with a newfound confidence bound by daylight's coming down, bayonet in ye withered streets, doughnuts crumbling from ye prosthetic jaw!

"Hath I five dumplings, one pancake, one soda, and sayeth no more.

"The food was thrust forth. Within brisk minutes I was done and yet no sign of Mustard showed. I would have to accept his memory and be content. The bag-eyed counterwoman coughed an oyster of phlegm, another, and another. Ye pigeon outside struck with a slingshot! I stepped through the carnage, and back again past the razor-thin shoulder of ye cashier. And there, ye comrades, he stood.

"At once he caught my eye with the grip of a wound vise. He wore an old eye-patch and scratched at his collarbone until he knew it was I. He wore his stained smock, battered sneakers, his teeth random and discolored as tombstones, silver shining in scattered hours like places of ye psychedelic dreams! The sole fell out from his shoe; he tucked it back in with embarrassment.

"By the look in his eye I could tell he belonged less in ye hallowed kitchen than at a roundtable meeting of the rulers of the world.

"Me want break, he said to the boss-man. His breakage of the silence brought a tear to my eye. The children had long taken the pigeon away and all was calm. My friend here—

"No! Back!

"I was quite depressed and knew not what to do. Rather this is my implication, then, of being ye storyteller; one ought to know these things. Consider the universe in terms of the compass; hath thy begun to regard meteoric north, south, or stepped away for chemical coaxing! Thou art not alone. I was ready, dear friends, to jump off the Brooklyn Bridge, for I could find no way to live, nor any reason. I felt it just then, too—

"Mustard broke away. He wobbled toward the counter, past the stunned cashier, as pots and pans clamored throughout the small kitchen. Anarchy, I tell ye, anarchy, and isn't she a beauty! Fire-marks and boils I hadn't noticed ran across Mustard's hands and determined, tight-lipped face. Steam broke from a broiler. Yet he at once shook my hand with the intensity of registered philosophies.

"Me Mustard, he said.

"I remember ye, Mustard, responded I, concealing my undiagnosed joy.

"Seconds passed. The boss began to rise from the ground; we observed in parallel the ground beneath our shoes. Mustard pointed with his half-thumb to the overflowing trash bin.

"Day lazy, he announced.

"Mustard, man, shouted I—we must get going!

"The cashier held back the boss beneath a burnt-out bulb.

"Mustard! Mustard! You son of a—

"Back, Mustarr, back!

"Let he speak! Let he breathe! The cashier cried out, repeating herself, her eyes thrashing through the spectral, vagrant dusk.

"Go! said I, as we took off running down the street.

"At Bowery we stood breathless, on the way; I offered Mustard a coffee and dinner.

"No, no! Airplane! JFK!

"He took a wad of hundred-dollar bills from his pocket and smiled for a moment. Lifesaving! I want to get to train, my friend, but no small bills!

"Damn, Mustard, said I; is that what's keeping ye around!

"No, no, just now, to bank, he spoke between breaths. We ran at once down into the subway. I bought him a transfer. He knew the way to the airport; he had the handwritten directions from his day of arrival intact. At the turnstile he looked around as dozens past through in disarray, going one way, the next; he reached into his pocket and gave me a pencil-inscribed self-portrait, turned around, and vanished into the crowd."

El sat still a moment, exhaling.

"And that's it," William said, "He just turned around and vanished."

"I know not what I did that night, nor the next, but I know that Mustard made it all right."

"How do you, like, know," Daniel doubted, passing around the bottle of whiskey, tying up his shoelaces.

"Because the day before my sister and I traveled back west, some weeks later, I stopped into Prosperity Dumpling, and there was the thin-shouldered cashier. She recognized me at once and pointed to the wall; there was a photograph of Mustard on the beach; he and his wife, and three children."

William and Daniel watched entranced as El leaned over, pulled his wallet from his pocket. He carefully removed the self-portrait from his wallet and spread it out across the desk.

There he was, there was Mustard; his half-thumb extended north across the sky, his smock stained with debris, big belly, traces of a mustache, and chipped teeth in a grin. El took a thumbtack from the drawer and nailed the portrait to the wall with gentle precision; Mustard shone in the outstretched light of the lamp.

"Mustard, ye know, is mankind—Now, verily, to the Hemlock!"

18

WILLIAM WAS ALONE FOR the first time in weeks, walking down to the subway in the Sunday San Francisco afternoon, out to Berkeley to meet the man on Telegraph with Raleigh bicycles. He traded his found Raleigh in with fifty dollars for another and rode it back to the train. From there is was out to Market Street, then all the way out to, across the Golden Gate Bridge, Sausalito, Tiburon, and stopped when the fog was far too thick, depletion coming on strong. Harold Smith had at last gotten in touch; they were set to meet in days. William stopped into the seaside café.

The café was that depraved, accumulative blend of old men and old women and youngish yuppies sterilizing pacifiers with hand wipes, dropping torn packets of raw sugar to the luxurious carpet of ivy and somersaulting sail boats, and discussing all the aspects of politics they'd advocate for and donate to behind the security of armed guards, walls, fences, and gates. Aged, bloated lesbians with rainbow visors looked around at one another and took ninety-five-dollar glasses of wine, heaving through crisp editions of the Chronicle; one understood why the world looked at the nation with such contempt, among other reasons, in their deplorably draining presence. It was thus not long before William stepped out and washed the chain-grease and sweat from his hands and face; but first a dash of people-watching over wine, and notes-to-self.

In the parking lot a stuttering woman, apparently some type of artist living at home—how else could she have ended up here?—cross-eyed with deformedly turned-in feet, webbed sputtering hands, and a pallid color reminiscent less of purity than disease, tipped her straw hat to the pilgrim. William imagined himself, revisiting the menu, placing coin into her cup. From a strange angle as a nearby siren climaxed and dissolved, he envisioned her being once his age. That hypothetical yesterday, with all its seaside fireworks and memories of the future, rendered the deformed woman something of a Gertie MacDowell in the fleshbut now he was not thinking of a deformed gal's stockings, but that mysterious Melody Nelson's.

The vision was interrupted by exiting patrons, some poor soul's agonizing wife decrying "I kissed her flat belly but almost vomited at once from a horrific stench."

William considered that not all of the world was San Francisco, that perhaps San Francisco was no longer even San Francisco; he longed to return to his room at once, averting his eyes to the hotel artwork as to avoid the bewildered, economical stares of customers drugged with music. He sat secluded beside the window engulfed with spray-on mist, his half-bottle of chilled white wine, pasta, and a loaf of bread, eating and drinking.

The waiter reappeared.

"What did you do with your wine glass?"

"I was not given one," William admitted, indicating his drained water glass. Onlookers tried to demagnetize their eyes, restrain their blissful gesticulations in some anonymous concentration or another. But it made them feel good, vindicated, to watch the black sheep caught in some kind of ambiguous accusation.

"No, no; the waitress gave you one."

"Oh, alright." William could tell by the look in his eyes that linguistic specification was irrelevant—the stumbling tuxedoed man had an emotion he was content on conveying, perhaps having been tossed around the dish room for several anxious minutes. William saw in the American elite, as he had seen in the Caravan backyard, just why so many citizens of the world despised Americans. "In that case I suppose I dropped it. It may be along the floor somewhere. I do not remember."

"We will add the price of the glass to your check."

"No, no, you oughtn't."

The management stepped forth. Everyone took turns speaking. The entire restaurant watched on, no longer embarrassed, licking sauce from their lips, thumbing at their bibs, sightless, patting children upon the head.

"Are you positive you brought out a glass?"

"How could I be positive?"

"So you're not positive," the chef said to her.

"Listen," the second entity said, readjusting the rumpled column of his graying head. "We won't add it to your check. Just make it quick, it's already been a scene. We are busy on Sundays."

Janine had been right; this grotesque experience lent credence to the idea that San Francisco, like a lover, did resemble a taste of honey upon return as William finished his wine and longed to leave without further ado. He tore the check in two, cycled through the autumnal paths and trails stopping once to eat wild berries. He watched a couple in love pass by; the girl unafraid to smile in front of strangers.

"And I know what that is like," William said to himself, dampened winds cooling his body, past the last set of decoratively-trimmed storefronts, laughing aloud. "Someday when the ashes of heaven and the blossoms of hell converge. Some fine day I'll fall in love again."

Late in the night pebbles began to tap at his window. He pulled himself from a dream, the torn blinds apart, and there she was. Part of him wanted to go back to bed and the other half felt risqué.

The parade, the parade, after-all, for stillness is outlined death, uninvestigated comfort more dangerous than missiles.

He switched on the lamp once, stronger, and held down the buzzer. Satin turquoise and a loose-lipped description of the day in Dolores Park.

"Oh but come on," she said, whispering to herself in French, "Why do one glass at a time when you know we should each just have our own bottle and enjoy it by leisure!"

"Because I don't feel like a whole bottle of wine right now," William said. "It's late!"

"Oh but you always say that in the beginning!"

"I do?"

"Everyone does!"

"Well still, we'll share our bottle here and talk. Can't people just talk at midnight? Shouldn't you be in school? It's a school night—"

"Shut-up! You don't know a thing about me! I'm older than you!"

"No."

"You don't know much at all."

"Fine, madam, fine."

"I want my own bottle of pinot noir!"

"Once you learn pronunciation!"

"You've got half a case!"

"No, no," William explained, "This is the last of it. I saved this one for a special occasion."

"You didn't know I was coming," she asserted.

"If you're coming, I'm coming; we come together, like all happy, and hence deluded, couples."

"Shut-up; there's a case of French wine behind you! I was there when you bought it, you bum! *Homme stupide!*"

"Well listen, listen; it's much better to share a bottle than to hog one."

"You don't know anything! You're in *denial*. You don't mean any hogging around, you're afraid of, of enjoyment, of commitment to anything! Wine, women, life! I know your kind!"

"You think so swell of me," William said, "Of course I knew you'd come. But dear, dear, can't you comprehend the difference between indulgence and elegance? It is much more elegant to go bottle by bottle. It is the sole way the night can shine through in the morning. Greed would ruin us in the morning if we sat here with private stashes. Even if the source remains the same, friends ought to always share one bottle at a time. In the morning you become better friends that way. If I had the money, we'd go ice-fishing, but for now we may as well have drinks and share thoughts. In fact I'm beginning to understand that the latter might be far more worth cherishing. No more debate. Finis," he concluded, in a hoary, Brooklynese tongue of French.

"What do you know with all of your big talk?"

She sat straight up, her ample breasts before his eyes. He liked them much more before they were his; now one was becoming animal, all too animal, comprehending well-kept, bow-tied udders.

"I know I have you tonight," said William, tugging for a moment at her rustled brown hair. "What do you know?"

"That you don't know anything."

"We shall alternate between city and forestry, circles of forest that lead to circles of the holy mountain. I make myself the half arch of a bridge."

"But witches live up on that hill, their heels strike the earth and their eyes are lured by great poisonous ideas, rolling around their empty heads like little wheels; the ones who burnt them at the stake knew well what they were doing!"

"But no one is chosen by God," suggested William. "One is rather suffering from monomania, most likely genetic. Yes, hope and justice make sufferings less harsh, their right hands extended before they dissolve with a whimper into the dying light—but enough of that, woman, suspend your greatest care tonight, for the poem is a naked person!"

"I knew a mortal named after a certain river, and see the great deal of mammalian burdens with the lightness of a feather, after all I have been through."

"Tell me about your old boyfriends. Tell me all about them. I want to know that much about you but little else, with you and your bowl-cut hair and big bad rich family from Prague with two houses in the Catskills and studying abroad and marrying a real estate tycoon. There, I've written your biography."

"Stop it."

"Did they hold you like this, and touch your soft neck, and hold you like this and then kiss your earlobe like plucking grapes from a vine? Oh, I know, and then come, my love, and lay down beside me, we're getting too old for all of this pretend."

She explained, with the pilgrim's aid, that rehab is like a mountain of inverted souls, most of whom know that not even this shall save them; they are the rest of the *Pequod*, and one is Ishmael, or Job, or Melville, only escaping to tell thee. "So you are a fellow-servant of one Power, collecting alms for oblivion? Your dignity makes my conscience reproach itself."

It took till just before dawn before she let go, and let her innocence be known, and began to fall asleep within his arms. She kissed him once, looked into his eyes, and fell asleep with a beautiful smile, as if she were weeping.

He looked through her purse for matches and came across her name: Melody; Melody Nelson: "I would have sworn it was a pseudonym. It makes one wonder what her parents were, are like."

$\sim$

William sat at the café watching the people pass through, flipping through a borrowed book. At last Janine reappeared.

"William!" she gasped. He took her hand in his and kissed it over and over and explained to her all that had happened, and how Harold Smith had gotten a room at Page and Webster and didn't start waiting tables for another month, the franks-trade and its declination in the absence of summer, Phil Cohen and Heather and everybody else. Janine had just returned from Italy.

"I was at the park all afternoon," she relayed, breathless, sitting beside him. They drank iced tea in the vista, absorbed by one another's eyes and the cold crisp air. William listened to her travel tales smiling, speechless, observing Janine's longer hair, her jet-black outfit and beige wingtips, her pink lips parting as she asked of Isaac, of the apartment, "And you need a phone!"

"I will get one soon, if just for you."

"Don't you remember when you first got here!"

They went for a walk through the park as fog nestled within the initial evening light. He interlocked his coarse hands within hers, soft as lace, and could feel the pulse beat upon his through her palm, and at once felt motivated, a longing to be productive, to prove himself to Janine and Janine alone as he walked at her side—how much she resembled Octavia, Octavia Savonarola.

"Look at you!" she laughed, "Showing me around, now!"

She awoke in the night and explained she'd have to go home. William yearned to convince her to stay, but in his heart he knew it just could not work. There was no reason at all, as she dressed in the moonlight, but why couldn't she just lay beside him for weeks at a time?

"Is there anything I can do to help, bubby? I am a terrible girlfriend."

William ignored the latter and pondered just what he could have delivered from the nocturnal streets:

"A doughnut from Bob's?"

Janine kissed him on the forehead, returned with a box of doughnuts and coffee. She kissed William once more, instructed him to call her soon, and left. He listened to the door click shut, Janine stepping to a cab, and could not bring himself to watch. He sat in silence for several minutes, fingering, twirling his beard, when it suddenly struck him: there was a force in the air that would not allow him any further chances at love. It was as if his soul itself fell over, awakening to enter a monastery without explanation. There would remain Epicurean aspects of being, at least for the short term; but its particles were all at once disconnected with heavy terrible clarity.

When he opened the box, he was astonished to find a note, and money wrapped in napkins:

> Quit that stupid job! Pursue your craft and art! Love, J

William sat dumbfounded counting the thousand dollars out, knowing nothing of craft nor art, but loving Janine, and feeling rich, and awake at sunrise again, content.

"Beautiful girl!"

> Password for the first night is Hiram; for the second night, 'neque nubent'—now let me to leave, so we can resume our weeping.

19

WILLIAM RETIRED FROM FRANKLIN'S while the nocturnal parade continued straight through all of October, November.

And he was outside of the world, more and yet quite still a conscientious microbe; and he beheld the melting of the world.

And there in the middle of the city he found himself anxious beyond measure, as though at the foot of a cliff, or contemplating one of one of those valley bridges made of glass; for what is a planet, but a spherical cliff suspended temporally through immeasurable nothingness?

"A she-wolf stoned to death in Iraq last night, and all I hear about is your hollow hunger!"

Riches are nothing, said the oceanic wind, are but symbolic variations on invidious carnality and object-accumulation. Power, too: that is weakness.

William Fellows seldom left Harold Smith's side.

"See I pulled a knife on him, the junkie, see, but I have a warrant out, so I went south, LA with my folks, and I'm back! Heather Daily? Ah, forget her anyway. She's the one that called the cops on me in the first place! Ha!"

The pair of pages torn from some heretical essay of the flesh convened at Blondie's and encompassed every last corner of the city drenched in soul music, the docks, sunset, fresh meals, sunrise, all of this and that. It was as if the summer had returned.

In the beginning each young man wore a suit and drank martinis with beautiful women; in the end it was a can of beer and awakening in the dirt, vomiting through car windows, and waking up and carrying ahead through life in staggering, fortuitous disarray. When he looked back on it, William liked to consider the entire month kaleidoscopic, still yet held together by piercing, beautiful moments constructed with the precision and tenderness of a million Faustian harbor lights luminescent across the cities of the mind, whereby a sort of psychological dawn fell upon him.

"Damn," Smith said on the final night, December in looming, the drizzle coming down for days at a time, sitting out on the porch and laughing at random intervals and unable to speak any longer: "The wine goes by so fast, doesn't it?"

"It does, but there is always more."

"What are you going to do for money, William?"

"I've still got a bit saved up. I'm still in fine shape."

"I can't imagine myself working tomorrow. It seems like such a shame."

"I know," sighed William. "Saturnalia is coming to an end."

Harold looked up in a final burst of enthusiasm.

"No!" he shouted, over and over, his arms outspread to Page Street, Webster Street. "It's going to stay summer! Shake on it!"

They shook on it, and it seemed that marching bands could be heard along Haight Street.

"You hear that, m'boy? We're all just getting started!"

Smith collapsed. William took to staggering home delirious, against his will, trying to comprehend just what he would do. He consulted a log, whom he made promise to come drink at his grave when he was dead. What did anyone do? What could anyone do any longer? He solved the problem by collapsing in bed and staying there for days, and yet the question bothered him when he awoke. He felt as if he were letting the women in his life down, all of them, except for that Melody Nelson; this he knew in the way she would not leave his mind when two days had passed and still she hadn't stopped by in the night with her pebbles and her voice.

"My mother's died," she said. "She quit smoking, see, and found herself so fixed on the idea of a cigarette that she had a heart attack! Do you believe it?!"

She looked through the window and away, caving into William's arms and crying, and even in mourning had an amorous touch to her arm. He began to feel affection for her once more, but even in the catatonic fusion of green vodka and hashish the idea of venerating pleasure opened itself to the necessary disintegration that dwelt at the twofold heart of filial reconsideration, the piety of the fifth commandment, and the cosmic prospect of redemption. Such thoughts made the pilgrim wince; and thus even Melody Nelson remained an incomplete affection.

He refused his emotions, summoning a skeptical blend of vinegar and wormwood.

"I see him killed between living thieves. I was taken with a chill reminiscent of my night at the holographic mountain, shaken once and again, falling through a dream to the *Days of Heaven* soundtrack, vinyl, which I saw the next day used at Amoeba—I was a disciple of Daniel Dennett, William, working in biomechanics and molecular physics; but now I see the sky as a cosmic tarp, or age-old quilt, with some holes poked out. And as for what we call the sun, the moon? Oh, that's just the eye of Diana on one hand and Apollo on the other. I named my two dogs after them; we live at the compound, or as I call it, Hamlet's Mill, over in Sausalito."

Then they took up their holy way again, gazing out through the last vestiges of dissolving fog, over traces of souls below, some lying upon the earth and weeping.

"I've got to get out the city," she wept. "Will you come with me, this weekend?"

"Where?"

"Death Valley."

"Alright."

"I go there to take LSD," Melody said.

It was so strange that in life all of the fierce, serious women seemed to cave in as if their exterior was far less methodical than an adverse reaction to the looming despair within, which could be resolved by excessively meaningless intercourse and hallucinating in Death Valley.

"I've got the car outside—let's go now."

William tied his shoelaces and locked the door behind him. And walking to Melody's window, he kissed her forehead and wished her the best of luck, providing her with half a dozen phone numbers of persons who he believed would love to get and keep her indulgent company he was unsure what he would in time cease becoming, but knew at least that he was no longer the type of person who would get into Melody's car to go partake in that awaiting oblivion of perception and interior narrative.

William walked on, timidly thoughtful, feeling the poetics of space upon him.

20

ATOP POTRERO HILL THERE was a mansion owned by a great big woman who Melody had been friends with since high school. Postponing Death Valley, she took William all throughout the contours and the people, the shelves of books, the drawers and refrigerators filled with weed, cocaine, heroin, ecstasy, DMT, and varieties of tablets. Everyone spun around in circles and wore tutus, body paint, or nothing at all. Everyone came in and out on the bus and took turns with the telescope, overlooking the Mission and out to Twin Peaks.

At once William felt a desire to speak with no one, coupled by a second desire, as he listened to just what these persons were talking about, howling over, and laughing hysterically concerning, the complimentary desire then being to borrow a gun somehow and shoot himself in the head. The hammock was reportedly brand new, swayed well, and he drank Anchor Steam as Melody slipped away. She had determination in her voice when she spoke of leaving, an awful bliss in her voice when she thanked the pilgrim for inadvertently talking her out of Death Valley, picking him up two blocks down the road from where she'd sat some seconds gnawing on the skin beneath where nails once grew.

The crowd chanted on about saving the planet, incoherent revelations serving the chorus-function which proved they could not even save themselves, and that was the whole truth of the matter. Everyone had a phone in their face and was taking pictures and screaming about movies and the Castro, Barack Obama and Portland, blends of marijuana and miscellaneous trust fund lamentations.

Without much conscious effort, William hated all of them and all their body-paint. The lights of the city shone beyond them. Sirens wailed below; winter was on its way and there was nothing worse that could have happened than to become one of these insufferable rooftop moralists.

Melody returned with a batch of transvestites, artists, environmentalists. William had met some of them somewhere, and recalled caring as little then as now, albeit at present adding, "I have come to despise people who want me to judge them based on external circumstances, no matter how scarce or endangered"; and Melody took William inside to the mirroring maze of hallways.

"Look," she said, like 'Luck,' and pronouncing the *k* unclenching her fist and displaying the contents on her foreign palm: Two tablets, a gram of cocaine, a gram of weed. People passed around rags of ether, went through dozens of canisters of nitrous until their faces turned blue. She closed her fist and pecked William on the cheek. He had never seen her so happy as when her palm was filled with drugs.

"So who are thee, sexy boy," inquired the man with breasts and diapers.

"I come here by way of Hell's wide throat, and I see its hounds still here and there roam thy once pristine streets—was it just some months ago that heaven appeared a geographical rather than terminal matter?" A crowd grew, the cloaked pilgrim arose with his olive branch and chalice. "For if you paused just for a moment, you would see that your bliss is torture. Look at dictators and political theology: give up the ghost of refusal and see with meteoric clarity that you are tortured against your will, so long as the degree to which you live to sin is inorganically impenetrable, like the script of any tyrant. Behold: as I depart from thee and thou whisperingly condemn me, know that a little voice called me, saying 'Tolle, lege!' and so I dispense the dispensations themselves, I and my little pocket-book given to me by a nun, in the soul of being, as being is the soul of being, unto the granularity of the beatific vision, it sings, 'Tolle, lege!' Help my unbelief! There are signs everywhere, reigning with and through the semiotics of the time; but the reign of the Thomistic good is all that ever matters—we see at last what the salt pillar was all about, when I take the little boat out past the fog of limbo at daybreak, and I come face to face with the larynx of Hell."

He excused himself for the bathroom. There he filled a thermos with whiskey.

Then he walked down Potrero Hill to more familiar land, as the drugged voices dissolved behind him. They sounded high up and far away, incarcerated in some sense.

In the morning he'd go to the bookstore, call Octavia, Nielsen, his mother, and begin to carry out some sort of goal again. He did not feel content: He felt more-so that he was growing malcontent with oblivion and could not conceal his displeasure with the drug culture, the drug attitude. He needed to recapture his life. Everything else seemed trite, convoluted ventriloquism.

"William! Wait!"

"Yes, Melody?"

"Have you lost your mind?"

"Whoever loses his mind shall find it."

"Do you have any concern for my reputation?"

"Melody, the time to beat around burning bush is over."

"Um, what? Why?"

"Because I said so. Now, listen: Virgil was my nurse and papa, thou whore, for we poor Italian skeptics still have nothing else to read or to compare our own compositions to; laughter and weeping are lost on they who see will and representation for what it truly is. And my love that burns toward Octavia, an angel you will never know, for the angels may as well abhor you and yours, reprobates of declination. Tis she, not thee, who is stamped into my mind every time that emptiness slips away from me, especially on Sunday morning; you cut one of us and we all bleed, as surely as the Second Temple incurred what was right and just, more than a thousand flames, through which the poet emerges nonetheless in a springtime of truth, gazing and smiling, eager and truthful. Yea, your collective presence has wounded me by volition of its stupidity; and laughter is but a flash of the soul, a light appearing as it feels within."

Melody could not make out every word but was visibly enraged, as hard rain rushed down. Later on William reflected, overlooking the streaks of rain through his window, that her eyes spelled out the death of a dream. The ladder of perfection turned in yet another new direction, erected in the midst of an earthquake whose tremors terrified the city for a night.

21

ONCE AGAIN IT WAS Film Night at the Application, and once again he took to his tan-red packet of Halfzware out in the pure marble air and began rolling cigarettes so quickly three of them broke clean in half, discarded in an ashen bottle of port.

"I'm going to miss the subway," William said to himself, "And there goes another thousand-dollar baby carriage!"

He bolted outside into the night; Paul could follow him down, Paul one of the last American puritans, from Isaac's professorial circle, who had also been at Casanova Lounge mid-day, himself with postdoctoral work examining one Statius, who like William had been unable to find sufficient cause for the earthquake and had subsequently thrown himself into study by tavern light.

By the time Paul stood to go his glass-green eyes had long been set intermittently upon Dolores Park, electronic moonlight through hallucinated pines, envisioning swarms of people encircling the illimitable frosted terraces come winter's end, and the night ahead, some strange movie or another playing the Berkeley Film Club over at the Application. He stood, switched down the lights, and took off for the bodega, running once and again his pale hands through a formulating auburn beard brought on by belligerent inactivity with the cold winds blowing his way, making his cheeks rosy and the vague warmth of the filthy, cardboard-floored bodega seem somewhat relieving.

Two girls sat outside of the hidden bar down off Valencia and 17th, their gloved hands entwined upon a cracked pottery of what looked like an apartment door; had one not known about the Application it would have appeared at a glance just another pair of rich girls who dressed poor smoking cigarettes in the spherical midst of thrownness, asphalt, eternity and death, flesh bare, horny, and furious should a man let the bones of his eyeballs live.

One wore a leather jacket and long hair on one side; the other had half of her dirty blonde hair shaved off. The taller girl beside her wore a corduroy coat with tousled frays dangling and from her swinging, animated arms, and the other broke into an unfortunate little dance.

The dancer held out a colorless plastic donation tub in which several one-dollar bills lay atop and beside one another, outlined by a couple of quarters and a half-dollar.

"How's it *goin*'?"

"Fine, fine. And how are you?"

William readjusted his coat collar.

"Care to give a donation?"

He exhaled:

"I've got to get cash I am sorry."

"Enjoy!"

At the middle of the horseshoe bar William stood with his long black coat still on, talking to the bartender and taking down notes for a recipe. The Application was not yet crowded when Paul set his coat upon the rack and let the heat rush through his body in waves.

The bartender polished off his neat array of multicolored bottles before a Chinese lantern, creating little flash patterns of pyramidal light. He readjusted one bottle, another, all the while listing off ingredients, and tucked the bottles back beneath the bar and took to customers at the end of the bar.

"I didn't know whether to tip those girls or not."

"Don't," William smiled, extending his hand. He seemed already to have been drinking. But how could that be? Had they not just had that sobering dinner and tea with the daughters of Mary Magdalene?

"Take off your coat?"

William did not acknowledge this inquiry:

"Fair-weather friends! Waiting for Godard. Death to Godard. I hate the whole thing incomplete whole the thing our father whose art's in heaven bliss back to pre-birth nothingness and thoughts on long grunting lines at Bi-Rite Market king come thy shall be done. And what were you saying—"

"I feel like an asshole."

"What are they doing? Putting on a movie? It was advertised as free. In—"

William checked his phone, snapped it back shut and tucked it away: "In ten minutes they have free Anchor Steam in the back. That's the only reason anyone comes to these things. Here, have some tequila."

Paul drank the tequila and let it burn through him.

"Much emptier than I thought it would be," he said.

They looked around. There were no more than seven people in the long candle-lit room, four of whom stood alone, nodding through distended frames. The projectionists dashed in through a doorway hidden by velvet sheets and carrying their equipment, rushed frantically to the back room.

"So," the bartender returned, "It should be a very good film tonight. Are you going to watch it?"

"I think so," said William. He turned to Paul: "Right?"

"Unless we stay at the bar."

"That is a possibility," said the bartender. "And you're—Paul—right? Right. I'll be here till four at least."

"If I am feeling lazy I probably will not watch the film."

"You know it is just around the corner from the bathroom there."

"Exactly."

"I have never heard of someone being too lazy to watch a film. What is the film called?"

"I don't know," said Paul. "That's a good question. Yeah, then I'll have another tequila. We descend again into the unknown!"

"We see the writing on the wall," swallowed William, "but it is in an archaic tongue; one cannot see if this sense of doubt is false so long as true reason remains clouded, unknowing."

"Far away from the shorn locks of ignorance."

William made way for the young vagrant, who strummed softly at another street corner's bucolic song.

"You were in Parnassus, Paul, anchored to an ocean floor of vanity and sin, when the exegetes introduced me to God, by way of desert pit and deathbed."

"Something to that affect."

"Our habits are our banner, the dented crown of debauchery and excess, watching with uneasiness one worthy soul's assent, at the cost of a dozen psychic deaths. All around us, in conceptual space historical and immediate, windowside gluttons, faces stuffed with food, turning together rightward for incessant group photo—but sometimes they walk ahead and one of them falls behind, and it is just enough of a programmatic crack in the procession to have one, say, recall a line from Rilke or Petrarch; and thus together, the living and the dead, and vice-versa, teach us all there is to know about poetics as autumn knowledge: like acorns, locust, and wild honey, after a mutinously uncompromising fast: here we standing, having stripped the altars of our minds."

22

THE HOLY NIGHT, THE young men decided over clinked glass and a charity of cigarettes, called for an oscillation between profundity and flesh.

"What did you do earlier today before Casanova? You said you were up before sunrise?"

"Nothing much," William slurred, unsure just who he was talking to, drinking tequila. "I read for a while and went on a bike ride to Sausalito and had lunch and drinks along in a secret bar under the bridge and then back out to Lower Haight and here. No, wait—I stopped at your place. Wait—who are you? You're Harold's friend, right? You mentioned something about the Wreck Room on Flushing Avenue last year when you lived in Bushwick or along the way here to drink—or was that—or did I walk alone?"

"You must be feeling good."

"You sweat it out quickly bike riding. I like to ride my bicycle across the Golden Gate bridge drunk with no hands. I have never heard of anyone else who likes that, so it makes it even more fun."

"I've got to start cycling again," Paul said.

"Sure."

"When did you start drinking tequila?"

"It's a temporary thing. The last time I fell in love I was drinking tequila. Maybe I'll fall in love again tonight. Anyhow after this one I'm sticking to the free drinks. Then what did you do today?"

A tired, tattooed man rolled half a dozen boxes of Anchor Steam into the back room.

"Excuse me—ay, excuse me!"

"I did not know Anchor Steam came in cans."

He came from the back room and set a milk crate against the wall and tossed a set of keys to the bartender. The projectionists came out and the donation girls came in. The music was turned down and from the back room came two dozen people.

"This is becoming fancier and fancier an event every month. That's why I don't even take my coat off anymore. Next I'm going to wear a scarf and earmuffs and gloves and shout about Glenn Gould all night."

"Excuse me—Excuse me," said the undergrad, perching himself atop the crate and clearing his clean-shaven throat: "We want to thank you all for coming out to our annual series here at the Application and we want to thank the Student Radio Fund for helping out with everyone and the wonderful owners of the Application who allowed all of this to happen. Tonight we are in for a good one."

There was a round of applause as the girl with half of her head shaved off handed him the donations. He looked in, swallowing and disappointed at the contents, coughed, and tried his best:

"And thank you all for donating. We believe this is a good cause and will enhance the artistic community of *East Bay*."

The dual syllables from the last word brought about abrupt, ravenous applause and whistling.

"We will leave the jar out in the back here where we are all set to go. The film will start in five minutes but the beer is good to go! For the first hour it is free and then—"

Paul and William joined in on that round of applause and followed the small group to the back.

"So many strained by pitiful wages," said Paul. "Balanced out by secretive parental gifts, yet still unable to ever truly untie the knot of their many debts—look at that one; a face that took its shape from ring of bone, eyes long dark and hollow. Doesn't she look familiar?"

The room was a cavernous dance hall with unconcealed walls of carved rock and the dampened feeling of caves beyond peeling posters and fliers. William looked about deftly, puzzled, for bats and crystals and hieroglyphics, and tried to take the weariness of a dance hall on an off night.

One of the owners of the Application struck up conversation with Paul and unlatched the first cardboard case. People slowly gravitated toward the black, green, and gold box showing one another absurd courtesy.

"Isn't the whole thing just absolutely *marvelous*?"

"Thank you *so* much. What's your name?"

"William, aesthetician. Job? No. Why? Because I never wanted one."

"Oh, this is *marvelous*."

It was sort of marvelous, William reflected, and he took his drink out to the backyard to smoke beneath the winter moonlight and reflect upon his endless summer now here at the Application in such a realm where time stood still once more. He found it strange how so many of the girls, the women, appeared for days, weeks at a time, and always then vanished never to be seen by anyone again. Or was it he who never stayed put at a single bar? San Francisco was a small city. One could not get lost there but just left one day instead wondering what'd ever taken so long. But the women, yes, appearing out of a thin air into which they in time vanished again, never seen at subways, the restaurants, the streets, the parks—they all vanished without a trace one day and it always seemed less melancholic than understandable in that way one can look reflectively to the night sky daydreaming of people one will never see again—that when it all slowed down, like on a Monday night, one began to wonder for a moment just how much futility was wrought up in the nothingness of carnality. But that little flame would spark in one's mind and was put out just as fast with a pull of beer.

"O sacrament of language," he sang taking a long sip, arching his crossed legs upon the adjacent bench, "O Lord."

The tin door swung open.

"I think she likes me," said Paul. He handed William a beer and lit his smoke.

"You're a good guy. She'd be crazy not to like you. She seems a bit old though."

"How old do you think she is? I kind of like older women. You know I'm almost thirty." William had forgotten Paul was almost thirty and realized the reason he had suggested the woman was old was because he was jealous. She may have been just past middle-aged, but in a way it made her seem all the more successful and young and beautiful—or it was her long denim shirt selectively buttoned with a silver necklace drawing all the more visual attention and distant intoxicated concentration. "Tell me again what brings you to the Bay Area, Monsieur William."

"I lost Jerusalem to find myself, warmly confronting Hell for a heavenly cause—"

Beside them a pair were comparing rings without gems, digressing upon standing in line for Fritz Lang's *M* followed by *Occult Forces*, screening at the Masonic Temple just yesterday.

"But that is all ancient history now. Thus to the maters at hand in glove, you are right," William explained, "You should go and get her. Kiss peck her neck during the movie. Do it in a way as if you're up against magnetic fields, like when you kiss them somewhere else. Don't hit the bull's eye right away. Be dramatic. Life is a drama and we are all looking to salivate from our mouths among other places before we perish."

"I can't do that yet," Paul laughed, knowing now that William had been drinking all day, where at Casanova and dinner it had been a mere possibility rendered unbalanced by bursts of seemingly sober discourse.

"Well of course you can."

"How?"

Paul eyed William suspiciously and felt the same anxious sensation he had early felt earlier on overlooking Dolores Park. November second; November of the soul.

"I'm telling you that there are certain places in the world one goes to for anonymous sex. No one is here to watch films but I appreciate the earthlings and animals that put it together because they bring people together to drink for free and not so much to watch art house movies but to project, if you will, a reason for young men and young women to get together and drink for free while a grainy film only one or two of us has ever seen or ever will remember plays on."

"I still don't know," said Paul.

"Play it by ear," William said. "First you sit beside her. If this does not work, you may buy her a cocktail later and see what is the word. If this does not work, you will have to do whatever you do in that situation—every man is different in that situation."

"Which situation?"

Paul curiously lit another cigarette.

He repeated himself.

"When you want someone so badly and fate seems misaligned; your questions are incorrect, your answers awkward, your voice foreign in that moment wherein your senses are deranged based on such heightened levels of attraction. Isn't it a pity! The ones we want so badly often cripple our sense of confidence—but you still must try, try!" William shouted, "Because sooner or later we will be disintegrated or buried!"

"My God," Paul said half seriously, overlooking the innumerable rows of apartment buildings, listening to the sirens sing and the last children of the night cry out joyously in the streets. "William, you are a morbid man."

"It is all in good humor. Say, go get that woman and I'll be inside then. Sometimes you cannot tell how someone is eyeing you when it is you they are looking at."

William looked through a hole cut in the bar's backyard fence at whatever was making an odd rustling sound. He beheld a black man in the fetal position strewn atop urine-dampened cardboard, scratching at scaly, bloody skin, falling apart and into little clumps at his withered elbows; and approaching him was a younger man in rags, whose face looked ominously like William's, blue eyes shining in an otherwise atrophied body, a skin disease that made one up close wince with nausea. He procured a fresh needle.

Through the bar doors came someone discussing Nella Larsen and her broken weeping. Her siren song had drawn the speaker to Oakland, Berkeley, where today she was making charcoal sketches out on the shore of waiting, receiving digital letters from the shameless lack of faith in politicians, and something about the utopian future right around the electoral corner.

'All their political howling at the doctrinal moon shall be destroyed,' thought William, putting out his cigarette in a defaced coffee tin half filled with liquid.

23

THE DOOR OPENED HALFWAY. Paul could hear voices crashing together, equipment being readjusted. He again stared at the rooftops of this neighborhood and reverted to his daydreams of fame, success, his true dream of escaping New York unscathed and start a family somewhere exotic, somewhere different in the future like Costa Rica, or Glasgow, only to return to his parents' home in Monterey before moving again back up to San Francisco. He knew not to go overboard tonight as he had work as a stagehand in the morning, something like economical sprinkles to the frosted cake that was his postdoctoral stipend amplified by trust fund— and yet so many of those nights and somehow he always made it through in the morning.

'That's the beauty of the city, I guess. Everyone is passing through and making it through and it is something you have in common with anyone. It's a damn beautiful tragedy, the most beautiful tragedy I've ever known.'

Beside him William wondered when he'd find another job, and how beautifully fragmented his day had been, when love breathed within him a spirit of mystical theology and divine names, signifying to the pilgrim a ladder of perfection present in everyday life. 'No longer,' thought William, 'does regurgitative revolution or critique of everyday life interest me at all; now I am interested in the miraculous, negative theology, and the exilic craft of thought of one who escapes a city or town stripped of goodness, bent on sad ruin, dragged by its tail as though by a beast, outmoded speech genres, and a disfigured corpse of its linguistic self. There is nothing to doubt or fear when one is on the right path; and let the right path be lethally rough at first, all the while maintaining constancy by way of wisdom of the heart'.

The tin door opened. The bartender stepped out for a smoke, lighting it, and tossing back his hair.

He came over and sat beside William. He patted him on the knee.

"How ya doing, bud?"

"Ah, wonderful," William said, overlooking the city and the rooftops, and listening to the children laugh and play in the distant woodchip park before the last of the closed up empanada carts rolling across the rickety sidewalk. "Good day, good evening. Just one of those fine successions."

"Good, good!"

"Yes, yes."

"Do you think the tequila will help you fall in love tonight?"

"I can't tell yet," he laughed, "But I'd rather be out here giving it a whirl than lying in bed with anxiety watching the wheels of the world go by in my head."

The bartender parted his hair to the side with his hand and drank lengthily from his ceramic mug.

"*Try* this," he exclaimed. "It is called the Celebration. It is a new cocktail."

"It tastes like licorice," William observed. He plucked liquid beads from the twirls of his mustache and rolled a cigarette from Paul's pouch.

"Mind rolling me one?"

"Of course not."

"I used to only roll my cigarettes," the bartender said, and motioned to his Adam's apple.

"Here you are."

Talk of travel, a dozen people swinging through the screened doorway. One could tell business was picking up and felt as though tonight would be a good one.

"Don't you think that the end of a pen sort of looks like a bullet once you take it out of its case?"

"I never thought of it that way."

"Let's go drink Fernet?"

William stood with the bartender as the door swung open, whipping up the silk of his black duster.

William was one step inside when Walter's ex-girlfriend showed up, which was particularly odd, for she was straight edge.

He stood upon an upturned crate and for a second looked out on the crowd, that eternal return of silly, petulant children, drowning in ideological vacuum bags of smoke and poisonous beer, their hands upraised and outstretched to take photographs of themselves—and he was one of them!

He could see that even the accursed share in creation up within the clouds, permanently drunk and raving, then stepping down, asking the three men before him where they were headed, they with eyes red like scorched glass or enflamed metal, and flesh like incandescent copper:

"I don't want no bread of life—I want justice!"

"Justice and the bread of life—but how does one grow so thoroughly sunburnt at this frigid time of year?"

"Don't mind him—he's drunk."

"Yes," said William. "And good for him—there is not much else to do!"

He hovered over to the bar, where an Irish coffee awaited him.

24

WILLIAM TRIED TO MAKE a last effort to recapture conversation with the bartender although the ex-girlfriend, he realized, was not Walter's; it was in fact a student he had gotten to know well over a particularly disastrous weekend; and now she had already set her glossy eyes upon him:

"Lately I have been drinking around the clock and listening to Beethoven. When I have free time, I work at the play you saw me working at once or twice. I generally cannot write in public. In fact I do little in public but share drinks with people and blow smoke at the moon as if it were some sort of reemerging language." He looked once, fleetingly, to Laura. "I have been reading the classics and their reviews on unspecific websites about how books should say profound things simply and I think a number, or a majority of people are irreversibly inexecrable. You see them all the time on the streets of the Mission, Brooklyn too. Huge glasses, vague glances, hollow heads. You see—"

"Oh William, lay off the tequila. Oh, I think you have a friend here waiting to talk to you."

"Christ," said William, looking helplessly to Paul.

The bartender nodded through a cloud of smoke, winked, and stepped back inside with one of the Berkeley students who had been standing around for a moment with multicolored cables in his hands.

"William!" she shouted, throwing her thin arms around him; she was wearing her nocturnal best.

'Since sunrise, since years past—'

And her heeled shoes, neurotic eyes glowed in the dark.

William looked to her with an immediate sense of remembrance and shock and looked instinctively and sincerely to press his lips against hers, to think of nothing but how good that felt, but since he knew she was soon to be engaged he instead pressed his lips to the bottle of beer in the cold wind.

Paul checked the weather on his phone. He had heard of Laura before although he had never met her and longed to talk again to the owner he'd met earlier.

Laura wore slim-fit denim pants cuffed at the ankle, beige wingtips without socks and a rose-red overcoat outlined by a swaying maze of golden necklaces.

"How long it's been," William said, "It has been so long."

They sat down on the steps and he nodded through long gulps and losing himself in the moonlight glowing in the frames of her glass lenses. Often it was sincerely overwhelming to see such clichés come alive in the middle of sentences concerning the past. He saw she was turning out just another girl.

"What have you been doing?"

"Nothing really—working at a vegetarian food store. Read a beautiful book earlier today, *Hogg* by Samuel Delaney. I am going back to school!"

"What are you studying?"

"Religion—not to be a nun or anything, but to teach religion myself."

"Oh?"

"And you! What are you studying!"

He knew better than to really begin speaking, for straight edge people often have photographic memories—and if they do not, they have a way of convincing subjects in a mix of neurotic persistence and a morose relationship with the catastrophic aspects of inventive memory.

"Looking for work—I am no longer in school. No gods, no masters, nothing positive but oblivion. But I say, nonetheless, that if there were a God we would be most sensible to praise Him for the gift of death. Look around you in horror—but it ends. That is the real joy in life—not working, not families, not degrees, not travel—its end. I would rather be drunk than famous. Fame! What is fame, anyhow? Fame is wet panties and a bandaged hand. Everything is a mess, everything, when you have faith neither in God nor politicians. No one who has read Herodotus can anticipate a bright future. So, yes, I am a failure too. It is better to get drunk and talk about doing things than it is to do them. Viva Voltaire! Viva le French Revolucion! Off with their heads! One nation, under Baal, divisible! The world is my ashtray! You were saying—"

She smacked him on the arm in a manner seeming simultaneously yearning and repelled.

"Oh my God!"

He thought quickly of something he had heard before:

"School, ahem," drinking, ". . . is not for everyone."

"Why didn't you go? My God, have you completely lost your mind? How since that one time in what, summer, can you look the same and healthy and yet be so deranged? I kind of like it."

"I looked at myself in the mirror and could not envision myself living in Texas. It seemed an incorrect assessment. I understand full well Nietzsche said that life without music would be an error, but then again Nietzsche was a virgin who was afraid of cows, so that settles that."

"Oh, alright."

"How'd you find out about this place?"

"A friend here is helping put it on! Want to meet him?"

"No."

"What do you think of Jonathan Safran-Foer or Jonathan Franzen?"

"I don't think of Jonathan Safran-Foer or Jonathan Franzen."

"Where do you live now?"

"Four blocks that way," she pointed. "Do you still live at Fort Mason?"

"I live on Polk Street now."

She paused and looked away as if to say something to herself that she knew better than to say aloud, thought William. She winced; *perhaps take a double shot in private and blurt it out anyway*?

She touched his twirling moustache:

"Come on, stupid—Let's go watch the film! You need more affection, and less insanity."

William recalled her insatiable way of saying rude things and why they had long ago broken up and took grave offense to her calling him stupid. He understood the vast, invariable stupidity of mankind well; he knew that progress was mythological banality and all politics propaganda; still, despite being mortal, he disliked being reminded of such. She knew this and smiled, for once upon a time she had called him a genius and perfect and beautiful and a daddy to their little babies instead.

"Let's just go to the bar."

"I thought you were going to quit drinking."

"I have many times," William admitted, blowing smoke at the starlit rafters of the sky. "At least a thousand times."

"That's so sad."

"Don't speak foolishly."

"Don't tell me what to do. Why are we out here right now—What have we done to deserve this?"

"The greatest people I've ever met have been in pubs and bars," William said. "Man or woman, for a moment or a sleepover, I never heard from them again, the way it should be. All of life is prostitution; becoming an innovator is simply to recognize this and make the entire process, life, one's whore. O fate, come hither; sing, ye birds."

"Have you always been possessed?"

"The world awaits another Machiavellian moment. Until then I just walk up the little steps of Romolo Place pondering, my dear, 'does semen become the soul of the fetus?'"

Laura unwrapped a sponge. She took a water bottle from her purse. She watered little lines on nearby plants, and wiped clean their counter.

"I don't know semen and fetus souls; it's like trees in a forest with nobody around. My husband had no soul, and I have no soul, so the question is irrelevant. You can turn to the Middle Ages all you want, William but in the end you're no better than taking rectangularly cut green and white construction paper to a cashier and demanding they accept your money. You must move from text to action."

"Yes, but I don't know about the specialized construction of organs . . . such is the sanctuary of self-preservation. Sun and God, seed and grape! The damned and blest alike move through here, in accordance with their Maker."

"Maker? Please, for the love of order, do not talk to me about God right now. You might as well be considering dangling meat from a car roof in a junkyard where the guard dogs' last meal was missed."

But Laura did look at him at him with a severe mercy; instinctually she longed to cast him off as hopelessly drunk, but the pilgrim did not strike her as vacuous; William struck her, oddly, as legitimate in his musings on God.

"The seal of the Trinity is within, upon the human mind, by way of memory, understanding, and will. Consider if you will, the fabric of the world—"

"William," she raised her hand, her eyes like two marbles signaling his speech come a halt. "We can discuss pious weeping, songs that are gracious, and pure hearts cleansed of stains—I was living with a Sister of Life who once prayed so long she passed out beneath my stuffed parrot—and the woes of life, like my father's diseased liver, burnt out with the same fire that encouraged and annihilated one's mindless lusts and vices—but not tonight."

William came to his senses. He nodded in bewildered approval, able for just a moment to exit his self-perception and pass it onto the rest of the patrons, all of whom would surely think outrageous were one to begin discussing religious matters in the midst of a hipster bar.

"I know not man," said the nocturnal pilgrim.

Paul listened in on fragments of their conversation. He was steadfast, resolute, unafraid to be William's friend. As in life it is in religion, where actions are much preferred at times to wishes and to words.

He ran into a daft patchwork of resemblances, dodging an ex-girlfriend, and then another, and then with the former had a mentholated cigarette and stepped into the bathroom. The sticker outside of the stall doors barring coitus seemed to invite it all the more. In a pornographic world, chivalry is head.

The bar had suddenly become jam-packed.

Laura looked cute, considered William, fumes of liquor making a misty ring around his delicate head; yes, cute as a button, deep within the madding crowd, and yet there was something in her that he knew to stay away from when the pressing fumes evaporated into nothingness.

He saw no ring on her finger. O heavens! Something went wrong. Tis a pity. Furthermore, it was the way she was never bored and always spoke, and spoke, and those people, William considered, are perpetually the most boring, those claiming never to be bored.

"I don't know. I don't believe in fate. I don't believe in belief. I just want enjoy myself and dance on stages and tables through sunrise and if I feel bad about anything in the morning I'll have a Bloody Mary or seven and mosey on down to the library at Grove and check out seven good books five minutes before closing and ride the subway home alone and shut my phone off because that's what I do anyway and smoke packs of organic cigarettes and make love."

"I don't understand how you live that way."

"You have answered your own question."

Paul reappeared in the doorway with a smile on his face and followed William's motioning for him to come outside. William reached over Paul's shoulder to clink his bottle with a smiling woman's whose shoulder-slung acoustic guitar was lined with Woody Guthrie stickers.

"Oh, right, that's the one who sells cassette tapes and reads Montaigne and Christina Rossetti. I—I introduced myself as R.W. Crump—or was it R.I. Dung?—and we even read Uwe Johnson, and we thought we were going to get married. Ah, but those days are gone! Don't look back. Yes, Laura, meet Paul. Paul is the greatest actor I've ever met. Paul, see, I have not seen Laura in weeks more like long years."

Paul set half a dozen bottles of beer on the concrete ledge and smilingly shook Laura's hand. She admitted a smile so wide William grew jealous for a second, before he understood that it was a part of the game everyone was at once involved in, metempsychosis preordained by shipwrecked nocturnal destiny.

"The Application," he laughed, checking his phone, considering both slowing down and grabbing another beer.

25

HE REVISITED HIS SCRIPT and sat down, chain-smoking and considering their conversation on the complexion of the painting of Mussolini and the Black Shirts beneath that particular lamp light on the third floor of MoMA wherein William had recently received pictures from Octavia who'd attained a lifelong membership which he now looked forward to mentioning for the sake of poisoning the potential kinetic energy between Paul and Laura—but he also knew this made no sense—but it was the way they shook hands which had, in its own multilayered way, sealed the deal. It was weary, William considered, but bearable, how ex-lovers seemed sometimes to fit into other friends' arms as if pieces of a desperate puzzle, albeit one inclusive to ex-lovers only.

"What do you think," Laura said, "Is the food here *really* that good?"

"It is pretty good. I eat here two to three meals a day but only recently. For months I came here but did not eat. Instead I spoke with people and had Fernet with an ice cube until four am. The owners of this place are from New York. Every so often we used to lock the doors up and smoke inside. Laura, right? I've got to go see a friend inside."

Paul stepped inside to speak with the older woman and Laura stood beside William, who could not definitively confirm whether he had even once left his outstretched position upon the plank of the bench since the film had begun.

"There is a reason we broke up," Laura said. "We were bad for one another."

"Why are you not wearing socks in the winter?"

A couple stepped out back and walked down to the iron bench at the edge of the steps and spoke to one another at a low pitch of the aquamarine tint of the tequila bottles in Spain they had seen spinning around on the preview to the film as the projectionist readjusted his lens for the last time.

"Oh so I guess they haven't even started yet."

Paul stepped back inside to meet the owner, tapping his fingertips along the peeled balustrade.

"Oh there you are," the middle-aged woman shouted over the voluminous crowd. "What are you drinking!"

"I thought that you studied religion," William said.

"There's no career in it."

"It took you all of those years to figure that out?"

"Don't start. I thought I wanted to teach religious history right up until I obtained my degree. Then I lost interest. No—don't even."

"I'm not," sighed William, "I just don't understand what you expected to happen."

Inside a light clapping of hands resounded in short bursts beyond the tin door. The couple below crushed their cigarettes with combat boots and pointed to the shed inscribed with jagged black spray paint before them:

ALL PIGS MUST DIE

"Well let's go in," Laura said. She stood up, blowing from her shoulder. "Months later and we still can't just be friends."

"I'll be in in a little while."

"What are you going to do, stupid? Sit out here by yourself?"

"It is so nice out."

"It is freezing!"

"Then the tranquility is nice. I'll go in with you to grab a beer."

William stood, taking Laura by the hand. At once her touch was familiar. He looked into her neutral nascent eyes and felt either transported several years back or further in touch with some sort of futuristically deranged realm of the senses, her touch an homage to the impossibility of heartbreak.

"I have to go to the bathroom."

She stepped inside and William listened to the men on the film screen shout in foreign languages, men upon distant streets and porches shout in foreign languages, all the while the infinitely familiar language of an ex-lover circulating through his mind. He looked around for Paul and didn't see him. He feared upon Laura's return she would seem even more neurotic and strange, perhaps a mirror of his own sudden mixed feelings, although he still had this strange feeling that if Paul wanted her, Paul could have her, Paul being someone William admired for his self-destructive erudition trapped in obscure antique poetics.

She returned with two bottles of Blue Moon.

"You drink?"

"No."

"There's free Anchor Steam right there."

"I like Blue Moon!"

"But there's no orange," William offered to the crowd.

He opened the bottle with his sky-blue Bic.

"More people have shown up."

"So what did you do over the years?"

"I was an assistant at Harper Collin's. I actually had a good stint there."

"Good."

"Do you remember we were on a date and I jumped off of the deck doing an impression and cut my head open on the ground?"

"Oh yes."

"You used your sock to stop the bleeding."

"It was a clean sock I can convince you."

"I went to that park two days ago," she said, smiling at William. "You should have been there."

He thought of the past, its images breaking suddenly in his mind, and took a long drink of the crisp beer.

"I saw your friend inside there, Paul."

"Is he having success?"

"He was speaking with an older woman and both were smiling. Well, even if we'll never be together again at least we can talk like it was just yesterday. But what about this Paul?"

"He is good. He is nearly a charming man. With a little luck he'd be a charming man," William said venomously.

"What do you mean?"

"He is older than he looks. He is due for success."

"I thought you said he was a big actor. He invited me to a big fund-raiser on 9th Avenue tomorrow. He's going to e-mail me the flier."

William twisted his beard lightly and knew not what to think of that nor if it were his place to think aloud of anything at all on the subject.

"Everyone is San Francisco, like New York, is a successful actor," William said, "But he, like many others, is a chimney sweeper at the end of the day. Many people are chimney sweepers at the end of the day but I suppose it depends on where your night begins and how many logs are burning beforehand and how many embers sift through the ashen viaducts afterward."

"You mean he sweeps chimneys to make money?"

"I heard something like that. I do not know him too well although it does not matter, really. You can explain with an ethics in the form of a fist of love in your eyes how you have not in fact succumbed to the net of anguish; but love is colder than death. Everyone is looking for a clean break and often you have to do something you dislike in the meantime unless you are rich or unless you commit suicide."

"Of course. Yes, how lovely. That is life."

"I know," said William. He blew lightly upon the opening of the bottle, looking around the long room for Paul. "You might despise the ones who cry 'Sodom and Gomorra' at you, but your hatred is more thoroughly borne in objection to the reference than it is in your inability to refute it. Dark columns smeared with dung where once an empire stood. Now what were you saying earlier?"

"We were at lunch," Laura said aglow, "Down by the financial district—and the streets were closed off with rioters and police! I heard on the news there were thousands down there today!"

For half an hour they discussed the present, the future, the past, their hands occasionally touching one another's shoulders and kneecaps.

"I have to go the bathroom again. Wait for me!"

William stepped inside and waved to Paul in between films and took two more beers out of the last case. He avoided eye contact, maneuvered past four people, approached Laura.

A young man was stepping away from her who William could not make clear if he had been speaking with her or not but the young man's teeth appeared permanently carved upon his face like a Jack O' Lantern. William took that as if some sort of panged reaffirmation and walked to the cold bench.

"We had good times," Laura horrifyingly reappeared. "Don't you think so?"

"I think so. Do I even know you?"

Her phone buzzed—she was staring into it, transfixed, a single finger upraised—before the rumbling ceased.

"Are you going to be here awhile?" asked sad-eyed Laura, in a tone whereof she could not breathe until she heard the answer.

"I think so."

"I mean, out here. A friend of mine wants me to meet him down the street and then we're coming back."

"Sure."

They stood and embraced, and she jogged up the steps.

William spent a half hour finishing his beer, ignoring the other smokers, and eventually the lights were up and he longed to go inside and have a Hot Toddy. He held the door for the doorwomen and from that angle noticed just behind the pillar opposite of Paul's spot in the cramped, cavernous room, Laura standing with the man of teeth. She did not see William and he quickly walked through the doorway.

"I don't understand women," said William, "I don't understand anything at all."

There were a good two dozen people at the bar, inadvertently swarming around one free stool.

"How was the film?"

"Oh it was al*right*," William shouted over the voices. "It was pretty good. But my mind's eye is elsewhere. I shall shed my blindness soon and, in time, return to NYC, first annihilating morality and mortality alike in Hell and Limbo."

The bartender smiled and set some water boiling. William looked vacantly through his phone.

"What are you reading?" asked the bespectacled girl beside him.

"What do you mean?"

"Oh," she laughed, setting her book aside. "I thought that your napkin was a book from the way the light was tilting."

William did not bother to see what book she was reading although she left it close to his elbow. He accepted his Hot Toddy with a smile.

"Thanks, sir."

"But of course."

"I'm Kate, by the way."

He looked around the bar and came to his senses: There was no Paul, Laura, or co-owner in sight and he did not feel drunk at all. He felt nervous and exhausted and sipped the Hot Toddy and at once felt much better.

"I'm Hamlet. Yes, Hamlet. My parents were either insane or prophetic, depending on who you ask. I know you."

"Do you?"

"Yes, I took your sister's virginity."

Her smile disintegrated. She reached quickly for her gin and with nothing left of it chewed at an ice cube.

"Oh," she shouted, "Oh but alright—Now, now don't go being a jerk—Don't put it that way! But yes I remember you!"

"A gin for the lady," William said to the bartender.

"A gin for the sweet lady!"

He turned to Kate:

"How is she?"

"Oh, she's good. She lives in Walnut Creek."

"Oh?"

"She is good. How are?"

"Be ye not lukewarm."

"Do you live in Oakland?"

"Yes, but moving soon to lower Haight."

"Fancy!"

"Rent control. Come over some time. We'll drink wine and force my neighbors to listen to the Magnetic Fields and smoke too many cigarettes."

"Do you do that often?"

"I only stop when it is forcibly brought upon me or against my will."

She took a long drink from her gin and tonic. William looked around the cavernous room. He at last saw Laura talking with Paul in one corner. The owner talked with a gay couple by candlelight in the next. In a sense William wished he were at home with a bottle of wine deep into a good book. He had been having reader's block, though, and for two weeks he had been unable to get further than 90 pages within any book, even books shorter than 90 pages.

"I'm just bored with everything," he said. "I think I have exhausted what I once believed indispensable."

"Which is?" Kate asked, squeezing her lime into the fizzing drink.

"Art."

Paul walked in stride toward William. Kate ordered three vodka-cranberries.

"Where the hell where were you," said William; he stood to yawn and fell backward through a pile of crates and trays.

He arose from the dead, covered in sawdust, excusing himself.

"Ahem."

"In the movie room." Paul rolled a cigarette. "They brought out one last case of beer."

"Any luck with what's her name?"

"A little luck. I can't tell if she's drunk or crazy. I talked with Laura awhile. She is pretty cool. She went to Spain for bull fights."

"Did she, Ernest? Well I suppose that, truth be known, the truth remains unknown; still, isn't it pretty to think so?"

The beer man stomped cardboard cases flat and brought them outside through the bar to the dumpster. Roman candles.

"It's not even midnight," Kate smiled, wiping clean her glass lenses with a napkin. "That just is the best news always. Where'd your friend go? I bought him a drink."

William studied her ghostly complexion, her spotless and prescriptionless eyeglasses, shrugging his shoulders.

"Are you going to stay here a long while? My sister might come!"

"Let's take the train to Far Rockaway," William said, "We'll get a big bottle of wine and pass it around on the three-day blow."

"No, no," said Kate, "No, no! I've got work in the morning."

"So what?"

"I have to pay rent!"

"Oh, OK."

"Don't you?"

"Sometimes you just forget about that."

Kate formally introduced herself to Paul and they talked briskly. Everyone lifted their vodka-cranberries and drank them halfway down.

"What sort of vodka?" William asked, wiping liquid from the edge of his mustache.

"Grey Goose!"

"Oh, that explains it. Can we have three more?"

Kate stepped to the jukebox and put on the Magnetic Fields.

"Yeah—oh yeah!"

"Be careful what you play—I may come for you next," whispered William.

"Oh, but I'm taken. Wait—what did you say?" She tucked her book into her bag.

"It's dangerous for any single man or woman to come out for innumerable drinks."

"I am not out for innumerable drinks."

"Surely."

"How do you know?"

"Your smile and the look in your eyes."

She cleaned the perspiration from her glass lenses with her t-shirt, sightlessly relaying:

"What of them?"

"They're saintly, yet in some perverted way."

"What did you say?"

The music increased voluminously.

"Let's go have a smoke," said Paul. He handed William his pouch of tobacco. "Freshly grown from Massachusetts!"

William declined the cigarette. He washed his face in the bathroom. Bodies cut around him and one another apologizing with an agonizing, mindless repetition, and cutting in through swaying wooden doors.

When he returned to the bar he halted; then noticed Laura through the windowpane. He scanned the room for Paul, who reappeared at once beside him with his house keys dangling from his extended ring finger.

"Tell me monsieur, but please make it brief—"

"Doth thou needeth vomit? Should I seek the donations bucket?"

"No, no, William—snap me out of my imaginative coma. Why am I bored with everything?"

"Render unto thyself a cargo cult of experience in order to die better, having traversed both sets of borderlands: the borderlands of night and day, and those of exteriority and interiority," said William.

"And?"

"They seek reputation over truth, with opinions fixed before, and thus against, art or reason; these are the ledges of avarice, pride, lust, wrath, and envy; these are your inmates; this is your purgatorial city, and it is the culmination of all of your euphemistic promises and utopian fantasies; let a rustic be amazed, but not quite go like Jonah . . . your veneer is dazzling for twelve or so weeks; but let him who has more than an adjectival city to add to the concept-world sober up before the twilight of his mind, and recapture what it means to live."

"Can you say that again so I can record it?"

"No. Now I must turn to go, comrade: chaos and night awaiteth me!"

"Well here is the extra set of keys," Paul shouted. "Come by anytime tonight! We'll drink! I'm going to run some errands and be there in two hours or so—Meet me there then!"

Through the gift-ribbon red window William watched Laura leave, her arm interlocked with Paul's. He sat still, stunned, offended and relieved, bloodshot sleepless eyes drowning in a garrulous sea of the age's self-images. Either end remained stifled, drowned, at the currently unreachable core of his senses and he turned swiftly to the packed bar.

"Don't get me wrong, I like William and all—but I like you too."

"I know," sighed Laura. "Why don't we take a cab instead? I feel strange whenever I do coke on the subway. I get paranoid."

"Taxi!"

No matter what he decided to do, William vaguely considered, it would be a delayed reaction. He scratched at his hair, pensively fingering his upper lip with thumb and index fingers. He could not bring himself to drink just yet, opting instead to stare into the dozen enclosed conversations over melting ice cubes going on around him, the somber night tinted and shaped by octagonal glass and candlelight. He reached for the house keys in his pocket and held them tightly.

A middle-aged man beside him held his pint of ale to the light while William's sight shifted from this toast to the next, left and right, when suddenly, like the softly-spreading hues of a collage, that messy bowl cut of hazel hair, perhaps purposely disarrayed, was suddenly just above his shoulder.

"Our friend's left!" cried the co-owner, her dampened hair breezing past his neck. Her silver necklace glittered in the night. She laughed with a deep tone. Kate had not returned from where she'd vanished. The bartender talked still with the couple. William laughed with the co-owner without visually addressing her and felt as though his laughter was guided at something deeply profound that in the morning would seem insane.

He looked to her expressionlessly and could not bring himself to ask what she meant, for what she meant by the look in her eyes was that either of them had been screwed in the worst way possible.

"That guy, your friend, I was going to buy him a drink! And he's gone! How dare he!"

As she introduced herself and extended her hand William knew at once that he felt very comfortable around her, she who he'd only ever seen a handful of high epochs from absinthe-summoned distances, yet she whose warm intoxicated voice evoked tones that expressed more about herself, her carefree attitude toward life, than Laura had ever alluded to expressing in hours. He cherished the presence of this mature, hard-drinking woman. It was like a privative version of a healthy upbringing compressed and recaptured.

William complimented her on the development of the bar. He began to point this way and that, to one work of art or another, the critical lack of TV sets, and quickly grasped how fiercely her assumptive age scattered along its imaginative scale with either side, angle of her face.

There, to the rubber crocodile: 32, 33? Yet there, to the triangle of exposed gas-blue fluorescent bulbs: 26? Still more, to the model ships mounted within liters of wine just beside sequences of heeled leather boots: 37, 39?

She wore a bracelet of seashells strung together by floss, which added one last childish anecdote to her aging face and neck as she leant her temple against her palm and sat down.

"I invited him over and everything!"

"You did?"

"Yes," she said desperately, and although she looked away, she looked straight to the menu, which William knew she'd long known by heart. Also considering the kitchen had long been closed he took this as an impromptu invitation.

'An invitation to what, though? If only they had Bruckner on the jukebox I would play "no. 4" on full blast.'

Instead he said nothing. He glanced at Kate's bag; an exposed book edge. What is she reading? Oh. She was reading *Mrs. Dalloway*.

He felt the owner's tired eyes upon. For a moment he considered himself pompous or ridiculous in his silence and nearly decided upon decency.

"How about I go instead with you," William blurted out. He drank from his steaming cup and looked to her with eyes he had long studied in the mirror, then photographically in his imagination whenever he could not sleep and dreamt instead consciously of women. "We'll sit on the roof and drink. It's so loud here I cannot think."

"You come to the bar to think?"

"On Tuesdays."

Alas, she turned to the bartender and clicked her glass to his, ignoring William. He noticed at once their matching wedding rings shining in the reflection of the flickering melon-colored set of candles. He turned away, slightly shaken, and let the warmth of his drink rush through him. Soon enough the thoughts swimming through his mind would come together in such compacted fury he would feel suffocated if he went on any longer speaking to no one.

Kate tucked her hand below her thighs and pulled her stool ahead.

"I forgive you, I've decided," she said.

"For what?"

"For being rude."

"I was not rude. I just had to tell you. I think you would enjoy it. My studio is enormous. We'll drink wine out on the roof and at sunrise go dancing."

"I hate dancing," said Kate. "My sister won't be here after all."

"Oh, I had forgotten that. Then we'll—"

"You have to get real. It's not going to happen."

"Forget you, then!"

That pushed the minor situation over its edge. Either was drunk enough now to lucidly argue till blows, or to thoroughly enjoy bad food, as the room spun round and around.

He was saved solely by the co-owner, who placed her ringed hand upon William's shoulder as his words broke from his lips. She tugged at his shirt sleeves. He disguised his shock with confidence and followed her outside into the brisk, tranquil nocturne. One by one his senses began to work more clearly. He lit a cigarette and followed her through seas of leather ventriloquists and polo dummies.

She stopped beneath the blinking lights of the bodega and pinned him to the wall, kissing him deeply. At first, the sole pleasure he received from her warm wild untamed tongue was that of Paul, Laura, or even Kate then witnessing this mauling. The woman whom he had once just known as in charge of the Application felt him up and down against the ivy-strewn gates, their bodies periodically lit blue and red by spinning police lights. She pulled away, breathless, and smiled triumphantly, wiping her tight wet little mouth.

"I've been eyeing you a long time."

"You have?"

"Don't be silly, little man."

"Common sense, or the general consensus—that too is inexecrable hysteria."

"10th Street and Prospect Park West," she jokingly said to the driver, with whom she was familiar. William's scorched eyes bolted open, his mind jolted, feverish with the luminescent moon dangling above their heads and the nascent fear and trembling of hallucination.

"Wait—we're in New York?"

"Be quiet. We're going like three blocks away. You're just unreliable by foot right now."

"Really," the pilgrim whispered, clutching once more the spare set of copper keys. "What a coincidence."

She threw money at the driver and pinned William against the window. There was something insane, yet thoroughly comforting, contained in her aging colorless eyes. She whispered passionate things he could not make out entirely, nor did he try, understanding long ago that such details don't matter in the dawns following such nihilistic dereliction, as the cab went up and down over potholes and the driver shouted into his blinking earpiece.

'Both she and Paul live off 20th Street,' William attempted to understand; 'Paul with his curved brownstone-type of thing, no, whatever it is,
she describing a second-floor studio on what 18th Avenue? No—no, it's
streets here. How can this be?'

They passed Paul's apartment en route to hers. William did not see
any lights on, nor anyone on the little porch up above.

"Let's go!"

Through ancient uncarpeted hallways, past stacks of outdated newspapers and unnoticed packages, up the old-fashioned elevator kissing
and whispering, her studio was unlike anything William had ever seen.

Everything revolved around the orbit of the unmade queen-sized
bed, situated in the center of the room. Men's clothing dangled from each
last piece of IKEA furniture, strewn almost in synchronized patterns about
the colorless walls and coffee tables. The small room was one of masculine
extravagance, perhaps belonging rather to a chambermaid centuries-dead,
who even in unconsciousness could never escape the bifurcated slobbery
equalized by wealth after some week-long bender's inexorable end.

William walked with her around the corner of an apparently unused
kitchenette, which led into another room just bigger than a walk-in closet; she explained drunkenly and emotionlessly that this was her room.

"How wonderful."

"Isn't it? Come in!"

Beast-shaped planks, corporate statuettes, framed little gloss por-
traiture refined by fire amidst centuries of alterity and vengeance.

Her room was bare saved the twin-sized bed, an unframed charcoal self-portrait taped beside the slight window of iron bars, and the old
wooden desk beneath it. The desk appeared decades old, as if stolen from
a ghosted schoolyard, and William ran his fingertips across the metal
ruler-engraved initials and words, long bleach-white and illegible. He
placed his hand to the cold navy blue seal strapped around the chair,
sat down, and propped open the desk: A locked diary embroidered with
roses, two unopened bottles of white wine, sandwich bag of cocaine, and
the Polaroid photograph of a child. William squinted, and made out the
impressions of a young girl at the San Diego Zoo.

26

Fancy that!

"Nosey! The problem with young men is that they're too damned curious and confidence only really begins when the curiosity has been rubbed out of you! Open a bottle of wine!"

He looked up to the middle-aged lady and felt it too late to ask her name.

"Thou hast opened my eyes."

He examined the bottles as if he knew what he was doing and opened the bottle of wine that was 13.5 percent instead of the bottle that was 13 percent. In this seemingly obscure, irrelevant gesture, he liked to think, he had made the grandest decision of all.

"I like to think that my husband won't mind me not sleeping with him if I keep all of my belongings outside of this little room, you see. All the pictures. Let me show you some of the pictures!"

"I saw them," William lied. "They were beautiful. Especially the one of the Grand Canyon."

For several minutes they drank in silence, each facing the fate of sex in their own way—She by examining her bitten fingernails, William by looking through the window to the moonlight coming in through the skeletons of Dolores Park and thinking, lightheartedly, of nothing. He waited for her to make a move on him with one odd pass of the bottle or another. She did not.

He turned to the moonlight, to Dolores Park once more. The cramped element of the room, its roaring hush, and blank slates of walls, made him feel more like a prisoner of war, a prisoner of sex. He contemplated that everyone you got to know in life, whatever that meant, was more so a matter of understanding their insanities. That was the charm of running into someone you knew well on the streets of the cities, where millions march forward furiously at each hour as if beyond collected and confident—then you caught someone you knew, and you could look into one another's eyes, and at last the annihilating sky reflected in each last shape of reflective chrome died away. Casual sex, then, was little different than the berated language of the streets.

If the self-portrait had been sketched so recently, then she must have thought herself much younger. William grew unsure of his actions while simultaneously standing and delicately positioning himself before her. He grew curious to see how she would react to sex. That seemed a good enough reason, and so he broke away from despair with a smile on his face and walked to her bed. She smiled, too—And in that moment she did in fact look young again.

When it was over, William longed to return to the squarish frontal room. Her bedroom seemed possessed by her love-making sounds, his mind compact with the images of her aging body; he heard repetitively her long, shrill cries which made him feel as though he was stabbing her rather than making love to her.

She made no motion to leave, contentedly smoking cigarettes, stamping each out with an unexpectedly warm, yellow-toothed smile, and discussing the history of her bar between exhales:

"See the whole thing started upstate. My husband and I, when we were still together all the time, decided one day to go in on property in the Mission and make it a bar. We predicted that ghetto would become trendy. We were right. The next thing I knew—"

The tone of her voice was shaky, shrill, gulpy, forcedly proud beyond atonal pride. William thought of the little bar, that it was nice, and that it was just a place to drink. One could drink anywhere, really, depending on whether one was looking to enjoy the company of friends, to enjoy the company of no one, to get laid, or to be seen, still better yet, photographed. It was not complicated. William found decors nice, and wax flowers had a nice glow in the dark, but her bar was a place to get laid—

Which reminded him of Paul and Laura.

As she spoke on of the biographical doctrine of the little bar, he took many sips of wine. He nodded occasionally, every two minutes pressing her pierced nipples between index finger and thumb. When she began to react, he stopped as if unaware. She continued her recitation. He attempted to pretend he was in a haunted house and that there were occasions in his life he'd been more drunk out of nowhere.

Eventually he dressed, recalling his books and tobacco and Japanese tea at Paul's. He was ready to leave her behind and to never acknowledge her again at the bar. If it became more complicated than that he would find another. That was the nice thing about bars in the city, he thought. A bolt of clarifying lightning struck his head: the bars were not yet closed.

"In 2007 we had to call in a lawyer, you know, and my cousin—"

Her voice drifted away when he leapt onto the bed in his shoes, shouted with his arms outspread to the sky:

"I am the Rimbaud of the Bay! I don't care about anything! I'm going back out! The more the world ignores me, the closer I get! When I die, bury me with Dylan Thomas and Schopenhauer!"

With that he leapt from her bed.

She stood, aroused and infuriated, dressing briskly. William bolted to the main entrance as to escape her and return to Paul's apartment and found it horrifying that she would dare follow him out.

She caught him at the door and vampirized his neck. He found himself leant against the love seat armchair strewn with long unbuttoned denim shirts, listening to the sounds of distant doors opening and slamming shut, sets of keys jangling while she pressed her wet lips ardently to his.

"Oh," she gasped. "You've got lipstick all over your face!"

William wiped at his face with the palm of his free hand.

"I have to leave," he said. "Please, let me out of here."

"And oh, oh, where is *Jim*?"

"Who? Please, let me though! I have an appointment to make!"

"*Jim*," stretching the 'I.'

"Oh, Jim," William smiled. "He's down the street I bet. He's at his apartment."

"That girl he was with was ador*able*. In a crazy way. With her skirt suit. No, not skirt suit," she nearly toppled over. "What was—was—she, she wear*ing*?"

"She is crazy. I dated her for two days."

"Really?"

"Yes."

"How interesting."

Heavy feet, as if within steel-toed boots, marched up the stairwell and resounded through the hollow hallway. Keys crashed against the doorknob. William sat up, straightening out his coat and hair, too drunk to feel a total sense of alarm.

"Oh, my husband is here."

"What?"

A middle-aged man, muscular and blonde-haired, teeth white as milk and a ceramic smile, stepped inside the room. He looked once expressionlessly to the bulletin board, then mordantly to the woman, and locked the door behind him.

"Paul! Meet William! He's a regular at the Application!"

He turned to William and all froze, save a helplessly expanding grin. He spoke effeminately, his bolted open eyes glistening with a thousand stories:

"Hello, *you!*" They shook hands. William noticed he too wore matching rings to the owner of the Application. "What Paul is it!" he shouted at the chandelier; "It's cocktail Paul!"

Paul took off for the wine cabinet, his buttocks breaking to and fro, narrowly confined within suffocating denim jeans. William interlocked his hands and looked to the electric fireplace.

"What's wrong?" she whispered, outstretching her thin hands. "Come lay with me! Hey, Paul, William's a regular at the Application!"

"I *heard!*"

"You," she said stubbornly and with a smile; "You come here, now."

William looked at her. He reached for his keyset and sneezing, smelt the copper upon his fingertips.

"What's the matter, young gun?"

"I forget."

"Oh, I don't even know what you've said. We're so drunk. Everyone should always be drunk. Oh, I love it. I love owning a Mission bar. Oh, I love it and I love you."

"I love you too," William whispered, placing his hand upon her inner thigh.

"Wine!" Paul screamed. "Winey-wine wine!"

He sat between them, removed his shirt, and flexed his abs.

"I was going to say you said you were going to the gym, silly, you liar, but you may as well have been there. Look at you!"

"The gym! Never! Let's drink!"

They were halfway through the liter of wine and warm, laughing hysterically and chain-smoking William's hand-rolled cigarettes. The wine, in its way, relayed to him that he ought to not question the scenario, the latent homosexuality of the married man whose hand was then periodically placed upon his kneecap, or anything in the world at all.

"This is better than any film playing at the Application," William announced.

He understood at last who the owner of the bar reminded him of, as she and Paul determinedly discussed who William reminded them of and drowning away to memory:

He, the Second Paul, had recently visited home and had run into the prettiest girl from his high school. She was still strikingly attractive and smiled when she spoke. They met at the cashier of a pizza shop called Big Thing's. They made a date. He bought a big bottle of good Californian wine for them. She never arrived. He drank a pot of Chinese tea, read Richard Ellmann's *Oscar Wilde*, and smoked his pipe till dawn. But where, in all this, is meaning? O muse—where is thine *Logos*? That had been a strange night, he knew, and still stranger was his desire to know nothing of the details of the couple before him. But this owner, Crystal it was, he saw in a flash what she looked like when she was younger, and late at night his heart underwent random, sharp pains at the most basic fact: Everyday life was moving faster, and everyone was getting older, and it wasn't so much that there was no time left to lose, but that time was an unattainable object, and he could do nothing but try his best to let the impossibilities of the transitions go on unmagnified. And William rubbed his eyes, knowing now that he was so drunk his own thoughts and memories were literally colliding with this strange swinger couple's words, and felt sick with the madness of the night, and that in a sense we longed to weep, and pray, and be anywhere other than where he was.

"So we married because things are cheaper when you're married," Paul announced, tilting his head back and swallowing wine. "Wine! He-he! Lights in my brainy-brain brain! He! William you're the *best*!"

"Isn't his just the biggest Adam's Apple you've ever seen? Look at it, William, just look at it!"

"I have to go!" shouted William. It was getting late. He stood up.

"Not yet!" Paul shouted, extending his wiry hands. "Not yet!"

"My friend's sleeping with my ex-girlfriend for God's sake! I can't sit still! All I wanted was to drink Anchor Steam and watch a movie, what was it even called?"

"The Disintegration Loop."

"Oh, right, my phone's dead too."

"What time—William didn't you say you dated her for like two days? God never mind—what time is it, Paul?"

"Two fifty."

Crystal bolted up, laughing, and rushed into her room.

"Isn't she the most marvelous bird! Isn't she just incredible! Not a finer dame on this street! Admit it! Admit it!"

She stepped out in Marilyn Monroe makeup, long black coat to her tennis shoes, and her hair in slight disarray. The long coat had a dazzling effect. One could not stand to not remove it from her. William reconsidered himself and this lady.

"So long, Paul!"

"No!" piped Paul. "What about cocktail! Me want cocky-tail!"

"Goodbye!"

They ran giddily down the steps and out into the freezing street.

"Which way, bubs," she shivered.

William guided her toward First Paul's apartment, passing a quiet Irish pub on the way.

"Want to go in?"

"Sure," she shivered. "Just look inside."

The old freshly-stocked bar of waxen oak sat no more than fifteen before tunneling into a long billiards and darts room, concealed by lack of light yet evident in the periodical clacking of pool balls. The air smelt of stale smoke and fried food.

"Evenin'!" shouted the stately Irish woman whose accent was thick, thick as the syrup stains upon her apron; she was missing several teeth yet smiling. Her ample cheeks were enflamed, and that regenerative observation filled William with warmth, all of this and more, "What'll it be, lad?"

"Two Fernet with ice—"

"And two pints of Harp," said Crystal, throwing a fifty-dollar bill on the dampened counter.

William stood to tilt the electric heater in their direction and noticed they were the only two at the bar.

"Quiet night," he sang, "Holy night."

"So Mr. William, isn't it right and natural we got to know one another?"

"Oh but of course. Take off your coat, stay awhile."

"I'm naked beneath it, though."

William did not ask if she was serious, as he knew she was, and smiled to her in awe.

"You are a wild woman, just doing as you please. I've seen you for days at the Application and never did I think we'd be here. Did you?"

"I never noticed you," she laughed. "Well, once I noticed you. I must have. Because I knew tonight that I recognized you from somewhere."

"So once you saw me and liked me, even though fleetingly, and here we are now."

"I knew that you were too young, but sometimes I am in that mood. For a bunny rabbit. Many women get in that mood sometimes, though few refuse denial. We know much more about the agony which follows impulsive flings much more clearly than men do. When it's over for a man he's looking in 45 minutes to go again, and if he's single, probably anywhere will do."

"Did you enjoy yourself earlier? You must know much more about sex than me. I've been at it less than a decade."

The swaying drinks, glistening beneath a bath of dimly-lit multicolored lanterns, came forward

"You're a doll," said the bartender, "Both of ya. For what's it worth, next one's on me. Till we shut the place down, ya know. I'll be scrubbin' o'er here. Call me if you need."

"I'm Rose, by the way."

"Rose?"

"Yes."

"Paul called you Crystal."

"Paul makes up names for everyone."

They shook hands as if having just met.

"It's been a pleasure knowing you. Cheers."

"The night has only begun, little man."

"I could have sworn I smelt perfume as we crossed that Cathedral lot. Did you?"

"No, but we can go back and see. It would be poetic. I need more poets in my life."

"You, Rose, are a woman of all seasons. Cheers to you."

Rose discussed at length taking a freighter ship to Europe with the bartender. No one knew the specific way but felt they'd heard of it somewhere before; the idea was not completely extinct.

"Tell me something about yourself," Rose said, seductively tilting her line of vision, "Tell me something I'll remember so that, so that whenever you're in my bar I'll go to you at once and not care what anyone thinks. I don't want to care what anyone thinks anymore."

He leant to Rose, placed his hand softly to her neck, and kissed once her scarlet lips.

"That is all I have to say to you."

Rose blushed, lengthily concealed by her pint glass. She smiled innocently and looking away, made a nostalgic, slow shake of her head while the pool balls clacked on.

"For once, William, you cannibal, I wish this bar was crowded so we could sneak into the bathroom," she whispered. "Well, perhaps we shouldn't."

"Paul lives two minutes away, my Rose; but I know."

He glanced to the bartender, looking through, rather than at, the television screen, the weather channel, high above her head.

"I would like to, of course."

"We'll go to Europe together," said Rose, "Why don't we just buy the tickets and go to Europe? Where do you even live?"

"I'm staying at Paul's tonight."

"Paul?"

"He's a friend of mine."

Her face lit up.

"Oh, *oh*, that reminds me—What happened to *Jim*?"

"We're going to see him soon."

"I'm awful with names. He'll let us in this late? We could go to my apartment but then we'll have drink gin with Paul and listen to Divine 45s until sunrise."

"He gave me the spare keys."

"I'm so confused."

"Jim is Paul. See?"

"Oh!" she cried, "Oh, but of *course!*" She shook her head. "I knew it!"

An old man pouted upon the pool table. The bartender turned up Brian Roebuck.

"He's on a bender," she sighed, nodding at the man. "Bad one. Two-year spell since his wife died. You can't blame a man for being drunk all of the time like that. It ain't his fault. He breaks into tears sometimes, plays pool by himself all night. Made up a whole elaborate game, a tournament he plays alone. Sometimes I see him walk by in the night and glance into the window and if anyone's at the pool table he walks on by. Only comes in late at night when no one's at the pool table."

"What's he do for a living?"

"He's an old man, hun. Collects some money somehow or annutter. Says he needs no possessions, no vacations. Rather drink and sing, and play the bill'ards. I must say that when he is happy, which seems most of the time, he's the happiest fool you ever met. I envy him for that, that look on his face he's usually got in, got on his face. Sometimes he falls asleep under the pool table."

The old man stepped forth. With gloved hands he wiped brief tears from his acne-torn, emaciated face, threw the three of them a sullen sightless wave, and departed through the doorway.

"What did you want to be when you grew up, William?"

"William, hun? My brodder's name's William."

"I don't really remember." He looked away. "You?"

The bartender looked on with eyes squinted in a way as to signal her own recollections and her eagerness to not let them go on undisclosed; but then Rose was yelling:.

"I wanted to be in the circus. My daddy used to hate it. I think I wanted to be in the circus just to infuriate him. He was a beastly man, just terrible. Inaudibly violent, totally irrational, that sort of insanity just barely cloaked by picket fences, fancy mailboxes, and stylized license plates." She left William dumbfounded with a sudden lyrical rapport. He assumed her coffee mug contained not coffee and smiled at her with Rose, intoxicated and entranced by her resounding Brogue. "I used to tell 'im I was going to join the trapeze, that I'd spit fire f'r a livin' and travel all over the world from carnival to carnival." Rose reflected with a sigh and took William's hand in her own, less romantically than as if to convey the steady, hot blood bursting through her heart and to her palms. "Don't you ever wonder about carnival people? I want to do a photography book on it love, I tell ye! That's what I'll do! I've got enough spare time! I've got a camera, a good one too! A thousand bucks! Oh, I've got to write this down!"

The bartender reappeared with pens and paper napkins and poured herself a glass of whiskey.

"My childhood dream came true long ago when I sailed from Dublin straight through t' here. I was the last of my brothers and sisters to arrive. In fact they arrived decades earlier; I'd just mustered the courage months ago. What a feeling it is to be at sea in the modern age! No computer, no phone service, no nothing! You realize, once you break away, how sudden everything we considered to be old-hat has been because technology moves so quickly, too quickly anymore—and what we consider necessity is just the opposite—only it's got to be marketed as necessity, because nobody knows where these gadgets lead. I love to travel see, and Cheers to a winter night, because traveling I found as I get older is the only way to *dissolve* boredom! Drinking works, but the drink, see, more so destroys many a lad and lassies' perception of the good. Shatters it. Travel though; traveling is the only way to escape time—by breaking through it, against the grain they say, against the normalcy of everyday life, see. And a toast to a fine young couple, and a toast to being alive. Cheers!"

"Cheers!" said William and Rose together.

Just after four o'clock the trio cleaned up shop and departed as a last taxicab broke forth, its headlights stretching across the silent concrete.

"What a fine woman," William shivered, "And to think I'd never been to that pub before."

"Does that mean you'll not come to *my* bar anymore," Rose smiled, kissing William once, delicately as a flower petal, upon the earlobe.

"And—and what do you do for a living?"

They laughed hysterically along the edge of Dolores Park, their voices sifting and echoing through the trees and pathways and grand, pluming breaths of peppermint fog.

Rose led him by the hand in silence, either sadly or reflectively, and pointed to the glowing moon as William staggered just behind her.

"I can never remember if that's waxing or waning."

"Waning, I think."

"One of us cannot be wrong."

Beneath the dreaming moon stood Paul's apartment building. All his lights were on. Figures danced to and fro across the screenless windows.

"Look—Someone's dancing up there!"

William and Rose stood shivering and dumbfounded.

The window facing another direction flung open. Paul propped himself up and against the railing. He motioned to the other figure with his hand and music burst through, as he sang uproariously, arms out-spread, "The Impossible Dream" in a tremendous baritone falsetto in accordance with Sinatra.

"Paul!" slurred William through cupped hands, "Paul, slave and apostle!"

Rose took her turn too, to no avail. William threw his arms around her and danced to rhythm of, and across, the street streaked with a thousand wavering shadows of bare trees.

The volume went down abruptly as Paul caught sight of William and Rose below. He waved his cigarette of success like a maestro's wand, and belted out the last lines at the top of his lungs.

"Bravo!" shouted William, staggering through a slow dance, "Bravo! I'm—I'm drunk!"

"Bravo monsieur!"

"Laura, dear—Buzz our guests in!"

Paul disappeared through howling laughter.

Rose pinned William against the elevator wall and pressed his hand, with hers intact, across her naked body.

"You're going to catch a cold!"

"Oh no," Rose said confidently. William marveled her apparent sobriety through the chaos of the evening. "I am immune to everything. Now, sweetie, where *are* we?"

Through narrow hallways, a loose left, there to the heavy door swung open before William could get to his set of keys.

"I know him!" Rose shouted, laughing lightly, "You were at my bar!"

"And now you're at mine! Come on in, everybody! It's time to drink!" He shuffled and twisted to the ice box: "And away we go!"

Beside the stereo and beneath the fish tank William watched Laura roll around in a gray t-shirt and navy-blue pajama shorts.

"Is she alright," William said.

"Just drunk. A little drunk," said Paul. "Laura, get some whiskey from the cellar while you're down there!"

William overlooked his former love, set for some skyscraper in less than six hours, and noticed she was so drunk she could tell neither cellar nor ceiling, and blindly reached for various bits of furniture, of matter. She lay sprawled, convulsing across the carpet through hysterical laughter as if on a dash of nitrous oxide.

"I don't mean this in any sort of bad way, of offensive way, see," Paul whispered, "But William—she was exceptional in bed. That is all I can say. *Exceptional.* How was she, owner lady?"

Paul, in a moment of clarity, set aside his mixers and shakers and looked curiously into William's eyes. He knew there was no way to respond to what he had said.

"I've crossed the line, Mr. O'Brien, crossed it clean good. Perhaps, now, I ought to—to make a change in my life . . ."

He felt Rose's eyes upon him as Paul returned to his cocktails. Laura stood up and washed her face. She whistled aimlessly before the mirror.

"Why don't you take your coat off and stay awhile?"

"Do either of you work?"

"Ontology."

With that, Rose stood and removed her coat. She stood naked before Paul and William, who overlooked her slightly misshapen body with drunken curiosity. The immediacy with which the owner of the Application was naked before them, standing in all her disheveled, caramel-colored glory, put a silence into the room that seemed as if it would stay forever.

Rose looked into Paul's eyes. He reached for a blanket, wrapped her in it, and took her away to his bedroom.

William stared at his hands. He observed the untouched cocktails. A hand tugged at his collar.

"Oh!" cried Laura. "Will*iam*? When did you—What—*get* here?"

"I sort of actually forget. Alien hearts."

"Tuck me into bed, then. Where's Jim? Listen—"

They listened to Rose down the hallway. They laughed together.

"Boys will be boys," she said.

"Don't you have work tomorrow?"

"I called off."

"Good."

"I had to. I'm drunk. I'm sorry." She started to sob. "I'm sorry about everything."

"What do you mean?"

"I don't know," Laura pouted, "I don't know what I'm talking about, and it's frightening."

"You need to go to sleep," said William.

"I hate sleeping alone!"

"Then we'll go to sleep together and just sleep."

"And what," she sniffled, "Listen to those two all night?"

"We will fight fire with fire," William said, taking an outrageous sip from a dirty martini, spilling some on his barely buttoned shirt. "I will be The Faerie Queene, and you will be The Faerie Queene."

"Oh my God," laughed Laura, wiping away her tears and William laughed with her. Insomnia overcame him and he laughed for two minutes straight.

"You left with Rose, didn't you? That's her in there."

"How did you know? How do you know?"

"Sometimes you can see things happening from the beginning. I know everyone. Sometimes you can't see anything coming. And then sometimes you just see the wrong things coming. Tonight I knew what was going to happen before it happened. Give me a little tiny sip, William."

He gave her the martini and softly wiped a tear from her cheek.

"What happens next?" William inquired.

"We won't go all the way, but we'll have fun. I'll always like you William, but I won't ever love you, because I'll always be capable of betraying you, because you betrayed me first."

"Stop talking about the past! Stop living there. I don't recognize you when you talk that way! You won't cry anymore when you stop living in the past!"

For an hour they drank and reminisced, decided either one of them still hated dreams of the unconscious sorts, eventually laying down together.

"Well, I'll always like running into you."

"Maybe I'll see you next Tuesday."

"Tell me a story. Some people just want to touch another person—I just want to hear your voice."

He cleared his throat and tried to decipher the past, not unlike working from a mountain of three different 1000-piece puzzle sets, their final portrait models destroyed in bouts of drunkenness, and wondering where to begin.

"A group of them drove down to Death Valley for a weekend of LSD. Melody drove, one of them, Leah or Rachel, had a car—LSD or whatever its modern equivalent is—I clasped my hands together and envisioned bodies I had once known, burning. And not dying, mind you, but just burning forever, torment without death.

"And there was a man down there. And between another man and lady he'd revered since childhood stood a little mulberry tree, which when the drugs kicked in, acceleratingly potent, it was said that the tree turned crimson.

"And all of the people, the women, random men, an occasional couple—they could not convince one or the other to move to *their* side of the crimson tree, having entered into a game of chess, with absolute darkness over the west on the razor-thin line of sanity. As in a session of rough perversity, the druggists had a code word and a person ordained to keep it; but this person was higher than anyone, and we'll see how he ended in a moment.

"And the rays of sunlight glittering upon the sole pathway, Rachel claimed, indicated the true way of proceeding, incidentally on *her* side. She said, sometimes I sit back and for a moment can recall the scene of a record store where cigarettes and cigars had been smoked inside daily for 17 years; such is serenity.

"And they together hallucinated William Fellows had joined them for laced tea, as faces morphed less into monsters than far more horrifying things: the hallucinator's father, when he was his son's age; a lifelong friend morphing into one's gynecologist; Leah reincarnated as a gas station attendant with diabetes; and these things were, at least according to them, less hallucinated than experienced. There were even screaming elves present to explain, at long last, just how and why the universe came into being. It was, of course, the elves, with the help of someone named Horselover Fat and the god Sirius. A patristic fish shone gilded in the roaring sky.

"And William Fellows was there. And he dreamt he was a shepherd, wide awake and dreaming, singing the colors of Saturnalia's sky at sunset to himself, protecting his flock from evil beasts, ready to turn from his dreamt protection to a ferocious hunter in one fell swoop—when a lady appeared, walking through the last edge of meadow unto him, cradling a bouquet of flowers: 'Now you have seen temporality and the psalm of the tide that goes; not even I, an angel, can discern further than this: but you are my drawing, my quilt and cup, flesh of wit and bone of art. I crown you over yourself, sweet shepherd prince.'

"But as for Giordano, he remains alone in Death Valley, camping at his crimson tree. Today he goes by "Norris McTeague", or "Octopus", I hear.—Why, you might ask?—Well, first you'll have to riddle me this: who ain't a slave?"

Laura had fallen asleep as dawn broke with the winter sun rushing through the skylight, William beside her smiling, smoking, tapping ash into a miniature game of downturned bottle caps, and let the cool breeze of the fan rush across his body. A part of him was tempted to continue reciting the story: the poetic space of his mind was full of imaginative conviction.

But instead the pilgrim tiptoed out to the porch. There he heard sounds from inside, way down the hall, as slight as the rattling chord to a fan. A little tapping that, naturally, in time moved faster. Thus he overlooked the winter morning below and beyond, rubbing at the smoke-swept bags beneath his eyes.

27

FOR A WHILE HE reflectively drank by himself and soaked in the misty morning of Dolores Park, once or twice nearly getting to a point of justifying the night's chaos, when Paul emerged and sat down beside William.

"Don't you feel as if we've won some sort of conquest," Paul sang through whispers, outstretching his arms to the sky, his cigarette tracing a ladder: "Isn't life beautiful, and this city beautiful, and to be young and alive and crazy in the winter night there, there now, see, the old men and women will be out in fifteen minutes to walk through the park, to have coffee in diners down in North Beach, to walk across town, and look at us tonight, it began as just another Film Night at the Application and we both fell in love, twice! God I feel good, good, don't you! Let me tell you of my dream—but first—"

"Nothing happened," William exhaled, "With Laura."

"Really?"

"We just talked. We can only speak anymore when our mouths are not interlocked or pointing like dissolving arrows in that direction."

"Well then I might as well admit I did nothing with Rose."

"Oh, yes, she was just kicking and screaming and moaning for ninety minutes out of sheer boredom?"

"William, I swear to you—She fell right asleep and into, I guess, sex dreams. I sat at the laptop all night."

"Doing what," William said skeptically.

"None of your business!"

"Well that is fine. And it is true."

William looked out upon the park, fingertips to his temples, and watched as sudden streams of snow began to race down from the pale gray sky in sheets of white across the pathways and the hallucinated pines. Not a soul was out on the streets which in the snowfall took on that photographically iridescent glow of dusk in the still city morning, snowfall breaking across streetlamps which remained lit, as the invisible sun stood surrounded by sifting clouds of snow.

"Breakfast, that's it!" cried Paul. "Oh, it's snowing! It's snowing! Let's go, let's go, man—I'm buying breakfast for us! Come on! I'm starving!"

"Listen closely," said William. "Listen to the hallucinated snow."

Something like a foghorn bellowed faintly across the land as the door distended. Divine forest and the last construction of the human root, needled fragrance cut with ashen blue tobacco fumes, ale, sliced tangerine, and vodka from every side. The sweet unchanging breeze through pliant branches, en route to the holy mountain, some little birds, into the mythology of Muir Woods and nocturnal song among the last leaves; hymnals to Classe porter and Aeolus red—scarcely setting one foot before the other, visions of tomorrow's grassy-glassy knoll, a fractured morning submerged by lovely river and her succulent mouth, that gift of raising up her eyes—dusting off Xerxes, and, bewailed their hostess, the return of the rat.

"What are you looking at," Paul laughed, counting his money in his hands; "Sixty bucks should do it! Breakfast! Let's finish these drinks and go!"

He stood beside William and stretched out his arms. He overlooked Dolores Park, cast in thin scintillating streams of snow, and patted William on the back. He buttoned his coat and rolled a cigarette. He turned, latched his window closed, and walked through the apartment concealing hysterical laughter, and on the street following William's lead bolted through the whirlwind and streams of sleet and snow to the diner some blocks away, side by side, howling through fits of laughter straight ahead to the diner, whose neon sign amidst that black heaven of delirium and hunger burned meteorically:

OPEN

/

OPEN

\

"I know what I'm getting. You get whatever you want," Paul said.

"You don't mind?"

"Not one single bit."

They looked back once to the snowfall coming down from the white sky down upon the park, walked inside the diner, where a new day was beginning to the tune of fresh hot coffee, and a newspaper man was rifling off newspapers across the porch, muttering something beneath his thick, frozen breath.

"I'm just lazy in love," said Paul.

"With what?"

"Just about everything in my life."

"Really?"

"Just about, William," said Paul, "I could say honestly just about, but tonight I may tell you something different, but right now let us feel good and take in this feast, and watch the people on the streets come alive again, and think to yourself how lucky you are, then stop thinking, and then stop talking altogether, and just listen, listen to the wind blow."

"I can't tell if I hear it," William said. "I just feel like I'm in a state of wonder."

"That too," said Paul, "Is as fine beginning as any. But now let us take a break from the Application. It's becoming too scandalous. I like waking up in the Village little more. I love the Village in the morning."

A school bus adorned with a fresh bit of Hebrew came to a brief stop at the intersection right outside their polished window. The waitress emerged through swinging doors with two black coffees laced with whiskey.

"I thank God there is no God," said Paul, "So that now anything goes. Barbarism."

Heavy fog and blinding smoke at last evaporated into crisp, misty late autumn morning.

Octavia sang to me, thought William, *Delectasti*, destined to uncloud my mind, and resurrect my intellect; she said to me, I will purge the fog that strikes you, as surely as the sphere of air moves in a circle, following a first unbroken turning/when they dreamed poetic dreams in Parnassus, we are what they saw; let me leave syntax and logic in the hall, and taste your milk and honey.

Chiming bells held together by tape, uniform veering tires slick with damp; at the right hand of bliss, falling for nine days straight.

28

TWO WEEKS PASSED.

William got back into the habit of writing articles; he dared not send them out save in a rare, digital burst at the SFPL, for he was rusty, but it was nice to spend two or three days alone, writing whatever came into one's head concerning the minor and major events of the world at large, to respond to yourself, leave the window open, and listen to the classical radio station by night, the Catholic station by day. He was neither ready to return to Mass nor repulsed by the idea; he was both stuck between the stations and on the cusp of something new. At times he read Augustine, the Church Fathers, *Philokalia*, *The Way of the Pilgrim*, John Henry Newman, though it absorbed him most when the wine bottle had been dented. It was terrible, yes, but also true, as with Schopenhauer's stages of truth and remarks on both the educational system and women. But then one afternoon in an unforeseen turn of events even the atheists began to bore him to death; he noticed himself soberly becoming more enamored with a Chrysostom, or Angela of Foligno. Waves of brutal anxiety crushed his mind and spirit: he had failed his mother, himself, and had nothing to show for it save nocturnal predilection and a mind consumed by the futility of lust; he was a proper child of his generation but one who had begun to see at last the cave walls for what they were; he crossed himself and said a boyhood prayer from Arthur Avenue, the Seven Graces, and outstretched his arm in the used bookstore: Bernard Lonergan: *The Triune God*. If he was seldom in a natural frame of mind he at least knew something more than the ever-present dice throw of drowned men's bones: that he was willing to surrender, and knew neither the hour nor process, but that he was willing—and this spirit kept the flame of his heart aglow.

His final hypothetical plan was to get freelance work, make enough money to visit home with nice presents, return to Sacramento Street, plagued with a lip so dry it clung to his ragged white teeth, shuddering: *Roman Orgy Parade in miniature: A series of lights shone through the forest, equivalent to horizontal lightning; a melody ran through the luminous air. This was the background scene of supposed eternal pleasure. Discussions of a painting—but does anyone even care about paintings anymore? No matter: now must Helicon pour forth for me and Urania with her chorus & things difficult to conceive?*

He did not worry about Melody and even knew what had happened the moment he had left the party: she'd found another droll man with whom to take drugs in the desert, one she may herself never see again. That was the way the scene worked, and the way one could agree with it was to care nothing for it, which was simple enough, and yet at the end of the day simplicity seemed undesirable for he with a mind of ceaseless layers, of abstractions and complexities.

William set his notepad down and recalled Man Ray and took off for Buchanan.

"You have to give your mother a call back," Man Ray said, over a glass of filtered ice water. "She's been calling every other week—I had no way of contacting you!"

William left without eating and felt nervous as the digits of the phone number rushed through him. Keeping in touch with anyone on the east coast was difficult in that most people could any longer communicate through the arched thumbs of a contagious mental illness entitled, in English, 'social networking', and therein contemplative voices seemed as if threats from another world.

At last he called, and again the reality of the world came down; Pennsylvania, the country, was in appalling shape. His heart was rattled, less like dynamite exploding beneath a bridge than being the one talked into detonating it. Austerity and barbarism had left him high and dry, and now the furies put forth cyclical political psychoses; for there has never been a power in history, thought the pilgrim, his mind shattered by the cries and whispers of his poor mother, that has not ended up precisely where it first set out to conquer. Every land is a captured land; the scales are never balanced because less because humanity is still on the way, but because the scales shall never be balanced because they needn't be. Reality is, he thought further, in the last of all last analyses beating around the bush, of conceptual power. Liberation is a disease; a chimney that has built itself beyond even treetops and is now heading for the sky and cosmos. Helpless is he who puts his dreams into the temporal, yesterday's epiphanies already outdated, promises like cloth fluttering in the wind.

But what were all these lamentations when Ms. Fellows had been laid off weeks ago? Reality was itself a theory. She no longer cared about college nor inquired as to how William had been managing—soon she would be evicted. She spoke in a strained voice that had considered making light of the incident and had found itself unable to do so. The landlord wanted to sue her. William spoke for a long time on Valencia Street as the city streamed past, sunlight breaking through the sky, steam rising from the street. Soon all of it would be a vast memory. He went down to Casanova and had a drink, four, and realized he'd have to go east, that oblivion would be postponed. Something was not right in the country at all; he had forgotten for so long. He called his mother back.

"I'll be back in two weeks, then," he surmised with a sense of shame.

"I've got you a bus ticket for next week."

He stood and stared at his hands for a minute. He got on the phone and let everyone know. He knew this would be bad, but at the end of the day if one needed to one could thrust everything aside, including oneself, and keep going again, and again, for each blow he took could all but make him more of a man.

Then to think of his mother in that state, and all the dreams of the land going down in flames. It seemed a fine time as any to jump into the fire.

He walked the wintry streets alone combating terminal depression, his eyes fixed upon the sidewalk, tormented by memories of things that had seemed so definitively aligned with the prospect of cultural freedom, but in turn haunted the detoxified unconscious like so:

Then came the two-wheeled chariot down Dolores, where the missionaries once walked with sacrament, canticle, and hearts on fire, now this debauched vehicle drawn harnessed to the gryphon's neck, white mixed with crimson. And three ladies I thought I recognized dancing in a circle like of red right wheel, and another bursting rush of fire. Flesh and bones like emeralds, then four rejoicing dancers clad in purple, one with a third eye.

After the procession there were four final stragglers, some clunky heifers whose footwear damned them to the rungs of touristry, followed by a lone sleepwalker, his withered face alert. But was this even the night of the Application? No more lilies garlanding their heads, no; just domestic beer and plastic roses, some paper crimson abounding burnt eyebrows. We see that the difference between Marxists and anti-Marxists, I would tell Prof. Booty somebody had said in the wine-dark see of Mission nocturne, is the latter have actually read him. And his system, joked my friend, offers this: take a scenario that could use some good works and make it unfathomably worse.

William could make little sense of the face that this idea—that never once in the history of mankind has a revolutionary overtaken power with anything but apparently sacred intentions, only to get his hands on the controls, and carry out infinitely more grotesque violence that the apparent claim he and his odious minions set out to 'free' the people from in the first place—haunted him at the end of all his liberation. But life was too short to even do anything about this epiphanic nightmare, borne of exile and chemical alterity.

"Even my bones feel dead."

At last he gave in and drank a double vodka with Anchor Steam.

Ten minutes in and it was, he solidified with both himself and the holy muses, the greatest decision he had ever made in his life.

"And we'll get to the bottom of just what this means at a later date. For now I must save my mother's life and see Octavia. And if I must drink, and even pray, to do this—then let it be."

29

THERE IN THE CITY's diseased bowels a hooker set fire to advertised palmistry and a dog-eared copy of the *Owl of Minerva* fell from the attaché of one Professor Headphones. Closing in on a day-long study of sacred and profane prostitution, both ancient and present-day archetypes, the pilgrim crossed paths with a prostitute. He sat atop what appeared a discarded tanning bed, overlooking the candle-lit hutch before him: white veil girt with olive, a younger whore despicably tattooed with the Star of David, stained with fingerprint; a green mantle of ointments and coins, postcards in the color of living flame; and as she massaged him he felt the force of an ancient love, signs of the ancient flame, strange memories of an abstract garden, thinking, 'we could only use woods in the garden.' She directed her dark eyes to his as she overturned his body, lapping up a little golden stream of ale—but then it was sunrise again, and he was not satisfied, making him ransom to the foliage of being, and the hermeneutics of exilic psalm.

Now the days were shorter. Either that or William had just taken to noticing this in his looming departure: that now there were not only less parties, but less daylight in which to feign preparation for a hypothetical unexpected invitation. These were the handful of quiet days in San Francisco, as William resolved to ensure his mother went on living, consult Octavia, and—critically—to think no further on the matter. Pure reason took its curtsy and bow; now one walked alone beneath the late afternoon sky all rosily adorned with the evaporation of cloudless blue, the face of the rising, shadowed crescent, so that by the tempering of vapors the eye endured it for a long while, in the next hour oneself within a cloud of flowers.

"Damnit and I was about to say we have to go up Portland, Seattle, all of that!" Daniel cried, stepping from his motorcycle. He and William

tucked the bomber helmets beneath their arms and had coffee on Guerrero. "Next year, ten months from now, fall is the perfect time, when all of
the leaves are changing along the highway. We'll go then!"

Autumnal solace passed through the spirit of each afternoon; these
moments worked upon the pilgrim's heart strings—whether or not he
liked it, or even noticed it—like unseen echoing church bells in the distended aberrations of wintry evening light.

"I heard Heather ended up in Los Angeles."

"I forgot all about her," William lied; his optimistic tone rang hollow.

"Yep," Daniel said, "UCLA, I think. The academics are, or academia
is, I should say, really its own cult. I used to wonder how such learned
people could be so hopelessly hive-minded and addicted to newspaper
propaganda, so pathetically unoriginal on the world-stage yet connected
to endless streams of resource, but then you realize most of them have
never known anything else. From diapers to tenure, and from there, as
you so optimistically put it, a diet of worms or dust. Hence their ideas by
and large fail in the world: it is less the dictatorship of the proletariat than
it is full-term corpses wailing from their ultra-conformist crib. But then
life is worth losing, so in the end whether Heather or anybody goes that
way is extraneous. I don't know if that's true, where she is, but, oh—oh
well. It's a transient city I guess."

Closing in on both things to say and the energy to contemplate a
new dialogical avenue, the young men slowed to a stop down the street
from Sasha's apartment at Post. Divas' graffitied awnings creakily rose
across the street at Divas.

"I thought that place opened at 7:00," William said. He longed to
correct Daniel in that there was much good in academics, but he no longer had the energy. He had tragically realized that neither side of the
oligarchical divide would hear the other out. It truly was technological
feudalism; let one thereby condemn not one side but the system whose
mythology proffers two bogus, manufactured bogeymen. "And yes, the
wind is my reference. I thought," he exhaustedly repeated, "Divas opened
at 7:00."

"Someone was shot."

"Are you still going to the library?"

"I went earlier," sighed Daniel, stretching his arms. "Well you'd better e-mail when you get home!"

"I will, I'll be back soon! Tell Sasha I'll see her soon."

"We'll mail you out a bowl of soup."

"Please do."

They embraced. William gave a final wave of the hand. Daniel turned:

"Farewell!"

"Farewell—I'll be back soon."

"That's it?"

"That's it," William said, turning around to take a speedball balanced by scotch, and walked back up to Sacramento.

～

Phil sat beneath the sketch of Mustard. He had grown a beard and looked like a different man. William had walked past him just a moment earlier at the top of the steps, although this could have also had something to do with the pilgrim's unceasing metaphysical preoccupations, secular conjectures against them, and amidst this violent civil war unfolding in his mind, trying to refrain from drinking in the morning.

"A little something before we hit the town," El said, taking a pint of Old Crow, a liter of seltzer-water, and a tattered edition of Proust from his backpack. He stood to prop the window which had been long propped-open. "Damned optical illusion! What do you think going home will be like?" William had been awaiting to respond to this question.

"People working so much that they can't read. People who therefore do not grow at all but in the extent to which their thought patterns go on unstructured. People where even if the whole thing splits open with retirement, one at last has time to think, and he cracks and gets put in assisted living. People who wager their emotional livelihoods on professional athletes and overcrowded drive-thrus, fade into the next funeral. They believe without question in God all their lives and then one day admit it, which means they feel life is halfway over. Now a lot of them don't have work, though, so I assume it will be people watching TV and worthless movies drugged on pharmaceuticals, driving around in their wonderful cars, looking and talking unfashionable, despising themselves and anything different from themselves. I won't be there long, comrade, but long enough to see old friends and help out my mother. It'd do me some good to go out there and do nothing. Then I'll come back and write my essays and publish them and we can go out and discuss our progress and ideas."

"We'll meet out in some state when you decide to return."

"How about Reno?"

"Sure," El said.

"That'll be the plan. I am serious about this, all of this."

"As am I."

By the end of the pint their voices rose with the radio to the direction of hands waving blue smoke through the isomorphic quarters, the limitless array of bars and cafes breaking through the air like music.

"Rather we ought to just climb up Sacramento to the Cathedral, sit and chat."

"That is a much better idea."

William bundled up with scarf and coat and followed the towering philosopher through the stuffy hallway, pressing his finger first to the place upon the glass where all of that dust had been, next to the acrylic painting of the cowgirl and the alien hearts.

Buses crept by, inquisitive eyes following El and William down to Polk. William buttoned up his black peacoat and they walked ahead through the cold, tranquil night, smoking fresh tobacco from a porcelain pipe.

"We must quit bad jobs, trek long mountains, and listen to the heart, for the night belongs to us, and that is one thing that will never slip away."

"A-ha!" shouted William, as if to the full, bright moon. His voice resounded through the alleyways and streets of Nob Hill.

The fountains streamed in the park at the tip of Sacramento. They took a seat overlooking the wavering flags atop the historic hotel, the Embarcadero way out.

"You know," William said, "For as much as has been said about love, I still think that one of the strangest notions is that strange inability to fathom anything else in life. All your rationality is absorbed by sex, mental and physical contact, proximity and faithfulness, and it makes me wonder. It is bliss, no doubt, to know nothing lest yearn. Then know everything thus moan, moaning always, lusting for life unfathomable, sometimes you are so alone you get to know yourself so well that others become insufferable unless they're just like you, and yet they never are, so the road may be remote but then loneliness might be all there is. The closest we can get to another is in creating a whole new other. Love lost, love regained, and that's it. You cross your fingers and hope you'll no longer awaken alone, you awaken beside someone and you cannot take them anymore, nor explain, even to yourself, why."

"The conscious, living, shall always have a dual interest in domination and death, I believe. That is the political ingredient, and relationships are political as anything."

"It'll be good to see Octavia," William thought aloud, breaking away: "El, do you think on some level the American goal is to police the world while we disintegrate, thus leaving the sole available jobs any longer sorts of police and security jobs?"

"At times," El exhaled, "I can see it that way."

"The rest divvied up as informants and acolytes."

Wind swept through the dark trees and chimes, foreign couples on tiptoe tossing coins into the pond and waving.

The subservient night wore on, romping all around downtown. In the late hours they shared a last bottle of Dante in the park. At dawn they departed at the subway.

"Reno," El said, extending his hand.

"You got it, O comrade, and we'll go see Isaac, too! If I could do anything over, it'd be that night. I'll miss you, man!"

"Never think of what has passed when you must leave—but focus instead on your arrival into the next psychological realm, the next unknown city, the next leap of faith."

After a long embrace William watched Phil descend into the subway and sat down upon the wet, marble bench, swallowing at something within his throat, breathing through his nose.

One by one the parade breaks away as one by one we pass through each other's lives, and one by one the music stops, and again we must walk, whether waving hello or goodbye, yet going ahead, for the people walking in darkness have seen a great light; on those living in the land of deep darkness a light has dawned.

There can no longer be any doubt, thought William, that today's liberalism is indeed the dialectical mutation of pure bourgeoise thinking and the *nihil obstat* of stringent nunneries. It is right and just to have a hand in ruining this unending cultural production of pathological altruism.

~

Melody and William walked through the Mission after dinner, agreeing to keep in touch, each other let down by failing to spend more time together, sharing kisses and secrets and—

Then Harold Smith was walking by out front of Hemlock; William called out his name, having missed him over on Page, Harold having missed William at his apartment. He bolted inside to the table, the exact table it seemed yesterday William had set his weary elbows upon after leaving San Diego.

"I heard," Smith said, looking down, up, and away, unable to say the words, "But—but you're coming back, bud, right?"

"Of course!" William shouted, to the delight of the bartender, though the sobriety in Smith's eyes was the way William knew he'd feel soon enough. "I'll be back out in San Francisco in no time. I just have to make sure they don't lock away my mother. The whole state's in disarray."

"We're next," Harold said, taking the Chronicle from his bag. Reports on bankruptcy and job loss circulated through the pages with an agonizing repetition. William took the paper in his hands; he hadn't bothered much with newspapers in months.

Harold looked to the street, lit a pipe of hashish, exhaled toward the sky, and then returned his eyes to William's. The parade had not ended. The parade had not even begun.

"Well God-damnit!" he shouted, smashing his fists to the table, "If all the best artists are dead, then God-damnit we got to live! All the good ones are dead! There's not a writer today that can speak for his generation! What do you *say*! We must die in order to live!"

"Stop," the bartender interjected, sensing that Harold was—in his incoherent, fatalistic way—serious. "Don't go getting yourselves killed!"

But it was too late; William Fellows kissed her on the forehead and stormed out of Hemlock with Harold Smith. If he were to take death trip, so be it. He was tempted to get everyone together before he realized he ought to just carry it out with Harold. There was no one better for the job.

"Listen up," Harold said at midnight, "Let's just wing the whole thing and throw away the map, the compass, the premonition! What is premonition anyway! We'll just go, and have a day of it, and your last in the city for a while!"

"No, no, no while. I'll go home for a day and return. That's what it'll feel like."

"I know, I know, man, but we're still right *here*! You'll go home and figure everything out, we all do that sometimes, but the main thing is that we're here, here right *now*." His hands and fingers twisted with the words as if conducting an orchestra on fire. "We ought to live in a way that stamps itself into our indelible minds, man, because when it's all over and we're alone in the tomorrow of existence, we'll have memories!"

Coming to his senses, he retrieved the Goncourt Brothers' journals from the bookstore. Reading up on the lives behind the French literary works he had cherished as a teenager, the pilgrim cared not whether the accounts were literal or gross exaggerations. Indeed William kept ever-closer to his heart the maxim that he had been developing for years, namely that all memory, informed by language, is a matter of imprecise ideality; the very intangible phenomenon of recollection was one that even its most arduously collective form was but one of many, ever-unfolding forms of phenomenal cognition. To this end one needn't enjoy Homer or Plato to understand that our mental movements are precisely Athenian, entwined with the dubious elixir of technological enslavement; our linguistic processes and formulations are essentially Platonic, composed of Ideas and Forms. And this mode of thinking, alongside reacquainting himself with Gustave Flaubert, among others, made his heart grow near to bursting with a desire for Octavia, who had been his guiding light in those legendarily formative years.

"Octavia?"

"William! I just got in! Are you still visiting east?"

"Truly, you are my angel. I have received an urgent message to tell you that, though I know not where the vision comes from. The Brothers Goncourt?"

"Well, perhaps; although they were none too fond of the fairer sex."

"Honesty and fondness owe one another nothing, my dear. But do you have a moment? Perhaps one hundred moments?"

"Yes. No, really, I'm glad you called."

"I have climbed the mountain whereby one finds out what happiness is," spoke the pilgrim slowly, "And why so few have it in earnest, despite everyone's claim. It is much like giving up on the vanities of life—everyone says 'I don't care anymore', but they, of course, care very much. Their whole shtick is predicated upon sociological dogmatic. Yet bitter, my angel, is the flavor of unripe compassion."

Octavia was silent. William could hear her little radio sing with angels, '*In te, Domine, speravi*', up till '*pedes meos.*'

"And the idea of happiness came to me as behind the little perfect flame of candle might sneak a windblown gust atop part of a candle's glass square encasing, melting the candle and dripping little trickling bits of wax. And there we see that the ice that had tightened around my heart became spirit and water."

"William, I do not understand all of this, nor am I going to grant you absolute comprehension; but when I was volunteering with the Sisters of Life today you came up, or I brought you up, and Sister Therese said to me, 'All means for his salvation have already fallen short, except to show him the lost people. Now God is doing that, and he must pray to Him to stay on the right path. Magic Hell is swallowing flies, Octavia—don't trust this old nun, pick up any newspaper; click open any news link; ask any stranger, or better yet, a confidante.'

"Oh William, I love these women! I wept in a way I had not since I don' know," turning tearfully away to her former studio, now a prayerful room of study, her heart lit with something like an interior lantern.

William, neither glass nor smoke in sight, listened.

"I thirst for holiness."

30

TOURISTS WERE OUT WITH bags and binoculars, sunscreen and scarves, waving hello and goodbye beside the rushing water, tilting their heads before unfolded maps, styling their hair with misty hands, on that December day at Lands End. William stood on the ledge and looked out for a last time to the Pacific, watched the sun glittering across the water, and felt vague anxiety about returning home. His memories of the town were disfigured, incoherent, and he did not delight in the prospect of the bus ride. There seemed nothing enticing nor exciting about the journey alone and it seemed like it was over-dramatic, and one would grow less inspired than bored and claustrophobic on such a trek. The fact that Ms. Fellows could not even afford a one-way plane ticket disturbed him. He shuddered to think where that might lead a frail woman, here in Gomorrah. The pilgrim did not look forward to seeing her new one-bedroom apartment. There seemed nothing glamorous about poverty now that he had lived it; it was something one drank, snapped springs, and screamed one's way through, stripping the altars of exterior perception in pursuit of degraded survival. Rather than sit around waiting to return to Jerusalem, William met Harold downstairs for double whiskeys.

"It's happening," Harold leading the way, "The whole thing's already over."

Harold had a crisp black suit tailored for the occasion, which at last brought out the bleak interior of his building. The sense of artificial newness even reckoned William to smell the insulated place afresh—it smelt of cigar smoke and maple syrup trapped in a vacuum bag from the 1970s, topped off with dashes of bodily fluid and garbage. Yet even the pauper's suit, with its urgent sense of dignity and style, could not conceal Smith's anguish. William looked into his whiskey tumbler, brushing ash from the outfit Janine had bought him on Polk Street as they prepared a cab to Geary and 44th.

"The one option was to let a bad situation get worse. I couldn't bring myself to do it. I felt terrible for my mother. Of course, miscellaneous sages offered me their varied proems of advice, namely to leave her to her own devices. But I am no longer looking at the American program with hatred, bitterness, or indifference; it is all, beneath the dualling veneers of ecstasy and crisis, a tragedy that is not worth the hallucinatory effort to force into a tragicomedy. One must help another while one can, having first thrown a brick through one's television set."

"O but William, a boy and his wine—do you think giving money to beggars is actually making anything better?"

"Time is thin and money worthless," said William, "So let the meaningless chips fall where they may."

"Well your mother, though—doesn't talk your dad at all, huh?"

"There is no father to speak of; to this extent I'm a perfect product of the age."

"I never met my dad either. Or, now, I guess I just don't remember him. It seems like no one has both parents in their life anymore. We should just get on a damn ship ourselves and get the hell out of here! I'm sick of this country. You keep in touch with anyone on the east? Let's hop on a cargo ship!"

"No one in Pennsylvania. Just Octavia in New York; but no one else. Thousands of people that are just the same person. The people hate the truth, and I despise the people; to that end we are all squared away. Something will go right for me someday," William said. "Some-day."

"What time's your bus leavin'?"

"5:00 am."

"Damn, damn; Fort Mason in the past tense is sadder'n hell, like the electric kool-aid acid test to end just with old Cassady dead on the tracks, made me whimper when I was a ked; we can't waste any more time, no more some-day!"

As with all things ordained by the furies, bits and pieces of the plan transpired while others did otherwise. By their seventh or so drink a hoard of destitute drunks had joined them. William explained he had to run an errand and vanished.

"My voice gave out, like buckled legs," he said to Octavia. "There is nothing left to say, I fear, over makeshift poison. It is all infinitely continual exaggeration."

"You say you've run into religious problems—I say this pleases me immensely. What are you thinking about in these moments, though? Your memories cannot have been erased yet by holy waters."

"Your face was hidden from me when I was learning all the things that I have learned in recent years. You become to me a notion within a thought; I did not assume you were swept up by the unreal city but hoped so, that I could journey into consciousness alone. Guides appear in many forms, some more archetypal than others. But for me it is the spirit that guides the excursion, and the journey, or excursion, is itself the leap of faith that is the attempt to understand the spirit. Therefore I did not fall away in order to bury myself within myself, but to better understand being and time in a culture dedicated to the decimation of the authentic living and solitude that is preliminarily demanded for the prolegomena of any future differential distinctiveness, or identarian discrepancy. If one has nothing to fall back on, one must then fall forward. And there I burned in lust, and my masters were my vices rather than the One. My dear Octavia, I thought of you as I walked along the water, skipping stones, listening for the sirens and the fog horns, dreaming of your touch, that lays aside the seed of weeping. 'My God,' I echoed, 'What is a heart?' A young girl and a short duration; such was Helena."

"Your wings were clipped, but who can blame you? She spread her net, and you shot your arrows in vain. Hell is the fire that does not kill, but burns and burns alone."

"You know me," said William, nearly taken out of himself. "But could you ever forgive me for vanishing?"

"O William, dear William," said Octavia, "There is no venom in my heart, my breast—but please tell me you have at least shaved that rabbinical abomination."

"Woman," said William. "Behold thy pilgrim: now I seek the nettle of repentance. Should I go on to live without you, the signs that mock me shall recognize me here and there; but in truth I shall have died, as I have longed to, would they let me."

"I will make a painting for you, William, of one who could walk on water, light as a little boat; that you too may turn away at last from the temporal, the odious, the meaningless, and step into the Light that is your birthright."

"I hunger for more than bread; I am weary, disconsolate, and despise extremes in an age composed of them. Like Robert Musil, against both Communist and Nazi—and about as many people at my funeral!"

"But listen, William my own personal Giannozzo Manetti: you may well find however that just this sort of thing, in the end, gives you a greater hope for the future. Let us move together toward a great faith in the future. We must wait for better times—I am daily praying that I regain vitality, and that the future is an Elysian field rather than crushing walls that are forever closing in."

"Yes", said the pilgrim, "I hear you."

"O to open my arms to you, William, to embrace your head, sub-merge you to the depths of holiness with me, of potency and act, contemplation and solitude—to drink from the fountain together—like the sun in a convex mirror! As I moved from Husserl to Stein, angels sang to me, William! Brucker no. 4; let your eyes be holy and know real faith; I pray you come to visit me, or I you."

"I close my eyes and taste your lips."

31

Now it was time to confront the vicious minute at last, and to gather dynamite to bring to the equatorial ties that bind. Walking through the streets to KoKo's Cocktails in an incoherent flash at half past four with everyone falling through the doorway, needling sirens like a ball to some collapsing pins, a weightlessness, or a lightness in the gravity of time, was upon the pilgrim. Now he would partake in order to bid his farewell, rather than to understand; and he took off for Mission and made the Owl bus in time, looking once to the lights of the Bay Bridge, and then ahead, returning to the first and everlasting wisdom of the East. He was warm with whiskey and a headful of brilliant memories as the red sun broke across the sky, and he was heading back across the country once more, feeling much less alone than he had presumed, with the skyline of Manhattan as seen in the winter from Kent Avenue as his sanctuary.

It had all happened so fast that one had little time to feel any pain; then time slowed down sifting out of the night and the state of California as the bus roared across the land and William thought back to everyone, and every last destination in San Francisco, and the tears of bliss broke from his eyes. He would make it back to San Francisco regardless of what the newspapers said, and upon his arrival the unvanquished artistry one sang of would be set into action. In the numbest hour he felt that flame burning somewhere, however microscopic, within his heart.

But to the first and everlasting wisdom of New York City, Brooklyn, that Octavia Savonarola—and what was more, was that sudden clarity with which the summer of San Francisco came to an end, to let the future disrupt in meteoric waves, to no longer walk beneath watercolor portraits of poplar trees; and what was the east if not that infernal compulsion, New York City, and the way one felt walking through Brooklyn in the winter and passing through Graham Avenue over blanketed pine needles in the tranquility of dusk as the subway broke beneath dented grates and night would fall, to the first and everlasting wisdom as the land pressed ahead in its gilded, inconceivable hallucination of time broken down, entrances at last, from land's end to land's end, from the furthest west to the furthest east, to the first and everlasting wisdom.

For what is intoxication, William pondered, but the attempt to paralyze time, and what could be nobler?

Much, it would seem, when one moved from instantaneity to intuition, as concerns the ascent of artistry; the ascent of the mind; the second coming of renaissance—

Now was the fractal hour wherein visionary fragments connected that had hitherto been segregated by forces diametrically opposed to *cura personalis*, sheep in wolves' clothing, moving from abject repetition to immutable interiority: *I met Octavia some years ago when, what, she was publishing and beginning to see through things; and ever since my senses have been extinguished in her presence—this was and remains a mystical negativity of the other: everywhere she is not, she is; for I know she is not there, and thus her heart beats in unison with mine*—like chain links done in at last by obstinate droplets all of the excess of the visible, lesser beings and lesser objects, dancing and making suitable accommodations in the house of desecrated reason—*a mural on the wall, seven flames bursting from some army machine's head*—and a thought disconnected by repackaged by church bells, the whispers of soldiers of the heavenly kingdom, and spiritual combat—*night owls in the moonlit pines when she longed to hear 'The Prayers of Kierkegaard'*—no longer may I bear to watch these repulsive birds of night circling round their skeletal trees of degradation and manufactured subcultures—*mystical annihilation and great lights coming down when one dared to close one's burning eyes—dissolving rose, arisen violet*—whereby I long for hymns and melodies that I both seem to hear for the first time and yet know by heart, when her hand is fixed in mine—*cruel eyes and a voice that had broken deeper sleep than theirs, accumulating bottlecaps for prisoners of the flesh*—where once she sought hollow company and lesser words, now she ponders potency and act, and when I think of her my mind's eye sees nothing else; eyes colliding with the world's recall through immeasurable space that for all our technologies of critique, nothing makes sense; that language (numerology) will not allow it—*father against son, mother against daughter, families and citizens who despise each other, beneath portraits of a Roman Christ*—
"Be sure that you write, William," said Octavia, "Photography is an idea,

thence we move to Writing and Idea'—*her attic footsteps commanded me,*
I and all my correlative abdication—dense clouds dissolving fast, and a
little bird falling from a tree—*the flight of fleshless bones*—I retrieved the
baby bird, with its little mutant silent screams, and returned her to her
little brother and sister; and later that day, much older then, I returned
to find a joyous little family gathering, all the precious birdies in good
health, and who there upon the bench of reason pausing to listen to, she
was then the white goddess of Jerusalem University—"What a blessing to
have a little nest outside one's door!"—invitation to the gallery exhibition,
'The Ark of the Chariot.'

"Is one who is promoting ungirt whoredom as ironical nihilism still
carrying out eschatological plans? Or if one who finds the Bible a work of
madness and stupidity, but models foreign policy after Revelation just to
keep believers foaming at the mouth—is this still divine providence? Let's
talk about this when we meet again! Octavia."

He held tight to the fragment of his heart and mind sent on a theolog-
ical geography, formulating bulwark against incessant animal seduction.

32

ABSORBING MEMORY AND EXPERIENCE in the process of aesthetic judgment, the pilgrim recalled those little foxes in the desert he had seen so many months ago as symbolic of something—or was he just admiring the moment? Either way, his lucid stream of thought was cut short by falling fast asleep, and into a simultaneous nightmare and memory, where and whence the pilgrim was down on Market Street before remnants of a sort of costume ball passing by. As he cupped his ear he could hear the masses chanting something about the body as a choice. Four of the parade's leaders had horns glued to their heads, and three behind wore pairs of horns; two, and then one of them, dual-horned, formed an inverted triangle. Through glittery megaphone one of the leaders screamed that come morning, they must take a baseball bat to a pregnant sister's stomach; they must kill whiteness; they must incinerate western civilization; they must castrate white men ("I prefer European-American, whispered William through a glass of wine"); they must defund the police; they must reeducate racists, and all white people were racist; one must become totalitarian in order to prevent beings from becoming totalitarian; untold numbers of persons screaming bloody murder, burning classical literature as at the Jerusalem University event, though here there were also bricks suddenly being thrown at bystanders with strollers and dogs, as well as police officers, and whatever independent business was within destructive reach.

William, wincing, turned away becloaked, aghast; now began his process of his gradually coming to hate them.

At the edge of Nevada two battered men got on board and took to discussing rumored work in Maine. There had been an avalanche and men out of work with good hands and nothing to lose were rushing that way. Those men were the first in a series of individuals William encountered passing through, across the country, and it was the look in their copper eyes and in the eyes of lonesome mothers that said more about the current state of America he had neglected far too long than any of their words he'd managed to overhear: something catastrophic was looming, and one drank gas station wine divided by Grey Goose airplane bottles, smoking at rest stops, return to Melville and the little black book, and sleep.

33

ALTHOUGH HE HAD GRADUALLY ceased bringing it into public since his life had quieted down, William now retrieved his palm-wreathed staff, and stood by candlelight overlooking the city, in what was to be his last prophetic dream before the bus ride had commenced in New York, with a vision of Octavia; Octavia, he reflected, was right to lament the death of culture. It was both meaningless and heartbreaking, but strangest still was to be anything at all.

"My work is independent, a blessing and curse. Sometimes the solitude grows too loud, and far less charmingly than that little book about the garbage-picker you had sent me. I believe both of us would benefit from an exchange of thoughts and ideas. God knows what we consider second-hand nature today shall in the historical tomorrow be outlawed, and imperceptible to later generations. Come more quickly—a plane?"

"No, my love; for now I must again see the land. Let me be unlike those revolting bipeds who claim to speak for all of America while having never left her insulated coasts. But my lady, yes, you know my soul and what is good for it. My body is like a magnet unto thee; here I stand at my window, prepared to bid this purgatorial mountain farewell, and thou make me stand while standing. We shall save all that for Brooklyn."

"Shame and fear die," the angel said, "And I disentangle you at last. To breathe the air you breathe; for this I live; because the worldly spirit departeth, I can see clearly now, I need not a stupid boy but you, my Walter Hilton. We put an end to the life that is nothing more than a race to death; we follow Ficino, and cast down Virgilian dungeons blind."

"My lady love, God's justice is his prohibition, and solitude is freedom. Now I read Jerome and Schopenhauer. You take care of me in my life, that one's mind is never cemented nor succumbs to stone."

"Do you truly stand there with your stick, wrapped in unraveled palm trees?"

"Doth the letter killeth?"

"We'll read books about waxen seals, memory, and the craft of thought, in the Williamsburg Grand Street afternoon."

"I stand once, twice, in soreness, cradled by aches and soothed by pain, wondering, is my Octavia mad? What of that Boethian Fortuna? Spin, O luminous wheel!"

At dusk the bus depot appeared to exist on the edge of a pale shadow according to sleepless eyes, in the midst of mountains and evaporated branches, black boughs and skeletal scaffolding, cascaded in the pin-drop dusk. Walls adorned with watercolor elk and cold streams; the Milky Way. Euphrates, conjured the pilgrim, seemed like Tigris to run from a single stream; and this heuristic debris of Loeb Library nocturnes gave abrupt way to an epiphanic vision, as though an interior light had been clicked on: *Octavia shall revive my waning powers, now that she has done the right thing and despised her peers for the sake of Truth; free from the mortal chains of freedom, en route, beneath the dreaming moon; O God, the bread of life and the chalice of salvation, to drink though never satiated; let me return from all this holy war like a parched mountaineer, who after fearing for his life and on the verge of hallucination has at last found a creek of cold, clear running waters, and nothing matters but to stay alive for some more days, till all these trees are again renewed with harmonious leaves, and ready to rise up to the stars. You say, 'Take thine own unto contemplation', and I pray that like these the little saplings, the messengers of peace that dwell and bring up life among them, that I might stand still like the hummingbird, beginning to see the Light.*

⌇

Flash of bar lights and sirens, something about an eagle, one ejected soul worse off than William whispering apocalypses, heroin needles and pickup trucks, roads blocked off and drivers checked, overturned cars on fire and in pieces, limbs strewn like theories of intelligibility.

On board and exiting, drugged and sober, the ecstasy of vanquished regret, pressing wayward into delirium nocturne at 80 miles an hour where the highway lamps flash across and through the tinted windowpanes, spray painted DXV, five hundred going fast, five, ten, the cartography of holy lights, skeletal forestry and flashing shadows, winter desolation unto sediments of decampment, by night in America.